I0534559

CROWN OF FLAMES

THE WINTER QUEEN SERIES—*BOOK 3*

ENDORSEMENTS

With storytelling that draws you in and heroes that carve themselves into your heart, *Crown of Flames* is a masterpiece that will stay with you long after the final page has been turned.
—**Tabitha Bouldin**, author of *Trial by Courage*

Erica Marie Hogan's *Winter Queen* series grabbed a hold of me with book one and continues to keep me turning the pages in her latest book, *Crown of Flames*. Her use of mystery, magic, and allegory give a nod to J.R.R. Tolkien's *Lord of the Rings*—one of my all-time favorites. From the depth of characters to her beautiful prose, Erica's storytelling kept me up late many nights!
—**Beckie Lindsey**, author of the award-winning series *Beauties from Ashes* and editor of *SoCal Christian Voice.*

Just when I thought Hogan couldn't possibly add more depth and complexity to her story world and characters, she blew me away yet again. *Crown of Flames* brings forth more relationships, hidden powers, challenges, intrigue, and, most importantly, hope. Nothing is easy in this battle between good and evil and every character is tested, but behind it all shines the Creator's beautiful design. I can't wait to see this epic journey through to its conclusion!
—**Laurie Lucking**, author of *Common*

CROWN OF FLAMES

THE WINTER QUEEN SERIES—*BOOK 3*

ERICA MARIE HOGAN

PUBLISHING THE POSITIVE

ELK LAKE PUBLISHING INC
Plymouth, Massachusetts

Copyright Notice

Crown of Flames: The Winter Queen Book Three

First edition. Copyright © 2019 by Erica Marie Hogan. The information contained in this book is the intellectual property of Erica Marie Hogan and is governed by United States and International copyright laws. All rights reserved. No part of this publication, either text or image, may be used for any purpose other than personal use. Therefore, reproduction, modification, storage in a retrieval system, or retransmission, in any form or by any means, electronic, mechanical, or otherwise, for reasons other than personal use, except for brief quotations for reviews or articles and promotions, is strictly prohibited without prior written permission by the publisher.

This book is a work of fiction. Characters are the product of the author's imagination. Any resemblance to actual events or persons, living or dead, is entirely coincidental.

Cover and Interior Design: Derinda Babcock

Editor(s): Cristel Phelps, Deb Haggerty

Author Represented by Hartline Literary Agency

PUBLISHED BY: Elk Lake Publishing, Inc., 35 Dogwood Dr., Plymouth, MA 02360, 2019

Library Cataloging Data

Names: Hogan, Erica Marie (Erica Marie Hogan)

Crown of Flames: The Winter Queen Book Three / Erica Marie Hogan

268 p. 23cm × 15cm (9in × 6 in.)

Description:

Identifiers: ISBN-13: 978-1-950051-86-1 (trade) | 978-1-950051-87-8 (POD) | 978-1-950051-88-5 (e-book.)

Key Words: Fantasy, Speculative, Kingdoms, Magic, Love, Power, Legacy

LCCN: 2019943229 Fiction

DEDICATION

For MaMa.

You have loved my work from the very beginning,
have read every one of my published books,
and have been such a wonderful support.
I love you so much!

ACKNOWLEDGMENTS

As always, many thanks to my family and friends for their wonderful support in my writing journey. *Crown of Flames* took a bit longer than expected to complete, but with the loving encouragement of the people around me, I managed to complete book 3!

Deb Haggerty—my wonderful publisher, without whom none of this would have ever happened.

Cristel Phelps—my marvelous, lovely editor who helped me polish and improve *Crown of Flames*! And who has given me such wonderful support by being such an awesome fan of this series.

Derinda Babcock—thank you for my beautiful cover! Once again, you've done an absolutely fantastic job of capturing what was locked away in my mind that I struggled to express.

Jim Hart—my agent, for whom I am always thankful.

Tabitha Bouldin, Beckie Lindsey, and Laurie Lucking—Thank you for agreeing to read and endorse *Crown of Flames*! I am so happy you all enjoyed the book, and I am blessed by your beautiful words.

CHARACTER GLOSSARY

THE SUNDRAGON SISTERS

Adlae Sundragon—The Winter Queen and rightful heir to the throne of Sunkai, she is a fierce creature of magic and the eldest of the Sundragon sisters. With the ability to command the Frostlings and bring winter to the land of Nfaros, she will stop at nothing to regain what is hers by blood and birthright.

Brae Sundragon-Jandry—Princess, wife to Brecken Jandry, and mother to Noelle Jandry, she is the middle of Vihaan Sundragon's three daughters. Gentle, quiet, but secretly courageous, the Abyss thought her the ideal sister to be sacrificed for the use of blood magic to strengthen Raphaela Kael as of the three, she was the purest of heart.

Mirae Sundragon—Princess of Sunkai, Queen of the Woodlands and youngest of Vihaan Sundragon's daughters, she has always been bold and strong. Trained by Jaeger Senne from the age of fifteen, she quickly won the love and trust of the Woodland People, leading them in the fight against the usurper Roderick Kael.

THE JANDRY FAMILY

Brecken Jandry—Former friend and captain of Roderick Kael's armies, eldest of the Jandry siblings, and widower of Brae Sundragon-Jandry. Filled with the need for vengeance after his wife's murder, he abandons everything he thought he believed in to join the Sundragon cause and defeat Roderick and Raphaela Kael.

Lathan Jandry—Former lieutenant in Roderick Kael's armies, second eldest of the Jandry siblings and the new *Chalqüin* to the *Almaër Dominÿe*. He has fought in many battles, his body bearing the scars of severe wounds he took in the name of the usurper, Roderick Kael. Following his heart, he is now reborn a Son of the Haven Star and will live a life of immortality because of his love for Damari Kael.

Maxx Jandry—Former lieutenant in Roderick Kael's armies and the middle of the five Jandry siblings. He has always had a sense of humor, but is considered a bit strange by many. Strong and protective, he will do anything for the people he loves, but his odd connection to the forest always unsettled his younger sisters, Afra and Clea.

Afra Jandry-Malaki—Eldest daughter of the Jandry family, widow of Brax Malaki, and a Passer. She is the gentlest among her siblings, keeping the strength of her power as a Passer hidden from them for the most part. Able to transport pure souls from the mortal body into the Creator's realm, her magic weighs heavy on her, weakening her in times of war. Also considered plain, she has never held herself in very high esteem, remaining humble and preferring a quiet life in shadow instead of a bold life among the gentry.

Clea Jandry—Youngest of the Jandry siblings, a Lady of Quintaria, and the Heir of Molderëin. She remained unaware of her responsibility to the country of Molderëin for most of her life, crowned queen in the direst of circumstances. A strong creature of magic, she sometimes stretches the limits of her power, putting her mortal soul at risk. She also chose not to join the Eventide Sisters when she was a child, instead choosing her love for her family over a life hidden away in the Night Wood.

Noelle Jandry—Only daughter of Brecken and Brae Jandry. She has been given a unique gift of magic which could save the whole of Nfaros, but could also cause her death. Under the protection of first, Damari Kael, then her Uncle Maxx since the death of her mother, she must now learn from the Eventide Sisters how to control her magic and preserve her mortal soul.

THE KAEL FAMILY

Roderick Kael—Current King of Sunkai, usurper of the throne, and murderer of Vihaan Sundragon. Believing himself to be more worthy of the throne, Roderick overthrew Vihaan Sundragon, murdering him and forcing two of his daughters to flee the city. A cruel king, he has fallen under the influence of his powerful sister, Raphaela, but now begins to grow tired of her dominance over him.

Raphaela Kael—Princess of Sunkai, Intermediate of the Eventide Sisters, and murderer of Brae Sundragon-Jandry. Raphaela has grown strong in her power under the tutelage of the Eventide Sister, Jhaedra. Vulnerable to the Abyss, she has joined his evil ranks and allowed herself to be his puppet, serving him and seeking the death of every Sundragon who walks the earth.

Damari Kael—Princess of Sunkai, youngest of the Kael siblings, and *Almaër Dominje* of the People of the Dragon. She has lived in the shadow of her brother and sister for most of her life, secretly plotting with Brae to overthrow her own brother and take back the throne in the name of the Sundragon. Her journey takes her far across the sea where she awakens what has been sleeping inside her for years and takes her rightful place among the People of the Dragon.

Bridie Kael—Cousin of Roderick, Raphaela, and Damari Kael. Meek, shy, and withdrawn, she long ago separated herself from society. Now returned to Sunkai by order of Roderick, she sits upon the throne as Queen Regent while he marches across the land to Kaldon in search of Adlae Sundragon.

THE LIGHTMAKER SIBLINGS

Navaria Lightmaker—Considered royalty among her people, she always knew her bloodline was meant for great things. The true mother of Damari Kael, she has fulfilled her purpose in bringing the *Almaër Dominje* back to Hadroul's Mountain in an attempt to save her people from the Abyss once and for all.

Evingar Lightmaker—Brother of Navaria and Kalea and uncle by blood of Damari Kael, he was once reborn as a Son of the Haven Star. Husband and *Chalqüin* to Malindra as well as a great warrior, he is protective of his home and those he loves.

Kalea Lightmaker—Younger sister of Navaria and Evingar she is considered a princess in her lands. A captive of Rhoydaen Molten for many years and now rescued by the hand of Clea Jandry, those she loves have assumed she is long dead.

THE MOLTEN FAMILY

Rhoydaen Molten—Lord Ruler of Molderëin in the absence of the Heir, he has allowed Molderëin to fall back into its savage ways. A greedy tyrant, he dreads the day the true Heir of Molderëin comes to the city to take back the throne he considers his.

Grange Molten—Son of Rhoydaen Molten and a creature of magic in his own right, he has kept his power a secret from his father since he was a boy. Raised in fear, he has come to despise the man he must call father, but believes himself powerless to move against him.

THE MALAKI SIBLINGS

Jabon Malaki—Older brother of Tyrese and Gelsey, nobleman of Kaldon, and a fierce warrior. He has bent the knee to Roderick Kael for five years, biding his time in the hopes that one day Nfaros would rise against the man, break tradition, and put Brae Sundragon on the throne. Now, with the return of Adlae Sundragon—the love he thought lost forever—he rallies his men to her cause to bring down Roderick and Raphaela.

Tyrese Malaki—Brother of Jabon and Gelsey, former officer in Roderick Kael's army. He remained loyal to Roderick the longest before finally fleeing from Sunkai and has not been seen since.

Gelsey Malaki—Only sister of Jabon and Tyrese, she has been named the Lady of the Night Wood. Having left home when Roderick took the throne, Gelsey has watched and waited from her hiding place for her opportunity to fight back in the name of the Sundragon, alongside those she now considers to be her people, the men and women of the Night Wood.

THE EVENTIDE SISTERS

Gwylan—A Dominant of the Eventide Sisters, she was born in Draedin and left for the northern lands as a young girl. Now one of the strongest Eventide Sisters north of Sunkai, she is loyal to her Superiors and hides her true feelings deep within her for fear of the vulnerability that comes with them.

Ellia—Dominant of the Eventide Sisters and best friend of Gwylan. She was born in Draedin, traveling across the Nfaros Sea as a young girl when her power emerged within her. Lighter of heart than Gwylan, she does not possess the same strength as her friend, but her loyalty to their Eventide ways never wavers.

Symber—Dominant of the Eventide Sisters and a Kaldoner. Among Gwylan's company in their search for the Winter Queen, she is wise and sensible.

Haileah—Dominant of the Eventide Sisters, and strongest in the company second only to Gwylan. She is stubborn, bitter, and sometimes cruel, with a secret held deep in her heart.

CLEA'S COMPANY

Morgren Lanfira—Loyal friend and mentor of the Jandry siblings and born of Molderëin. He helped raise the younger Jandry children when they lost their parents, teaching them the ways of the sword and forming a particular attachment to young Clea Jandry, who he follows across the Peace Bridge into Molderëin.

Rheatha—Once a slave in Molderëin, she was freed by the hand of Clea Jandry and remained loyal to her. Like a second mother to the child, she remains by her side, despite her fear in returning to her home country where she could easily be enslaved again.

Izeana—Former slave in Molderëin and freed by Clea Jandry. She is very young and fearful, but her trust in Clea keeps her moving forward.

Ryker—A young soldier in Clea Jandry's army. He is anxious to see battle, though Clea does her best to keep him away from conflict in the hopes of preserving his young life.

THE DRAGON PEOPLE

Krow—Husband and *Chalqüin* of Navaria Lightmaker. He has stood by Navaria's side since she was young, even denying his own heart when duty called her to marry another twenty years ago. Reborn a Son of the Haven Star, he is immortal.

Glaydin—Captain of the *Almaër Dominÿe* guard and now fierce protector of the Winter Queen, Adlae Sundragon, with whom he has fallen in love.

Malindra—Wife of Evingar Lightmaker and sister by law of Navaria and Kalea Lightmaker.

Paefra—A young woman of the Dragon, blessed with fire magic.

Lyssia—A young woman of the Dragon, blessed with fire magic.

THE WOODLANDERS

Jaeger Senne—Mentor to Mirae Sundragon and captain of the Woodland armies. He raised Mirae after her flight from Sunkai five years ago, helping her gain the title of Queen of the Woodlands and determined to see her on the throne of Sunkai.

Astra, Tree Prophetess—A mysterious woman, no one knows exactly where she came from. Overwhelmed at times with visions, she is considered slightly mad, but her love for her loyal guard, Braven—and his love for her—keeps her anchored.

Braven—Husband of Astra and loyal soldier in the Woodland armies.

Cohdel—Guard over the Tree Prophetess Astra, and a soldier in the Woodland armies. His origin is unclear to many, but he has the look of a Shadow Lander and he is fiercely protective of anyone who possesses magic.

THE FROSTLINGS

Taleah—Commander of the Frostlings. She takes her orders directly from her connection with the Winter Queen to bring winter to the land of Nfaros.

M'kela—Frostling under the command of Taleah.

Ilicya—Frostling under the command of Taleah.

THE NIGHT WOOD PEOPLE

Nic Colney—Betrothed to Gelsey Malaki and a strong, yet gentle soldier in the Night Wood army. He adores the woman Nfaros has named the Lady of the Night Wood and is her voice of reason when she begins to lose control.

Maksim—Loyal soldier of the Night Wood, he is often at the side of Nic Colney or Gelsey Malaki.

Embry—Loyal soldier of the Night Wood, she is Gelsey Malaki's right hand, ordered to take command should anything happen to Gelsey.

THE DEVAREIGH FAMILY

Analli Devareigh—A loyal subject of the Sundragon, she is the wife of innkeeper Rufus and the mother of sons, Dedric and Thane. She was a good friend of Brae Sundragon-Jandry and adored the young woman's daughter, Noelle.

Rufus Devareigh—A loyal subject of the Sundragon and innkeeper in Sunkai, he is the husband of Analli Devareigh and father of sons, Dedric and Thane.

Dedric Devareigh—Oldest son of Analli and Rufus Devareigh, he flees Sunkai when under threat of arrest for treason against Roderick Kael.

Thane Devareigh—Youngest son of Analli and Rufus Devareigh, he flees Sunkai with his brother when under threat of arrest for treason against Roderick Kael.

THE SISTER OF THE CREED

Sister of the Creed—She dedicated her entire life to the study and worship of the Creator, remaining unmarried in a pledge of loyalty. But her life did not remain untouched, as the Abyss came to take the lives of her fellow Brothers and Sisters of the Creed. Only her own will and strength preserved her against such evil, leaving her the only one left alive.

THE SHADOW LANDERS

Healer Faw—An elderly man, rumored to be over one-hundred-years-old, the people in his village consider him their leader. He knows a great deal about magic but can only practice to a certain extent.

Elias—A young boy of the Shadow Lands who is more than he seems.

PROLOGUE

Deep in the Heart of Hadroul's Mountain
Many Years Ago

Screams echoed against the walls of Hadroul's Chamber. The air shifted, sending ripples of heat through the caves. The stone city of Hadroul was silent, the clan praying to their Creator for the Blessed One. Years had passed since the Mountain Mother appeared before them. The time had finally come, and only the Creator's blessing could save them now.

Another scream rent the air, bouncing off the shimmering black stone walls. Evingar moved out of the shadows, walking cautiously down the hall toward the screams. Sweat gathered on his brow, hands trembling at his sides as the woman's agony grew louder. He turned the corner, pressing a palm against the wall as he peeked into the hall.

His sister was on the floor, at the very center of the room. Her round stomach had dropped low, skirts bunched up and knees bent. Paefra and Malindra cooed and sang to her, Paefra supporting her back while Malindra knelt in front of her, hands to her knees.

Evingar took another step, his heart thundering when he saw blood staining the ground beneath her. Then she looked at him, her golden eyes glistening as her pupils flashed into horizontal lines.

"Navaria?" he whispered.

His sister raised her hand to him. "It's all right, little brother."

"No, Navaria ..." Malindra hissed.

"Let him come to me. Please!" Navaria groaned on the last word, squeezing her eyes closed. "Come to my side, Evingar."

Malindra glared at him when he took another step into the room. "It is not done ... but if it is what she wants, then come."

Evingar strode forward, falling to his knees at his sister's side. Navaria gripped his hand, her breaths coming short and strained.

"Where is he?" she cried, tears sliding down her face, making the sapphire scales on the right side of her face glitter. "Where is Kordon?"

"He waits beneath the Haven Star," Evingar answered soothingly, stroking his sister's hair. He looked to Malindra. "How much longer?"

"The child is coming," Malindra replied. "Hold fast, Evingar."

Evingar sandwiched Navaria's hand between his palms, holding onto her tight. His sister tilted her head back against Paefra's shoulder, a low groan starting in the base of her throat. Her fingers curled around Evingar's hand, squeezing until his skin tingled. Malindra made a soft sound of encouragement before she released a gasp.

Evingar turned his head sharply, his eyes widening as Malindra lifted the squirming, squealing infant in her hands.

"A girl," Malindra said, breathless. "She is the one, Navaria! Just as was prophesied!"

"Let me see her," Navaria rasped, holding out her arms.

Evingar watched as the babe was passed from one woman to the other, his insides trembling.

"Sweet child," Navaria whispered, nuzzling her face against the round cheek of the child. "You bear the mark of prophecy. You will save us all."

"You're certain, Navaria?" Evingar asked.

Navaria looked up at him, her eyes glistening. "Yes, brother. I am certain. This was foretold to me since I was a child. I always knew I would bear this burden."

Navaria smiled down at her daughter, tracing her finger lightly along the cooing infant's cheek.

"*Almaër Dominje* to our people. My daughter ..." Navaria's breath caught and Evingar put his arm around her.

"Kordon will come."

Navaria trembled. "No, he won't. I should have known."

"What, sister? What's wrong?"

Navaria rested her temple on Evingar's shoulder, cradling the babe close against her chest.

"She is in danger. I knew in my heart even before she left my body. This is the curse of being the savior of our people, Evingar."

"What do you mean, Navaria?"

"Don't you see, little brother? She does not belong to me, but to our people and because of that ... I cannot keep her."

2

Hadroul's Mountain
Years Later ...

Navaria paced beside the lake. The water rippled softly, and she paused, staring at the expanse of water. Moments passed with no other movement. Navaria continued her pacing, rubbing her palms together. Hours had passed since she'd sent Damari Kael into the water, and she'd been met with silence this whole time. There wasn't even a whisper of the Creator's intentions. No hint of Damari being released into the world as the *Almaër Dominje*.

"Navaria," Krow whispered near her ear.

She turned away from him, facing the lake with arms folded across her ribs. Krow wrapped his arms around her, pulling her back against his strong chest. Navaria closed her eyes, trying to rest in her husband's arms.

"She will come back, Navaria," he said, rocking her softly. "From the moment she was born, you said this was her destiny."

"I know." Navaria's eyes stung. "Blessed Creator ... where is she?"

Krow didn't answer. Instead he kissed her hair and tightened his arms around her. The heavy thud of someone else coming echoed on the walls. Navaria turned her head, her temple resting against Krow's chest as she watched Evingar appear around the corner. Malindra went to him, raising her hand to touch his face tenderly.

They spoke in whispers before approaching, Malindra keeping a hand curled around Evingar's arm.

"Lathan Jandry?" Navaria asked.

Evingar shook his head. "He too waits upon the will of the Creator. We have received no answer as yet."

Navaria closed her eyes. "He is meant for her, I know this. Their love is real. He is her True Heart."

"Then he will be chosen," Krow purred against her ear. "We must have faith, my wife."

Faith. Navaria burrowed against Krow's warmth.

Another ripple made the surface of the water twinkle. Navaria held her breath ... and waited.

3

The City of Sunkai

"Quick with you! Quick with you!" Analli's hands trembled as she frantically waved them to the kitchens.

"Mother, you shouldn't be doing this."

"He'll find us."

"No, no! My boys, my beautiful boys."

Analli peeked out the door once she pushed her sons into the kitchens. The dining room was clear, Rufus standing calmly at his desk, watching the front door. She smiled, her heart warming. How she loved that man! How calmly he stood, as if he'd not just brought his deserter sons into their home.

"I told you we should've left the city, Thane," Dedric grumbled. "We should never have come home."

"We'd never have gotten pass the gate, Dedric." Thane grabbed his brother by the arm, yanking him across the kitchen.

"No bickering!" Analli scolded, giving them both a shove. "Quickly! Quickly! Coming, they are. Far away you must be."

She kept hold of their sleeves, tugging them to the back of the kitchens. After a hesitant glance over her shoulder, she placed her hand on the wall, giving the smallest push. The invisible door slid open silently. Analli reached in, pulling out two plain brown cloaks, old, worn boots, two pairs of gloves, and two baskets for them to wear on their backs.

"They will not stop two merchants," Analli murmured, tossing the first cloak around Dedric's shoulders. "You are of the Woodlands, rejoining your caravan on the road to Quintaria."

"I suppose it's a chance we will have to take," Thane muttered, tying off his cloak and hefting the basket of fruit on his back. "I don't like leaving you here, mother. You and father should come with us."

"No, no. Home here, we are. They will not drive us from the city." Analli took Thane's face between her palms, staring into the eyes of her youngest boy. "Good boys, I raised. Good boys to serve the Sundragon."

Her eyes flooded, the memory of a red-haired princess gracing her dining room with a small child playing in her mind. How she'd loved Brae

Sundragon's visits to her inn. How she missed the sweet laughter of little Noelle.

"Captain!" Rufus's voice boomed from the dining room. "What can I do for you?"

"Hurry! Hurry now!" Analli rushed the boys to the back door.

"No!" Dedric growled, spinning back around. "No, we can fight them!"

"Bring death to this house, you will!" Analli snapped, shoving her boys out the back door. "Go! Handle the soldiers, your father and I will! To the Shadow Lands, you must go, and find the little princess. Find Noelle Jandry! The first village you come to, stop and tell them your mission. They will help you. They will know what to do."

She paused, staring at her children where they stood in the alley. Thane, barely eighteen, and Dedric! A man of twenty-two. When had it happened?

"Live," she whispered. "Live to fight for Adlae Sundragon, my beautiful boys. We will meet again, when peace the Creator brings."

She closed the door, latching the lock tightly before turning. Taking a deep breath, she walked calmly to the kitchen door and stepped out into the dining room. The soldiers stood at the center of the room, Rufus a solid wall before them, his face pinched and red, hands fisted. Analli came to his side.

"Help you, can we?" Analli asked, taking her husband's hand. Rufus gripped her fingers tight, until she could no longer feel them.

"Madam," the captain said, hand on the hilt of his sword. "By order of King Roderick and Princess Raphaela, I must inform you, you are now prisoners of the crown."

"With what are we charged?" Rufus snarled.

"Harboring the traitors Thane and Dedric Devareigh, offering assistance to enemies of the crown, and plotting with the Princess Damari to overthrow the true King of Nfaros." The captain took a step closer. "Rufus and Analli Devareigh, I hereby place you under arrest to face trial and judgment according to the laws of old."

Analli tilted her head up proudly. Rufus looked down at her and she smiled at him.

"Do what you must, captain. Afraid, we are not."

5

The Shadow Lands

The child raced across the frozen ground, his small feet slipping and sliding on the cracked ice covering the expanse of their village. The Ice Mountains loomed behind the forestry surrounding their cottages, glistening under the light of the winter sky. The sun's rays barely reached this far, casting their land in shadow nearly all year. There never were many visitors to these lands for that reason alone. So, the arrival of anyone from another part of the world was exciting news, indeed.

The boy came to a skidding halt outside the smallest cottage nearest the ridge. He inhaled deeply, breath steaming on the cold air, and readjusted the fur cloak draped on his shoulders before he stepped through the door.

"Healer Faw! There are riders coming!"

Healer Faw raised one finger to silence him, his eyes focused on the tiny woman whimpering on his table. The boy stared at her—the way her little wings released frost every time they trembled and her sky-blue hair glistening where it fell across the table, nearly a foot in length. Another fairy hovered close, sending shimmering flakes on the dirt floor of the cottage, hastily creating a pile of soft snow.

"The *Brakari* came from nowhere," she said, her voice barely above a whisper. "We won the day against the creature, but young Ilicya was struck by its red fire. My mistress sent me here straightaway with her. Will she live, Healer Faw?"

Healer Faw muttered something under his breath, stroking the poor Frostling's hair with his finger.

"Her frost is fading," he said, more clearly.

"But that is the source of her power and without it, her soul will fade!" The other Frostling shot forward, floating right in front of Healer Faw's face. "Please, Healer Faw! She is so young and has a family awaiting her return to the Ice Mountains!"

Healer Faw sighed, scooping up Ilicya in his palm. He held her out to the Frostling, his weathered eyes sad as she took Ilicya in her arms.

"Then take her to her family in haste, my lady, and await the Creator's will. This is beyond even my skill to heal. Only the ice can save her now."

The Frostling's bottom lip trembled. "If ice can save her ..."

"If you try to take her to the Winter Queen, you risk her death before you ever arrive. The Winter Queen has not been seen in days."

"I cannot give up, Healer Faw. My mistress entrusted her to me, and I must do everything to save her. I thank you for your attempt."

The Frostling spun, shooting pass the boy where he still stood in the door. He turned, watching the trail of snow dust she left behind as she flew. She disappeared almost instantly, leaving no evidence she'd ever come to their village.

"What is this about a rider, young Elias?" Healer Faw's question brought the boy around.

Elias swallowed, staring up at the aged healer. Their people said Healer Faw was nearly one-hundred and fifty years old, the oldest Healer who ever lived. If he remained another year, the people believed he might never die.

"Two riders, Healer Faw! They approach from the Caravan Road and wear cloaks of the Woodlanders. You must come see!" Elias grabbed the old man's hand, tugging him from his cottage.

Healer Faw went quietly, a smile wrinkling his leathery cheeks as Elias half-walked, half-skipped down the village streets. Others had gathered, blocking the riders from entering the village—the men holding fishing spears and the women rushing children into their homes. Elias shoved his way around the men, pulling Healer Faw along with him the whole way. They stopped at the edge of the village.

One of the young men looked down at them, his dark hair flopping over his forehead and head tilted. His nose was red from the cold, the thin cloak around his shoulders barely protecting him from winter's wind.

"What brings you here, friends?" Healer Faw asked.

The two men exchanged glances.

"Are you the ruler of the village?" one responded.

Healer Faw chuckled. "We have no ruler here, young man. I am, however, the oldest member of this community."

"Our mother sent us," the boy said cautiously. "My name is Dedric Devareigh, and this is my younger brother, Thane."

The other rider—Thane—nodded slightly. Healer Faw placed his free hand on his heart.

"I am called Healer Faw. Tell me what you seek, and I shall do my utmost to assist you."

"We are looking for a child and her protector. Our mother told us they were coming this way. We've ridden these many days to find them and be sure they came to you safely."

Healer Faw's brow wrinkled. "You seek a single child in all this chaos?"

"Not just any child," Thane replied, leaning forward in the saddle. "We seek Noelle Jandry, daughter of Brae Sundragon."

Elias looked up at Healer Faw, watching his cloudy eyes clear, his lips parted slightly.

"You seek Zelaria Sundragon's granddaughter?"

"Yes, is she here? Is she safe?"

Healer Faw took another step forward. "Who was it who sent you? Who is your mother that so desperately wants to protect the line of Sundragon?"

The two boys shared another look, confusion clouding their eyes.

"Analli Devareigh."

Healer Faw's knees trembled, and Elias put a cautious arm around his waist.

"Analli of Quintaria, of course!" Healer Faw's mouth spread in a smile, and he turned facing the people. "The time has come! She has sent her message!"

The villagers looked at each other strangely as Healer Faw laughed. He turned back to the Devareigh brothers, and Elias found himself grinning for no reason.

"The time is finally upon us!"

"What, Healer Faw?" Elias asked, pulling on the man's robes. "What is it?"

Healer Faw looked down at him, his eyes suddenly clear of age and exhaustion.

"Our people will finally no longer live in shadow, child. For the first time in years, we will leave our homes, as was prophesied in days of old." Healer Faw turned, looking out over the great expanse of snow-covered land. "We shall once again stand beside the Winter Queen and ignite the flames of the Sundragon for all the world to see."

CHAPTER ONE

The City of Sunkai

For four years, rumors abounded of the fate of Gelsey Malaki. Women at the wash fountain spoke of the young beauty who'd vanished into the Night Wood, never to be seen again. Men told tales of the youngest Malaki sibling's rise to power among the wild men and women who lived far to the north. Children fell asleep to whispered stories of the courageous young woman whose arrows fly straight and true. A woman who would come one day, the Lady of the Night Wood, to free them from the hateful Roderick Kael's rule.

Gelsey Malaki knew full well how powerful rumors could be.

Crouching low in the shadow of the Blood Keep, she watched. There were only three guards upon the gate tonight, perhaps a dozen more inside. Roderick had taken the rest of his soldiers with him out of the city to meet Raphaela in the Gracian. His arrogance allowed him to believe his little cousin could hold Sunkai with only a few hundred men in the barracks while he was gone.

How progressive of him, to offer his female cousin a chance such as this. Gelsey scowled, then looked over her shoulder.

Nic grinned at her, the twinkle in his steel grey eyes shining brighter out of his dark face and making her heart skip a beat. The moonlight glistened on his ebony skin, reflecting on the snow clinging to his long, thick dreadlocks. He'd been the first to find her when she ran from Kaldon, abandoning everything her father had wanted her to be in her desire to redeem the People of the Night Wood. Instead, she'd found herself the one in need of redemption. Taking their traditions and their home as her own was made simple when she realized everything she'd been missing as a captive of her own heart. The People of the Night Wood had freed her, and she intended to return the favor.

She felt Nic's body heat when he moved closer, the brush of a dreadlock tickling her arm. Absently she reached over, twining one of the strands round her finger. She'd done them herself this morning as they were preparing to depart. Until then, Nic had worn his hair loose and ratty round his shoulders, not caring how unkempt he looked. Gelsey cared, however, so she'd begged and pleaded until he'd finally given in.

He'd fussed and grumbled the entire time. Yet even as complaints poured from his mouth, his eyes glimmered with a sparkle reserved just for her, and his lip tilted with the warm smile that declared how much he loved her. She twisted the ring on her right hand, reminded of the promise they'd made to wed as soon as Adlae Sundragon sat upon Sunkai's throne.

"You're sure our people are in position around the barracks?" Gelsey asked.

"Ready to pull the Kael woman's soldiers from their beds at your signal, Gelsey," Nic confirmed.

"If they're not prepared to go when I say, this will go bad—quickly."

"I know, love. They're ready, trust me."

Gelsey looked at him, locking gazes. "I always trust you, Nic, you know that."

He leaned in, kissing her softly. "Be careful. I'll see you in the throne room."

Gelsey nodded, a lump forming in her throat when he jogged away, keeping close to the shadows so the guards patrolling the battlements wouldn't see him and give away Gelsey's position.

She waited until his silhouette disappeared completely before turning to the small group of men and women behind her.

"You all know what to do," she whispered. "Vintra, you run back and give our men the signal to raid the barracks. We uphold our Mercy Statement, even for the soldiers who agree to surrender and especially for the women and children."

Vintra nodded, her bobbed hair bouncing before she took off. Gelsey turned her gaze back to the Blood Keep gates. The guards were coming around again, their hands firmly on their swords and gazes locked on the streets below.

That Roderick would be so foolish as to leave Sunkai in the hands of his timid cousin only proved how anxious he was. To travel outside the city with nearly all of his men to find Adlae Sundragon himself?

He has a death wish, for certain. Gelsey smirked.

True, it had been days since anyone had a sighting of the Winter Queen, which was troubling to most for many different reasons. The number of arrests in Sunkai had risen with the tension of knowing she was out there somewhere, waiting for her opportunity to strike. Gelsey knew her actions here today would only help the progress of the war. If she could take the Blood Keep, it would either draw Roderick back or leave the grand city vulnerable for Adlae or Mirae to finally swoop in, grab a hold of the country, changing the course of the war.

Gelsey breathed in and out slowly, giving Vintra a chance to get back to the barracks. If she was even a moment off in her timing, it could mean the slaughter of her people right here on the streets.

With one last nod to her troop she stepped out into the moonlight, skidding to a halt before the gates.

"Greetings good soldiers!" she called, waving her arm wide over her head.

The three men turned. "Who goes there?" one shouted.

"Just a passing woman of the city." Gelsey held her arms wide, moving forward toward the gate. "Tell me, is it true the king has abandoned us?"

"Be off with you!" the soldier answered, waving a dismissive hand at her. "Go before we have you arrested!"

"Arrested?" Gelsey squawked. Hands on hips, she laughed. "For what? For this?"

She grabbed hold of the gates in both hands, shaking them. They rattled and shrieked, the sounds filling the quiet of the night.

"Cease!" the soldier bellowed. "Take your hands off the gate—now!"

"Why? Did I hurt them?" Gelsey shook the iron bars again.

The soldiers turned, disappearing when they took the steps. Gelsey shuffled back, stretching her fingers at her sides as she waited for them to appear. Each breath she took was slow and steady, her heart pounding faster against her chest as the sound of their boots thundering against stone steps came closer. The next moment, the three of them appeared, two grabbing for the gate handles while the third drew his sword. Gelsey grinned.

"Ooh," she murmured. "I'm so scared! Forgive me, good sirs, please!"

"Enough of that!" the soldier with the sword spat. "Who do you think you are?"

The gates shrieked as the two soldiers tossed them open, stepping out toward her, flanked by the third. Her grin faded as she slowly lifted her hand toward her sword hilt.

"Who am I?" she murmured. "I'm Gelsey Malaki."

Her troop raced out of hiding, leaping behind the soldiers with bows and arrows ready.

"Don't move!" Quinten shouted.

"Put down your swords now!" Embry added.

Gelsey stepped forward, relieving one of the soldiers of his weapons. "Perhaps you've heard of my brother, Jabon Malaki? One of the most powerful men among the nobility of Nfaros?"

The soldier scowled.

"Oh, and I'll want a full report on my other brother, Tyrese. I hear he fled the city with Roderick's dogs on his heels. If he's hurt, you'll pay for it."

"You'll never get away with this!" one of the other soldiers yelled as Quinten and Embry tied their hands behind them. "You'll never be able to hold Sunkai! When King Roderick finds out—"

Gelsey grabbed the man by the scruff of the neck, shoving him against the gates. He grunted, his eyes bugging in his head when she clasped her hand around his neck, digging her fingernails deep against his flesh.

"Do not call him king," she hissed against his ear. "He's not the king. He never was." She shoved him away and Quinten grabbed hold of him. "Get them out of my sight, Quinten. Embry, Maksim, and Oda with me. Camari, Zaire, and Haiden, around the back to meet up with Nic."

Gelsey jogged through the gates, her shoulders hunched as she tried to keep low to the shadows. She remembered the Blood Keep from years ago when she used to run the halls and courtyards with Mirae and Brae as children. Jabon never once let Adlae out of his sight. They were always going off into the gardens together for secret talks, their love blooming before the eyes of all in Sunkai.

They thought they kept it a secret. Thought they were so clever ... Gelsey shook her head. They'd hardly any time together before Vihaan was murdered—it was a crime against love and life. To this day, Gelsey dreamt of them having the happy life they'd always deserved. The happy life they'd all deserved. It was wrong they were denied such a dream.

Please, good Creator, let the rumors be true. Let it be that they found each other. Gelsey breathed deeply, slipping silently through the door to the armory in the south wing of the castle. She moved on her tiptoes along the dark corridor, her fingers tight round the hilt of her sword. Her companions moved slowly with her, keeping close to her back as they climbed the steps.

Gelsey stopped at the top, resting her hand on the stone door. It was slightly ajar, allowing a small whisper of air through. She glanced back at Embry. The young woman winked at her, a rebellious brown curl falling across her forehead when she nodded vigorously. Gelsey pushed the door open. The stone groaned, scraping against the floor as Gelsey cautiously stepped into the hall.

Empty. Gelsey jerked her hand at them and they started down the hall, moving swiftly.

A soldier appeared around the corner. Gelsey's breath caught, then, with one sharp upward thrust of her arm, she slammed the heel of her hand into his nose. His head jerked back, and he landed on the ground, head lolling to the side.

"Tie him up," she hissed, moving forward without missing a beat.

A quick glance back told her Oda stayed to tie up the soldier while Embry and Maksim continued on with her. The throne room doors suddenly loomed before her, and her heart shot down into the pit of her stomach. Gelsey paused for a moment, resting her palms flat on the large doors. One good push and they would open easily, despite their weight.

"Now, Gelsey!" Embry hissed. "Nic will be coming up the back way any moment!"

Gelsey nodded. Holding her breath, she shoved.

The doors slid open, gaining speed until they rebounded against the walls. Gelsey strolled inside, holding out her arms to either side of her.

"Well, well, well," she laughed, her voice echoing against the high glass ceilings. "If it isn't Bridie Kael, Queen Regent!"

Bridie Kael leaped off the humble throne of Sunkai, her golden hair thickly braided over one shoulder and blue eyes going wide. A white-haired man stood near her side, perhaps one of her advisors, and three soldiers jumped down before the throne, swords ready to protect the Queen Regent.

"Gelsey Malaki?" Bridie gasped, her voice raspy with fear. "How is this possible?"

"Hello, Bridie." Gelsey tilted her head and slacked a hip. "Is it my imagination or have you grown? Oh, well, perhaps I am not accustomed to seeing you wearing a crown that rightfully belongs to Adlae Sundragon.

And I simply do not remember the stench of loyalty to the Abyss emanating from your person when last we met."

Bridie sucked in a breath, her face blanching. Gelsey tugged at the cuffs of her coat sleeves, taking another step forward as she continued.

"How your cousin must love you, to leave you guarded by so few men! Oh, yes, Roderick Kael truly does care about Sunkai."

"Gelsey, please, you do not understand the circumstances—"

"Circumstances?" Gelsey's voice rose to a shriek, her smile gone. "What circumstances demand the arrests of poor, innocent people? What circumstances demand that citizens of Sunkai rot in the Blood Keep prisons?"

"I have been investigating—"

"Well, I have come to put an end to your investigations."

Gelsey drew her sword, the steel hissing loudly in the chamber. The soldiers surged forward. Embry and Maksim jumped in front of her, ready for a fight.

The back door to the throne room burst open, her people flooding in with Nic walking calmly amongst them. Gelsey's heart soared when he jumped the steps to the throne, grabbing Bridie by the arm.

"Good evening, my lady," he said to Bridie, then turned, winking at Gelsey. "Gentlemen, may I suggest you point your swords at something other than my betrothed?"

"W-What do you intend to do?" Bridie stuttered, turning her big eyes from Nic back to Gelsey.

Gelsey tilted her head up, a smirk twisting her upper lip. "Well, Bridie, I do not intend to do anything, because I've already done what I came to do. In the name of the Creator, I take this throne for Adlae Sundragon, to hold in trust until she sits upon it."

Gelsey turned her back on the Queen Regent before she could answer, holding her arms wide to the Night Wood people.

"My loves," she shouted, her voice vibrating throughout the room. "We have taken the Blood Keep! Long live the Sundragon!"

Hadroul's Mountain
In the Mirror

14

You must awaken what you have held prisoner in your soul all these years ...

Damari Kael ran through the woods, her pearly legs glistening in the sunlight where her dress had torn, arms pumping wildly in rhythm with her racing heart. The sun beat down on her relentlessly, but she barely felt the heat. It strengthened her power, bringing her fire to the surface stronger than ever before.

She broke through the trees, skidding to a halt at the cliff's edge. Her shriek of surprise echoed against the ravine walls. The drop seemed to have no bottom, going deeper and deeper into the earth until all she could see was darkness. Damari looked up at the other side of the cliff. Lush grass covered the plains beyond. Rolling hills beckoned her, the mountains beyond calling her name. But the expanse was too far to jump and there was no way around.

"Where are you?" she shouted, the words bouncing back to her in the emptiness. "I need you! My people need you! Why won't you show yourself?"

She waited, her hands fisted at her sides in frustration.

Whoosh ... whoosh ...

Damari looked up, excitement bubbling in her belly as she felt the wind shift with the distant sound. The soft thud of wings batting against the air getting closer ... closer ...

The dragon descended toward the center of the canyon, facing Damari. Her white scales were smooth like marble, sky blue eyes that nearly matched Damari's exactly, staring back at her with curiosity. Then she rose again, her large wings flapping in gentle strokes as she came to hover over Damari. Carefully, Damari raised her arm toward the creature.

The dragon lowered herself, clasping Damari's entire arm within her huge talons. Then they rose. The breath left her as the dragon lifted her off the ground, carrying her across the gorge to the other side. When her feet touched ground again, she stumbled, the weightlessness offered by the dragon coming over her in waves as she fell on all fours.

She twisted, looking over her shoulder ... but the dragon was already gone.

CHAPTER TWO

The Aulend Forest

"This is impossible! She's far too young!"

"Are you denying what your own eyes have seen, Haileah?"

"Do not take that tone with me, Ellia. The child is cursed!"

"Says the woman whose magic manifested at ten years?"

"She is far from ten years, Symber. She is a baby!"

"Enough!"

Gwylan's voice echoed in the woods, every eye turning to her. She paid no attention to them, instead watching Maxx Jandry from across the encampment with his niece, Noelle, on his hip. He was distracting the child as best he could, encouraging her to catch snowflakes on her tongue, keeping her eyes on the sky instead of on the four bickering women he'd brought her to for help.

The gentle way he held Noelle was oddly endearing to Gwylan, stirring a warmth in her belly she'd not felt in years. She could still remember the way he looked at her upon their first meeting, could still feel his hand through her glove when he touched her.

Touched. I am touched by a man. Gwylan's breath deepened, and she turned away from the man who had, with a simple gesture, changed her future. Her mouth pursed. *Creator's Night, I despise my Draedin customs.*

"The Creator has a reason for everything, even the early manifestation of magic in little Noelle Jandry. Her mother and aunts held great magic in their souls, and if rumor is to be believed, the Jandry women also possess great power. If the Creator has given Noelle such a gift now, it is because he is in need of her."

"But even the Creator would not do such a thing. He would not place a baby at the center of this war! What could she possibly accomplish? How will she ever survive?" Haileah argued.

"Do I detect a hint of fear in your voice, Haileah?" Gwylan frowned at the older woman. "Maxx Jandry has come to us for help, and Noelle most certainly needs us. I believe the Creator wishes us to teach the child. Perhaps, we were meant to find her, not the Winter Queen."

"But, Gwylan," Ellia murmured, hesitantly. "The Superiors gave us specific orders. We are to find Adlae Sundragon, the One Thought Dead."

"And we shall, Ellia," Gwylan assured her. "However, the Superiors never said we should abandon our purpose in life. We turn away no one with the Gift. Noelle Jandry has a future of magic now, and it is our sacred duty to help her cultivate her power."

Gwylan paused, taking a breath as she looked upon the child again. Noelle was laughing, spreading her arms wide with her head tilted back. She stuck out her little pink tongue, wiggling it as she tried to catch as many snowflakes as she could.

"I see what this is," Haileah sniffed, chin up. "You are allowing your Draedinian traditions to muddle your brain! Because you are bound to the man, you are becoming submissive to his will!" Haileah wagged a finger in Gwylan's face.

Heat flushed her cheeks, and her hand came up sharply, snapping around Haileah's finger and squeezing. The woman's eyes widened, mouth parting in pain as she tried to tug herself loose from Gwylan's grasp.

"You question my heart, Haileah? You question my loyalty to my vows as a Sister of Eventide? Have you so soon forgotten your own vows, to protect those with the Gift? If you wish to turn your back on a child with powers capable of killing her, if you desire to forsake your vows, then go, for I will not forsake mine. And Maxx Jandry's foolish action, binding us to a custom of my homeland, has nothing to do with my wish to help Noelle. It is our duty to make sure she survives, no matter the cost."

Gwylan shoved Haileah away. Before any of them could speak again, she walked away, raising her feet high in the deep snow to close the distance between her and Maxx. He turned at the sound of her boots crunching snow, drawing Noelle's attention away from the sky as well. Gwylan hesitated, her hands unsteady and stomach fluttering with nerves. The way Maxx stared at her, his dark eyes so riveting, her knees trembled ... he provoked something within her she didn't recognize, and for the first time in years she was frightened.

"May I?" she whispered hoarsely, holding out her arms to Noelle.

He nodded solemnly, transferring the child to her. Noelle came into her arms with ease, wrapping one of her small arms across Gwylan's shoulders and her little legs around Gwylan's waist, ankles crossed.

"Noelle, do you know who I am?" she asked.

The child stared at her blankly, bright green eyes wide.

"What you can do, I can do also," Gwylan continued softly. "The Creator gives some people a Gift, to be protected and cherished. I am here to make sure little girls like you, who have this Gift, live to see its purpose. Do you understand?"

Noelle tilted her head. "Like my Mama Damari?"

Gwylan frowned, her gaze darting to Maxx.

"Damari Kael," he murmured, threading his arms across his chest. "They became close during their escape from Sunkai. I've tried to explain to her that Damari wasn't her mother but ..."

"Such a love between a woman and a child has no explanation. Noelle needed her and loved her for the care she offered. It does not mean she forgot her true mother." Gwylan smiled, nuzzling her nose to Noelle's cheek. The little girl giggled, drawing away slightly from the tickle.

"Allow me to take her?" Ellia's voice purred beside Gwylan and she turned.

Maxx hesitated, moving forward slightly as Ellia reached for Noelle.

"I will take great care with her, Maxx Jandry. You and Dominant Gwylan should speak privately."

"Yes." Gwylan passed Noelle over to her friend. "We should, indeed."

Gwylan watched Ellia walk away, joining a smiling Symber and scowling Haileah, who stood apart from the two Dominants now fawning over little Noelle. She turned back, gesturing for Maxx to walk with her across the clearing. He kept his distance, his arms firmly crossed at his chest, keeping his hands from view. Gwylan tightened her lips to keep from smiling. What other customs of her country did he not understand?

Doesn't he realize the damage has been done? She shook her head.

"Tell me," she murmured, rubbing her palms together thoughtfully. "How did you find us?"

Maxx cleared his throat. "We were on the Woodland Paths for a time. I found your trail, and when the snow became too thick to find the stones, I continued on the way I believed you would go."

19

"Hmm." They stopped near the trees, Gwylan turning to lean slightly back into one.

From here she had a full view of their camp, a clear sight of Ellia and Symber playing with Noelle in the snow and Haileah sharpening her daggers a few feet away.

"When did you discover the Gift in your niece?"

"Right after we were forced to abandon the Paths. I couldn't light a fire and she ..." Maxx shuddered, his arms clenching tighter at his chest. "When rumors abounded that my sister Clea had magic, I never questioned it. She never revealed her power to me or our other siblings, but we all knew the rumors were true. I wasn't worried because she was older, stronger. But Noelle ..."

"I understand your concerns, Maxx Jandry. You did well, bringing her to us with such haste."

"Lady Gwylan," he paused, clearing his throat again. "I wanted to apologize for my earlier ... error. I had no idea—"

"Let's not speak of that." Gwylan waved him off, hoping he didn't see her true desire to discuss the Draedinian law of betrothal in her eyes. "The custom is an old one and may not even stand in this country."

"Then there's a chance we're not ...?"

Gwylan tilted her head back, staring at the sky. "I have done my utmost to maintain the traditions of my homeland, even in this northern country. By Draedin law, I am bound to see this betrothal through. But we are not in Draedin, are we?"

"No, we're not. It was just a touch on the hand, after all."

Gwylan smirked. "Hardly worth mentioning."

"No one needs to know."

"Indeed. It's a silly custom, really. For the brush of a hand to bind two people together forever ...?"

Maxx chuckled. "I could hardly believe it when my brother told me what the touch meant to you."

Gwylan tilted her head to look at him. "Don't laugh too hard, Maxx Jandry. I could still have your head if I wanted."

Maxx sobered, his eyes wary. She grinned.

"Do not look so worried. Don't you know when you're being teased?" Gwylan pushed slightly against the tree, taking a few steps forward. Her attention returned to the child, brow creasing with a slight frown. "Maxx Jandry, how old is your niece?"

Maxx came alongside her, studying Noelle with the same intensity.

"She turned four mere days ago."

"Is she not rather big for four years?"

Maxx didn't answer, his brow furrowing deeply. Gwylan's heart raced a little faster, the chill rushing over her having nothing to do with the winter storm.

"Impossible," she whispered.

"What? What is it?" The edge of fear in Maxx's voice forced Gwylan to offer him her attention.

"I've not seen something like this since I myself was a little girl. Sometimes the early manifestation of power in one so young can cause the child to grow at a rapid rate, in both body and mind. I saw such a thing happen to a young boy from Draedin. His purpose, given by the Creator, was to rescue Draedin from the Abyss."

"But he was all right, wasn't he?" Maxx asked, his hands falling to his sides to form fists. "He just grew up faster, yes? He was all right?"

Gwylan's throat dried, blocking words. Maxx lunged closer to her, his hands trembling at his sides as he resisted grabbing hold of her.

"Tell me he was all right," he hissed, the rush of tears in his eyes breaking her heart.

"I'm sorry, Maxx," Gwylan rasped. "Perhaps with Noelle, the outcome will be different. Perhaps the Creator has another purpose for her, or perhaps I am seeing something that isn't there. But Maxx, when his mission was fulfilled, the boy from Draedin died."

Maxx stared at her, his mouth thinning. The mixed glimmer of grief and terror in his eyes called out to her heart. Gwylan moved a little closer to him and felt the rush of his breath on her cheek.

"Do not lose hope. I am going to do everything I can for her."

"I won't let her die," he snapped. "The Frostling said evil would not touch her again. You have to save her!"

Gwylan's heart skipped. "I will do everything in my power for her, Maxx Jandry. Then her fate is up to the Creator."

His fear turned to determination. Maxx raised a hand, as if to touch her, thought better and returned it to his side. "Is it possible she is merely a tall child?"

"Of course." Gwylan dipped her head.

"But because of her magic, you think it unlikely." Spoken more as a statement than a question, Maxx turned from her, his focus solely on his niece. "How am I supposed to tell my brother? How do I tell Brecken that he's lost his wife and will, most likely, lose his child once her purpose is served?"

"We still do not know that, Maxx. The Creator's intentions are never clear to us. We need only trust and hope."

"Hope ... what hope does Noelle have, Gwylan? She's lost so much already. Must she also lose her own life? Her childhood?"

"Maxx ..."

He walked away without a backward glance.

Maxx crouched beside the fire in the center of the tent, rubbing his palms together above the sparking flames. The wind had intensified to a furious howl, the snow and ice falling from the sky chasing Maxx, Noelle, and the Eventide Sisters into the tent. He stared across the tent where Gwylan was settling Noelle on one of the bedrolls. He froze, watching her.

Gwylan seemed not to notice him, humming softly to Noelle as she began to unwind her braids. The child was nearly asleep, her head resting deeply against the rolled blanket substituting a cushion and her knees curled against her chest. Gwylan didn't stop humming, releasing her raven hair from their bindings slowly. Maxx swallowed. The first time he'd seen her, he thought her cold. But her reaction to Noelle earlier told a different story, revealing a woman with emotion buried deeply inside her.

And those eyes ... he'd thought her eyes a simple brown the first time he'd seen her. There was so much more to them—deep, round pools of chocolate with flecks of gold he'd not noticed before. Her hair fell softly against her back as she finished with the last braid, the ends of the thick strands nearly reaching her waist despite the tight waves from being bound so long in braids. If straight, he imagined her hair was even longer, perhaps reaching passed her hips.

A lump clogged his throat, and he looked away, putting his imaginings aside. Her attitude toward her country's tradition had, oddly, troubled him earlier. Not to mention her lack of concern for her own reputation. In

Draedin, he had dishonored her by daring to place his hand on her. The moment it happened, he was certain the gesture meant far more to her than she intimated now.

Maxx sat back against the heels of his boots, subtly keeping an eye on the other three women in the tent. The other Draedin woman—Ellia—was going through a similar routine as Gwylan, unwinding her dark braids as she settled in for the night. The Kaldoner, Symber, was nose-deep in a thick book, a strand of her short blonde hair twisted around her finger and her bottom lip clamped between her teeth in concentration.

As for Haileah—the oldest of the four women—she was scowling at his niece. Maxx's skin chilled at the sight, watching the woman furiously brush her tightly curled brown hair with her cold eyes fixed on Noelle and Gwylan. Why did his niece frighten her so much, having seen so many young girls with magic in her time? He couldn't understand.

"You should sleep, Maxx Jandry."

Maxx jerked to the right at the soft voice. Ellia smiled gently, her dark hair falling all around her shoulders. She'd removed her gloves, hands bare as she held them out to the flames. Her leather bodice was also removed, revealing a thinner silk bodice beneath. The split in her skirt was loose, subtle so you might not notice, and she'd replaced her boots with soft slippers to wear during sleep.

Ellia sat, tucking her feet beneath her knees. "Gwylan and I traveled from Draedin to Sunkai together when we were twelve years of age, did you know that?"

Maxx shook his head.

"Our Gift manifested nearly at the same time, and our families sent us away immediately. In Draedin, the Gifted are revered but feared. In these northern lands, they are loved." Ellia tilted her head, staring at the flames. "Becoming a Sister of the Blood of Eventide was our greatest joy, as well as the hardest decision we ever made. The strongest commitment of our lives and most certainly a solitary one. Except for our other sisters, we live alone."

"I think I understand what you're trying to say," Maxx murmured.

"Do you?" Ellia tilted her head, eyeing him. "Our lives can be lonely, though we be surrounded by sisters. Gwylan's life has not been the easiest, and if you were to continue with the betrothal tradition, you might find her more agreeable than you first thought."

"Continue?"

Ellia's smile turned to a grin, her eyes twinkling mischievously. "There are three steps to a Draedinian betrothal. You have touched her, to place a claim. Next, you must complete an act of loyalty. Thirdly, you must make a vow."

"And that completes betrothal?"

"Yes, it completes betrothal. When she returns the vow, you are married. Then you need only a Holy Man to bind you under the Creator publicly, so the world knows."

Heat crawled up the back of his neck, and he cleared his throat. "That is not exactly the way we do it in the North."

"No, I suppose not. But despite appearances, Gwylan loves our homeland and their traditions. You would greatly please her, were you to follow Draedinian custom."

Maxx watched her walk away, a knot forming in the pit of his stomach. *So much for not being betrothed.* He buffed the back of his neck. Ellia clearly thought he had an obligation, no matter what Gwylan said to him.

"Are you all right?"

Startled, Maxx fell back, his head snapping up sharply at the sound of her voice. Gwylan's mouth tightened, but her eyes revealed her amusement as she settled in the place Ellia had just vacated.

"I'm fine," he grumbled. "Noelle?"

"Asleep. It didn't take her long to find peace. I wish my heart and mind were as light as a child's again."

"Where do we go from here? What happens next?" he asked, steering the conversation from a more personal subject.

Gwylan straightened her shoulders, interlocking her fingers together in her lap. "We will continue as we have done. My sisters and I have our mission. We will seek the Winter Queen, and as we travel, I will do my best to help Noelle in her … transition."

"Transition," Maxx grunted. "I've always believed such power was a gift, given by the Creator. But if it means her death …"

"We don't know for certain," Gwylan said, her voice lowering.

"But you suspect. That's good enough for me."

Maxx stood up, striding across the space to Noelle's side. He knelt beside her, reaching to place his hand on her head. She didn't stir. Instead, deep, quick breaths of sleep slipped between her lips. He bent over her, kissing her temple softly.

"I'm not going to let anything happen to you," he murmured against her ear. "I promise you. You're going to be fine, Noelle. You have to be."

A Forest with No Name

Brakari. A creature of darkness so fierce even the strongest of Frostling magic struggled to defeat one. M'kela looked up through the shelter of the tree branches. She stood perfectly balanced on one of the twigs, her tiny wings fluttering nervously against her back. The moment she'd heard the growl—felt the vibration of the creature's wings on the air—she'd taken Ilicya to the cover of the forest. They couldn't stay for long. Ilicya didn't have enough time for a prolonged delay.

When Taleah sent her to the Healer in the Shadow Lands, M'kela had been certain he could help Ilicya. Now alone and so far from her people, M'kela feared her quest to find the Winter Queen was in vain. Their Keeper hadn't been seen in days, not since word had reached them she'd taken a journey through the Tower of the Dead.

M'kela shuddered, crouching low and crawling along the branch to the hollow in the tree where she'd laid Ilicya. Her Frostling friend moaned, tightly packed beneath fresh snow M'kela had created herself. If ice could save her friend, then surely keeping her cold would prolong her life long enough to give them a chance to discover the Winter Queen's whereabouts.

Though nothing is certain ... M'kela swallowed the lump in her throat, ignored the sting of tears.

A low roar shattered the peaceful silence of the forest, and M'Kela spun, her wings trembling violently in preparation for flight.

"You should go before the *Brakari* comes," Ilicya's weak voice whispered behind her. "Leave me, M'kela. Return to Taleah and see the Creator's will done."

"No," M'kela said between deep breaths. "It is not your time."

"That is not for you to say, Sister. Perhaps the Creator wants me with him."

M'kela looked over her shoulder. Ilicya smiled, her lips warming to a ripe apple red.

No! If she is that warm while covered in snow ... M'kela fell to her knees beside the younger Frostling.

"Hold on, Ilicya, please! We are going to find the Winter Queen."

"The *Brakari's* fire is too strong, M'kela. I cannot fight anymore."

"Yes, you can! You must!" M'kela stood quickly, turning back.

The heavy *whoosh* of the *Brakari's* wings drew closer. M'kela closed her eyes, summoning the frost in her heart. She smiled, her wings sending thousands of snowflakes to the ground beneath her feet as she floated slowly into the air.

A crash shook the trees, and M'kela fell hard on the branch. She gasped, clutching a hand across her ribs as she twisted her neck around to see what had happened. A streak of solid ice flew through the air from the ground, whistling against the wind. M'kela watched the wintery spear go by, her eyes widening when it stabbed the *Brakari* in the shoulder.

The animal shrieked, snapping at the frosty weapon with its teeth. Another came up, bouncing off the hard scales protecting the *Brakari's* heart. M'kela looked in the direction the ice had come from, and her heart soared. The Winter Queen came from among the trees. The train of her white fur cloak dragging the ground, and her pure white hair separated in multiple braids brought behind her and joined in one long, thick rope down her back. Her crystal blue eyes pierced the *Brakari*, the staff in her hand shimmering and bright with magic.

Her snowy lips moved, but M'kela was too far to hear what she said before she raised the staff, sending another bolt at the *Brakari*. M'kela watched as the animal dipped, his wings shuddering before he fell in a heap in the snow.

More voices murmured below her as M'kela crawled back into the hollow of the tree.

"Come, Ilicya," she gasped, scraping the snow away from Ilicya's body before gathering her up in her arms. "The Winter Queen is here!"

Her friend was warm to the touch, and M'kela's heart sank toward the pit of her stomach. Was she too late? She leaped from the tree, her wings catching in the wind as she fluttered down toward the forest floor.

"Where did it come from?" a male voice said as she approached the Winter Queen from behind.

"Raphaela grows desperate to summon such dark magic to her side," the Winter Queen said, her voice gentle and surprisingly indifferent. "I pity the creature for its weakness to be drawn to the dark."

"What do you mean?" another man asked.

"The People of the Dragon once believed the *Brakari* are what is left of the mountain dragons that once roamed the skies of Southern Nfaros. But in their weakness, they fell prey to the Abyss, and even the *Almaër Dominÿe* could not save them."

M'kela huffed, rising a little higher before spinning around to face the Winter Queen. The two men jolted back slightly at her sudden appearance, but the Queen stood stoic, tilting her head slightly in curiosity.

"Forgive me, Your Majesty," M'kela cried, unable to hold her tears at bay a moment longer. "A Healer of the Shadow Lands told me that a *Brakari's* fire could be vanquished by the strongest of ice magic. You are the only one who can save Ilicya."

The Winter Queen stepped forward, carefully avoiding brushing against the dead *Brakari.* She lifted her hand, brushing her finger along Ilicya's forehead.

"My poor child," the Winter Queen whispered. "So warm. Too warm."

"Please tell me I'm not too late!" M'kela held Ilicya tighter.

The Winter Queen raised her hand, palm up. "Place her here, M'kela."

M'kela's eyes widened when the Queen spoke her name, as she'd not given it. But she put her surprise aside, gently placing Ilicya in the Keeper of Winter's palm.

"Now," the Winter Queen said with a smile. "Let us see what the Creator wills for young Ilicya."

CHAPTER THREE

Outskirts of Kaldon

Raphaela absently stroked the *Brakari's* head, her fingers catching on the leather-like scales curving in gentle horns down his neck. Winter's wind pressed in on her from the north, catching her raven hair up in a whirlwind around her head, veiling her sight. From here, she could see clear to the Ice Mountains, the city of Kaldon rising against the horizon, surrounded by forest and field.

The Kliat Plains spanned to the Pilvaa and beyond, to unnamed forests very few dared pass into. Only upon the Caravan Road would people dare travel that far and then rarely. Creatures of magic ventured there, as they could protect themselves. All others feared those places, for beyond them lay the Shadow Lands.

The Shadow Lands ... Raphaela breathed deeply.

Her magic rippled unsteadily within her, warning her of a change coming. She'd seen the light growing brighter near the mountains hovering over the Shadow Lands. Zelaria Sundragon's birthplace was coming to life once again—the strength of the Sundragon power growing ever since the shadows danced over the Tower of the Dead.

Do not listen, my child, his voice whispered in her mind. *Listen only to me. Heed my words. Go to the woods.*

Raphaela dug the sharp heels of her boots into the *Brakari's* sides. The creature shrieked then dove, flying hastily toward the earth. Raphaela held on, her legs gripped around the animal's rounded belly and her hands digging into the softer scales on his neck. She pulled up sharply before they reached the ground, and the *Brakari* flattened his wings against his sides, shooting straight into the woods and skillfully avoiding the trees.

Find the bark which bleeds black, her master ordered.

Raphaela's head swung from side to side. Deep within her, she called to her magic, drawing her power out to sharpen her vision. A low gasp slipped between her lips, and she yanked back sharply.

The *Brakari* roared, landing hard on the icy ground, his talons overturning snow and dirt alike before he came to a skidding halt. Raphaela slipped lightly down from its back, marching across the woodland floor to the tree she'd spotted. Black sap oozed from between the cracks in the bark, darkening the trunk of the magnificent oak.

Find the longest branch, my child.

Raphaela circled the tree, running her fingers along the rough exterior, catching a few drops of the thick liquid on her fingertips. A grin curved her lip, and she reached up, snapping the longest branch she could see from the trunk of the tree.

Now, remember your loyalty. Remember your vow to me. Let your allegiance fill you to overflowing. Think only of it.

Raphaela's heart thundered wildly in her chest, her breathing growing rapid. The branch began to bleed in her hand, black droplets flowing thicker and thicker from within the wood out until the entire branch was stained. The pole cracked and groaned in her hand, the top beginning to take its own shape. Rounding, then curling until it formed a perfectly twined bulb, twisted to a point.

A bubble of laughter rose in her throat. Raphaela thrust the staff toward the sky and a bolt of black lightning shot from the top, stabbing the winter blue sky in shadow.

The snowfall ceased, and the world went suddenly still.

"Is this how I will defeat her?" Raphaela whispered into the quiet forest. "Is this how I will kill Adlae Sundragon?"

The Abyss cackled inside her.

Yes, my child. It has begun, and soon the Sundragon will be no more.

Raphaela stared at the sky, watching her shadow grow and spread. Swallowing the winter clouds and halting the snowfall for miles beyond the forest—thick like smoke, roiling across the sky, covering the world in shadow. A deep, throaty laugh lifted from her lips, and her eyes gleamed with malice.

"Without winter, Adlae will be nothing," Raphaela murmured. "Now they will truly see what I am capable of."

Her new weapon in hand, Raphaela remounted the *Brakari* and they flew to the sky, disappearing into the thick of the shadow.

A Forest with No Name

Adlae Sundragon bent at the waist to watch the little Frostling beneath the dome of ice she'd formed on the tree stump. The faint noises of the men setting up camp near the heart of the forest reached her, offering her some semblance of comfort. It had taken days for her to banish the whispers of the dead from her mind.

Even now, they fought for control of her, pressing her with their strength. They wanted her to tell her men their prophecy. They wanted her to tell them *everything*, even the things she'd chosen to keep hidden in her heart—things her soldiers didn't need to know.

Things that will only harm them, Winter agreed. Adlae smiled.

"Your Majesty?" M'kela whispered, the soft hum of her wings filling Adlae's ears. "Does she improve?"

"I believe so, child," Adlae replied, lightly tracing her finger over the delicate ice she'd encased Ilicya in. "Her skin returns to the pale white of winter magic, and her breath grows stronger. I believe the Creator has a larger plan for this young one."

M'kela gasped and her wings faltered for a moment with her relief. Adlae gestured for the tiny creature to take rest on her shoulder. M'kela did so, settling comfortably in the curve where Adlae's neck and shoulder met. Adlae straightened, turning back toward the camp. The end of her staff sunk into the thick snow, a flurry of white flakes falling heavily between the tree branches overhead.

"We have been hard at work for you, my queen," M'kela murmured, curling her arms around her knees. "Nfaros has not seen a winter this fierce in a hundred years."

"Your mistress has done well." Adlae frowned. "She no longer comes to me in my dreams."

"The darkness fights us. My mistress has scattered the Frostlings to every corner of the land, even to the Nfaros Sea, in an attempt to do your

31

bidding, Your Majesty. She grows weary, for only she can hold the darkness at bay so it may not hinder the frost."

Adlae stopped at the edge of the camp, leaning on her staff as she watched the men raise their tents. Jabon and Glaydin were walking the line, pointing and talking amongst themselves about their next move. After they left the Tower of the Dead, her Second and Third seemed to finally gain common ground. Moving further north seemed the best decision, considering Mirae was rumored to be heading for the Tower of Tears. They were far past the time she should've joined her sister, uniting their armies against Roderick and Raphaela.

Your sister would not go to Tears without you, surely! She must know Roderick has the tower under heavy guard. Winter murmured.

Adlae shook her head. Mirae had always been impulsive. Her stubborn will had gotten them into trouble more than once as children. One thing was for certain, Adlae was glad her sister hadn't changed. She'd need Mirae's strength in the days to come and knowing the kind of woman she'd become was a great comfort.

Thunder rumbled across the sky, and Adlae looked up. A frown creased her brow when she saw the clouds roiling, dimming to a dull grey, and continuing to darken as they thickened. M'kela stood on Adlae's shoulder, wings batting wildly as she lifted a few feet into the air.

"That is not the work of my mistress," M'kela whispered.

Adlae's heart stuttered.

The Abyss! Winter shrieked.

"M'kela, go to Ilicya! Protect her!" Adlae ordered, spinning away.

A bolt of red fire burst from the sky, slamming into one of the tents. Screams and shouts erupted in the camp as Adlae ran for her men.

"Glaydin! Jabon!" Adlae skidded along the slick ice, stopping before them. "Gather the men to the center of the camp—*now!*"

The two ran to do her bidding without question, roaring orders to the soldiers, even pulling some of them from their tents, too shocked were they to move. Another fireball tumbled from the sky, lighting the trees in a spectacular display of flames. Adlae could feel the darkness in the fire, felt the evil stirring overhead as she raised her staff to the sky.

Her eyes darted to M'kela, watching the little Frostling create a protection spell of her own over herself and Ilicya on the tree stump nearby.

Adlae returned her attention to the task at hand, watching the glittering mist lift from her staff, reaching high toward the sky before stretching out, forming a dome around the camp. The edges were closing, reaching toward the ground as Jabon and Glaydin packed the men close within her barrier.

Adlae Sundragon! Look to the sky! Winter cried.

Adlae's neck twisted, her eyes widening when she saw the black tendril slither from the sky, as a snake from its hiding place. The vine twirled and dipped, shimmering like onyx stones before striking her barrier.

The breath sucked out of her, Adlae went flying, a force she'd neither anticipated nor encountered before slamming into her so fiercely her heart stopped. She landed hard on the icy ground, wheezing in her attempt to breathe. The men raised their swords, panicked shouting echoing all around her, but the dark magic whipped them aside, knocking them into trees, raising them by their throats before dropping them violently to the ground.

Get up, Adlae! You must leave this place! Winter begged her.

"Adlae!" Jabon appeared at her side, taking her arm. "We have to move!"

She nodded, groaning as she forced herself to her feet. Her knees trembled, her power draining from her so quickly she thought her heart was failing. Adlae gripped her staff firmly, tears rushing to her eyes against her will as she watched the darkness overcome her men, some of them escaping deeper into the forest, while others fell prey to the evil.

"This cannot be happening ..." Adlae gasped.

The moment she spoke, the darkness shifted. The vine twirling in her direction. Jabon tugged on her arm, his mouth moving, but she could no longer hear his voice. A low ringing filled her ears, drowning all other sounds. She was paralyzed, that single tendril of darkness hissing and slithering toward her.

"Go, Jabon," she said—or she thought she said the words, she could barely hear her own voice. "You must go now. Find Mirae."

Adlae shoved him aside, raised her staff—

An animal cry rent the air. Adlae had no time to react before he flashed before her eyes, throwing himself in front of the darkness.

"NO!" Adlae screamed.

The tendrils wrapped around Glaydin, lifting him into the air above her head. His long, copper hair swung as he struggled in the hold of the Abyss, waving his wide curved sword in all directions. The steel shattered when it touched the blackness, falling in shards to the snow below. Glaydin shouted in pain, wrapping his hands around the vines, squeezing.

Bones crunched, he writhed.

Adlae sobbed, falling to her knees.

"Creator have mercy!" she wailed.

"My queen!"

M'kela and Ilicya swung before her, wings fluttering and bodies glowing with their power. Ilicya was pale and bright-eyed, as she should be, looking stronger than ever before as she leaned close.

"Together, my queen!" M'kela shouted above Glaydin's moans. "We can send this evil thing back to the sky together!"

Her staff pulsed in her grasp, fresh ice crackling and twining around her knuckles.

Rise, Adlae. Help him. Winter urged gently.

Adlae trembled, her hands sinking into the snow as she pushed herself unsteadily to her feet. The Frostlings faced the darkness, floating back until they were on either side of her.

Drawing on what strength she had left, she thrust her staff toward the darkness, sending a steady stream of ice into the shadow. The thing—whatever it might be—screeched and twisted, tightening around Glaydin. Adlae shouted, her body writhing as she poured out everything she had left. The Frostlings' magic seeped into her, reinforcing her power.

The tendrils loosened around Glaydin and he dropped, falling limply in the snow. Adlae swung her staff over her head then sent another bolt of ice at the creature.

The vine retreated, twisting in a whirlwind up into the sky before disappearing among the blackening clouds overhead. The world was awash in darkness—not a hint of blue sky or sun overhead as Adlae's knees buckled beneath her. She fell in the snow, her staff rolling from her palm and tears freezing on her cheeks.

"My lady?" Ilicya murmured near her ear.

She ignored her, crawling across the small space between her and Glaydin. A sob wrenched from her throat as she turned him over, his head falling in her lap. His skin was now cool to her touch when it should have burned her, the sensation sending ripples of horror through her.

"No! No, my friend, please!" Adlae pressed her cheek to his, rocking him back and forth.

He moaned, and she raised her head. Glaydin stared at her, small coughs splattering blood on his lips.

"I-I can try ..." she reached for his chest, but he grabbed her hand, clutching her fingers in his palm.

"Only fire magic could save me now," he said hoarsely.

Adlae shook her head, tears flowing as she looked into his eyes. His beautiful, strange eyes—one blue, one green—watching her with the same intensity they'd held for her almost from the moment they met. How cautious he'd been when first they'd been introduced! How much suspicion she'd seen in his eyes, only to watch those feelings change to the love that comes with loyalty.

"I swore I would protect you," Glaydin whispered. "You knew I would die for you, and now ... now my time has come."

Adlae shook her head fiercely, squeezing her eyes closed.

"You must live, Adlae," he continued. His fingertips grazed her cheek, and her throat tightened, breathing unbearable. "I know you could never love me, my queen. But you must know by now ... you were my True Heart."

"Oh, Glaydin!" Adlae opened her eyes, smiling down at him. "You are wrong, you dear, dear man. I loved you before I knew you. My soul cried for you. My heart ached for you. To watch such a one as you come to my side in my time of need—to swear your sword to me when this fight was mine alone to bear—awakened a hope in my heart I thought long dead. Knowing you, a creature of fire, could love me, a creature of winter, brought me back to life, and I will always be in your debt for that. I will always *love* you for that."

Glaydin smiled, his hand tightening on hers. Adlae bent over, pressing her lips to his. Clinging desperately to him as she prayed for mercy.

When she broke the kiss, he did not open his eyes. His hand slipped from hers, falling into the snow.

"No," Adlae sobbed, hugging him close with her forehead on his. "Come back. Please, come back!"

The wind whipped around her, her men groaning as they rose from where they'd fallen. The crunch of snow beneath boots and whispers filled the air as they gathered around her.

Then something else ... a softness covered the wind. Peace settling over the ruined encampment. Adlae looked up, her heart thundering out of control.

Afra Malaki stepped forward, her light footsteps barely leaving an imprint in the snow as she came to kneel before her. Gentle brown eyes glowed at Adlae, full of compassion.

"Let me take him now, Adlae," she whispered, her voice like a song. "Let me pass him to the Creator, for he has done well and shall now be at peace."

Adlae nodded slowly. Afra reached over, placing her hand on Glaydin's chest. A fierce glow rose from his chest—red and golden—his soul glistened even in the darkness shrouding the woods. His soul settled on Afra's palms, and she smiled.

"Such an old soul," she whispered. "With so much greatness. He lived for the Creator with a pure heart."

"Yes," Adlae replied, her voice gravelly. "He truly did."

Afra closed her eyes, and when Adlae blinked, she'd vanished. Glaydin's body remained, tucked firmly in her arms. Adlae looked up, watching the blackness overhead deepen and coil, consuming any light that remained. Only the fires from the Abyss brightened the forest now, cracking and eating away at the trees. Even her staff grew dim, the ice snapping and hissing as the darkness overcame its light.

Blessed Creator ... what do I do now?

The City of Sunkai

Gelsey stepped gingerly down the rough stone steps, holding the torch out before her. Nic was close on her heels, his over-protective nature hanging over her like a shroud. She smiled. His need to keep her safe didn't bother her, truly, she only pretended it did. There was something nice about being loved so much. A feeling she'd not had for a long time.

Her thoughts shifted to her big brothers, and her heart sank. She'd declared for the Sundragon long ago, forcing herself into hiding in the Night Wood to escape Roderick Kael's executioner. Her brothers, as a result, had disowned her. Whether they still spoke of her in private—or

36

even spared a moment to think of her—she didn't know. She only knew since Adlae declared herself, they were doing the right thing, and for now, it was enough.

The groans grew louder the further she went, and she reached out, grabbing Nic's hand.

"Time to see Roderick's damage," she muttered. Gelsey glared over her shoulder.

Bridie stood there, blonde hair disheveled and wrists tied together with rough rope in front of her. There'd been many opinions on what to do with Roderick's mouse-like cousin, none of which Gelsey was willing to consider. There was something wrong about this whole situation. Bridie might be a Kael, but she'd never been cruel.

What did Roderick threaten her with to make her sit on the throne and keep these innocent people in his dungeons? Gelsey shook her head.

They stepped onto a smooth surface, Gelsey holding the torch high as she followed the corridor deeper beneath the Blood Keep. Iron bars greeted her on either side, prisoners filling the cells. Some approached, softly begging for their release. Others cowered in the light of the torches, holding each other and mumbling prayers to the Creator.

"Did you even come down here when your cousin handed you Sunkai's throne?" Gelsey whispered, stopping at one of the cells. "Did you bother to look at their faces?"

Bridie cringed. "I wanted to—"

"No. I don't think you did." Gelsey peeked through the bars here and there as she searched for one face in particular. "Nic, have Embry and Quinten release them as soon as possible. They are to be treated well and housed in the royal quarters until we know it is safe for them to venture home."

Her betrothed turned, heading back the way they'd come to do her bidding. Gelsey continued on, Bridie close on her heels.

"Please, Gelsey," Bridie whispered. "We have known each other since we were children. You cannot believe this is what I wanted."

"Then perhaps you'd care to explain why all of these people are still here? Why half of the inhabitants of Sunkai's Lower Village are imprisoned?" Gelsey arched a brow. "Roderick and Raphaela left for Kaldon days ago."

"I had a plan, Gelsey. Don't you think Roderick would have come back had I released all his prisoners right away? Don't you think Raphaela would have received word from her spies? I had to tread carefully!" Bridie stomped her foot in frustration.

"If you say so."

Gelsey stopped in front of another cell, leaning close to look into the dim room. Her heart thundered.

"Blessed Sun ..." The keys trembled in her hands as she thrust them at the keyhole, twisting the lock with a rusty *clunk*. Gelsey burst in, shoving the torch into one of the sconces on the wall before she fell to her knees beside the one she sought.

He wheezed, his skin pale and clammy. Evidence of torture with black magic covered him, darkening his veins and slowly stealing his life.

"Oh, Rufus," Gelsey whispered, stroking the man's thinning hair. "Why would they do this to you?"

Rufus Devareigh coughed, his swollen eyes squinting open. A soft smile touched his lips, and he squeezed her hand.

"M-my boys ..."

"They passed through the Night Wood days ago, telling us of Roderick's plan to leave the Mother City and secure Kaldon. We would not be here now had they not given us all the information they could in service of the Sundragon."

Rufus nodded. "A-Analli ... they t-took her ... my wife ..."

Gelsey's throat clogged, and she looked back. Bridie had closed her eyes, her skin paler than before.

"I tried to convince Roderick not to take her, but Raphaela was insistent," she whispered. "I don't know why they would take an innkeeper's wife but ..."

"Oh, little one," Rufus murmured, drawing both their gazes. "My sweet Analli is so much more than a mere innkeeper's wife. She has hidden her true name well."

Gelsey sniffled, blinking the tears from her eyes. She knew why they'd taken Analli, but realizing Bridie wasn't privy to the secret altered her perspective of the young woman. Perhaps she was telling the truth. Perhaps she *was* trying to use her position as Regent to fight her cousin.

Or perhaps she is playing you ... Gelsey breathed deeply.

"Gelsey!" Maksim burst into the cell, his eyes big and hair wild. "Gelsey, something's happening!"

Gelsey stood quickly. "Maksim, get Rufus upstairs and take Bridie with you."

She pushed passed him before he could argue, racing back up the corridor to the stairs. Shouts and screams echoed down to her as she broke from the dungeon entrance and out into the courtyard.

Her heart stopped. The blackness rolled across the sky, creeping ever closer to the city. Bursts of red lightning flashed among the thick clouds that swallowed the winter snow.

"Creator's Mercy," Gelsey breathed. "What evil thing is this?"

Flames burst from the cloud, barreling down to the city and igniting the Lower Village. Shrieks filled the air as Gelsey ran for the gates.

"Oda! Zaire! Gather our people! We head for the Lower Village—*now*!"

"What is it, Gelsey?" Oda cried, her face stricken with terror.

Gelsey stopped at the gate, looking over her shoulder at her people.

"Hurry, my loves. The Abyss has returned to Sunkai."

CHAPTER FOUR

Molderëin

Clea Jandry stood before the south windows of the Queen's council chamber, staring across the great expanse of glistening mountains. Behind her, the nobles of Molderëin roared with anger, their words jumbling together with their haste to be heard. The black dress she'd donned after her coronation lay heavy on her body, as did the cold, golden circlet atop her head. Everything seemed to happen quickly here, so far from the northern home she'd become accustomed to. She had done what no other who'd been crowned in Molderëin had done. Upon receiving the crown, she'd instantly brought charges against the Lord Ruler.

A gentle presence came to her side. Clea could feel the woman's power, pulsing between them. An invisible bond between two creatures of magic no one could understand. No one except another who held the same amount of power Clea and Kalea did. The Mountain Woman had somehow managed to anchor Clea's power, bringing a renewed sense of strength to her soul she thought she'd lost forever. Soon, the Summer Flower would also be in her possession, and she would be unstoppable.

If the people of Molderëin will truly rally to me. Clea took a deep breath and turned.

"Enough!" her voice echoed on the stone walls, instantly silencing the five men gathered round her table. "I have heard all of you and do take heed. But the charges against Rhoydaen Molten stand."

"My queen, please allow me to speak?"

Clea turned slightly, meeting Lord Brimley's eyes. He was shorter than she, his belly overlapping his belt and a neatly trimmed silver beard coming to a perfect point beneath his chin. Aside from two bushy eyebrows, there was not another hair on the man's head, and his eyes looked like two white bulbs with dark brown dots, they were so wide.

She gestured slightly with her hand, giving him permission to continue.

"Your Majesty, Lord Molten has been a faithful servant of Molderëin for over twenty years. We have never suffered under his rule and these allegations ..." Lord Brimley glanced nervously Kalea's way, sweat beginning to bead on his brow. "How can they truly be believed? A woman so deformed—who does not hide her nature the way her people do—how can we—?"

Clea raised her hand to silence him. "If you call the beauty of a mountain creature a deformity, then you have lost all privileges here, Lord Brimley. Women of the Mountain do not hide their faces because they are ashamed, they hide their faces so they will not frighten mortal men."

Clea took a few steps forward. "As for the allegations against Lord Molten, let me tell you I saw with my own eyes the crimes he committed against Kalea Lightmaker. I am the one who found her, bound by iron and half-starved in the Tower dungeon. Her wounds, now healed with her own magic, covered her entire body. Lord Molten failed to inform me she was even here, and I have it on the authority of his own son he had no intention of ever telling me about her."

"Where is Grange Molten?" another of them—Lord Cravell—asked irritably. "Should he not have a say in his father's fate?"

"Grange Molten requested to only be called upon for the trial—as a witness. He has no wish to be a part of the debate." Clea came closer to the table. "Lord Brimley, you say Lord Molten has been a faithful servant of Molderëin for over twenty years?"

"Yes, my queen."

"How?" Clea clasped her hands in front of her, tilting her head. "Do you mean he has lined your and your fellow noblemen's pockets at the expense of hardworking country men? Do you mean he has seen himself and the nobles of Molderëin prosper by encouraging public fights in the street, provoking gambling debts? Molderëin is a disgrace, and if the kings and queens of old could see their city now, they would turn in their graves for what it has become."

"Molderëin has always been a fierce country!" Lord Cravell sputtered. "Our city is known for its savagery!"

"How proud you sound!" Clea exclaimed. "Perhaps that is why my family relinquished the throne. Perhaps that is why they could not bear to even be known as the heirs. I do not—cannot—believe the Creator brought me here to change nothing. I will not rule a city bent on killing itself and its people. Whether you like it or not, my lords, I have come to make sure Molderëin turns with the rest of the world. You do not have to like my choices, but you do have to abide by them. The first thing I intend to do is see justice done for Kalea Lightmaker, our mountain neighbor and a woman revered as a princess in her own land."

She looked at all five men in turn, waiting for her words to fully sink in before she spoke again.

"The charges stand. You all know the penalty in Molderëin for harming a noblewoman or a woman of royal blood."

They each nodded, Lord Brimley and Lord Cravell's faces bright red with frustration.

"Then he will go to trial as a formality. Once we have adhered to the laws of old, we will see justice served."

"You said you came to end the savagery," Lord Brimley hissed. "Yet your first act as queen will be to take a sword to your own Lord Ruler?"

Clea tilted her head up, her heart thudding a little harder in her chest.

"I have no Lord Ruler. Rhoydaen Molten lost his right to the title long ago." She turned her back again, returning to the windows. "You are dismissed, my lords. I will announce the trial date before the sunset."

Clea waited until the doors thundered after them before she released the breath she'd been holding. Her shoulders drooped, her eyes fluttering closed. The weight of her new place in the world nearly buckled her knees, but suddenly all she could think about was her niece. Was she safe? Was she protected?

Is my niece alive? Is my brother alive? Clea shuddered, buffing her arms.

"We will find the Summer Flower," Kalea murmured beside her. "You needn't worry."

"I'm not," Clea replied on a sigh. "I just wish I knew what was happening further north. I left my family behind, Kalea, to pursue a future I never expected or wanted. How do I do this? How do I rule this wild country while my family fights for another?"

"You will find a way. The world is turning, Clea Jandry. Nothing will ever be the same."

Clea frowned, her gaze lifting.

"Kalea ... what is that?"

Before her friend could answer, Clea turned, swinging the long train of her gown behind her. She jumped back when she opened the doors, her eyes wide when she saw servants and guards alike rushing toward the door to one of the bridges between the towers. Clea stepped out among them, Kalea close on her heels as she followed the people.

Their worried whispers and frightened eyes made her stomach flutter, her hands shaking as she pushed her way to the front of the crowd and stepped out into the sunlight. A hot wind grabbed her hair, swinging her loose tresses all around her face as she turned, facing the north. Slowly, she walked to the center of the bridge, her gaze fixed to the sky.

The darkness crept ever closer to Molderëin. Thick and chilling, a mass of evil was inching closer and closer from the north, reaching fingerlike black tendrils toward the city she'd just claimed as her own mere hours ago. Terror was prevalent in the wind all around her, the people standing in shocked silence as they watched the darkness overtake the north. A heavy hand settled on her shoulder and Clea's own flew up, gripping rough fingers tightly.

"Is that …?" Grange couldn't finish the question, and she did not blame him.

"Yes," Clea croaked, her throat aching. "I believe it is."

She spun to face him, fear fueling her determination.

"No more games," she said, staring into his sharp green eyes. "No more secrets. No more lies. The Abyss has taken the north, Grange Molten, and is on his way here. I need the Summer Flower."

Grange stared at her, his lips thinning and eyes darting. He raked a hand through his hair, huffing softly with a tight breath. Clea waited, the sense of the Abyss growing stronger tingling her spine. She could feel the power in the cloud coming closer to the city, could feel the strength of the evil within. Thunder rumbled across the sky, reaching them from miles away, and Clea shuddered.

"Come with me," he whispered, cupping his hand under her elbow.

She nodded, keeping close to his side as he guided her to the other side of the bridge, shoving the door open with his shoulder. Grange led her down a corridor, pausing to snatch a lit torch from a sconce. His green eyes glowed in the darkness, reminding her this man possessed a magic she neither knew existed or understood. A male creature of magic was so rare in the north, Clea had never encountered one before. The urge to ask him about his magic right now tightened her chest, excitement pulsing in her blood at the thought he could teach her something new. He could show her his world, his power.

How much power does he have? Clea bit her lip, tempering her curiosity. Now wasn't the time.

Grange kept his stride in check so she might keep up with him, walking side by side down the long hallway. The corridor came to an end abruptly, smooth stone wall staring at her. Clea's nose wrinkled.

"What—?"

He glared at her. Clea's teeth clicked shut, and she pressed her lips tight. Grange leaned forward, lightly passing his hand over the stone. He muttered something she didn't understand, and suddenly, the wall cracked. Clea squeaked, taking a small leap back as dust burst in puffs from the one invisible line, revealing a hidden door. Grange laid his palm flat on it and pushed. The door scraped and growled along the floor, revealing a spiraling staircase within.

Fear gripped her when Grange stepped inside first, turning with his hand outstretched to her in a silent beckon. What if this was a trap? She didn't know this man, not really, and despite his honor in allowing the charges against his father to proceed, he could be looking for a way to gain the throne for himself.

This could be a trap. Clea held her breath. *But what choice do I have?*

She took his hand, gripping his fingers hard as they hurried down the stairs. The tower trembled and Clea gasped, slamming her back into the wall.

"W-What was that?" she asked, her chest tightening and breaths quick.

"The Abyss," Grange snarled, lip curling. "He's getting closer."

Grange tugged on her hand, and she rushed to his side, tilting her head up. He stood still for a moment, staring down at her, their noses nearly touching. Gently, he curled a comforting arm around her shoulders, keeping her pressed to his side.

"Quickly now, Your Majesty," he said huskily.

Clea nodded. He kept his arm around her as they continued on, faster than before, down the stairs. They reached the bottom in moments, the only light to be had from Grange's torch. Abruptly, he let her go, and she nearly stumbled. A chill rushed over her at the loss of his warm touch and she stood still at the bottom of the staircase, watching him march across the room to light another torch on the wall.

"My father prized this flower above all other things," his voice reached her as he moved to the next torch, the room beginning to brighten in the flickering firelight. "Even he, born without magic as he was, could feel the power it held. Long ago, tales of the Avarys reached us. Tales of a place long dead where the Summer King once ruled."

Clea tilted her head, listening to him speak with such reverence as he took another few steps. The more he lit the torches, the more was revealed until she realized she was standing in a circular room, the torches arranged a few feet apart on the wall to offer the same amount of light to each section of the chamber.

"This flower holds a piece of the Summer King's power. He was so strong his magic could not be contained. So to anchor his strength, he plucked the fairest flower in the land and embodied the blossom with his magic, keeping only a little for himself so he might continue to rule. No one has been able to draw magic from the flower since. Many who touch it die instantaneously, which is why we keep it hidden from the people."

Grange finished lighting the torches and turned. Clea stared at the center of the circular chamber, the pedestal standing four feet high, domed at the top and covered with a blue velvet drape. She took one step forward, then another. A soft buzzing filled her ears, her blood pounding harder the closer she came to the object. She could feel the pulse of the power beneath the drape. The magic reached for her, called to her soul in a way no power ever had.

Clea licked her lips, finding her upper lip moist with sweat. She shivered, her fingers curling around the soft cloth. With one motion, she slid the covering from the pedestal. A gasp slipped from her lips, her face awash in a silver glow. Tears sprang to her eyes when she leaned closer, keeping her hands at her sides as she stared at the blossom beneath the dome of glass.

Petals rose to sharp, thin points, glittering bright silver in the torchlight. She counted at least eighty, all surrounding a soft golden center. The stem was ivory-colored and a foot long, the thorns glistening with silver tips.

"I never imagined it would be so beautiful," she whispered, her throat swollen with her tears. Clea raised her eyes to Grange, finding him as enthralled as she was. "You know what I must do."

He nodded mutely.

Clea clamped her bottom lip between her teeth and lifted the glass cover from the Summer Flower. The blossom seemed to glow brighter as she set the cover aside. She rubbed her palms against her skirts nervously, trying to calm her racing heart. Then she reached for the flower.

Grange's hand slapped around her wrist, stopping her.

"I ... I can't ..." He shook his head furiously, the glint of fear in his eyes making her smile. "You could die."

Clea placed her hand over his.

"You know we don't have a choice, Grange Molten. I am in the Creator's hands now, and he has brought me to this place. Let us see what he intends for Molderëin's future."

Grange struggled, his brow furrowed and mouth tight. He pulled in a shuddering breath, then let her go, turning away. Clea gathered her courage and ever so gently placed her fingers on the Summer Flower.

Hadroul's Mountain
In the Mirror ...

Damari rolled onto her belly, peeking up over the grass whispering in the breeze. She twirled a strand of her hair around her finger tightly, watching the dragon pause to take a drink from the lake. She was so beautiful, her pure white scales glittering in the sunlight, smooth like marble and sharp blue eyes half-closed as she bent to dip her tongue in the cool liquid. Damari bit her nail, rising slowly from the ground.

The dragon lifted her head, turning to watch Damari approach impassively. She'd not been this still since the moment Damari first saw her. Her wings were neatly folded on her broad back, front claws tucked against her chest and her long tail curled in a near complete circle across the meadow. Damari stopped a few feet away, her head tilted back sharply to stare at the magnificent creature.

"I know what this is," she whispered, and the dragon tilted her head. "I understand now. We are the People of the Dragon which means you are a part—"

A thunderous crash drowned her words. Damari spun, eyes widening as she watched the darkness coil overhead, balls of fire tumbling from the

47

sky to light the trees aflame. The dragon roared, and Damari screamed, covering her ears and falling to her knees. Terror seized her, stealing the fire from her center, stealing her magic source.

Then the dragon's shadow fell over her, covering her completely. Damari looked up, the fierceness in the creature's eyes igniting her own strength. She tightened her lips and reached out, grabbing the dragon by the claw.

The creature swung her into the air, and Damari landed lightly on the animal's spine, holding her arms out to balance herself. A smile spread across her face, and she laughed when the fire returned to her heart, stronger than ever.

The darkness grew, fast and strong overhead. Damari glared.

"We're ready now," she hissed.

The dragon roared again and shot off the ground, carrying Damari up, up, up into the sky.

Water burned his nose and throat, choking the breath out of him. His arms pumped, fire churning in his belly as he reached for the Haven Star. The golden glow of the star fueled the burn in his veins, making him stronger. He fought harder, reaching for the top of the pond as quickly as possible. He was so hot now the once warm water felt cold.

Lathan Jandry broke the surface of the water, thrashing and gasping as steam rose from his body upon contact with the mountain air. Hands gripped his arms, strong fingers digging into his hardened biceps as he was pulled from the pond and across the rough stones of the mountain floor. He rolled onto his back, wheezing and coughing, as water spurted from his mouth, emptying his lungs.

Evingar bent over him, his golden hair falling across his shoulder and a curious tilt to his head. Krow was on his other side, looking at him just as deeply, a spark of pride shining in his eyes.

"Is it done?" Lathan gasped, voice hoarse and throat sore.

Evingar and Krow looked at each other briefly before both nodded. They took him under the arms, lifting him to his feet. He bent over, palms pressed to his knees and ribs aching as he regained his breath. Flames swam through his veins, igniting in him a heat he'd never known before. Lathan raised his hands, his brow furrowing as he looked at the enhanced thickness of his arms, felt the strength in his back and legs and the firmness of his torso.

He felt light, his heart beating faster, stronger. There was something different. Lathan could nearly feel his soul, stronger and fiercer. Endowed with a magic he'd never understood before but could not deny now. His gaze lifted, looking up through the round opening at the top of the mountain. The Haven Star had shifted away, nearly out of sight, and Lathan's insides tightened.

"How long?" He looked at Krow, eyes wide. "How long have I been … away?"

Krow hesitated. "Three days."

Lathan's knees nearly buckled, his stomach plummeting. "Damari!"

Ignoring Evingar's call of protest, he ran, his boots thundering on the stones as he followed the trail of torches through the mountain. He seemed faster, strides longer and stronger, as he raced toward the cave entrance. Lathan skidded to a halt at the cave opening, his eyes widening.

The village was in chaos, men and women rushing the children into their stone houses, Navaria calling to her people as she appeared from behind the waterfall crashing from the top of Hadroul's Mountain. The women gathered, their many-colored scales glittering brighter as they formed a circle in the center of the village, Navaria standing in the middle of all of them. Lathan watched enthralled, when they all threw off their simple brown robes. Each woman wore a dress to match their dragon skin, shimmering and bold, with ragged hems barely brushing their knees and scooped backs, revealing every woman bore identical scars, thick and long coming to a pointed V near the small of their backs.

Their wings. Lathan breathed again, his gaze shifting to see what Navaria was staring at.

He moved forward slowly, watching the darkness curl and growl overhead, covering the mountain in shadow. Thick black tendrils twirled in the cloud, reaching down toward the Mountain People as they prepared for battle.

Navaria was shouting something in her language, gesturing wildly to the other women. Lathan strode forward, reaching for his sword and stopped when his hand met air. He looked down, cursing softly when he remembered they'd taken his weapons. A hiss and crackle made him look up, watching as the women called on their fire magic, creating a glittering circle of flames with Navaria at the center, her hands rolling in circular motions over her head, twining the fire together.

Something cold slipped into his hand, and he looked down, finding a wide-curved sword placed in his palm. Krow was at his side, his eyes never wavering from the evil descending on their home.

"The Abyss has come," he murmured. "*Skätherin helgair.*"

"Prepare yourself, Lathan," Evingar added, appearing to his left. "We do not know what evil things will come from this darkness."

Lathan nodded and then froze. His head swung back and forth between the two of them, from Evingar's smirk to Krow's confused frown.

"Is something wrong, Lathan Jandry?" Krow asked.

"I … you're …" He shook his head, his thoughts stuttering as much as his tongue.

Three days ago, he had to look up to meet Krow and Evingar's eyes. Now … he looked directly into them. Level, shoulder to shoulder, equal now in every way.

"Time for that later," Evingar muttered, the smirk smoothing from his face as the shadows rumbled overhead.

Lathan tightened his hand around the sword hilt, raising the blade in front of him, his head arced back, as all three braced themselves. A black web slithered from the shadow, clasping around Lyssia where she stood in the circle. The girl screamed, writhing as the darkness swarmed her.

Navaria spun, sending a bolt of fire toward the girl. Lyssia caught the flames, turning them on the black threads tightening around her. The whole shadow seemed to scream, releasing Lyssia and sending her in a heap to the ground. Lathan groaned, the sounds ringing in his ears, making his head spin. Krow and Evingar shuddered beside him, all of them faltering under the weight of evil bearing down on the village.

The ground trembled beneath their feet, and Lathan looked up, watching. A low roar resonated from within Hadroul's Mountain. He frowned, watching the waterfall part into two streams. Something white— shimmering like diamonds—flew from behind the waterfall, dragon wings flattened against her back as she soared toward the shadow.

She turned, twirling through the air before stopping. Lathan stared at her, the long white gown rippling in the air, wings spread wide and so familiar. Her hair flowed nearly to her waist, pure gold, the color sharper, more distinct than he remembered. Darker than the gentle corn yellow her tresses once were.

The shadow pulsed, but she didn't flinch, floating high above the ground facing the darkness.

"So," a raspy voice boomed across the sky. "You have been reborn. The *Almaër Dominÿe*."

Lathan shuddered, the new fire in his blood chilling to ice. He felt it all around him. A sudden gust of cold settling over the village. The fire the women had created diffused in moments. They fell to their knees, trembling and clutching their hearts.

"Malindra!" Evingar roared, racing across the space where his wife toppled to the ground.

Lathan stood stunned, staring up at *her*. She didn't falter. She barely moved at all. Instead, she raised her hand, palm up.

Her flesh ignited in a burst of white fire, glittering and growing at her side, spurting from her fingertips.

"You do not belong here," she said, her voice echoing across the mountain. "These are my people. And you cannot touch them!"

She spun.

A flash of crystal blue eyes and the glimmer of white dragon skin. Lathan placed a hand over his heart, falling to his knees as the breath was knocked from his lungs. With a swift swing of her arm, she sent her white fire down upon the village. Lathan raised an arm automatically, shielding himself as the light came crashing down on them.

The chill vanished from the air, replaced with a roaring heat that pulsed through him so strongly he thought he was burning from the inside. Lathan raised his eyes and lowered his arm. Her fire fell upon the Mountain People like a shield, sinking into them, igniting the women's dragon skin and making the men tremble. Slowly, the people began to rise again, groaning softly. Evingar assisting Malindra carefully to her feet, Krow wrapping an arm around Navaria as they both stared up at their *Almaër Dominÿe*.

Lathan forced himself to his feet as well, even though his knees still trembled. Then her eyes met his, the horizontal lines of her pupils and crystal shine of her blue irises warming his center.

Damari. My Damari. He could breathe again.

Then she turned, wings pumping the air, arms stretched wide.

51

"You cannot touch them!" she repeated. "Winter cannot touch them! They are protected by a power so much greater than this evil thing you've made. Now go! Return to your master and show him how you've failed!"

Fire whipped from her hands, pulsing into the shadow. The darkness shrieked and quivered, whirling into itself and sliding away. The sun peeked from above the shadow, sending rays of light back down on the mountain village. Everyone stood still, silence engulfing the mountain.

Damari floated from the sky, her bare feet sinking into the soft grass. Lathan stared at her, watching her wings slide gently into her back, her skin stitching back together, smooth once again. She turned around, her gaze centering on him. Lathan couldn't move, staring into the eyes of the woman he loved. They were perfect, round and normal, clear and glowing. She walked toward him, her dark golden tresses glowing like diamonds where they fell over her shoulder and her skin ... oh her skin! Smooth, marble scales covering her, white as snow.

The Mountain People bowed as she passed, some of the women reaching out to brush their fingers against her scales. Unlike the others, her entire body had been transformed with the dragon skin. She was so different, yet every bit of her was as much Damari Kael as she'd ever been. He could see it in her eyes, could feel it in the air around her the closer she came to him.

She reached him, tilting her head back.

"You look different," she said.

Lathan smirked, the sound of her voice raising the hair on the back of his neck.

"So do you," he commented. He took a step, closing the small distance between them to cup her face in his hands. Damari rested her hands on his waist, her neck arched sharply so she could look into his eyes, making him realize just how much he'd changed. She'd always been small to him ... but not like this.

"Either I've shrunk," Damari whispered. "Or you've grown."

He chuckled. But Damari's eyes hardened, her hands falling to her sides.

"Y-You didn't ..." She stepped back, and he let her go. He knew this would come, but he'd hoped maybe she wouldn't notice. "You promised you wouldn't! How could you?"

"Because I love you, and I couldn't protect you as I was."

"But now you're ..." She shook her head, her eyes flooding.

"Shh." Lathan took hold of her again, bending over to lay his forehead on hers. "We can discuss this later. Right now ... look. Look behind you, Damari. Look how you've helped them."

He whirled her around, resting his hands on her shoulders. Lathan felt her breathe in and out deeply, his hands lifting when her shoulders rose and fell. The people were staring at them, crowded together in the center of the village, the sun restored to its full glory as the shadow sunk away toward Draedin.

"I've only saved our little piece of the world," Damari whispered. "The shadow will take its wrath out on all of Nfaros, Lathan. Molderëin, Draedin, Sunkai ... the Abyss is covering our world in darkness, and I cannot stop him. Not completely."

Lathan wrapped his arms around her, tugging her back against him. Damari melted into him, placing her hand on his wrist and squeezing. He couldn't feel her heat anymore. Her warmth blended with his perfectly now, both possessing a power beyond understanding. A power Lathan never thought would be his.

They looked up, the darkness nearly gone now, giving way to clear blue sky. Damari took a deep breath.

"Oh, my love," she murmured. "This is only the beginning."

CHAPTER FIVE

The Aulend Forest

It's true. It's all true. Maxx's chest tightened as he watched Gwylan with Noelle.

Since coming into the company of the women, she'd grown another foot, the top of her head now reaching Gwylan's waist. So far removed from everything, Ellia and Symber had been forced to work through the night, taking apart some of their own clothes to a size that would fit the unnaturally growing girl.

Noelle's big green eyes flitted to him, trepidation lighting them. Maxx forced a smile, dipping his head slightly in an encouraging nod as Noelle attempted one of the practice spells Gwylan had been teaching her. She urged her to call on her magic at least once a day, to make her stronger, she said. Gwylan claimed the lessons were a way for Noelle to learn how to control her newfound power, so in the future the strength of her magic wouldn't overtake her and leave her half-dead.

The hardest part in all of this was trying to make Noelle understand what was happening to her. Growing as she was, her mind was changing and her power was getting stronger, confusing her. She couldn't sleep and barely ate. Instead, she would stare off into the distant forest, twirling her light between her fingers and humming. Sometimes, the detached expression in her eyes frightened him. The feeling she wasn't with him anymore overwhelming him to the point of panic. He'd sworn he would protect her. He'd sworn he would return her to her father.

Now, how can I? How can I bring this girl to him, a mere shadow of the daughter he once knew? Maxx buffed the back of his neck, turning away.

He stumbled backward, barely avoiding running into Symber. The tall Kaldoner woman grinned, tucking her bobbed yellow hair behind her ears and staring at him with big blue eyes. She was slightly taller than he with a more muscular figure than the other women and a bulbous nose less common among women of Kaldon.

"You are troubled by her growth," Symber stated, getting directly to the point.

He'd started to become accustomed to the bluntness of these women, though he did on occasion wish they would leave him alone. Maxx knew they didn't care what happened to him. As soon as they discovered Noelle's gift, everything changed, and they tolerated his presence because he refused to leave his niece.

Gwylan doesn't just tolerate you. He frowned, shoving the thought aside.

"Of course, I'm troubled," he said behind clenched teeth. "She's four-years-old and looks ten. In a matter of days, she's grown another foot and has the heart and soul of a young woman. By the time I find my brother, he won't even know her anymore."

Symber's eyes softened. "It is a difficult thing, when the Creator calls on the life of one so young. Not only for her, but for those who love her as well. Please believe me, I know."

"How do you know?" Maxx mumbled. "How could you possibly understand this?"

Symber tilted her head, her secretive smile and compassionate gaze easing him for a moment. Gently, she patted his arm.

"You will understand, too, Maxx Jandry. One day, the world will make sense again."

Before he could question her further, she turned away, stepping across the encampment to join Ellia at the fire. Haileah had disappeared hours ago, mumbling something about scouting the woods and bringing back supper. There was something strange about the older Eventide Sister. Something about her set Maxx's teeth on edge, but he couldn't quite put his finger on what it was. Perhaps it was the fear he saw in her eyes every time she observed Noelle's progress. Or perhaps it was the way she scowled at Gwylan. He didn't know and supposed he shouldn't care.

Maxx stomped through the thick snow, glancing up at the darkness overhead. They'd been without the sun for two days now, ever since the dark cloud crept its way across Nfaros, reaching far across the sea toward the distant Mountain Lands. His thoughts had turned to Clea, somewhere in Molderëin at Brecken's request. Was she safe from this evil? Was anyone?

Where is Adlae? Where is the Creator and his light? Maxx shook his head.

"Uncle Maxx," Noelle's voice pulled him from his thoughts. "Look, Uncle Maxx."

He crouched in front of her, watching as Noelle brought her palms together in front of her. White light gathered, twinkling between her fingers and crackling like flames. Maxx smiled.

"Isn't it pretty?" Noelle murmured.

"Yes, sweetheart. Very pretty." He leaned forward, kissing the center of her forehead. Noelle didn't raise her eyes from her hands, watching the light closely.

"She's stronger," Gwylan announced.

Maxx straightened, stepping around his niece to stand at Gwylan's side.

"The faster she grows, the stronger she becomes," she continued. Her fingers brushed his hand, and Maxx looked down at her, brow raised in surprise. Gwylan didn't seem to notice, her focus entirely on his niece. "I've tried, Maxx. I've tried so hard to see what the Creator wants of her, so we might be prepared but ..."

"Such things are not for us to know," he finished for her. He caught her eye, and she faced him fully, searching his gaze. "Do you regret my coming after you? Do you wish I'd stayed away so you might not have been burdened with this?"

Gwylan tilted her head, one of her braids falling from her shoulder. "A child such as Noelle is no burden to me, Maxx Jandry."

Her brow creased, the gentle tightening at the corners of her mouth alerting Maxx to her suddenly deep thoughts. He took a step forward, and she moved with him, both beginning a slow stroll around the perimeter of the camp and all the while keeping a close eye on Noelle.

"Will your Superiors punish you for the delay in your mission?" he wondered, clasping his hands tightly behind him, ignoring the strange urge to take one of hers.

"I think not," Gwylan replied. "Our Superiors ordered us to find Adlae Sundragon, they did not say when or how. We have not abandoned our mission—we have only taken a pause. If Noelle grows as powerful as I suspect, then my Superiors will understand."

Maxx frowned. "Have you ever seen your Superiors?"

Gwylan's brow winged up. "Of course not! They dwell in a higher realm than this, Maxx Jandry. They are not of this world and do the Creator's bidding as he tells it to them."

"My mother once told me stories of the Superiors of Eventide." Maxx buffed the back of his neck, readjusting the blue and yellow kerchief at the base of his throat. "She said they lived among the Immortals in a realm between worlds. The—"

"The Eventide Sky," Gwylan finished. She smiled at him. "Yes. Every Novice of Eventide is told the same story."

"So you believe that women who were once just like you actually live on another plane, listening to the whispers of the Creator and sending messages down to you?" Maxx smirked.

"You do not?" Gwylan frowned.

"Oh, I think you have Superiors. I think they live in one of the Woodland Towers, staring into their crystals and *imagining* they are higher beings. If they're so immortal, then why do you continue to raise women to Superior? There should be thousands of them by now." Maxx shook his head. "I don't think you're a fool, Gwylan. But I do think you've been manipulated."

"There is very little you believe in, isn't there, Maxx?" Gwylan's voice lowered and she stopped.

He turned to face her, staring steadily into her wide, curious eyes.

"I believe there is a Creator because I have to," he replied. "There are too many things in this world that cannot be explained any other way. But if you expect me to believe our Creator would raise imperfect beings to a realm beyond understanding and without the consequence of death ..." He shook his head, letting the unfinished thought rest between them.

Gwylan broke from his gaze, staring across the space at Noelle. She threaded her arms across her chest and took a deep breath.

"Perhaps the more you see, the more you'll believe," she murmured. "I did not have to see to know there were places I could not touch. I did not have to see, to feel the presence of something greater than myself. I did not have to see him to know the Creator had touched my very soul." Gwylan shuddered.

When she looked at him again, a chill rushed down his spine.

"I feel very little, Maxx Jandry. I do not let myself feel these emotions that stretch beyond comprehension. I do not let my heart run wild with passion. But when the Creator entered my soul and bestowed on me this gift of power, I felt a warmth that needed no explanation. So I believe, without doubt or hesitation, in things I cannot see." She shrugged slightly, the corner of her mouth trembling with a resistant smile. "I think, if you were to ask your niece about what is happening to her, she'd tell you much the same. The Creator has spoken to her, and to you. You've just forgotten how to hear him."

"Don't you ever grow weary of belief?" Maxx grumbled.

Gwylan tugged on one of her braids, a curious glint in her eye. He thought she was going to reply when Haileah came stomping passed him, mumbling under her breath and effectively distracting his companion.

"Sister?" Gwylan turned, reaching out to lightly touch Haileah's sleeve. "Is something troubling you?"

Haileah stopped, glaring at her. "No, Gwylan, of course not. The shadow doesn't trouble me. The child doesn't trouble me," she paused, scowling at Maxx. "*He* doesn't trouble me. The world is clouded in the image of the Abyss, and that most *certainly* doesn't trouble me."

The older Dominant stuck her nose in the air and shuffled through the snow, disappearing into the large tent at the center of their circle. Maxx whistled softly.

"She hates me, doesn't she?"

Gwylan shook her head, her eyes clouded in worry. "Haileah endured much during her lifetime. As a child she was forced to suppress her magic, hidden from the Sisters of Eventide, and became a wife at the tender age of thirteen. She lost three husbands and five children within ten years and was nearly forced to marry a fourth time before she escaped."

Maxx's chest tightened, and he clenched a fist around the hilt of his sword.

"Where was she from?" he wondered, voice low with anger.

"An island that cannot be found on any map. Such things do not usually stop the Eventide Sisters from sensing a powerful woman like her, but Haileah's family was clever. They wanted to use her in any way they could to gain status and wealth, so they did. When the Superiors finally located her, they did not even have to ask if she wished to take the vows." Gwylan glanced his way. "You can understand why her trust in men is limited, yes?"

Maxx nodded, unable to speak.

"Haileah is made fearful by her experiences, but I have faith she will be strong when we need her most." Gwylan's deep inhale and subtle tremor of her lower lip made Maxx doubt.

Is she as trusting of her Dominant Sister as she says? Maxx bit his tongue. It wasn't his place to question her.

"Uncle Maxx?" Noelle tugged on his trousers, and he looked down. She smiled, the new definition in her high cheekbones and rich, maturing color of her blood-red hair taking him by surprise for the hundredth time. Had she grown again in the space of moments? She certainly looked like she had.

"Yes, darling?" He placed his hand on the crown of her head.

"Damari looks like a dragon," she announced.

Maxx felt Gwylan tense beside him. Heart pounding, he slowly crouched down before his niece, placing his hands on her shoulders as he came eye level with the little girl.

"What did you say?" he whispered.

Noelle blinked at him, her pupils widening then thinning to pinpoints.

"Damari Kael," she said. "My Mama Damari. She looks like a dragon now. She has wings and shiny white skin like the marble floors in Aunt Clea's house in Quintaria."

Noelle smiled widely, the sparkle in her eye raising gooseflesh on Maxx's arms.

"And she's coming, Uncle Maxx. She's coming to save Sunkai."

Noelle blinked twice, spun and skipped back to Symber's side. Maxx stayed where he was, crouched in the snow, hands trembling.

"In the name of eternity," he rasped, spinning on his heels and rising to tower over Gwylan. "What was that?"

"The visions have started," she whispered, staring beyond him at Noelle. "I hoped she wouldn't have them ..."

She skirted around him, hurrying after his niece. Maxx watched her gently take Noelle's hand, whispering as she urged her into the tent. Gwylan locked eyes with him right before they disappeared inside, giving him a small glimpse of what was hidden behind her over-confident smile.

Fear.

Maxx whirled and slammed his fist into the nearest tree.

A Forest with No Name

Adlae stared at the circle of ash on the white snow. Smoke still rose from charred pieces of wood, the last bits of the pyre lying scattered on the ground. Jabon thought it unwise to delay so near the encampment where the darkness had attacked, but Adlae could not bear to leave Glaydin's body in the snow. The Mountain Men who'd remained with their leader requested the traditional burning of their captain's body, and she'd readily agreed, seeing their ritual through.

This isn't your fault, Adlae. Winter comforted, her sweet presence filling Adlae's heart with warmth.

"I wish that were true, Winter," she whispered.

A hesitant hand on her shoulder brought her around. Jabon watched her warily, his gaze darting to the ashes before returning to her.

"The men grow restless, Adlae," he said, his voice low and gruff. "The shadow covers the sky as far as the eye can see. I can feel the fear in them, and if we do not show leadership now—"

Adlae held up her hand, silencing him.

"I understand," she murmured.

Jabon stepped aside, letting her pass. What was left of her army were gathering their supplies into wagons. The clatter of weapons and nervous stomping of the horses overwhelmed the soft forest sounds all around them. Adlae stopped before the Mountain Men, catching the eye of one. He turned, bowing low, his long brown hair shifting over his shoulder.

"Return to your people," she ordered.

He looked up at her, surprise lighting his dark eyes.

"Tell them of your Captain's death. Give the *Almaër Dominÿe* a message from me." Adlae paused, inhaling deeply. "Tell her the time has come. The Sundragon is in dire need. For fire is stronger even than winter."

He bowed again. "Your wish is my command, Your Majesty."

Adlae turned before she could change her mind, feeling Jabon following her as she crossed the camp.

"Klade Overlage," she called.

The young soldier turned from packing one of the wagons, dropping his task to come to her. When he lifted his gaze after offering her a deep bow, her heart tightened. Knowing what she had to do next troubled her, and they would not understand.

But there is no other choice. Winter reminded her.

"Klade, you will take the rest of the men and journey toward the Tower of Tears."

Klade's brow rose. "Your Highness ..."

"My sister is on her way there," Adlae continued as if he'd not spoken. "You will find her and join her company. Tell her I am close and will see her soon."

"Adlae, what are you doing?" Jabon hissed near her ear.

"You are not to delay. You are not to stop for anything. I am placing you in command of this company until you reach Mirae. Do you understand your orders, soldier?"

He hesitated, his eyes darting between her and Jabon before he bowed at the waist again.

"Yes, my queen."

Adlae spun, her braid whipping against her back as she walked away. Jabon grabbed her arm, halting her halfway across the encampment.

"Would you care to explain to me what is happening?" he growled, the bridge of his nose pinched with concern. "Why are you sending our army away?"

"Because all that is needed for what's next is me ... and you."

His hand dropped from her arm, uncertainty lighting his eyes.

"This darkness cannot be conquered with an army. I do not have the answers yet, and I cannot find them if I remain with these men. I cannot discover what I am meant to do if I am in constant fear they will die simply because they travel with me." Adlae looked away staring into the pitch black of the woods. "But I also cannot do this alone. I need someone I trust at my side for this, Jabon. And I trust you, more than anyone."

His eyes softened, the tenderness in his gaze fluttering her stomach. Adlae opened her mouth to say something more when M'kela and Ilicya appeared before her.

"Let us go with you, my lady," Ilicya requested.

"No." Adlae shook her head. "Find Taleah. The Frostlings are in grave danger of this shadow, and they will need you. I have already felt the cries of my friend. I have felt the agony in her body. You must go to her, my children."

M'kela and Ilicya anxiously looked at each other, their bright wings sending thousands of flurries to the snow-covered ground.

"Forgive me," M'kela said, avoiding Adlae's gaze. "But ... my queen ... your strength is not sufficient against this evil."

Adlae smiled. "No, it is not."

Both Frostlings met her eyes now, unblinking and surprised.

"But there is a call I cannot ignore. This shadow reaches all across Nfaros, even to the far north. I must go where I am called, no matter the risks. You must unite your sisters and battle to reclaim winter's light." Adlae beckoned them closer. "When you find Taleah, tell her the Winter Queen orders her retreat to the Ice Mountains where the shadows cannot touch her. Wait there until I send for you."

"But Your Majesty—!"

"Obey without question, little Frostling. No matter what comes, this next generation of Frostlings must survive. *Winter* must survive." Adlae looked up at the shadow, swirling ominously overhead. "Now go and may the Creator's mercy be with you."

"And with you, my queen," Ilicya answered.

In a flash of light and stream of snow dust, the two Frostlings disappeared into the darkness. Adlae released a breath she'd not realized she was holding, turning to face Jabon. He frowned at her, one hand clenched around the hilt of his sword and the other in a tight fist at his side.

"Are you going to tell me what's happening?" he asked, voice low.

"How can I, when I hardly know myself?"

"But you know *something*, Adlae."

Her heart raced, a chill that had nothing to do with her power pulsing through her.

You cannot tell him what the shadows revealed, Adlae, Winter warned.

"You must trust me, Jabon." She raised her hand, cradling the side of his face in her palm. Jabon closed his eyes, seeming unaffected when ice crackled across his cheek at her touch. "I am doing what I must, and I need you by my side. Do you trust me?"

He opened his eyes to stare into hers. Gently, he raised his hand, covering hers with his.

"Always."

Though he whispered, his voice resonated in her heart like a caress.

63

This is a strange thing, Winter murmured. **This love you feel. Never in my hundreds of years on the earth did I feel what you feel for this man. Never did I feel what you felt for Glaydin, either.**

Adlae lowered her hand from Jabon's face, biting her tongue to avoid answering Winter's musings.

"We need to go," she said.

Jabon seemed to return to himself, his eyes glinting with determination and back straightening abruptly.

"I will gather what provisions are necessary and see the men start on the correct path toward Tears."

"Good."

Adlae watched him walk away, resting a hand over her middle to calm the fluttering inside.

"I am sorry you never knew love," she said quietly. "But at the same time, I am glad you never knew this pain."

What pain is that, Adlae Sundragon?

An icy tear slipped down her cheek as she watched Jabon order the men about, all while taking down his own tent and preparing their horses. He moved with the same confidence and strength she'd always known him for, always with a lightness in his eyes that brightened and broke her heart at the same time.

"The pain of knowing he can never be mine." She turned her back, facing the darkness ahead. "Immortals and mortals do not belong together, Winter. No matter how I want him, no matter how he wants me ... I could not live knowing we would never have a true forever. My heart darkens at the thought of it. In the end, such a life would destroy me."

So you sacrifice your own heart because of the gift of Winter upon you? Winter *tsked* softly. **Would not the Creator have taken the love from you if He did not intend for you to feel it?**

"It does not matter." Adlae shook her head, firming her grip around her staff. "We have other things to think of now."

She stared into the pitch black of the forest, her heart pounding for another reason now.

Yes, Winter concurred. **How *do* you intend to defeat this shadow, Adlae Sundragon?**

Adlae's chest expanded with a long inhale.

"I wish I knew, Winter."

64

CHAPTER SIX

Kaldon

I've always hated this city. Raphaela scowled, the soft click of her staff echoing down the empty streets of Kaldon. The Kaldoners who'd remained when Roderick took the city were hiding in their homes, doors and windows shut tight. Up the hill, sequestered behind the battlement's surrounding Thornlay Neverly's mansion, were Roderick's men. Or what was left of them, more like. Since Jabon Malaki's betrayal, Kaldon had been even more insufferable than before.

Raphaela climbed the narrow stone steps toward the Malaki manor where they'd been lodging. Roderick's insistence on living in the house of the traitor instead of taking lodging in Neverly's house had annoyed her to no end. But until this war was over and the true strength of the Kael family was revealed to all of Nfaros, he was still her king, and indulging his childish tantrums was all part of her plan.

The gates squealed when she flung them open with a wave of her hand. The guards snapped to attention, eyes forward, and she smirked. None of them dared look directly at her anymore, their fear of what she now carried was rank in the air all around her, the knowledge of it thrilling.

Malaki Manor wasn't nearly as large or elegant as Neverly's. Raphaela knew her brother's only intention in staying in the smaller house was to rile Jabon and Gelsey Malaki's followers. Whether he would be successful she didn't know, nor did she care. By the end of this conflict, every Malaki, Jandry, and Sundragon that walked the earth would be dead, along with any who followed them. She paused at the door, looking straight up into the sky at her creation. A smile curled her upper lip, watching her master coil and rumble overhead in all his shadowy glory.

She could feel him, a heavy pressure resting on her shoulders, filling her veins with his life and knowledge. How could the Creator hold a candle to him? His power surpassed anything she'd ever felt before. He could give life from death, where the Creator offered nothing more than the fragile hope of a realm for departed souls.

Raphaela stepped inside, turning sharply toward the winding stairs to Jabon's study. As she approached, she could hear her brother in the throes of a tantrum. She pushed open the door without knocking in time to see a storm of papers fly from the desk followed by a golden paperweight the shape of a wolf. Arching a brow, she looked up from where the paperweight fell, finding Thornlay Neverly standing before Jabon Malaki's desk, arms raised to protect his head with her brother, face red and blond hair askew glaring at him.

"Get out!" Roderick roared at Thornlay. "You worthless, sniveling coward! OUT!"

Thornlay blubbered as he backed away from the desk, bowing every two steps before spinning and racing from the room.

Raphaela tsked softly, closing the door after the man.

"Brother, you must control your temper."

Roderick leaned forward, palms flat on the desk, and harsh breaths slipping through his lips.

"Why am I here, Raphaela?"

"Must we do this again, Roderick?"

He punched the desk.

"Kaldon might be the largest city this far north, but Sunkai is the prize. And at this very moment, the so-called Lady of the Night Wood, Gelsey Malaki, is sitting on MY THRONE!"

Roderick shoved what remained on the desk to the floor. Raphaela sighed heavily, resting her staff in front of her, both hands curled around it. She stared into the pointed globe at the top, grey clouds roiling inside, her chest tightening when sparks of fire glittered within, reflecting the shadows covering the sky outside.

"I wanted to turn back," Roderick hissed, "the minute I heard that *girl* had invaded the Blood Keep. I knew we didn't leave enough men. Where was that in your prophecy, sister?"

Raphaela's head snapped up. "Are you doubting my power, brother?"

"Why didn't you see Gelsey Malaki coming? Why didn't you see how many people she'd rallied in the darkness of the Night Wood?" He smirked, eyeing her up and down. "Why did your precious master keep her movements a secret from you?"

"How dare you!" Raphaela shrieked, storming forward. "You should be on your knees, brother. I am more powerful than any creature of magic in Nfaros, and you would do well to fear me!"

Roderick squawked, leaning back and crossing his arms at his chest. "Fear you? Really, Raphaela?"

"Do not laugh at me," she growled. Her grip tightened on the staff, making it tremble. Closing her eyes, she took a long breath in, calming herself.

He does not see. He will never see, my child, he murmured in her ear. *Soon—very, very soon—he will be out of our way too.*

Raphaela smiled and opened her eyes.

"Patience, brother," she cooed, moving a little closer. "You will regain Sunkai. With the storm overhead, Gelsey cannot hold the city long. Not while it burns."

Roderick rolled his eyes and leaned forward.

"Tell me something, Raphaela."

She tilted her head and waited.

"If you are the most powerful creature of magic in Nfaros ... then why is Adlae Sundragon still alive?"

A harsh inhale hissed through her lips and she jolted back as though he'd struck her. Roderick strode around the desk, marching for the doors.

"If you can't kill her, then you're of no use to me," he said as he passed.

Her blood burned. The door slammed behind him, and Raphaela stood in the silence of the room, staff trembling in her right hand and heart bursting out of control. Her power flaming inside her so strong and sweet and agonizing she could not contain it a moment longer.

Her scream shattered every window and crystal in Malaki Manor.

Analli Devareigh cautiously raised her head, shards of glass slipping from her shoulders and hair. They'd locked her in the smallest bedchamber in Malaki Manor, a constant guard at the door and boards on the windows, forcing the glass inside when they shattered. Analli rose, brushing the glass from her skirts and tossing her braid from her shoulder. She shook her head, the echo of Raphaela's scream still ringing in her ears.

She reached up, tugging on the golden chain concealed beneath her high collar. The wind shifted through the boards on the windows, tickling the loose strands of her hair against the side of her neck. Analli turned, catching a glimpse of the plains beyond through the cracks in the boards.

"Don't worry, brother," she whispered. "I will find your sweet girls and help them in their quest, just as I promised."

She raised the chain over her head, lifting it until she was eye level with the pendant. The curled, golden dragon stared back at her with ruby eyes, igniting a fire in her chest. Analli smiled.

CHAPTER SEVEN

The Aulend Forest

"Are we lost?"

Gwylan looked up from braiding her hair, smiling at the child sitting across from her. The wind howled wildly against the tent walls—the sudden storm having driven them from the path hours ago. The moment the shadow had descended on the forest, Gwylan knew everything she'd ever known was in danger. She could feel it in the center of her heart where her power pulsed its strongest.

And there's nothing I can do to stop it. Gwylan sighed, tying off the end of her braid before leaning forward to stroke Noelle's cheek.

She'd grown another few inches, gaining on Gwylan's own height more rapidly than she'd expected. She could see how the change frightened Maxx. Could see how he wanted this to stop, and that his helplessness frustrated him. There was something almost endearing in the way he struggled, making her wonder if he'd ever, in all his life, been powerless. If he'd ever been unable to control anyone or anything in his life.

"I don't think so, Noelle," she replied. "We cannot go on in this storm, that is all."

"I don't like the shadows," Noelle commented, twining a strand of her hair around her finger. "There's something ... *in* them."

Gwylan frowned. "Did you see something, dearest?"

"Well ..." Noelle's lips puckered, and she snapped them a couple of times in frustration, twirling her hair more furiously. "They looked like hands, I suppose. Almost like long vines or something. Veins? I don't know."

She shrugged, lowering her hand to her side. "Does it mean something, Aunt Gwylan?"

Gwylan's brow rose, the title taking her aback. Noelle didn't seem to notice her surprise or lack of an answer, tucking her feet beneath her and bounding to her feet. She skipped across the tent and dropped beside Symber, peeking over her shoulder at the book she was reading. Her Kaldoner Sister never looked up from her book as she tucked an arm around Noelle's shoulders and pulled her close.

We're all becoming so accustomed to her presence. Gwylan sighed, pulling worriedly on one of her braids.

"She's nearly your size."

She jumped, his voice beside her ear sudden. Gwylan twisted to look a him as he settled on the cushion beside her, stretched his legs before him, crossed his ankles, and leaned back on his elbows. Maxx shot her a warm grin that wreaked havoc in her center. She looked away quickly, clearing her throat.

"I noticed. But I am not particularly tall."

"No, you're not," Maxx agreed, looking her over. "But what you lack in size, you make up for in your ..."

The unfinished thought got her attention. Gwylan turned slowly to him, arching a curious brow while eyeing him heatedly.

"In my what, exactly?"

Maxx coughed, the sparkle in his eye turning her fluttering stomach to stone.

"Your ... delightful personality?"

Gwylan sneered, shoving her hands into the cushions to launch herself to her feet. Before she could stomp away, he grabbed her wrist.

"Don't," he murmured.

She stared at his fingers, curled around her wrist, her heart thundering. His hand was warm but calloused. Fingers thick and large, wrapping all the way around her small wrist to hold her firmly, yet gently, in place. He didn't flinch, barely even blinked when he caught her eye and held her gaze.

The first time he's touched me since we met ... A lump clogged her throat, a threatening sting in her eyes warning her of a loss of control she'd worked so hard to achieve.

"Please, sit down," Maxx rasped.

Slowly, she lowered herself back to the cushions, slipping her wrist from his grasp.

"I didn't mean to insult you," he continued once she was settled. "My brother always told me I never knew when to hold my tongue."

"Would that be the same brother who tried to stop you from making the biggest mistake of your life when you first met me?" Gwylan wondered, the corner of her mouth twitching with a restrained smile.

Maxx relaxed again, an easy smile curving his mouth. "The very same. You'd think it would be my eldest brother, Brecken, who would chastise me for not paying attention to our lessons as children. But it was Lathan who was always after me. Turns out I should've listened to him."

"Indeed." Gwylan readjusted onto her side, sitting up on her elbow to face him.

The firelight danced over his face, giving a natural sheen to his olive skin, head tilted back so his dark curly hair rippled in the air. He seemed not to notice her scrutiny, shifting side to side to get a bit more comfortable and staring at the tent ceiling.

"Tell me something," he said, clearing his throat.

"Hmm?"

"How is this," he paused, gesturing widely with one arm at the tent and beddings, "possible? You don't have a wagon, and Haileah makes me look away when you set up the tents so ..."

Gwylan grinned. "Haileah is very protective of Eventide secrets." She leaned closer to him confidentially. "The truth is, Maxx Jandry ... none of this is actually here."

His brow winged up.

"The fire is quite real, as are the small things we can fit in our packs like our blankets, but as for the tent and the pillows, well, it's all part of an ancient bit of trickery. We have at least the illusion of true shelter and comfort to protect us while also keeping us invisible from our enemies. Ellia and I learned how to create such an illusion when we were girls in Draedin right before we left."

"Clever," Maxx whispered, a half-smile tilting his mouth.

"Have you ever been to Draedin?" she asked.

He scrunched his nose. "No, actually. I've never been one for ships. Couldn't stand the water as a boy, and dry land was far more appealing. I did cross the Peace Bridge once, though, to enter Molderëin. My father took us all there when we were of a certain age. All except Clea, she was far too little, but I suppose he sensed his time was coming and he wanted to take his youngest on the trip."

His smile slipped away as easily as it had come, replaced with a furrowed brow. Gwylan dug her nails into her palms, resisting reaching out to touch his arm in comfort.

"I'd never crossed the sea, either, until my power awoke. My family were more than happy to be rid of me. They feared my magic."

"That's unusual isn't it?"

"Not always. Noble families in Draedin were meant to have children who married well and bore many heirs, not join a nation of women who cultivate their magic and infuse their power to help the turning of the world." Gwylan sighed. "My uncle was killed by magic, and my family forbade it in our house ... until they couldn't."

"So, like Noelle, this was just something that was in you, and you couldn't stop it from coming out." Maxx turned toward her, looking into her eyes.

"Magic is in all of us, Maxx," she answered. "You just need to know how to find and nurture it."

"If you say so."

"You don't think you have magic in you, do you?" Gwylan smirked.

"The only person in my family who cultivated any magic at all was my sister Clea, and I didn't even see her do anything like what you've been teaching Noelle." Maxx wagged a finger at her. "Besides, men don't have magic. Never have."

"Oh, really?"

Gwylan sat up, tucking her feet beneath her and facing him. Before he could protest, she pulled on his wrist, forcing him into an upright position as well. He faced her, his longsuffering look burning the back of her neck, which she ignored.

"In Draedin, there are as many male sorcerers as female," she announced. "Did you never meet one in Molderëin?"

He shook his head, a glitter of uncertainty flashing in his eyes.

"Hmm, interesting. Perhaps they'd no cause to reveal themselves while you were visiting the city, though they do usually go after young, vulnerable children." Gwylan shrugged.

She raised his hands, palms facing hers. After a moment of hesitation, she placed hers flat against his, her shorter fingers barely reaching the tips of his.

"And don't forget the boy I told you about," Gwylan reminded him. "The one like Noelle?"

Maxx averted his gaze, but only for a moment. Taking a breath, she straightened her back.

"Now, breathe deeply. Relax your body, your mind. We are alone here. Just the two of us and there is nothing to fear."

Maxx's brow tightened, and he closed his eyes, shoulders rising and falling as he tried to do as she said.

"Good," Gwylan whispered. "Now, I want you to think of a place. A place where you felt happiest. Where you felt alive and safe. Where you felt loved."

His frown started to fade, the tremble at the corner of his mouth alerting her it was working. Slowly, he pushed his fingers against hers, sliding his in-between hers to clutch her knuckles. Gwylan gulped the lump in her throat and continued.

"Do you feel it? The warmth rising inside your heart?"

Maxx nodded, a small, deep sound slipping from him. He held her hands tighter. A spark twinkled from between their palms and she leaned forward.

"Embrace those feelings Maxx, let your body do the work, your mind focus. Breathe through the feeling until it consumes you."

Gwylan began to smile, the light glimmering between their palms growing stronger, brighter. Then, he opened his eyes.

Maxx gasped, releasing her hands, but the rays only shone brighter, rising toward the ceiling of the tent. He laughed, eyes wide with awe.

"You're doing this," he said.

Gwylan shook her head. "No, Maxx. This is you."

The light vanished, suddenly.

Maxx stared at his hands as he lowered them back to his lap, shaking his head slowly. The confusion in his eyes struck her when he looked at her again.

"But, if I can do that …"

"Then why can't you do more?" Gwylan finished for him. "Because some have a little, and others have more. Your sister, Clea, has more. Noelle has more. You have a little, and it is yours to keep and do with as you please."

Maxx bent closer to her, arms on his knees. "So you're telling me, if I wanted to, I could be as powerful as my sister."

Gwylan nodded. "If you wish to practice and strengthen your power, then yes. But the road to such a life is long and difficult, and you are starting late."

"You're saying I'm old?" Maxx's gaze narrowed.

Gwylan laughed, shaking her head. "No, I'm saying perhaps this isn't something you should pursue. Perhaps, it should be enough that you know the Creator has gifted you. How complicated the world would be, should everyone awaken the little bit of magic inside them."

A shadow fell over them, drawing both their gazes up. Gwylan stiffened, staring up into Haileah's blazing eyes.

"Are you teaching this *man* the ways of Eventide?" Haileah hissed.

"Haileah, please …"

"I was right." Haileah backed away slowly. "Your heart has softened because of what he's done. You are not fit to lead this company."

She spun away, and Gwylan shot to her feet, hurrying after her. A gust of wind tore at her clothes as she followed Haileah out of the tent into the darkness of the woods.

"What have I done to deserve your anger, sister?" Gwylan shouted above the wind, snatching a handful of Haileah's sleeve.

The older Dominant yanked away, her hair whipping into her face but the glare of her eyes shining through the thick strands.

"You swore an oath!" Haileah yelled. "This man has twisted your mind and heart. He's a charmer, Gwylan, and like a foolish little girl you've fallen for him!"

"Do not presume to tell me where my weaknesses lie. You know nothing of my heart!"

"I know you will destroy everything! You and the Jandry boy will compromise our mission, and you will turn your back on the only thing that matters in the world you've chosen!" Haileah moved closer, nearly nose to nose with Gwylan. "I always knew you would never be worthy of true power. You think you can do as you please without consequence."

"I never took a vow of solitude," Gwylan said on a strained breath. "I did not take a vow against marriage … or love."

74

"You're a disgrace! Now you teach him the ways of an Eventide Sister? You dishonor yourself and every woman you took as a sister the day you came to this land!"

A harsh, throaty sound burst from Gwylan. She shoved her hand up, sending Haileah flying across the clearing. She turned her hands palms up, silver flames igniting from her skin. Haileah was on her feet in a moment, amber fire shooting down her arms, through the tips of her fingers. The older woman's mouth curved in an elated smile and Gwylan hesitated, head spinning.

Have I been tricked into this? She shook the thought from her head, anger bubbling in her chest.

Their fire brightened the pitch black of night, reflecting into the darkened sky. Haileah raised her hand, a streak of flames shooting toward her. Gwylan deflected, her own fire slamming into Haileah's and locking in a stream at the center of the clearing. Gwylan pushed harder, sweat beading on her brow and her feet slipping in the thick layer of snow as Haileah tested her.

"Stop!" Ellia's voice echoed through the forest. "Stop this now!"

With a shout, Gwylan slashed her hand through the air, sending Haileah and her fire into the snow. Her shoulders rose and fell with quick breaths. Her fire left a line of melted snow and charred earth from one end of the clearing to the other. Haileah was curled beneath a tree, eyes closed.

"What is the meaning of this?" Symber growled.

Gwylan spun to face the taller woman.

"She questioned my loyalty." She jutted her chin defiantly, hands fisted at her sides to resist her magic.

"So you attack her?" Ellia shook her head, a stern set to her mouth.

"She has questioned me from the moment we left on our mission! I will not tolerate dissent, Ellia!"

"You have weaved fire magic in the Aulend," Symber grumbled. "It will have been noticed, not just by the enemy but by our Superiors."

"Let them notice." Gwylan straightened her clothing, rubbing her palms together a few times.

"And what will happen the next time Haileah makes you angry?" Ellia wondered. "What has gotten into you, Gwylan?"

She opened her mouth to answer, but Ellia brushed passed her, hurrying to help Haileah back to her feet. A soft hand on her shoulder brought her back around. She found Symber smiling softly.

"Having so much power isn't easy, Gwylan," she whispered. "And leading a company on the greatest mission of our time? Even harder. But remember what we were taught. Our light comes first. A winter light so powerful no flame we possess could overwhelm it. Seek your light now, my friend, before the flames ignite your anger and hold you in its vice."

Symber stepped around her, going to Ellia and Haileah. Gwylan moved toward the tent, stopping short when she nearly ran into Maxx in the dark. He watched her, a light of worry in his eyes and brow tilting uncertainly.

"Are you all right?" he asked softly.

Gwylan shook her head, pushing passed him into the warmth of the tent. She exhaled a breath she hadn't realized she was holding, resting a hand over her heart. How had she let Haileah provoke her like that? Why had what she'd said gotten to her so badly?

Noelle stirred across the tent. Gwylan stepped over the cushions and blankets, kneeling beside the child where she prepared for sleep.

"Noelle?" she murmured.

The little girl turned her head, staring up at her with big green eyes.

"Why did you call me Aunt Gwylan?"

Noelle smiled sweetly. "Because you'll be my aunt really soon. You love my Uncle Maxx ... you just don't know it yet."

Her eyes brimmed. Noelle tugged her blanket up over her shoulder to settle in for the night, as if she'd not just changed Gwylan's life forever.

If she's seen it, why haven't I? Gwylan tilted her head back, looking straight up. *Tell me. Why have You taken my visions? Why can I not see what is to come? Why are You doing this to me?*

Sniffling, she rubbed unshed tears from her eyes and curled up beside the child, seeking the elusive peace of sleep.

Maxx ... she is in danger ... wake, Maxx, wake!

He opened his eyes. Maxx sat up slowly, reaching for his sword as he looked around the tent. The night was quiet. The Sisters sleeping peacefully. He released the breath he'd been holding, dismissing the voice for a ridiculous dream. As he started to settle himself on his blankets once again, he saw it. A small, crouched shadow, creeping across the tent just outside the glow of the fire. Something glittered in each hand, and when the figure turned slightly toward the fire, he saw they were daggers.

Haileah? Maxx rose, easing his sword from its scabbard silently. She was moving away from her bedding, her feet silent on the soft floor of the tent. His heart picked up when he realized she was heading for Gwylan. *What is she doing?*

Then, before another thought could enter his mind, he lunged. Haileah was raising her daggers over the sleeping figure of his betrothed, preparing to strike. Maxx let out a roar to put her off balance then shoved her away, knocking her into a sea of cushions and blankets. He pressed the tip of his sword against her throat when she spun onto her back, glaring up at him.

"Maxx!" Gwylan exclaimed, leaping to her feet. "What are you doing?"

"She intended to kill you," he hissed, looking over his shoulder.

Gwylan stared at him wide-eyed as the others began to awaken.

"What happened?"

"What's going on?"

"How dare you hold a sword to our sister!"

Their exclamations battered him from all sides, but Maxx kept his sword steady against the hollow of Haileah's throat.

"She was going to kill Gwylan! Look at her daggers for evidence!"

"I merely drew them to defend myself," Haileah purred, smirking at him. "*He* attacked *me*."

"That's a lie! Why is she so far from her bed?" Maxx looked at Gwylan again.

She stared at him unmoving, her eyes wide. He couldn't read them. Then, he held out his free hand to her. "I have never lied to you. I came back for your help because I respect and honor you. If you truly believe I would lie, then kill me now. But if you trust me, take my hand. For I swear before the Creator, she was going to kill you in your sleep."

Gwylan's gaze shifted between him and Haileah, a flicker of uncertainty lighting her gaze. Then she stepped forward. Maxx held his breath as she slipped her hand into his.

"I trust you," she whispered. "Symber, see to it Haileah is chained and her weapons removed. She has tried to kill a Sister and must be taken back for the Superiors to punish her."

"You will never succeed!" Haileah spat suddenly, drawing their gazes. "Raphaela is stronger than all of you! She is coming, and no one will stop the Abyss when he arrives at her side. She will take all the Novices and Intermediates! You Dominants and Superiors will stand alone!"

An insane cackle slipped between the woman's lips as Symber grabbed her by the arms, dragging her away. Maxx breathed once the two women disappeared outside. Ellia followed, casting a wide-eyed look over her shoulder at them before she ducked out of the tent as well. He started to turn when Gwylan grabbed him, dropping her forehead to his chest.

Maxx stood still, his free hand hovering over her, unsure whether he should hug her or offer her a sympathetic pat on the head.

Creator's Night, man! She is your betrothed wife. Maxx swallowed the lump in his throat and wrapped his arm around her.

"You're safe," he whispered. "You'll always be safe with me."

"Never did I think any of my sisters would turn against me," she replied. "We are family! First, she provoked me into violence against her and now this? How could she?"

"Evil tempts the purest of hearts and magic," Maxx said. He placed his hand on the back of her head and she raised it, looking up into his eyes. His gaze lowered briefly to her full, lush mouth. He corrected his sight, ignoring the burn on the back of his neck.

"Haileah was weak," he continued huskily. "She fell prey and is a victim to Raphaela. To the Abyss. What will you do with her?"

Gwylan's chest rose with a breath. "What I must. She must be delivered to the Superiors for punishment, whatever that may be."

"Why did she target you?"

"Because I am strongest among our small company and proved earlier her power was nothing against mine. I think that's really why she provoked me, to fully test my strength. With me gone, she could easily control Symber and Ellia. They would have been lost to her treachery. Compelled by her power to do whatever she desired." Gwylan trembled.

Maxx put his sword away and rubbed her arms roughly with his palms to warm her.

"I am glad you were here," Gwylan murmured, looking up at him again. Her eyes glimmered with expectation and question. "We have been bound by accident, Maxx Jandry ... but I always believed the Creator knew what he was about."

Maxx grinned. "Then you're glad I came back?"

Gwylan rolled her lips but not before he caught a glimpse of her smile. "Yes," she breathed. "I suppose I am."

"Uncle Maxx?" Noelle's little voice drew his gaze. He let Gwylan go, turning to crouch beside his niece.

"Shh," he purred, tucking the blanket around her tightly. "Everything's fine, sweetheart. Go back to sleep."

"It was Haileah, wasn't it?" Noelle wondered, barely opening her eyes.

Maxx frowned. "Yes. How did you know?"

"She never liked me." Noelle sighed. "Aunt Gwylan is safe?"

He grinned, stroking her hair. "Yes, she's just ..." his voice faded when he turned, finding the space beside him empty. Looking over his shoulder, he caught a glimpse of her shadow before she vanished out into the night.

When they woke the next morning, the shadows overhead roiled with their darkest fury yet, and Haileah's chains lay empty round a tree.

CHAPTER EIGHT

The Tower of Righteousness

The soft *hiss* of blade on stone echoed in her ears as Mirae Sundragon stared at the blackened sky. The shadow had descended over the Tower of Righteousness two days ago, striking fear in the hearts of her people. Some wanted to run from the darkness, others were frozen, whispering of staying right here. Where they were *safe*.

No place is safe. Mirae pulled in a ragged breath, lowering her gaze to her dagger glimmering against the stone. Inside, she could hear the last surviving Sister of the Creed pacing and mumbling. She'd barely moved from her spot on the steps of the Tower, determined to keep the poor woman safe as Ahmet and Astra searched for a way to save her.

How do you expel the Abyss from a body without bringing death to the innocent soul within? Is such a thing even possible? Mirae closed her eyes, the same questions she'd asked Astra repeating in her mind.

Brecken was the one who convinced her to delay their journey to the Tower of Tears. She'd wanted to take the possessed woman away from here, even if doing so meant tying her up in the back of one of their wagons. Delaying their progress to the Tower that held all the weaponry they'd need against Roderick and Raphaela did not sit well with her, but she knew Brecken was right. The poor Sister of the Creed would only suffer should they force her departure from Righteousness.

The gentle thud of boots on the steps brought Mirae's head up. Brecken sat down on the step beside her, folding his hands and resting his elbows on his knees. Mirae continued sharpening her dagger in silence, ignoring the tingle of his warm body beside hers.

"Afra hasn't returned," he murmured, breaking the silence.

"I'm sure she is well, Brecken," Mirae replied. "The Creator must've required a Passing from her."

Brecken nodded. "I thought she would be back by now."

"Do you think the Creator needed her elsewhere?"

"That's what troubles me. She will be needed by many in the days to come." Brecken bowed his head, avoiding her eyes. "Perhaps you will think me selfish, but I want her by my side. I do not see her as a Passer. She's just my little sister, and I need her."

Mirae smiled. "I understand, Brecken. I know how it feels to desperately need your family and they are nowhere near."

A muffled moan from within the Tower made her turn sharply, heart pounding as she listened to the agony of the woman inside. Brecken placed his hand on her wrist.

"We cannot stay here much longer, Mirae," he murmured.

"I won't leave her behind in agony."

"So you will risk the lives of your people?"

Mirae frowned, turning a harsh glare on him. "I don't know what terrible things Roderick made you do while in his service, Brecken, but out here we do not leave innocents to suffer and die alone."

She rolled the dagger between her fingers before securing the blade in its sheath and rising.

"Mirae ..."

She marched down the stone steps, ignoring him. The snow crunched beneath her boots, blackened by the lack of sunlight hidden by the shadows coating the sky. She followed the line of torches ensconced on the walls around the Tower of Righteousness, the soft, muffled sounds of the Woodlanders moving about the camp carrying on the wind. She combed a hand through her hair, jagged fingernails catching on the delicate crimson strands which had grown out a bit, lying just under the top of her shoulders. She'd always made a point to keep her hair short, more manageable, so she blended better with the Woodlanders.

Mirae stopped at the edge of the camp, threading her arms across her chest.

"Trouble with the captain, Your Majesty?" Jaeger asked near her ear.

Mirae smirked. "You wish, Jaeger Senne. I take it your patrol was a peaceful one?"

"Too dark for a successful patrol," Jaeger muttered, his shoulder brushing hers as he came to stand close. "No clouds. No stars. No moon. Just blackness and an occasional fiery light. It covers the sky for miles, Mirae. No end. I fear this darkness has even reached the Shadow Lands."

Mirae looked up at him, the mention of her mother's birthplace tightening her chest.

"Are you sure you want to continue to the Tower of Tears while we're under the eye of this evil? The darkness will hinder our journey—"

"But it could work for us once we reach our destination." Mirae arched a brow. "If I could use this darkness to hide our soldiers, we could gain an advantage at Tears. I think, in the end, we'll have a better chance."

Jaeger grunted and strode forward, his form moving in and out of the shadows as he made his way to his tent. Mirae reached for her necklace, tugging on the chain until she felt the sharp tail of the golden dragon pendant in her palm. She closed her eyes, lifting the necklace to her lips. The dragon eyes seemed to glow in the darkness, the red shining brighter than earlier. She smiled.

Adlae. Mirae closed her eyes, the golden figure strangely warm on her lips with the presence of one who was far away from her.

"Not for long, dear sister," she whispered. "I'm coming."

Brecken crouched low to the ground, cupping a hand through the hardened layer of ice to soft powder beneath. There hadn't been a fresh snowfall since the shadow descended upon Nfaros, covering the world in a darkness so complete one would be lost without a lit torch constantly at one's side. He moved the softer snow between his fingers, watching it slowly melt against the warmth of his skin. He closed his eyes, trying to draw the image of his wife from the back of his mind, trying to separate her features from the striking resemblance he saw of her in Mirae. Yet the harder he tried, the more she slipped away from him.

As does Noelle ... Brecken dropped the bits of snow from between his fingers.

He'd always wondered what Noelle's first snow would be like. He'd pictured her, playing in the fields outside Sunkai's walls, laughing with Brae, throwing snowballs at him. An almost-smile trembled the corner of his mouth as he straightened.

Looking back, the pit in his stomach hardened. The last remaining Sister of the Creed still paced within the walls of the Tower of Righteousness.

None of the others held on as long as this one, her courage and strength surpassing his own understanding.

How unwavering her faith must be to resist the Abyss this long. Brecken shook his head, turning toward the encampment.

He stopped short, nearly running into the woman before him. She was wrapped in thick woolens, her brown hair cut short like many of the Woodlander women, and dark circles framed her wide, pale blue eyes. She clutched her hands before her, knuckles whitening with her tight grip. She moved a little closer to him, and a sinking feeling twisted his stomach. Most of the Woodlanders avoided him and he understood why. Despite Mirae's quick decision to make him a captain of her army, he knew most of the Woodlanders still didn't trust him.

Why should they?

"You don't know me," she said, her voice a low croak. "But, how could you? You know nothing about any of us."

Brecken cleared his throat. "I-I'm sorry, miss, I—"

"You killed my husband."

The abrupt, stark statement took him aback. Brecken clasped his hands behind his back, his heart thundering a little harder in his chest.

"He fought on the Kliat Plains, wounded by your hand. He died slowly of a horrible infection." Her eyes flooded, glistening in the flickering lights of the torches.

Brecken bowed his head, the block in his throat growing larger.

"I don't know why Mirae Sundragon has forgiven you so suddenly. I don't know why she's welcomed you amongst us and given you authority over our young men to lead them into battle. All I know is that weeks ago, you were one of our greatest enemies." She shuffled closer and he raised his head, looking into her eyes. "Have you nothing to say for yourself?"

Brecken straightened his shoulders, holding her gaze. "Only that in war, a soldier does what he must."

"You're as cold as the ice beneath our feet, Brecken Jandry. I pity our queen's sister for having been tied to a man like you."

He stiffened, his fingers tightening on his knuckles.

"Faël," Jaeger's voice startled her, and she took a step back. "Is there a problem?"

84

"Why is he here?" Faël replied, gesturing to Brecken. "Because of him, my son will grow up without a father! He doesn't belong here. Why do we welcome enemies into our camp?"

"Need I remind you, Faël, that we have had enemies amongst us before and called them allies. Even friends. Our people fought each other for centuries before we found someone to unite and lead us. Your husband was not the first to fall in battle and certainly will not be the last. This man's wife gave her life for the cause. Now his daughter is missing. He suffers as you do, and if you cannot show trust in our queen for her decisions, then perhaps you should come no further."

Faël inhaled sharply, taking a small step back. She looked back and forth between the two of them, shaking her head slowly.

"You have softened too much, Jaeger Senne," she hissed. "How could you? How could Queen Mirae?"

"Brecken Jandry is our queen's appointed captain. You will show him respect or take your son to the nearest village to wait out the war as you will. The choice is yours, Faël Eyres." Jaeger crossed his arms and tilted his head, fixing the woman with a hard stare.

Faël hesitated, her eyes still darting between the two of them. Abruptly, she spun on her heels, marching back among the tents. Brecken exhaled, moving to stand shoulder to shoulder with Jaeger. He took a breath to speak when Jaeger raised a hand.

"If you are about to offer words of thanks, don't," he muttered without looking at him. "I did not defend you for your sake. I did it for Mirae."

"I know that," Brecken replied. "I expected nothing else, especially not for you to come to my defense at all."

"The people need to trust our queen, and I cannot have them speaking thus about the man she's appointed to lead a portion of her army. There is no time for dissent, no room here for troublemakers." Jaeger shifted, lowering a hand to the hilt of his sword. "I watched you during the battle on the Kliat Plains. I watched you kill my men. My friends."

"War is war, Jaeger, you know that," Brecken answered, looking beyond the camp at the pitch black of the forest beyond. "But I will say this. I regret many things in my life. I regret following a man I thought was honorable down a road of darkness. I regret I was not strong enough to defend what was mine, to save the woman I loved, and keep my sword clean of the blood of good men. I wish, with all my heart I could change what happened, but I cannot."

"Well," Jaeger said, clearing his throat. "We all have regrets, Brecken Jandry. My sword, too, has been stained with the blood of good men."

"And may be again." Brecken stepped away. "For you forget, not all of Roderick and Raphaela's armies are made up of Wraith Spawn. I am not yet finished meeting familiar faces on the battlefield."

He turned, looking Jaeger in the eye.

"I made a choice when Raphaela Kael murdered my wife. In an instant, I was no longer the man I used to be. I know how your people feel about me. When this war is over, I will leave, and they need never look upon my face again. All I want, Jaeger, is justice for my Brae and my daughter returned safely to my arms."

Jaeger frowned, his stony eyes faltering. "The outcome of such a war is never certain, captain. You do know the chances of ever finding your daughter if you stay at Mirae's side are ... slim."

"Yes, I do." Brecken flexed his fingers around the hilt of his sword. "Yet, I am still here."

"Why?"

Brecken half-smiled. "Because if I don't fight for what's right, what sort of world will she grow up in when I do finally find her?"

Someone shouted for Jaeger, distracting him, and Brecken took his opportunity, striding away into the camp. The Woodlanders were preparing to depart, some loading wagons while others tended to the horses. The lights of the fires grew brighter the deeper into the camp he went, offering a nearly natural glow to the day. A few people noticed him, nodding in acknowledgment, while others turned their backs as he approached. Their reaction wasn't unusual, he'd been growing accustomed to their indifference.

Another reason I want Afra back. Without her, I'm alone here.

"Rickai!"

Brecken's gaze shifted at the sound of her voice, watching Faël duck out of her tent after a little boy, no more than six years of age. His dark brown hair curled over his ears, messy and wild as if he'd just rolled off his cot. He was draped in a thick woolen cloak, trousers a bit ragged at the hem, and worn brown boots a little too big for him, swallowing his feet. She caught him around the waist, lifting to perch him on her hip and nuzzle his neck. Rickai laughed, shoving against her shoulders.

"Let me go with the others, Ma!" he begged. "I just want to play."

"Not today, young man," Faël replied, dropping him lightly to his feet. "We will be leaving soon, and you must help me prepare. Go on, now." She gave him a playful pat on the backside, sending him back into the tent.

Brecken took a breath and marched across the camp. He caught her eye before she could follow her son, freezing her in a half-ducked position with fingers tightening around a handful of the tent flap.

"You have every reason to hate me," he said, his harsh breath steaming between his lips in the cold. "I admit I do not remember your husband. I've been a soldier for years, and one thing I learned to do well was distance myself from the violence I wrought under the command of others. To quickly put aside the many faces of the men I killed. But if you think I do not feel keenly the devastation ripe in your heart, you're wrong. Not a day—no, not a minute—goes by when I do not want to thrust my dagger into the heart of the woman who murdered my wife."

Faël released the tent flap, straightening her back. She stared into his eyes, her own softened and searching, taking in what he had to say.

"Your child is by your side, and mine ... has disappeared. You said I was cold, that you pitied your queen's sister for having been tied to me. Well, you were right. Because if not for me, she would still be alive today. If not for her ties to me, her life might've been better. So I take your judgment willingly. I deserve every bit of malice you can muster, but know this." He moved closer, nearly towering over her. "If the time comes, I will gladly give my life for you and your son. That is the oath I have taken as Mirae Sundragon's captain, and I will *never* break my word."

Faël remained silent, staring up at him, unblinking. Brecken shuddered as a gust of wind tugged his cloak from his shoulder, the winter chill ever present, but its full power muted by the shadow overhead.

"I'll leave you now, Mistress Eyres." He bowed at the waist before turning on his heels, marching toward his tent.

"Brecken Jandry!" Faël called after him.

He paused, looking over his shoulder with an arched brow.

"You judge yourself so harshly for things you could not control as well as for things you could," she said, clutching handfuls of her skirts. "Perhaps ... perhaps you do not need my judgment on your shoulders as well."

Before he could respond, she twirled away, disappearing back into her tent.

CHAPTER NINE

A Forest with No Name

The trees groaned and creaked against the harsh wind whistling through the woods. Jabon swayed with the movement of his horse, watching Adlae ride ahead of him, her staff lighting a path for them deeper to the north. After making certain Klade and the army were safely away, they'd moved out in the opposite direction, toward the Shadow Lands.

Adlae had barely spoken a word—at least to him. She whispered sometimes to an invisible companion, and it troubled him more than he cared to admit. Glaydin's death was taking its toll on her, he could see it in her eyes, and her light wasn't as bright as it had been before the shadow descended on Nfaros.

An icy layer over the softer powder of snow crunched beneath the horses' hooves, echoing through the forest. Adlae hadn't summoned another snow, something Jabon wanted to question her about but resisted. If the shadow had, somehow, blocked her from her power, it felt wrong to question her about where her loss left their position in this war.

I barely understand her power. How is it my place to question her about the secret workings of her magic? He raked a hand through his hair and tugged the reins to the side.

Jabon nudged his horse alongside Adlae's, moving his gaze between her and the path ahead of them.

"You said," he murmured. "When you came away from the Tower of the Dead that we were going to win. How? With this new evil from the Abyss, how will we win?"

"Some prophecies are conclusive, without change. Others bend as the world turns. The how of them is never clear," Adlae replied. She smiled at him, crystal blue eyes glowing.

"And our prophesied victory? Is that without change?"

Her smile trembled for an instant before she straightened her shoulders.

"I cannot say. The foretelling I received from the dead was for me and me alone to bear."

"Your faith in me is overwhelming," he mumbled.

Adlae pulled on her reins, coming up short beside him. Jabon did the same staring back at her stern brow warily.

"Do not think you understand what has been placed on my shoulders, Jabon. To know what is to come is a fearful thing. A burden so heavy it haunts my sleep." She trembled, new ice cracking on her staff around her fingers.

Jabon looked away, staring into the pitch black of the forest. "Forgive me. I only want …"

"I know." Adlae exhaled slowly, her body beginning to visibly relax again. "You find more comfort surrounded by hundreds of men with swords. I find my comfort in isolation. But if you will trust me, Jabon, I promise you there is a purpose to my actions."

He dipped his head once in answer. Adlae urged her white mare, Starlight, forward, tilting her staff toward the path. The smooth, round globe glowed brighter, casting shadows over the pure white ground. The icy way glittered like crystals, smooth and frozen over as the winter air grew ever colder. Jabon followed her cautiously, patting the warm, soft curve of his dapple-grey stallion's neck.

Adlae's white hair shimmered in the darkness, roped in multiple braids and brought together against her back in one large twist. Her restrained tresses offered a view of the delicate curve of her pearly neck, framed in the soft fur collar of her cloak.

He remembered her neck once draped in jewels, her hair as red as blood flowing like a river over her shoulders and down her back in silky waves. A time when her green eyes would smile at him the moment he walked into the room—when they would dance together in the Blood Keep gardens. When the only magic he could feel emanating from her was the connection between her and her sisters. Those days seemed so far away now. Completely out of his reach with no turning back. For her to come back after five years, bearing almost no resemblance to the young woman he knew … every day was torture.

Adlae lifted her staff suddenly toward the sky, eyes narrowing in confusion. Jabon looked up cautiously, his fingers tightening around the reins.

"What's wrong?" he asked as they brought their horses to a stop simultaneously.

"The clouds," she murmured. "They're ... circling."

"Adlae, they've been coiling for hours."

"No, this is different." She shook her head, the globe of her staff brightening to a blazing white light as she attempted to illuminate the sky. "The clouds are retreating."

Jabon scrunched his nose, squinting tightly at the sky. His brow winged when he realized she was right. The thick, blackened clouds were being pushed away, leaving clear black sky up above. The vines snapping and hissing as they were forced away from the Shadow Lands.

"Are you doing that, Adlae?" he asked.

"No, Jabon. I'm not."

Adlae dug her heels into Starlight's flanks, the animal leaping forward. Jabon followed hastily, keeping alongside her as she raced deeper into the forest. They skirted around the trees, the glaring light of her staff a mere blur as she pushed Starlight faster. Jabon shook his head, the cold freezing his breath when he tried to call out to her in an attempt to stop her. Something was wrong. Did she sense something? Was her magic telling her something was near?

Suddenly, they broke through the trees, skidding to a stop in a round clearing. Jabon gaped, his chest tight as he tried to catch his breath. He took in the sight slowly, his eyes moving around the strangest encampment he'd ever seen.

Caravans arranged in a semi-circle at the far end of the clearing, a roaring bonfire crackling in the very center of their circle as women and children danced in a circle around the flames, dressed in heavy robes to keep warm. The men sat nearby singing in a language he'd never heard, their baritone voices resonating on the wind. The flames only seemed to grow larger the more they sang.

Adlae leaped down from Starlight's back, not even sparing him a glance as she moved toward the dancers. Jabon hurried after her, nearly stumbling in the thick layer of snow in his haste to catch up to her. The further he went, the more he noticed the strands of red hair gracing the heads of nearly every inhabitant of the encampment. His eyes widened.

Like Adlae's hair before ... like her mother's ... Jabon's heart pounded harder against his chest as he wondered.

Had they passed into the Shadow Lands?

Adlae could barely breathe. The ice of her staff cracked and grew, twirling around her hand to hold her fingers captive. The singing stopped suddenly, the women and children stumbling slightly as they halted in their ritual dance. Adlae froze in the center of the camp, watching them as they were now watching her. The flames burst, booming as a log tumbled and spit embers into the blackened sky.

We have done it, Adlae Sundragon! We have found the people of the Shadow Lands! Winter exclaimed, her fear and excitement rushing through Adlae's own heart.

One of the women who'd been dancing moments ago stepped forward, pointing at Adlae.

"The Sundragon has come!" she cried, her big, pale eyes glistening with hope.

"The Sundragon has come," the rest of them repeated.

Adlae turned in a full circle slowly, watching the men rise slowly from where they sat, the children hurry to their mothers' sides.

"The Sundragon has come," they chanted on. "The Sundragon has come …"

"Adlae, I don't like this," Jabon hissed near her ear.

"Be calm," Adlae replied. "Just be …" her voice faded as her gaze was once again drawn to the bonfire.

They rose higher toward the sky, the flames rippling and waving, forming shapes so quickly she could barely make them out before they vanished once more. Adlae moved closer to the heat, unable to look away from the warm orange light.

Suddenly, the fire took the form of a dragon, its long neck swirling and thick snout puffing as the figure turned its face toward her.

"So you've come," the dragon hissed, spitting embers her way.

What magic is this? Winter wondered, curiosity and fear mixed in her tone.

"I do not know," Adlae whispered.

"You've come, yet cannot claim the power which I hold," the dragon continued, flickering yellow eyes glaring at her.

"You are of fire," she answered. "I am of winter. We cannot touch without destruction."

"Then you must find the answer and guide me to my wielder."

"How?"

The dragon appeared to smile.

"You know the answer, for it is already in your heart. But I will help you reveal the truth within yourself. With this circle of Sundragon fire, with this crown of flames, I will lead you through this darkness."

An earsplitting roar vibrated through the forest, nearly knocking Adlae from her feet. The flames shot upward in a swirling spiral, lifting and splitting from the ground as they formed a circle in the sky overhead. The flames illuminated the sky, sending a glow down upon them to light the forest. Adlae tilted her head back, neck arching at a sharp angle as she watched the fire turn in a continuous circle overhead. Glittering and crackling, they truly looked like a golden crown floating in the sky.

"We knew you would come."

The new voice drew her attention away from the magic. The elderly man smiled at her, his wrinkled face endearing and long white hair brushing his shoulders. He wore simple brown robes, a rope belt tied round his hips and sturdy boots on his feet. A little boy stood by his hip, peeking around him to watch her warily.

"Our journey began the moment the riders came to our camp in search of Zelaria Sundragon's granddaughter."

"Riders?" Adlae rasped, moving closer to him.

"You have awoken the flames of the Sundragon," the old man said, gesturing to the circle of fire above them. "But you cannot wield them."

"Who are you?" she asked.

"I am called Healer Faw," he replied, placing a hand over his heart. "I lead the people you see here. We are, all of us, of the Shadow Lands, as were your parents."

Adlae frowned. "You mean my mother. She was of the Shadow Lands."

Healer Faw smiled gently. "Of course. You would not know."

"Perhaps you should tell her," Jabon spoke up, making Adlae jump. She'd nearly forgotten he was there.

"Indeed, Jabon Malaki, you will both have your answers."

"Forgive me, I don't remember meeting you."

Healer Faw tilted his head, curiously. "Because we never have."

The old man turned, little boy following in his wake, toward one of the caravans. Adlae didn't hesitate, shuffling after him through the snow. She could hear Jabon following, mumbling something under his breath as Healer Faw took the three steps up into the caravan, ducking through the small door.

Adlae took a fistful of her skirt, raising the hem slightly so she wouldn't trip as she followed. The inside of the wagon was surprisingly warm to her senses, a heat that had to be formed from magic if she was able to feel it. The interior of the caravan was simply decorated with a small round table on one end and strings of plain brown beads hanging from the ceiling to separate them from the built-in bed. Adlae stared at the thick mattress, covered in a soft burgundy coverlet with a long, round pillow at one end. The sight alone made her body ache for the comfort of such sleeping accommodations. A bed fit for a king in one of the humblest dwellings in all of Nfaros.

Adlae turned away, noting the intricately stitched tapestries hanging from the walls of the caravan, giving the space a bit more character. Then her gaze fell on the two young men sitting at the table and she stilled.

"I know you," she said, tilting her head. "You are Analli Devareigh's sons."

The two men glanced at each other before rising, bowing deeply to her.

"Your Majesty," one murmured as they straightened. He placed his hand on his chest. "I am Dedric Devareigh, and this is my younger brother, Thane."

"My queen," Thane whispered.

"These are the riders who brought the message," Healer Faw said, taking a seat at the table. The Devareigh brothers sat back down as well, looking more uncomfortable than their host.

"What message?" Jabon asked, irritation laced in his voice. "What's going on here?"

"Sit, Master Malaki," Healer Faw replied calmly. "Have some warm food and I will explain."

"I'm not hungry," Jabon grumbled. "I could do with some answers, that is all."

"Jabon!" Adlae frowned at him.

Healer Faw held up his hand. "Do not worry, Your Majesty. He is right to demand answers. We are strangers, and in these times, there is little reason to place your trust in strangers."

"Those flames," Adlae said, mouth dry. "What do they mean? How will they help?"

"The flames of the Sundragon," Healer Faw uttered reverently. "They have been asleep for many years, even during King Vihaan's reign. But now, the Abyss has covered our world in shadow, and the flames have awakened to find the true rulers of our kingdom."

"But Adlae is of winter," Jabon reminded them, and Adlae cringed. "She cannot wield fire magic, as you know, yet she is the Sundragon. The true heir to the throne. How are a bunch of flames circling round and round in the sky going to help her?"

Healer Faw eyed Adlae, a silver brow crooked in question. "Do you not know the answer to his question already, Queen Adlae?"

Adlae rolled her lips, moistening them. "I … I am not sure."

Healer Faw sighed. The little boy who'd followed him sat down on the floor at his feet, leaning against his knees.

"She's awfully white, Healer Faw," the boy said. "There's no heat in her. Doesn't the crown need heat?"

"Hush, Elias," Healer Faw snapped.

"He's right," Adlae interjected, drawing the old man's gaze. "I do not have fire, Healer Faw. I cannot wield the flames. I can barely go near them without great struggle and pain. How will your flames of the Sundragon help me?"

Healer Faw leaned forward. "You were not always embodied with ice, Your Highness. At the moment of your birth, you were born of fire, and fire still lives within you."

"How? How is such a thing possible?"

"Ah." Healer Faw lifted a gnarly finger, his secretive smile raising gooseflesh on her arms. "Such a secret is for you to uncover."

"And what you said before? About my parents?"

"Born of the Shadow Lands, both of them," Healer Faw answered. "Long had the Sundragon's resided in Sunkai. So long, they forgot their true heritage. But Zelaria knew. She knew when she joined with your father of his ties to her country, and she reminded him. That is why he sent the Devareigh boys."

Adlae blinked slowly in surprise, her gaze shifting from Healer Faw to the two young men who looked just as puzzled as she felt.

"My father sent you?" she rasped.

"I ... we ..." Dedric shook his head, eyes darting frantically between her and Healer Faw. "Our mother sent us!"

"Analli? I knew of her loyalty to the Sundragon, but why would she risk such things while living in the heart of the Mother City?" Adlae shook her head.

"Can you not see the answer for yourself, Adlae Sundragon? Do you not see the truth, simply by looking at the sons of Analli Devareigh?"

Adlae's brow furrowed. She turned to the boys, staring at them in the twinkling candlelight. Their eyes were identical, soft hazel irises staring at her with as much question as she stared at them. Fair skin glistened in the light, straight noses—though Dedric's curved slightly, evidence of a breakage at one point in his young life—and strong jaws. They held themselves like soldiers, their experience in Roderick's army clear in their manner. Then, the light caught in Dedric's hair.

The floor seemed to shift beneath her feet, her head spinning. Unlike Thane's dark locks, there was a hint of another color in Dedric's. The accent caught the light perfectly, brightening his hair to a deep, rich auburn. Her heart thundered faster into her ribs, making breathing a chore.

"No," she gasped, spinning back to Healer Faw. "This ... this cannot be!"

Healer Faw just smiled.

"H-How?" she stuttered, her eyes brimming. "All these years, how did they keep this from me? From all of us?"

"What is it?" Thane wondered. "Healer Faw, what is she talking about?"

"You truly thought you were the last Sundragons to walk the whole of Nfaros," Healer Faw breathed. "I do not blame you. Your father wished it so ... as did his sister."

Adlae dropped into the nearest chair with a thud, closing her eyes.

"Analli Devareigh ..."

"Yes." Healer Faw nodded. "Analli Devareigh ... once Analli Sundragon."

"Wait, you're saying—?"

"Yes, Dedric," Adlae said. "He's saying your mother was my father's sister."

96

"How is that possible?" Jabon placed his hand on her shoulder, the strength and press of his palm comforting. "How could the whole of Nfaros never know Vihaan Sundragon had a sister? Married to an innkeeper no less!"

Thane scowled at him. "My father might be a mere innkeeper, but he is the best man to walk the streets of Sunkai."

"Jabon is right, though," Adlae whispered. "How could no one have known? She was a Princess of Sunkai!"

"Who lived in shadow her whole life," Healer Faw responded. "As a babe, she was taken from the palace to be raised in the Shadow Lands, a sacrifice freely given in the name of the Creator."

"Why?"

"Your grandfather, Your Majesty, had forgotten where the Sundragon bloodline first began, and where it should end. He could not, in all conscience, give his son Vihaan to the Shadow Lands as he was the heir to the throne. So when his wife gave birth to a girl-child, he sent her to be raised amongst us. But her purpose would be far beyond his understanding, for she was the one who gave us the power to find the flames of the Sundragon. She who dedicated her entire life, even from childhood, to seek this knowledge, cultivate and fortify it into a magic so unbreakable only the strongest of Sundragon blood could wield the power."

"How did she return to Sunkai? How did she end up ...?" Adlae paused, her eyes darting to Dedric and Thane.

Dedric's lips tightened. "How did she end up married to my father?"

"I mean no offense or disrespect. I know Rufus Devareigh, and his heart is true for the Sundragon. He is a good man."

"Lady Analli had no desire to claim her title as princess, and when she lost her heart to Rufus Devareigh, she relinquished the claim entirely. But Vihaan Sundragon always knew she was close. Such knowledge was enough for them both."

"I cannot believe he never told me." Adlae's eyes welled and she looked up at Jabon. "How could he keep such a thing from me? From all of us?"

"He was trying to protect Lady Analli," Healer Faw explained. "If the Abyss knew of the part she was to play in the future, he would have come for her. He would have tried to destroy her in her youth."

"You're saying Analli and my father knew this was coming? They knew the Abyss would take Sunkai and cover all of Nfaros in darkness?"

Healer Faw tilted his head, the light catching shadows in the crevices of his weathered face. "Such a future was foretold to them by the Tree Prophetess, Inaya, who traveled across the land from a place unknown to warn them. Lady Analli has been prepared ever since."

"So my father knew he was going to die," Adlae whispered. "He knew all of this would happen."

"He knew some, not all."

Adlae stood up, unable to bear another word. Jabon's hand tightened on her shoulder, but she brushed him off, stepping down out of the caravan and into the cold air. The flames circled overhead, casting amber rays down on the campsite.

The flames of the Sundragon. Winter contemplated. A great power, bursting in the sky. But who can wield them?

Adlae took a breath.

"I can think of only one," she replied.

Yes, Winter agreed. **As can I**.

The fire seemed to brighten suddenly, turning faster in the sky. The flames were moving away from the encampment, back toward Kaldon. This was the power she'd felt when the darkness settled over Nfaros. This was the pull drawing her through the woods, the great answer the Shadows had told her of when she visited the Tower of the Dead.

"A crown of flames ..." she breathed. "True Sundragon fire, lighting the sky like a beacon."

Do you think all of Nfaros can see them?

Adlae wrapped both hands around her staff leaning heavily into the pole.

"I hope so, Winter. If only to renew their faith during this time of darkness, I hope so."

CHAPTER TEN

Falshire
The Capital of Draedin

The lantern sent a ray of misty light down the street, making the cobblestones glisten. Zorina turned a slow circle, looking up at the pitch-black sky. Her quiver, laden with arrows, pressed firmly to her back, and she clutched her longbow in her left hand. She raised the lantern higher in her right hand, trying to pick out the barely formed images in the blackness. The city was full of whispers, guessing what resided in those clouds—Wraith Spawn, *Brakari*, the Abyss himself. The children had been banished indoors the moment the shadows came tumbling toward their city, only members of Draedin's finest armies allowed to roam the streets now as families hid themselves away, not wanting to be tainted by the darkness.

To her left, Kyros, captain of their unit, moved with her in silence, while to her right, her twin brother, Torin, strolled as if unperturbed by the blackness. Directly behind her, Bannon walked like a gloomy mountain unto himself. Zorina spared a glance his way, the corner of her mouth tilting in a smirk. Bannon was a hard shell to crack for certain—with his stony face and solemn demeanor. He was older than she, more than half her age, she suspected, but Zorina knew age did not matter in a unit, no matter what position you held.

And how can a man like Bannon, with so much experience, be a lieutenant while Kyros—a year younger than I—is a captain? Zorina shook her head. She knew why she held the place of Third instead of Captain. Her femininity prevented her from rising above a man like Kyros, though unjust the system be. Perhaps a similar prejudice fueled Bannon's humiliating position.

Half of Bannon's blood belonged to the mountain. They said this was the reason he was so large. That a man of the mountain had come down and fallen in love with Bannon's mother. But their union was not to be, for the Mountain Man was taken by the Abyss then threw himself into the sea before Bannon was ever born so he might not taint the woman he loved with the evil which had taken his soul. Zorina had always thought the story a romantic tale. Bannon never spoke of his history at all.

"Zo!" Torin nudged her with his elbow.

She glared at her twin, who stood Second in Command to Kyros. Torin grinned in return, cool brown eyes sparkling with mischief.

"What?" she growled, returning her attention to the street.

They'd nearly made it to the center of the city now, where they would meet up with Alok's patrol to change guards for the night. Zorina was looking forward to getting some sleep, especially since the perpetual darkness had made it nearly impossible for them to determine when was night and when was day.

"Just being certain you're still awake, Sis," Torin chuckled. "You know Bannon still doesn't know our last name."

Zorina arched a brow, looking over her shoulder. The man stared back at her, his olive skin and long, tightly braided black hair shimmering in her lantern light.

"You wouldn't be able to pronounce it," Zorina assured the man.

Bannon grunted in response, his honey-colored eyes tugging from her gaze to observe the streets.

"She's right, Bannon," Kyros commented. "I've known these two since we were scamps running the streets, and I still don't even try to say their name."

"What delightful conversation the four of us have," Zorina mumbled, the lantern swaying as she turned, backing her way up the hill so she was facing all three of them. "Contemplating the mystery behind Torin's and my last name."

"Say it."

They all stopped in their tracks. Zorina blinked slowly, eyes wide as she stared at Bannon. His rough, deep voice had been so unexpected none of them knew exactly what to do. Bannon shrugged his big shoulders.

"You know how to say your own name, do you not?"

Zorina cleared her throat. "Shämaendèriamna."

Bannon stared for a moment, then he started to smile.

"An ancient name from the Mountain," he commented.

"Yes, that it is." Zorina wrinkled her nose, turning away to quicken her pace up the hill.

Kyros shifted away from her hastily as they rounded the bend, and Zorina sighed. Being in a patrol where the only man who could touch her without risk of being bound to her in a betrothal was her brother was more difficult than she first thought it would be. The ancient customs of Draedin had been instilled in all of them from the moment they could walk. Zorina would never forget the first time a boy had touched her. She was only five years old, and such things did not matter until she came of age. But her father looked at her with such horror, she'd never gone out to play with her brother's friends ever again.

Then I joined the army. Father was none too pleased on that score ... Zorina exhaled heavily, her cheeks rounding. She knew her father was convinced long ago she'd been touched in some form by a man but would not admit to it. Persuading him otherwise was nearly impossible, and after the first four visits home from the barracks to receive concerned looks in the form of furrowed brows, pinched lips, and disapproving grunts, she realized her life might be better if she no longer accepted her home passes.

Torin inhaled, the sound hissing through clenched teeth. Zorina spun to see what was wrong, watching as her brother searched the sky, thick brows waggling in concern.

"Kyros," Torin murmured. "The shadows are moving."

Zorina's gaze collided with Bannon's before they both looked straight up at the sky. Her breath caught, heart thundering—her twin was right. The shadows were *moving*. Rolling and forming. Tumbling in great heaps toward the city.

"Black Ones!" Bannon growled, his blade hissing from its scabbard.

Zorina dropped the lantern. The metal rim clattered on the cobblestones as the light snuffed out, leaving them in darkness save for the glow of candles shining in the windows of the houses around them. In a flash, she fitted an arrow to her bow, crouching slightly as she kept a steady eye on the sky. She felt the men edge closer, tightening their little circle, each of them blackened silhouettes now the lantern was out.

Zorina evened her breathing, slowing her heart rate as she prepared for a fight. Suddenly, a shriek rent the air, stabbing her ears with its intensity. A flash of fiery light brought her head around quickly. Her eyes widened as she stared at what looked like a ring of fire lighting the blackened sky miles and miles across the sea.

Creator's Night! What is that?

"Zo!" Torin shouted.

She gasped, turning on her heel as the first heap of shadows tumbled to the street ahead of them. Another roared to the ground behind them, grabbing the attention of Bannon and Kyros. She felt her brother's shoulder brush against hers as he came fully to her side.

"With me?" she murmured.

"Always," he answered.

Zorina aimed, the feathers of the arrow tickling the corner of her mouth. Her bowstring creaked, the pull straining the muscles in her arm. Torin spun his sword between his fingers before raising the blade in both hands, waiting for the enemy to approach.

Her arrow whizzed through the air the moment one of the Black Ones took form, piercing straight through his heart and sending him to a heap of black ash on the ground. Zorina tugged another arrow as Torin charged with a shout, his blade glinting even in the darkness as he pushed his way into the torrent of screaming creatures. Zorina backed away, nearly running into Bannon before she abandoned her bow, pulling her own sword loose.

"Where is Alok?" Kyros shouted above the roar of battle as they were forced back to back from all sides.

Surrounded. Overwhelmed. Zorina's throat clogged as she thrust her sword upward through another Black One's chest. *We're already dead.*

"So this is how Falshire falls," Bannon said, his voice so near the sound startled her. Then she realized her arm was pressed against his.

So much for Draedin traditions. How little they matter at a moment like this. Zorina screeched, ducking from a claw before slicing the offensive creature in half. Its black blood splattered her face and lips, a drop touching her tongue and filling her mouth with the foulest thing she'd ever tasted.

The next moment she landed on her hip on the cobblestones, nearly losing her grip on her sword as she scrambled back on her elbows.

"Zorina!" Torin's frantic call was drowning in the growing boom of the Black Ones' cries.

A huge, clawed foot slammed into her belly, knocking the air from her lungs. Her skull slammed into the ground, making her head spin wildly and her eyes roll. The creature pinned her to the stones with his foot. Zorina lost her grip on her sword handle as she tried to focus, but she could see nothing except the murky yellow eyes of the horrid animal about to tear her heart from her chest.

So this is my death. Zorina started to close her eyes.

A flame of pure white fire burst through the Black One's chest. Zorina gasped for air when the creature's foot disintegrated in a clump of ash and blood on her chest, vanquished in an instant.

"Zo!" Torin grabbed her arm, lifting her back on her feet. "Are you all right?"

Zorina nodded without looking at him, too enraptured by the sight overhead. The sky was filling with figures. Slim silhouettes—framed in widespread dragon wings of all shapes and colors. At the center of all of them was *she.*

She glowed brighter than the rest, pure white diamond skin banishing the darkness with dark golden hair falling in a river of waves over her shoulder. Even from her position in the sky, Zorina could see her crystalline eyes glowing around thin, horizontal pupils. Then, she dove, wings flattened to her back as she came hurtling toward the ground and stopped just short of Zorina. She floated a foot off the ground, her light repelling the legion of Black Ones as they shrieked and recoiled, fearful of even coming near.

The dragon woman smiled.

"Good warriors of Draedin," she said, her voice smooth and warm, like a beautiful summer breeze. "Take up your swords. Fight for your homes."

Zorina's fingers curled around the hilt of her sword on the ground. She gaped, watching as large, shirtless men began to leap from the rooftops of Falshire, their wide-curved swords held high and guttural shouts echoing through the city. Turning, she watched the white dragon woman shoot back up into the sky, spears of white fire slicing through the darkness before she was engulfed by the roiling shadows.

Zorina's eyes locked with Torin's. He grinned at her, black blood smeared on his face and eyes wild with anticipation. With a shout, they raced into the chaos.

Damari landed on the cobblestones with a *crack*, her feet throbbing. Her wings slipped beneath her skin as if they'd never been. She turned a slow circle, her magic still pulsing through her veins, burning in her belly. Damari watched as the Wraith Spawn began to retreat, the surviving Draedin warriors chasing after them, blending with the *Chalqüins* and members of the *Almaër Dominÿe* Guard.

Suddenly, the Wraith Spawn were sucked up from the ground in twirls of black smoke, vanishing into the shadows overhead as the dark cloud began to pull back entirely from Falshire, allowing the first rays of sunlight in days to shine through. Damari smiled, watching glimpses of her white fire pulsating through the shadows, making the creature shriek and groan in pain. She had stared into the face of true evil and would not wish the sight on any other.

Damari shuddered, buffing her arms as the shadows began to roll across the sea toward Molderëin. The knot in her stomach tightened, waves of nausea attacking her full force. She had helped free one city, only to place another in even more danger. Looking into the blackness, she'd seen the Abyss's intent. She knew he would now attack Molderëin with his full force, as that was where the true threat lay.

To eliminate a new queen and weaken Adlae's chances once and for all. Damari closed her eyes, her blazing heart burned hotter in her chest.

"Damari."

Lathan's voice close behind her tugged her from her thoughts. Damari turned, watching him approach with Krow and Evingar close behind.

"Navaria and Malindra are making the streets safe while the others check the houses to ensure no Wraith Spawn remain." Lathan slid his sword into its sheath as he stopped in front of her.

"Good." Damari took Lathan's hand, turning toward Krow. "The Abyss will go to Molderëin."

Krow nodded solemnly. "The closer we move toward Sunkai, the more fearful our people will become, my lady. Winter barely touches Draedin, so leaving the Mountain to come this far was not difficult."

"I have dispelled the cold from them," Damari answered, brow pinching irritably. "They have nothing to fear."

"This is a people who has not been near a place with winter for centuries, *Almaër Dominÿe*," Evingar reminded her. "You cannot take their fear away with a mere word and a flash of fire in their hearts."

"Do you doubt my flame will protect them?" Damari glared at him. "I was not given this power so our people might sit under Hadroul's Mountain and watch Adlae Sundragon fight for the whole of Nfaros alone!"

"They know that, love," Lathan murmured, massaging her arm soothingly.

"I meant no offense," Evingar said. "I meant only they will be afraid until they feel winter's wind for themselves and the cold does not harm them."

"You think some will not come?"

Krow and Evingar shared a worried glance.

"We fear," Krow began slowly, "they will believe they have no choice but to follow your command. Many of the women have children they wish to protect. Will you bring the young ones across the sea to Molderëin as well? Or perhaps all the way to the snow-covered city of Sunkai?"

Damari hesitated, wishing she could shrink behind Lathan and out from under Krow's hard stare. Until a few weeks ago, she'd never even seen a person of the Mountain, much less understood their ways. Now, she stood here their leader, and she did not know how to command them. She didn't know how to speak to them as a queen would when she'd never held a position of authority in her entire life. She was one with her power now, that she could handle.

Using her magic came so naturally now. Almost no effort, the strength of it flowing out of her with a mere thought. Damari could feel the dragon in her soul roaring even now. All she wanted to do was spread her wings and disappear into the sky.

"Anyone who does not wish to venture further than Draedin may stay," she finally replied, squeezing Lathan's hand tighter. "But I am going to Molderëin, as I am the one who has driven this darkness back to their lands. From there, if the Creator wills my survival, I will continue to Sunkai."

She tugged on Lathan's hand, making her way up the hill where her people were gathering. She veered away from them toward the group of Draedin warriors, gathered in an uncomfortable crowd, keeping a few feet between them and the *Almaër Dominje* Guard.

The girl she'd seen when they arrived noticed her first, light brown eyes brightening at the sight of her, and she stood up a little straighter. She came to attention, tucking her arms behind her back with chin tilted up. The others mimicked her when Damari and Lathan stopped in front of them, looking over their heads.

Damari observed the warrior woman from her leather boots and trousers, over the matching bodice to the top of her black hair, twisted into dozens of braids. She was Draedinian to the very tips of her toes, anyone could see that, only she'd chosen a path not many young women of Draedin would.

To be a warrior.

"You all fought valiantly today," she said, shifting her gaze over all of them. "You should be proud."

Her eyes fell on a large man near the back of the crowd. Damari frowned, moved forward as her hand slipped from Lathan's. The soldiers parted for her, making a path clear to the man. He was taller than the rest, his dark eyes meeting hers warily and his long black hair pulled back by a rawhide string.

"You are no Draedinian," Damari murmured, curiously.

He cleared his throat, looking away. "My mother was of Draedin, my lady."

"Ah." Damari nodded slowly. "And your father was of the Mountain."

His brow rose in surprise. "Yes, he was."

"Have you served Draedin for many years?"

"My whole life, since I could hold a sword."

"And your name?"

"Bannon."

"Why have you never taken a place among the People of the Mountain, Bannon?" she wondered.

"I am neither of the Mountain nor of Draedin, *Almaër Dominje*. In Draedin, as a warrior, I was given purpose. On the Mountain, I would have no place, for I possess none of my father's power, save the gift of long life." Bannon's eyes softened. "I have made a fine life, my lady. Do not pity me my place in the world."

Damari nodded slowly, even as her heart sank. How sad, to never find your place. Not long ago, Damari felt the same way about herself. Reaching over, she placed her hand on his arm. She felt him tense under the touch, but she just smiled.

"The world is turning, Bannon. You will always have a place amongst my people, if you desire one."

Bannon nodded, the warmth in his gaze touching her. Damari turned, moving back to Lathan's side. She beamed at him as they clasped hands, struck once again by how much love she saw in his eyes. By the sacrifice he'd made in being reborn a Son of the Haven Star, just so he could be with her.

If not for him, I would never have survived. I would not have the courage to be what I am now.

"Warriors of Draedin," she addressed the company. "Your courage in the face of great danger has proven you among the greatest armies in Nfaros. Now I make a request of you, one you need feel no obligation to accept. Join me and my people. Board your ships. Sail to Molderëin and then to Sunkai, to destroy the Abyss once and for all."

Damari paused for a breath, watching the same girl standing at the front of the company.

"The choice is yours to make, for I am not your ruler. Creator's blessing on you all."

Lathan squeezed her fingers as they walked away, moving past their people down the hill. She caught sight of Navaria and Krow, talking at the bottom of the hill and beyond, the darkness slipping away from Falshire, leaving crisp sunlight behind to brighten Draedin. Damari stopped suddenly, Lathan nearly stumbling at her side.

"What's wrong?" he asked, brow creasing.

"Look." Damari pointed.

Far in the distance, across sea and land, a ring of fire turned in a slow circle in the sky. As far away as the Shadow Lands, if her estimate was correct, the flames broke through the darkness, the only light to be seen for miles.

"What is that?" Lathan wondered.

Damari's heart lifted.

"A beacon of hope," she answered. "For all of Nfaros to see. We are coming to it, now."

"To what, Damari?"

She looked up at him.

"Don't you see, Lathan? That is not just a ring of fire." Damari inhaled slowly, her next words slipping from her lips with reverence. "That, my love, is the Circle of the Sundragon."

Molderëin

"Kalea!" Grange shouted, racing across the bridge.

Torches lit the thick blackness covering the city, the clouds billowing fiercely in the sky as Grange carried Clea to her chamber. Her servants, Rheatha and Izeana met him in the hall, the fright etched across their faces making him cringe. Clea lay limp and pale in his arms, the Summer Flower clutched stiffly in her right hand against her heart.

The moment she'd laid her fingers on the blossom, she'd collapsed, a burst of white light engulfing the room and taking him to his knees. He didn't know how long they'd been locked in the torrent of magic below the towers. Hours? Days? In the moment, it felt like an eternity. But when the light had faded, and he'd regained the ability to stand, he'd found her prone on the ground with the Summer Flower slowly wrapping its stem around her wrist like an armband. She didn't move, her eyes never fluttered when he tried to wake her.

"Kalea!" he yelled again, kicking open the door to Clea's bedchamber.

He laid her on the bed gently, tucking strands of her hair from her face, being careful not to touch the Summer Flower. Rheatha and Izeana circled the bed, removing Clea's boots and slipping the crown from her head in an attempt to make her comfortable.

She won't know the difference. Grange's hand trembled as he covered her to her waist with the blanket.

Two hands grabbed him by the scruff of the neck, shoving him back into the wall. His head hit the hard stone, room spinning for a moment before he regained his focus enough to stare into the furious eyes of Morgren. Kalea came hurrying in a moment later, perching herself on the edge of the bed and placing her fingertips on Clea's temples.

"What did you do?" Morgren growled, his hands tightening at Grange's throat.

"Nothing!" Grange shoved his arms up, knocking the older man's hands away to free himself. "I led her to the Summer Flower, Morgren Lanfira, that is all! Is that not what you both wanted the moment you crossed the Peace Bridge into Molderëin?"

Morgren's lip curled in a scowl. "If anything happens to her …"

108

Grange shook his head, brushing past the man to Clea's bedside. Kalea sat back with a sigh, her amethyst-tinted hair swaying against her back when she shook her head.

"Can you heal her?" Grange asked.

Kalea looked up at him, white eyes gleaming. "This cannot be healed. She will wake when she is ready. The power pulsing through her right now is like nothing I've ever felt before."

"And the darkness? The Abyss has descended on Molderëin, and our new queen sleeps with no sign of waking! What are we to do about that, Kalea?"

The woman stood up slowly, her lavender-colored dragon skin glittering and her pupils trembling into horizontal slits.

"I can only tell you what I have Seen, Grange Molten. Our queen's condition … I did not foresee this."

Grange raked a hand through his hair, turning toward the windows. Not a single ray of light shimmered through the glass. Molderëin was awash in a darkness like he'd never seen before. But it was more than that. Closing his eyes, he reached into the recesses of his soul, drawing out the bloom of power deeply seeded in him. He inhaled through his teeth, hissing softly as his magic collided with the darkness, feeling the depth of evil within the shadow.

Kalea came to stand beside him, and he looked down at her, his heart thundering against his chest. The woman placed a gentle hand on his arm and Grange shivered.

"She needs to wake up," he whispered.

Kalea nodded, her eyes dim with sadness. Grange looked out the window again, his skin chilling.

"If she does not wake … we are lost."

In the Realm of Dreams …

A thick mist rose from the ground, swirling around her body as she turned a full circle. Clea could see nothing except the moist white clouds billowing up from the soft green grass. Around her arm, the Summer Flower tightened, the blossom twisting over the top of her middle finger

109

like a ring. She took a step, the mist parting for her as she moved blindly, arms outstretched so she wouldn't run into anything.

"Morgren?" she shouted, her voice bouncing back to her as if she were in a cave. "Rheatha? Where are you?"

"Who is this who thinks she is worthy of the Summer Flower's power?" a hoarse, masculine voice responded.

Clea turned back, trying to determine where the voice had come from.

"Clea Jandry, the Heir of Molderëin," she called back.

"A woman holds the Summer Flower? That is ... unexpected."

Clea arched a brow. "I have told you my name. Now what is yours?"

The mist billowed thicker around her, leaving nothing but white clouds shrouding her vision. She tried another step, but her feet wouldn't lift from the ground, stuck in the soft earth beneath her boots.

"What holds you in its grasp can be a dangerous thing, Clea Jandry, Heir of Molderëin. Yet, the flower seems to have chosen you. Are you ready to hold such a responsibility?"

"I have risked my life to claim this power. Do you think I would've done so if I wasn't ready?"

The mist hissed, rising higher and beginning to clear a path before her. Clea's heart raced faster when the figure appeared, draped in thick white robes nearly blending with the mist. Long, stringy, silver hair fell around his shoulders, and his pale, honey-colored eyes seemed to smile at her in his weathered face. The corners of his mouth tilted up, lips framed in a thin white mustache, hanging inches past his chin.

"So you think you are ready?" He held his hand out to her. Slowly, Clea raised hers to meet his, seeing no other choice. The strange man nodded his approval. "Then come, Clea Jandry, and understand this power you now hold."

CHAPTER ELEVEN

The City of Sunkai

Gelsey burst into the Blood Keep with a shriek, her hair sticky with blood and sweat dripping down her temples. She threw her sword to the floor, the steel clattering loudly on the marble. Bridie turned where she stood beside the throne, her blue eyes wide as she watched Gelsey stalk toward her.

The Lower Village was drowning in flames. For every fire they put out, another blaze came crashing down in a terrifying blast. Stronger, hotter, bigger than the first. Then the Wraith Spawn had come, destroying anything—and anyone—in their path. Children's screams, the cries of both men and women, still filled her ears. Gelsey screamed again, trying to drown them as she crouched on her haunches, covering her ears. The press of her palms did little to banish the echo of their terror, or their blood on her person, as they were slaughtered before her very eyes.

"Gelsey, calm down!" Nic shouted, following close behind her into the Blood Keep. "There is nothing you could've done!"

Gelsey dropped her hands, arms limp at her sides before she looked up. Her gaze locked on Bridie, and the girl took a subtle step back, uncertainty lighting her face. Gelsey shook her head.

She is the least of my worries now. She spun, rising from her crouched position to face Nic.

"I will *not* give up this city, Nic. Not after we took it with so little effort!"

"Then what is your desire, beloved?" Nic moved toward her cautiously, holding out a beckoning hand. "We have gathered all those who've survived behind the Blood Keep walls, but still this shadow grows. Still the Abyss reigns fire on the Lower Village, and his fury is spreading closer to this fortress."

"I swore I would hold the Blood Keep for Adlae Sundragon," Gelsey said between strained breaths. "Please, Nic, tell me there is another way."

"If we do not evacuate, we will all die. Queen Adlae disappeared into the woods weeks ago. Mirae Sundragon was last spotted in the Pilvaa, and there has been no word from Damari Kael. We do not even know if she survived the voyage across the sea." Nic paused for a breath, maintaining eye contact with her. "Gelsey, Sunkai is lost."

"No!" Gelsey stomped her foot, her hands curling into fists at her sides. "This is the Mother City, Nic Colney! The strongest city this side of Nfaros and I have it in my hands! It ... it was in my hands ..." Her eyes welled.

She turned away, hiding her weakness from him as she tried to regain some semblance of control.

"Gelsey," Bridie's soft, hoarse voice reached her ears. "You need to get Sunkai's people out of here safely. The passage from here to the gates is blocked, but there is a gate leading out on the other side of the gardens. We can get the people safely into the Gracian Wood from there and onto a Woodland Path to see them quickly to Quintaria."

"I did not ask for your opinion, Bridie Kael," Gelsey snapped.

"You know she's right," Nic interjected. "Only more of our people, as well as Sunkai's, will die. Is holding this throne worth such a sacrifice? I do not believe Adlae Sundragon would say so."

Gelsey turned away from them both, digging her hands into her hair. She battled the truth of their words, trying to work out the past days in her mind. Everything had gone wrong so quickly! The moment the shadow touched them, chaos like none she'd ever known had reigned down upon them so brutally she didn't think Sunkai would ever be the same. Half the Lower Village was gone, and the High Village wasn't too far behind. The flames would soon be at the Blood Keep gates, then escape would be impossible for all of them.

Her hands dropped limply to her sides, a weighty exhale slipping between her lips. Gelsey turned, looking up at Bridie. The girl's smile was full of compassion, a sincerity in her eyes that made Gelsey's suspicious nature falter.

"Bridie, will you please make certain Rufus is one of the first out of the city? Analli will need him before the end."

"Of course, Gelsey."

"Also, please tell Embry and Maksim to ready the people to move quickly from the city, on my command."

Bridie hesitated, Gelsey catching a glimpse of the girl's hands tremble before she hid them among her thick skirts.

"T-They will not l-l-listen to me," she stuttered.

Gelsey tried to soften her gaze. Tried to give the poor girl a small smile of encouragement.

"Tell them the order is from the Lady of the Night Wood. They will not argue."

Bridie gulped, the sound so loud it reached Gelsey's ears. Then she straightened her back, lifted her chin, and marched across the room. Gelsey watched her skirt a wide circle around Nic before hastening through the doors and out of sight. She breathed again once Bridie was gone, hugging her arms against her ribcage.

"How is this happening?" she asked, looking into Nic's eyes. "How, Nic? Why? I did not work so hard, I did not live in the Night Wood all this time, forsaking everything I knew and everyone I loved, to be stopped now!"

Nic stepped forward, cupping her face in his large palms. "We have lost this time, Gelsey. There's nothing for it. Now is the time to survive so we can fight again tomorrow."

"I was so sure." The words choked in her throat. She took hold of his wrists, gripping him tightly. "I was so *sure*, Nic. I just knew the Creator wanted me here. I knew His purpose was for me to hold this throne for Adlae Sundragon. To even face Raphaela Kael, if necessary."

Nic's eyes flickered with fear, his thumbs moving in gentle circles on her cheeks.

"You do not have magic, Gelsey. Raphaela Kael is now known as one of the strongest creatures of magic this side of Nfaros. Do not even think of seeking out that woman. You would never be able to defeat her."

"Perhaps, but nevertheless, I was certain! Certain the Creator had another purpose for me." Gelsey closed her eyes, inhaling deeply. "Now, I am sure of nothing."

She removed his hands from her face, softly kissing his knuckles.

"I don't want to retreat."

"Neither do I."

113

Nic rested his forehead against hers, squeezing her fingers tight. Gelsey closed her eyes, peace washing through her at his simple touch. Outside, she heard the roar of the fires, the frightful thunder of people racing through the Blood Keep, preparing to flee. Gelsey pushed those sounds aside, taking a moment—just a moment—to breathe with Nic. To feel his heart against her hand and know everything was going to be all right.

Blessed Creator, let everything be all right.

Kaldon

Raphaela sneered, a wicked glint lighting her eyes as she watched Sunkai burn. The vision, encased in the globe of her staff, flashed with images. The Lower Village, crumbling in a roaring blaze, Gelsey Malaki screaming in the halls of the Blood Keep. Citizens of Sunkai—traitors loyal to Adlae Sundragon—fleeing through the gates toward the Gracian. She looked over the top of her staff at the woman standing by the windows. She'd taken down the boards on the windows, allowing Analli Devareigh to look out upon the darkness.

Clever woman with her tricks. But not clever enough. The Abyss snickered.

"You can look all you want," Raphaela growled. "You will not find what you seek. There will be no charge by Adlae's troops to rescue you. No one knows you're here."

"Hmm," Analli hummed in reply.

She tries to provoke us with her silence. But her silly games will not work on us, will they, daughter?

Raphaela laughed. "Do you still think I do not know who you really are? That Sundragon blood flows through your veins?"

Analli glanced over her shoulder but still said not a word.

"Would you like to see your husband now? Would you like to see your fat little innkeeper?" Raphaela moved forward, swirling her hand over the top of her staff.

Analli's eyes flickered with a moment of doubt before she turned away, staring out the window once again.

"My Rufus is in good hands now," she said, finally breaking her silence. "I will see him again before the end."

Raphaela clucked her tongue. "So much certainty in your voice. Yet your hand trembles at your side. And how quickly your speech changes! Now you sound not like a Quintarian but like a woman of Sunkai!"

She reached out, snatching Analli's fingers in her hand. The woman didn't even flinch, her eyes steady and unblinking as she gazed through the broken windowpane. Raphaela squeezed until Analli's fingers whitened.

"Sunkai has fallen," Raphaela hissed in Analli's ear. "Molderëin will soon be overrun, and your precious Adlae will never leave the forest. She knows I'm coming for her, and like a coward, she fled into the darkness."

Analli turned slowly, looking straight into Raphaela's eyes.

"And yet Draedin is freed by the hand of Damari Kael," she announced.

Raphaela dropped Analli's hand, taking a small step back. Fire burned in her belly at the satisfactory beam on the older woman's face.

"If you think my little sister can defeat the force I have sent to destroy Molderëin with a few Draedinian warriors and a handful of winged mutants from the mountains then ..." her voice faded when Analli's attention drifted back to the window. Snarling under her breath, she shoved the woman to the side. "What are you staring at?"

"So consumed by the destruction of the Mother City, you did not even notice there is a break in the darkness," Analli said gleefully.

Raphaela looked out the window, staring at the fire in the sky. The blaze formed a perfect circle, the flames rising in dips and slopes like the points of a crown. They turned slowly, glowing bright orange against the pitch black of the sky. She scowled, presenting her back to the window.

"Is this meant to frighten me? A few pitiful flames in the sky not of my making?" Raphaela sniffed, her grip tightening around her staff.

Analli raised a finger. "Ah, but they are no normal flames. These flames ... are the Circle of the Sundragon."

Ice slithered up Raphaela's arms, her breath stopping in her lungs. Analli's lips spread in a triumphant smile, as if the woman felt the sudden fear sweeping over Raphaela.

"You are going to fail, Raphaela," Analli announced, fisting her hands at her sides.

Raphaela took a small step back, brow furrowing when Analli's fists started to tremble and redden, as if her skin was growing hot.

"Do you think your darkness is stronger than Sundragon fire? Did you truly believe your precious Abyss is greater than the Creator Himself?" Analli shook her head, her body beginning to steam.

"What magic is this?" Raphaela gasped, watching steady streams of sweat pour from Analli's skin, the woman's breath coming harder and hoarser. "What are you doing?"

"How quickly you forget." Analli's smile sharpened, her eyes glistening. "I am a Sundragon."

Then she screamed. Raphaela shrieked, slamming backward into the wall as Analli burst into bright orange flames, silvery smoke enveloping her before she vanished completely.

Raphaela stared, stunned. Not a single speck of ash, no evidence remained in the room that Analli had ever been there.

Raphaela screamed, racing for the door and yanked it open.

"Guard!" She grabbed the man by the scruff of his neck. "The prisoner has escaped. Find her!"

She spun back around, facing the empty room.

WHAT HAVE YOU DONE? he shouted in her head.

Raphaela groaned, pressing the heel of her hand to her temple when a shuddering throbbing began.

You let her escape? One of the greatest threats to my rule and you LET HER ESCAPE?

A tear rolled down her cheek. "I-I'll find her! I'll bring her back and kill her!"

ON YOUR KNEES.

Raphaela dropped heavily to the ground, her staff rolling out of her hand as she clutched her head in both palms.

"Please, master!" she begged, her throat convulsing with sobs. "I did not know she had such power! I was not prepared—"

No, you were not, he snarled. *You useless little sorceress! How could I have been so foolish as to entrust my mission to you? The other one was stronger!*

"No!" Raphaela slammed her fists on the ground. "I am strong! I can win all of Nfaros for you!"

I should have taken the other one. She would have brought a nation to me! A nation once loyal to my darkness would have returned to me if I had simply taken your—

"STOP!" Raphaela grabbed her staff raising it to the ceiling.

Black lightning scorched straight through the ceiling, the roar filling the room until she could hear nothing else. Gasping, she pulled back, the black stream dissipated in a light dusting of ash. He was silent in her head as Raphaela rose slowly to her feet, wiping the tears from her cheeks with her sleeve.

"My little sister," she hissed, "would never have been able to make the blood sacrifice you required. She was not strong enough, you know this. That is the reason you chose me. Because I am more worthy than she ever will be."

He remained quiet, the void in her head growing larger. Raphaela tilted her head up.

"I will find Analli Devareigh again. When I do, she will die and you will have another sacrifice of Sundragon blood, this one purer than the last. Imagine, master! The blood of Vihaan Sundragon's little sister!"

She waited with bated breath, fingers tightening around the smooth wood of her staff.

Then, he chuckled.

Clever girl, to restore my faith in you, he murmured. Then his tone changed again, fiery anger seething through her blood until her knees trembled. *But,* daughter ... *never fail me again.*

The Road to the Tower of Tears

"Make way!" Griyer shouted, shoving people aside as they crowded toward the front of the caravan.

Brecken followed close on the man's heels, his heart thundering against his ribs. Why had they stopped? Why would Mirae halt the wagons in the middle of the woods, where magic ran rampant, putting the entire company at risk? He shook his head, raking a hand through his hair as he followed Griyer through the crowd. Murmurs and gasps filled his ears on either side, stories of why they'd halted already racing amongst the people.

A hand grabbed his sleeve and Brecken frowned, looking down to find Faël there.

"They're saying it's a woman," she whispered, eyes wary. "A woman covered in blood."

117

Brecken placed his hand over hers. "Stay close to the wagons with your son."

She nodded and he moved on, catching up with Griyer hastily. They'd left Righteousness less than an hour ago, the tower still in sight if he looked over his shoulder. The last remaining Sister of the Creed was packed in Mirae's personal wagon, still writhing with the dark enchantment cast over her by the Abyss himself. Yet she did not seem to be in as much pain as had been expected. She groaned and whispered to herself, but as long as no one touched her, she seemed calm enough.

Still, foolish to bring her along. Brecken sighed. He was coming to learn Mirae would do what she wished, no matter how she was advised.

He and Griyer finally made it to the front of the line, coming to an abrupt stop. Mirae looked back at him, her eyes wide with a mixture of fright and curiosity. Brecken moved a little closer, his gaze shifting to the woman.

She was leaning against a tree, her skin reddened as if hot and a layer of silvery ash covering her. He understood why, by the time the word reached Faël, the people described her as being covered in blood. Her hair was wild, standing on end, and her head was bowed, keeping her face hidden for the moment. What he assumed was once a dress hung on her in burned rags, barely covering her and leaving most of her skin exposed to the cold air. Jaeger leaned closer, his torch illuminating the ash in the woman's hair.

"Mistress?" he said quietly. "Can we be of help?"

Slowly, the woman raised her head.

Brecken nearly stumbled when his eyes met hers, the blood rushing from his face and leaving him cold.

"Analli?"

CHAPTER TWELVE

Quintaria

The streets of Quintaria had never been so quiet. Maxx held tight to Noelle's hand as he navigated their way down the back streets toward Clea's mansion. Word had spread quickly when Clea closed up the place, boarding the windows and securely locking every door for her indefinite journey to Molderëin. His sister's house would be the perfect place for him to hide with Noelle and the Eventide Sisters until they worked out where Adlae had gone. The entire household had left with Clea, so there was no chance their presence would be revealed to the city if they broke in.

Noelle peeked at him from beneath the hood of her cloak, a mischievous smile playing across her lips. Maxx returned her sweet grin with a wink, pushing away his inability to ignore how much she'd already grown. She was as tall as Gwylan now—though considering the Eventide Sister herself was small, that wasn't saying too much—and her hair had grown as well. Long, sleek strands of red, loudly proclaiming her Sundragon heritage. She was beginning to look like a woman, the baby roundness of her cheeks fading to more mature, sculpted lines. In a matter of days, she'd grown from a babe of four to a young woman of sixteen. Thinking about how she'd changed made his head spin—looking at her made his heart stop.

Will Brecken even believe she is his daughter? Maxx shoved the thought aside, bounding across the street with his little band of women close on his heels.

"You are certain no one belonging to the house remains?" Symber hissed once in front of Clea's door. "Eventide Sisters in Quintaria are unheard of. If we were to be discovered, they would swarm us and innocently bring every soldier wearing Kael colors to our doors."

"Those under my sister's employ and protection are fiercely loyal to her. They would have all followed her to the ends of the Nfaros Sea if she asked them."

Maxx wrapped his hand tight with a handkerchief, moving away from the door to the window. Grunting and tugging, he tore the boards away, leaving just enough space for him to climb through. Checking over his shoulder for late-night stragglers, he took a breath and punched his hand through the glass. Once the latch was lifted, he climbed through, boots crunching shards of glass as he strode to the door. The women tumbled inside before he'd even opened the door halfway, Gwylan with a firm arm around Noelle's shoulders to keep her near.

He bolted the door quickly before turning to face them, watching Ellia and Symber move hastily around the house, whispering words he didn't understand. They held out their hands, fingertips glowing briefly before they'd move on to another part of the house.

"They're casting protection spells," Gwylan explained quietly. "This magic is subtle enough so as not to be sensed by Raphaela Kael."

Maxx nodded slowly. "I will start the search for Adlae tomorrow. You truly believe she is still somewhere in Quintaria?"

"No, I am sure of nothing. But we might be able to sense her magic if she was here and know where to go from there." Gwylan frowned, her little nose scrunching. "And you will not go on this search alone."

"Yes, I will. The danger to you and your Sisters is too great for you to leave this house."

"This is *my* mission, Maxx Jandry, not yours. Besides, how will you sense her magic? Have you suddenly been endowed with the power of an Eventide Sister? No, I will go with you into the city tomorrow."

"No, you will stay here and protect my niece."

"Symber and Ellia are sufficient protection."

"Then you will stay here and remain *safe*."

"I will go with you and find Adlae Sundragon as my Superiors ordered me to do!"

"I will not argue about this, Gwylan!"

"Good, because neither will I!"

They were nose to nose, their heavy breaths mingling. Her hands were on her hips. His arms were crossed tight over his chest. She smelled of lavender and wildflowers, her shimmering black hair slightly mussed from the journey and an aggravated flush in her cheeks. Noelle glanced between them nervously, clamping her bottom lip between her teeth before she inched slightly between them.

"Uncle Maxx, do you think Auntie Clea left my room the way it was?" she asked quietly.

"I'm sure she did, sweetheart," Maxx answered without breaking eye contact with Gwylan.

"I'll go up then."

The young girl rushed away, clattering up the stairs and out of sight. Once he knew Noelle was out of earshot, Maxx opened his mouth to yell again, but before he could get a word out, Gwylan spun braids flying as she marched into Clea's sitting room. Mumbling under his breath, Maxx followed, slamming the double doors behind him. She didn't seem to notice his wrath as she tugged sheets off the furnishings, meticulously folding and stacking them on one of the settees. Puffs of dust rose in the air as she yanked the last sheet from a wingback chair nearest the fireplace.

"Symber said Eventide Sisters in Quintaria are unheard of. If you come with me and are discovered ..."

"I won't be," she insisted without looking up from her task.

"You don't know that!" He raked a hand through his hair, frustration burning his chest. "If I am discovered, it will be the executioner's axe for me, Gwylan. I need to know Noelle is in good hands should that happen."

"Then perhaps you should stay here while I go looking for the Winter Queen," she said softly, head bowed.

Maxx's mouth tightened. "You cannot be serious."

"I failed Haileah, Maxx." Gwylan stroked the top of the folded sheet tucked against her chest. "Being blinded as I was to her true nature, I failed her, my other Sisters, and my Superiors. I was charged to lead this mission, and already I have let myself be distracted by—" she stopped abruptly, clamping her lip between her teeth. Her chest swelled with a long inhale. "I *have* to see the next part of this mission through, Maxx."

He stared at her, catching a note of vulnerability before she quickly schooled her features, holding her head high in the proud manner he'd come to expect from her.

"I am going, whether you wish me to or not," she said firmly.

He shook his head, hardly believing what he was about to do as he moved across the room toward her.

"We will take the back alleys," he demanded. "You will wear your cloak and keep your hair covered at all times. One look at those Draedin braids and half the city will trample us."

"Very well," Gwylan agreed. Then she looked up at him, a sparkle in her velvety eyes. "Then you will wear a hat and gloves."

Maxx smirked, threading his arms over his chest. "Will I now?"

"If I must walk about the city with my head down and my hood up like a criminal, then you will walk about the city in a hat. Don't you think the people will recognize those Jandry locks and Molderëinian skin?" Gwylan shrugged. "You are more recognizable than you believe, Maxx Jandry."

He grunted, dragging his feet as he made his way to the wingback chair by the fireplace. A chill swept through the room as he took a seat. He shivered, tucking his arms tighter against his body as he stretched his legs out. He closed his eyes, trying to ignore the fact there was no wood for a fire as he sought a little rest. Clearly, in this darkness, Quintaria had decided when was night and when was day. For all he knew, the city would begin to awaken within an hour. Gwylan stepped toward him, he could feel the gentle heat of her body when she came to a stop beside his shoulder.

"Maxx?"

"Hmm?"

"You do know, if we find Adlae Sundragon, everything will change," she announced.

Maxx opened one eye, looking up at her cautiously.

"How so?" he wondered.

"You are trying to take your niece to her father, I understand that, of course. But I was given orders to join Adlae Sundragon. If she is not also seeking Brecken Jandry then ..." she hesitated, staring into the empty fireplace. She looked far away suddenly, her eyes clouding so darkly he thought, for just a moment, she was going to cry. But instead, she licked her lips and continued, "Then our journey together will have come to an end."

Slowly, he sat up, planting his feet firmly on the floor as he met her gaze directly.

"But Noelle needs you," he argued.

"Not anymore. She knows how to control her power now, and there is little more I can do unless she wished to join the Eventide Sisters." Gwylan turned, placing the last sheet on the pile she'd made.

His throat went dry, a strange twinge tightening his chest as he tried to identify why her words were hitting him to his core. Perhaps it was simply his fear for Noelle's future—his worry he wouldn't be what the child needed going forward.

Or perhaps you've become a bit too used to Gwylan's presence.

"Is this what you want?" he asked.

She frowned, as if he'd placed a complicated puzzle before her.

"I'm not sure what you mean."

"Do you want us to part ways? If you find Adlae tomorrow, will you be glad to leave us behind?" He took a breath, then forced himself to say what was on his mind. "Will you be glad ... to leave *me* behind?"

Gwylan stared at him, eyes wide and unblinking. He couldn't read her, the vacant look on her face giving away nothing as he steadily held her gaze. Suddenly, she turned on her heel.

"I should check on Noelle."

Maxx watched her go, his heart sinking into the pit of his stomach. The lack of an answer from her gnawed at him. He sat back in the chair again, dragging his hand down his face with a heavy exhale. Until she'd voiced it, he'd not thought of what would happen should they find Adlae tomorrow. Because the truth was hitting him in waves, the longer he sat alone in his sister's sitting room.

If he lost Gwylan tomorrow, his world would never be the same.

Gwylan couldn't remember the last time she'd been in a city like Quintaria. The swarm of people in their brightly colored clothes, milling around dozens of market stalls in the Lower City. The flat streets, barely a slant separating Lower from High. Buildings pressed tight together, making narrow the paths to the back alleys Maxx insisted on taking. These curious Quintarians seemed unperturbed by the constant darkness shadowing their land. They brightened the streets with dozens of lamps to guide their way in the thickening black cloud overhead. She'd never expected the thrill rushing through her at the sight of so many people or the strange sense of peace permeating a city on the brink of war.

Or the adrenaline coursing through her when Maxx took her hand, interlocking their fingers tightly. Gwylan looked down at her much smaller hand clasped firmly in his large, calloused palm. Her fingers folded over his knuckles, a perfect fit. What a strange thing this was! To feel no

123

consternation in touching a man! To feel, after such a short time, that touching Maxx Jandry was as natural as any other part of her life. Being close to him, even his rough scent—a mixture of musk, soil, and trees— had become something so familiar she couldn't imagine her day without him.

Gwylan shook the thought from her mind, instead focusing on the task at hand. They'd visited two inns already, but there'd been no sign of Adlae Sundragon. Not even a wisp of leftover magic to indicate she'd been present at all in the city. The power of a Winter Queen would have left a trail for someone like Gwylan to follow.

Unless she masked herself. She rolled her lips, glancing up at Maxx.

His question from last night still burned inside her. Her heart and mind were in turmoil over an answer for him—her soul divided between duty and desire. Because no matter how indecisive her fickle heart, she knew one thing for certain. She'd grown far too attached to young Noelle Jandry and leaving the child to discover the full extent of her power on her own would be the hardest thing she'd ever have to do.

I don't want to leave her. Gwylan breathed deeply, pushing the melancholy thought away.

"How many more inns in the city?" she asked, keeping her voice low as they squeezed between two more buildings onto a back street.

"Not many," Maxx replied gruffly. "Golden Dragon's next."

"Did you live very long in Quintaria before going to the Mother City?" she wondered.

"A few years. Enough to know the city forward and backward. Our family really settled in Kaldon, but I moved around a lot with my brothers after our parents were killed." Maxx looked over his shoulder at her with a shrug. "Couldn't very well let my little sister be alone here when she first moved into the Manor. Once I saw her settled and cared for, I joined my brothers in Sunkai."

"Hmm," Gwylan hummed. "I adored Draedin before I left. I lived in a small village, just north of Falshire, but I would often accompany my father into the city for his trade. Once my power was discovered and I came across the Nfaros Sea, the woods became a home I never expected."

"Many think of the woods as a sanctuary," Maxx commented, his fingers tightening on her hand. "I would wander the woods outside Kaldon for hours, sometimes days. Worried my sisters to no end and certainly confused my brothers as to my attraction to the trees. There was just always something about them ..." He shrugged, looking side to side before hurrying her across an open path and behind another building.

Gwylan stared at him, remembering the magic she'd felt inside of him out in the woods. The spark he'd created, all on his own, had held more power than she'd let on at the time. Now looking at him in the ridiculous, wide-brimmed and feathered hat he'd agreed to wear for their outing today, she wondered how much strength he actually possessed. She'd felt a mere hint of his power before it vanished again, buried beneath a lifetime of inexperience.

Perhaps his connection to the trees means more than he realizes. Gwylan wrinkled her nose, shaking her head as her thoughts tumbled around. Her focus should be on the task at hand, not the man standing beside her. Once the Winter Queen was found, she and Maxx would go their separate ways, after all, most likely never to see one another again.

He guided her down another alley, the pathway so narrow now her shoulders brushed against the walls to either side. They squeezed through, briefly coming out onto the busy street before Maxx tugged her through a door. They stopped on the threshold, both staring at the sparsely filled dining room. A chill slithered through her, awakening her magic.

Maxx looked down at her, an inquisitive gleam in his eye.

"I'd enjoy a cup of tea here, I think," she announced softly.

He merely nodded, taking her across the room to an empty corner table. Gwylan scooted onto the bench against the wall so she could look out at the people while still keeping herself in some shadow, her hood pulled low against her forehead to completely hide her hair as she'd promised Maxx. He took the chair across from her, gesturing to the young girl moving from table to table.

She appeared a moment later with a tray, carefully placing a pot of tea in the center of the table before handing each of them a delicate red teacup. Gwylan poured in silence, watching Maxx fidget nervously as his dark eyes darted from table to table. She raised her cup to her lips, blowing softly and sending a stream of steam across the space between them. Maxx turned back, frowning down at his tea.

"Well?" he grumbled.

"I believe she was here," Gwylan replied, then took a sip. The hot liquid scalded her tongue, but she ignored the feeling, the sharp sting of mint leaves following the burn.

"But she is no longer here?"

"No. She left the city many days ago."

Maxx cleared his throat, the crease in his forehead deepening. "And … do you know where she went?"

Gwylan lowered her teacup from her mouth, staring as the beverage trembled against the edges. She reached deeply into the recesses of her magic, becoming keenly aware of every scent in the inn, the slightest movement of the occupants, every sound—every creak of every floorboard from here to the attic she could hear. There was a room. The smallest room in the building, two floors above her head. A whisper of the magic that rested there many days past rippled through her.

"She would have made her way to Kaldon first, in search of allies. But I do not believe she stayed long. From there her path is … shadowed."

"So what does that mean for you and your Sisters?" He set his cup aside, choosing not to drink as he waited for his answer.

Gwylan lowered her cup slowly to the table, unable to find the courage to look him in the eye. Her mind drifted to Noelle, the thought of walking away from the child forming a knot in her stomach. She'd watched her, in a matter of days, grow into a young woman. The overwhelming nature of her development had taken Gwylan by surprise, Noelle's rapid growth different from the boy from Draedin. His development had been hasty, indeed, but nothing like this.

What purpose will she serve? Blessed Creator, what is Your plan for her? She took a deep breath, finally raising her eyes from the table.

"I do not know, Maxx," she replied softly.

Something sharp stabbed the back of her shoulder. Gwylan winced, reaching to rub the spot. She glared over her shoulder but found no one there. A wrinkle of confusion rushed through her as she turned back to face Maxx, still massaging her shoulder.

"So we move on to Kaldon," he grumbled. Rubbing the back of his neck, he leaned back, setting his hat off-kilter.

"Yes, I suppose—ouch!" Gwylan squeaked, bouncing in her chair as another pinch cramped her shoulder.

Gwylan! An echoing hiss filled her ears.

126

She sat up straighter, the voice strangely familiar, yet she was certain she'd never heard it before.

"What's wrong?" Maxx tilted his head, eyes narrowing.

"I ... I'm not sure ..."

Gwylan!

She gasped, rising so fast her chair fell over. Several eyes turned, piercing her.

"We have to go." Gwylan hurried for the door before he could respond, stumbling around a couple of the tables before racing out into the street. She spun back to the alley, taking herself out of the sight of the Quintarians milling about.

Another sharp pain shot through her entire body this time. She cried out, falling against the wall. Flickering darkness scattered across her vision until she was encompassed, a magic she'd never felt before pulsing and dragging her, lifting her from her body until she was no longer standing in the alley in Quintaria.

Gwylan raised her head. The strange, floating feeling carrying her far away from everything that had become familiar. This was another plain, covered in murky clouds with a gentle breeze lifting her braids from her shoulders, as if they were suddenly weightless. Five silhouettes appeared in the darkness, remaining far enough away so she could not make out their features.

"Gwylan," the voice boomed now, vibrating between her and the figure that spoke.

"Who are you?" she rasped, throat dry.

"Do you doubt your senses, Sister of Eventide? Search deep within yourself and you will find your answer."

The silhouettes started to take more shape. Flowing, long hair waving around their shoulders, feminine figures becoming more apparent, taking solid forms in the mist. Gwylan inhaled sharply, her heart pounding frantically.

"Superiors," she whispered.

Gwylan bowed deeply, half bent as she tried to breathe. How was this happening? Even the extent of her power did not explain how this was even possible—how she'd been taken to another realm so suddenly.

"You are forgetting your purpose, Dominant," a new, silky voice announced.

"I'm not," Gwylan denied, shaking her head.

"This girl, Noelle Jandry, has clouded your mind. For you hold a secret, buried deep in your heart. A secret you have not revealed to anyone," the silky voice continued.

Gwylan stiffened, slowly straightening from her bent position. She placed her hand on her fluttering stomach.

"I am searching for the Winter Queen, your excellencies, as you asked me to. We believe she has moved on toward the city of Kaldon."

A deeper, raspy voice replied, "Who is *we*, Dominant Gwylan? You and this man you are so attached to?"

"I am not attached to Maxx Jandry."

"You have become betrothed to him, have you not?"

Gwylan cringed. "By an unfortunate accident, yes."

"I fear you feel more for him than you will admit, even to yourself," the first voice *tsked* softly. "Beware these feelings, Gwylan, for a difficult choice will come with them."

She closed her eyes, her throat tightening with the inability to speak.

"There is something else we require of you," the silky voice said. "A new task for you to fulfill and the reason we summoned you here."

"Ask anything of me, your excellencies." Gwylan bowed again.

"You must bring the girl to us."

Gwylan froze, her eyes going wide as she looked at them. "Noelle?"

"The child's magic is ... strong. Unpredictable. Her strange growth is too unknown. We must discover more."

Gwylan hesitated. "Do you intend to make her an Eventide Sister?"

Silence answered her.

"Do you intend to teach her?"

No answer.

"Do you mean to ... study her?"

A heavy sigh whispered across the air before the silky voice said, "You must understand, Dominant Gwylan, we do not know the Creator's purpose for her."

"No one knows the Creator's purpose for her," Gwylan replied sharply. "Perhaps this is not for us to know!"

"We are of Eventide!" the raspy voice shouted, her voice echoing all around Gwylan. "We are responsible for the turning of the world! No creature of magic roams the earth that we do not understand!"

Gwylan looked at each of them, squinting as she tried to make out their shadowed faces in the mist. But no matter how hard she looked, she could not see their features in the grey mist surrounding all of them. Yet she could feel them. Her eyes fluttered closed as she reached deep within herself, the crackle and burn of her magic flooding her belly as she reached out to them. She could feel them—their heartbeats thundering in their chests, their blood racing in their veins, their minds tumbling with unanswered questions.

She opened her eyes.

"You're afraid of her," she whispered.

Silence.

Gwylan shook her head. "I will not bring her to you."

"What?" the raspy voice growled.

"Creator save me, I will not bring her to you!" Gwylan's voice rose, her hands fisting at her sides. "You do not wish to help her! You do not wish for the Creator's purpose for her to be fulfilled! You wish to cage her like an animal because you *fear* her!"

"You are out of line, Dominant!"

"I will not do what you ask."

"If you refuse our orders, then you betray every Eventide Sister who walks the earth!"

Gwylan shook her head fiercely. "I will betray myself if I bring that innocent child to you."

"Do not let your past lead you into foolish choices, Gwylan Almandreya," the silky voice breathed.

Gwylan paused, the use of her family name rushing over her in shuddering waves. So many years since she'd heard her full name spoken aloud. So many memories it provoked, so many feelings.

"My past," Gwylan hissed, "has nothing to do with this. I can *feel* your intentions. You do not mean to do Noelle good, only harm. She is not meant to be hidden from the world! There is a reason this is happening to her!"

"Enough!" the raspy voice boomed. "You will bring the girl to us or face the consequences!"

Gwylan stared at their masked figures. Then, she unfurled her fisted hands, stretching her fingers as she settled herself in her magic.

"I will face the consequences," she declared.

Before any of them could speak, Gwylan surrendered to her magic, allowing the power to flood through her until she was hurtling from the mist. Down … down … down …

Gwylan gasped, falling limply against the wall in the back alley of Quintaria. Strong hands gripped her shoulders from behind, keeping her on her feet as her knees knocked and sweat trickled down her temples. Her mouth was dry as dust, throat sore as she wheezed, trying to fill her lungs with air.

"Gwylan, what happened?" Maxx asked, his breath tickling the hood of her cloak.

She turned into him, burying her face in his solid chest, leaning on his strength to keep her upright. His arms went around her, big hands rubbing her back and shoulders. She started to recapture her breath, her heart slowing as her power drained out of her.

"We need to get back to Noelle," she said. "I think I'm all right now."

"Can you tell me what happened?"

Gwylan tilted her head back to look up at him. "Not now. I will explain when we are securely behind closed doors."

Maxx nodded, his eyes shifting warily. Gently, he cupped her elbow, leading her down the alley, back the way they'd come. Gwylan used the edge of her cloak to dab the remaining beads of sweat from her forehead and temples, her mind still spinning with the odd encounter she'd just had.

You will bring the girl to us or face the consequences! The horrible, guttural shriek still echoed in her head.

Maxx paused at the end of the alley, gesturing for her to wait as he stepped forward to look out into the street, assessing how many people were crowding the streets. She stared at his back, the air hitching in her lungs, coming short and fast. Then, before she could change her mind, she opened her mouth.

"I need to tell you something."

He looked over his shoulder, forehead wrinkling as his brows drew together.

"Yes?"

Gwylan inhaled deeply, then released the words on a single breath, "The boy from Draedin was my little brother."

CHAPTER THIRTEEN

Maxx's stomach turned over. He stepped away from the street into the shadows, out of sight of any of the passing Quintarians. Her words were tumbling round and round in his mind, the truth of them in the sheen of tears in her eyes and the tremble of her bottom lip. Slowly, Gwylan lowered herself against the wall, hugging her legs to her chest with chin on her knees. She sniffled, a tear clinging to her long lashes as she stared across the alley.

He approached her cautiously, more stunned than anything. He never imagined he'd see this woman who exuded indifference at almost every turn—who'd so rarely shown him a hint of the soft heart behind the hard shell—reduced to a puddle of tears and trembling. He crouched down in front of her, loosely clasping his hands with arms on his knees. Gwylan looked up at him, their eyes locking.

"Tell me," he whispered.

Gwylan wiped the tears from her eyes, damp lashes fluttering. "He was taller than me by the time he was three and I five. My parents kept him hidden, because in Draedin, while those of magic are revered and respected, they are also feared. This magic had never been seen by any in Draedin. We did not know how our fellow countrymen would react to him. My mother wanted him protected."

"What was his name?"

Her eyes rounded, startled. "You are a strange one, Maxx Jandry."

"Why?" he chuckled.

"I stop you in a dark alley in the middle of Quintaria with a war brewing throughout Nfaros to tell you a rather strange story, and all you wish to know is my brother's name?" Gwylan shook her head.

"I see in your eyes that you loved him. I would like to put a name to the person who captured the heart of a woman such as you." Maxx reached out, tucking a stray strand of her hair from her temple.

Gwylan closed her eyes, a soft, loving smile illuminating her face.

"Aesir," she breathed. "As the months passed, and he became a man before his fifth birthday, we realized the Creator's plan for him must be great. When the Abyss came to tempt the hearts of the Draedinian people, my mother was convinced Aesir was meant to stop him. My brother revealed the true weakness of the Abyss."

"How?" Maxx wondered, drinking in every word.

"Despite his growth, in both body and wisdom, he still carried the innocence of a child in his heart. Such innocence, such purity, has the power to destroy the Abyss. To expel him from a city. Even perhaps ... to destroy him forever."

Maxx reached over, placing his hand over hers. "But he didn't succeed."

"No, he did!" Gwylan grabbed his hand, squeezing his fingers tight. "He wrestled with the Abyss on the highest peak of the greatest mountain overshadowing Falshire. He saved the city, its people, even the People of the Dragon!"

"How?"

"He took the Abyss into his soul." She gasped, a sob bursting from her as tears trailed down her cheeks. She slammed a fist into her chest, pounding her own heart. "Aesir used his power to draw the Abyss down from his shadow in the sky, pulling him in, allowing the evil creature to possess him ... and he trapped him there. But he was not strong enough to hold him."

"Hold him?" Maxx repeated.

Gwylan closed her eyes tight, as if trying to expel a bad memory. He held her hand tighter, leaning in close until he could smell the whiff of lavender in her hair.

"Aesir believed the only way to destroy the Abyss was to kill the body he possessed." She bowed her head, shoulders shaking. "He threw himself from the mountain. But the Abyss left him before he fell upon the rocks."

"Then the Abyss fled," Maxx finished the story for her, drawing her eyes back up to his face. "He did not return to Draedin again."

"I have told no one about Aesir. I even pushed him so far from my mind as to convince myself I dreamed him. He was real only in my imagination. But when I saw what was happening to Noelle ..."

"You saw your past repeating."

Gwylan sniffled, rubbing the moisture from her cheeks until they bloomed bright red from the rough treatment.

"My quest is to find Adlae Sundragon and join her ranks, Maxx. Such a task will take me from you and Noelle, perhaps forever. But I must know she is safe. I must know she will always be safe, that there is another way for her. I *must* discover the Creator's purpose for her." She sighed, her shoulders dropping heavily. "I do not know what to do."

Maxx moved closer, taking her face between his palms so she couldn't look away from him. His nose rubbed against hers and her mouth wobbled into the semblance of a smile. He came as close to her as he could, their foreheads nearly touching.

"I am so sorry, Gwylan," he murmured. "No child should have to endure what you did. If I'd lost any of my brothers or sisters so young …" He shuddered—the thought alone unbearable.

"I know the Creator's purpose for him was true. I have told myself I understand why everything happened … but I don't. I don't understand why Aesir had to be taken, and I will not—cannot—watch such a thing happen again." Gwylan fell forward, her brow pressing firmly against his. "When my magic awakened, I thought perhaps there would be a reason. I thought perhaps my power would lead me to an answer about Aesir. But as the years passed and no answer came, I found the pain was easier to manage if I put him far from myself."

Maxx stroked the top of her head, the hood of the cloak falling back to reveal her braids. The darkness overhead roared and coiled, the lamps on the streets barely shining any light into the little alley where they'd sequestered themselves. But he could see her eyes. He could see that sparkle of gold among the wide, dark pools of the eyes he saw every time he went to sleep.

He cleared his throat, a tingle moving across his skin, a rush of heat through his body. Gazing at her now, all he could think of was how close his mouth was to hers. His eyes lowered before he could stop himself, staring at her full lips, parted slightly as small, quick breaths slipped out. He leaned in, wondering if she'd let him …

Gwylan sat back abruptly, wide eyes unblinking. "We should go."

I suppose that's a no. Maxx smirked, taking hold of her hands to pull her to her feet. She squeaked from the force of his tug, bouncing a little on the balls of her feet before she regained her balance. He pulled her hood back up for her, hiding her silky braids from sight before taking her hand. She twined her fingers around his, holding on firmly as he led her onto the street toward Clea's manor.

"Maxx?" she whispered as they weaved through the thinning crowd on the street.

"Gwylan?" he replied, eyeing her over his shoulder.

"Thank you—for listening."

He paused, pulling her aside as a carriage went by. The glow of the lamps created a hazy light on the streets streaming through the damp air. The moisture all around them was fresh. Surprising, considering there'd not been a drop of rain or flake of snow since the shadow had encompassed the sky.

"Anytime," he said huskily.

He started to move again, but the pull of her hand stopped him. Frowning, he looked back, but she had turned away. Head tilted back, eyes drawn up toward the sky, she stood still as stone. Maxx returned to her side, following her gaze to the sky. He froze, staring as intently as she was.

The fiery circle turned in the sky, the flickering flames rising and falling in slopes like the points of a crown. Gwylan leaned against his side.

"I have never seen such a fierce display of fire magic," she said, breathlessly.

"The Abyss?" he inquired.

Gwylan shook her head slowly, an unsettling flicker lighting her eyes.

"I cannot tell, Maxx. But whoever created those flames is far more powerful than any creature of magic I have encountered." She spun away suddenly, pulling on his arm. "Come, we should return to Noelle and my Sisters."

Maxx moved with her, both of them hurrying down the street. Their quick pace turned to a run. The feeling something was coming came over him in waves, the need to run—feeling chased—overwhelming. Ignoring the people, no longer caring who might see them, they ran all the way back to Clea's manor.

Crackling flames sent shadows dancing across the dark room. Gwylan stared into them, holding her arms tight across her ribs. She could still feel the Superiors reaching out to her, trying to draw her in. But the more they fought to trap her, the stronger her own power became to resist them. She could sense them waiting, wondering if she was truly going to defy them. Would they try to come for Noelle themselves?

I could tell Maxx. I could send him and Noelle away to safety. She sighed rubbing the ache at the top of her breastbone. A tremor ratcheted through her, the memory of those faceless voices striking a fear she'd never known before in her heart. The Superiors had always been held to the highest degree of respect and love. Yet no one Gwylan knew among those of Eventide had ever actually laid eyes upon them.

They hide in mist and shadow, allowing their fear of the unknown to govern their choices. She shook her head, turning away from the fireplace.

The house was quiet now, Symber already sound asleep upstairs while Ellia studied the many books in Clea Jandry's library. Closing her eyes, she could sense Maxx sitting at Noelle's bedside, watching her sleep with his dagger in hand. The faster she'd grown, the less sleep he'd gotten, instead staying up to make sure she was safe and peaceful during the night. Gwylan had woken many times to find him in such a position—sitting mere feet away, hovering like an over-protective father.

Noelle seemed to find his presence comforting, so Gwylan hadn't told him to be at peace. He didn't understand yet that Noelle herself would soon be all the protection she'd need. The girl had nearly passed every test of Novice and Intermediate among the Eventide. She was well on her way to matching Gwylan's own ability as a Dominant if the increase of her visions were any indication.

When she opened her eyes, she found Ellia standing there, book tucked under her arm and dark eyes wide.

"What's happening to us, Gwylan?" she asked on a low breath.

Gwylan's eyes burned. "I don't know."

"We have never been divided." Ellia took a step closer, the firelight dancing across her black uniform. "Yet I feel you slipping away from me and Symber every moment you spend with the child ... and with *him*."

"Ellia, you more than anyone know how I am bound to him now."

"Bound by tradition, Gwylan, that is all!"

She tugged on one of her braids, wondering how she could possibly explain what was in her heart to the woman.

135

"You are faltering," Ellia stated. "You are the strongest Eventide Sister I have ever known. You never let your personal feelings get in the way of your missions before so why now? What has changed?"

"I have seen the impossible," she answered, moving nearer her sister. "I have witnessed such a thing only once before, and that event ended in tragedy. I cannot let history repeat itself with Noelle!"

Gwylan moved past her, hurrying for the doors to escape this conversation as quickly as possible. The decision was laid before her—the choice hers alone to make. But how could she make such a choice when her heart was split so thoroughly? Half for the sister she had in Ellia, the other half for a child with more power inside her than she'd ever felt in any Eventide Sister.

"You're going to leave us, aren't you?"

Ellia's whisper stopped her at the door, her heart plunging down into the pit of her stomach. She stood frozen, unable to bear looking her childhood friend in the eye but unable to walk away from her at the same time. She evened her breathing, calming the storm roiling in her belly.

Without answering, she left the sitting room, forcing one foot in front of the other away from the woman she'd once called sister.

"Uncle Maxx! Uncle Maxx wake up!"

Small hands jostling his shoulder roused Maxx from sleep. He shot up, dagger still in hand, eyes rolling about frantically. Noelle leaped away, holding up her hands in a calming way.

"I'm sorry!" she gasped, her green eyes round as saucers as she looked between him and the dagger warily. "Uncle Maxx, they're gone!"

"What?" Maxx gurgled, trying to blink the sleep from his eyes.

"The Eventide Sisters! They left! I checked Ellia and Symber's room. Their bags are gone!" Noelle's eyes flooded, a tremor filling her voice. "I ... I can't find Gwylan either."

His chest tightened. Maxx strode out of the room, slipping his dagger back into his belt as he went. He could hear Noelle scurrying after him, her lighter footsteps padding close on his heels as he went to the room Gwylan had chosen. He didn't bother to knock, instead shoving the door open.

The bed was perfectly made, the room left as if it had never been used with no sign of Gwylan's possessions anywhere. His stomach turned over.

No. She wouldn't leave like a thief in the night! She wouldn't leave Noelle. Not after what she told me yesterday ... Maxx slammed the door, panic sending him running down the stairs.

He checked the sitting room, the library, the kitchen. The house was empty, the only sign she'd ever been here, the sheets she'd folded and left on the settee in the sitting room. Maxx sat down on the bottom step, his heart racing from his search. Noelle sat down beside him, laying her head on his shoulder as she wrapped her arms tight around him. Maxx patted her arm, trying to think of something comforting to say.

What would Brecken say to her? He closed his eyes. He was no father, that much was certain. He couldn't even think of one reassuring thing to say to his niece. If Brecken was here, he'd know exactly what to say to her, to assure her everything was going to be all right.

A chill breeze swept over them, causing Maxx to raise his head as the front door opened. She swept through, hastily closing the door behind her before tugging her hood from her head. When she turned around to face them, she was smiling quite smugly, her braids tumbling around her shoulders and a sparkle in those golden-brown eyes rankling him to his very core.

"I must say," Gwylan said, breaking the silence, "your sister keeps very fine stables. If we are to make our way to the Tower of Tears to join Mirae Sundragon, we should be moving on. I took the liberty of taking your bags out."

Noelle gaped. Maxx laughed.

Gwylan stared at both of them, curiosity and confusion lighting her face.

"What about your mission?" he wondered, rising slowly to his feet.

"Ellia and Symber left long ago to find Adlae Sundragon. I have had a ... disagreement with my Superiors. I believe the best course is for us to part ways for now until the world is once again at peace and we understand one another again."

He closed the space between them, took hold of her waist, and pulled her to the very tips of her toes.

"What—?"

He cut her off with a kiss. Gwylan gasped against his lips, stiffening for a moment before she melted. Maxx pulled her closer, kissing her deeply, infusing all the longing he'd felt building inside over the past few days into this moment. Gwylan slid her hands up his arms to his shoulders, holding on. Then her mouth moved beneath his, kissing him in return, and he smiled.

Noelle cleared her throat loudly behind them, breaking his concentration. Maxx raised his head, catching his breath as he looked back at his niece. The grin splitting her mouth was so wide it nearly filled her face. She giggled, rushing forward to wrap her arms around both of them. Gwylan cleared her throat, bright red splotches filling her cheeks as she patted Noelle's shoulder.

"We really should go," she declared, spinning for the door.

Maxx watched her hurry outside, pulling up her hood to shadow herself in the darkness. He put an arm around Noelle's shoulders, pulling her against his side.

"I knew she wouldn't leave us," Noelle said. Her eyes glittered with more happiness than he'd seen from her in a while.

"Me too," Maxx agreed.

He lightly kissed her temple before taking her hand to lead her out to the stables.

CHAPTER FOURTEEN

The Gracian Woods

There were many things Bridie Kael feared.

Dying was not one of them.

Gently, she dabbed her handkerchief along Rufus Devareigh's forehead, drying the beads of sweat gathered after their vigorous race into the woods. Torches lit their way around the trees with Gelsey's soldiers, Maksim and Zaire, at the front of the line while Gelsey and Nic took up the rear, so they would know immediately if anyone—or anything—had followed them out of the city. The amount of people they'd managed to get out of the city practically filled the woods, making getting even a glimpse of Gelsey an impossibility.

Rufus smiled at her, patting her hand lightly. "You are very kind, my lady."

Bridie shook her head, tucking her handkerchief beneath her belt before pressing the back of her hand to Rufus's forehead.

"I am not so kind, Rufus," she replied, lowering her hand once satisfied his fever was gone. "I am one of the evil Kael spawn, am I not?"

Rufus chuckled. "Hardly. You, my dear, are cut from a very different cloth."

Bridie smiled, appreciation for his assessment of her warming her belly. A long time had passed since someone paid her any sort of compliment. Buried in the shadow of Roderick's cruel rule and hiding from Raphaela's ridicule, Bridie had sequestered herself in her home in the country. Rarely traveling to the Mother City, she'd thoroughly enjoyed her peaceful solitude. But when Roderick had called on her to take control of the Blood Keep while he traveled with Raphaela to Kaldon, she'd felt she had little choice but to obey.

Then Gelsey came. Bridie looked over her shoulder, searching the crowd in the hopes of catching sight of the strange lady.

A woman who couldn't be more different from Bridie in personality, Gelsey seemed to fit directly into a soldier's world. Rough, bold, and strong, she seemed to possess the hardness Bridie would expect from a man. Yet the way she looked at Nic ... oh, how her face softened! In those moments, she transformed from a hardened creature of the woods to a woman deeply in love. Bridie couldn't even imagine feeling what was so clearly between Gelsey and Nic. Those emotions were something she only dreamed of experiencing one day.

After what felt like an eternity of racing through the woods, they'd finally called for a halt to give the people a chance to rest and recover. Stopping now, however, only seemed to make them more keenly aware they were standing shin-deep in snow and ice. They were shivering beneath the trees, women holding their children close to keep them as warm as possible while the men attempted to build fires with soaked through sticks. Bridie herself clenched her teeth to keep them from chattering, the hem of her dress soaked nearly to the knee, her feet frozen inside her boots.

Despite there not having been a fresh snowfall in days, the winter chill remained in the air. Without the sun, there was no balance. The frozen air was beginning to pain her lungs, every breath difficult. Bridie coughed, bowing her head low as she covered her mouth. Rufus placed his hand on her shoulder, squeezing gently.

"We need tents," Bridie choked. "These people will freeze to death if we do not find shelter."

"The Tower of Truce must be close," Rufus said.

"If we're moving in the right direction," Bridie mumbled under her breath, tucking his cloak closer around his body. "I'm going to try to find some water."

Rufus nodded as he closed his eyes, resting the crown of his head against the tree trunk. Bridie stood, shaking out her skirts before stomping away, lifting her feet high over the mounds of snow. She tried to sink her feet into the many footprints created by the people in an attempt not to stumble. She hugged herself, trying to keep some warmth in her body as she moved among the now homeless men and women of Sunkai. Such a strange feeling, being so close among them. A mixture of Lower Village folk and High Village gentry flooded the woods, no longer caring about station as they formed groups to keep warm.

Bridie hurried when she saw one of the packhorses, searching for a waterskin among the chaotic mess of bags thrown across the saddle in haste during their departure. An elated giggle slipped out when she finally found one, tucked beneath one of the larger bags. The soft slosh of water within awakened her thirst. She popped off the cork, taking a slow, long sip. She sighed after swallowing, the liquid sliding down her throat refreshingly cool. Turning, she started back the way she'd come to offer some to Rufus when a shout echoed from the back of the line.

Bridie frowned, looking over her shoulder as the distant sound of a ruckus began to bounce among the trees. She tied the waterskin to her belt, pushing through toward the noise as the crowds of people ran in the opposite direction. The clatter of steel reached her ears and she stopped, frozen. Her heart raced, her breath quickening. Had they been followed by Wraith Spawn? Or perhaps something worse?

"The Tower of Truce!" The shout from the front of the line drew her back.

She looked over her shoulder, watching Maksim wave frantically as the crowd rushed past him.

"We are nearly there!" Maksim gasped, coming to a stop beside her. "Where's Gelsey?"

Bridie couldn't speak. Instead she pointed toward the sounds of battle. Maksim hissed something unintelligible, yanking his sword from its sheath before turning to her. He pressed the hilt of a dagger into her right hand and a torch in her left.

"If you see anything, a shadow, *anything*, you stab. Understood?"

Bridie nodded fiercely. Her hand trembled as he raced toward the noises out of sight. She realized she was completely alone now. The people were running in the direction Maksim said he saw the tower, leaving her behind in the clearing to listen to the frantic noises coming from deep in the darkness. The dagger faltered in her palm, the glitter of the steel in the torchlight reflecting on the pure white ground. She'd never picked up a weapon in her life, but in this panic, she wasn't about to tell Maksim that.

Silence abruptly encompassed the Gracian. Bridie moved the torch back and forth, searching the pitch black for any sign of Gelsey or Nic.

Or Wraith Spawn ... She held her breath.

The crunch of snow beneath several feet made her take a step forward, gripping the dagger so tight her knuckles paled. A gasp slipped between her lips when Nic came in sight, cradling Gelsey in his arms.

"What happened?" her voice returned as she held the torch out, catching the red bloom of blood on Gelsey's coat.

"Wraith Spawn," Nic growled, moving passed her with such ease, as if Gelsey weighed nothing at all.

Maksim appeared a moment later, breathing heavily as he tried to match Nic's pace. He took Bridie's arm without a word, dragging her after them toward Truce. Bridie lifted the torch high, guiding the way through the darkness.

Truce came in sight up ahead, the tall, cylindrical structure rising to a point high above the trees. Only a few of the Night Wood folk were still outside, standing guard with torches high and swords in hand. They let Nic pass, stepping away from the door so he could disappear within the tower.

"Maksim!" The girl named Embry stopped them before they could follow. "What happened?"

"Wraith Spawn attack. Nic said they came from the sky."

"The *sky?*"

"Gelsey was stabbed."

Maksim tugged on Bridie's arm, hastening her inside before Embry could ask anything more. Most of the people had made their way up the winding staircase, leaving the dark, round room mostly empty. Nic had set Gelsey down on her feet by one of the windows, allowing her to lean back against a table. Bridie hurried over, going up on tiptoe to place the torch in one of the wall sconces.

"What can I do?" she asked.

Gelsey opened her eyes, sweat beading on her forehead as she very slowly unbuttoned her coat.

"Water?" she rasped.

Bridie yanked the waterskin from her belt, the cork falling out of her trembling hand before she lifted it to Gelsey's lips. The woman coughed but swallowed several gulps before waving Bridie off.

"Here." Nic thrust a pile of linen shirts into her hands. "Tear these up for bandages."

She nodded, turning away and settling herself on the ground a few feet from them. The two of them whispered softly to each other, the words too muffled for Bridie to make out. She took the collar of one of the shirts between her teeth, tugging until the material ripped. Then, grasping the tiny tear in both hands, she yanked, the shredding sound filling the sudden silence in the tower. She finished the first shirt quickly, moving on to the next.

Bridie looked up just as Gelsey finally managed to remove her coat. The woman breathed deeply, wide eyes focused entirely on Nic as he examined the knife wound through the thin material of Gelsey's clothes. The bodice was the strangest she'd ever seen, leaving Gelsey's arms bare from her shoulder and laced tight in a crisscross down the back. Bridie couldn't look away, watching first how Nic cared for his betrothed and second, the strange tattoo on her arm.

Wispy strokes of color swirled over Gelsey's forearm, all coming together to form a set of wings curling around the fierce face of a phoenix. Bridie finally tore her eyes from the image, looking now at the woman who bore it. She realized as she watched the tightness of Gelsey's lips and the repressed pain in her eyes that she was truly in the presence of a warrior.

Nic cut away the lower half of Gelsey's bodice, leaving her midriff bare so he could clean the wound. She hissed through her teeth, squeezing her eyes closed as he probed the gash, fresh blood dripping from her ribs. She opened one eye, looking directly at Bridie. Then she said the last thing Bridie would've expected.

"Look away, sweet girl."

The poor girl's face had gone deathly pale. Gelsey placed her hand on Nic's shoulder, her fingernails digging into his flesh as he cleaned her wound. He didn't notice, too focused on his task. The loss of her coat and half her bodice left her skin chilled, the desperate need of a fire within the icy walls of the Tower of Truce becoming apparent with each passing moment. Gelsey kept an eye on Bridie, watching the girl quickly return to her work, head down and eyes averted from the two-inch long stab wound across the side of Gelsey's ribs.

Nic looked up at her, relief shining in his eyes. "Not deep and no poison."

Gelsey smiled, despite the pain. "Good news, I suppose."

"The best." He grabbed her face, pressing a hard kiss against her mouth before returning to his work.

Gelsey cringed as he finished wiping the blood from her skin. She returned her focus to the girl preparing her bandages.

"Have you ever seen a wounded soldier before?" she asked.

Bridie didn't answer for a moment, looking up at Gelsey. Her lips parted in surprise then she stuttered before managing to get out an answer.

"N-No. I haven't."

"You were never raised in the ways of a noblewoman of Sunkai, were you? Have you ever held a sword?"

Bridie shook her head, mouth still a little open. As if shocked Gelsey had deigned to speak to her.

"In Sunkai," Gelsey paused, wincing as Nic pressed a thick square piece of cloth over her wound. "Noblewomen learn to defend themselves with the sword. In Kaldon and Quintaria, they are also taught how to command a bow and arrow, as well as daggers."

Nic held out his hand to Bridie, and she passed him a few strips of cloth. He started to wrap the wound tight, every tug of the bandages sending shocks of pain shooting through Gelsey's body. She gritted her teeth, trying to concentrate on anything else.

"In the Night Wood, we are not divided by the classes. Every man, woman, and child is treated equally and taught everything to the fullest." Gelsey looked at Nic, and he stopped bandaging her side for a moment to stare into her eyes. "We are a people who teach fairness, never to revere one human being above another."

He stroked her cheek, the rough callouses on his fingertips scraping along her soft skin. She looked at Bridie, smirking when she caught the tilt of the girl's head and the embarrassed flush filling her cheeks for having been caught watching an intimate moment. Nic returned to his task. Gelsey started to relax, the pain beginning to slowly subside to a throbbing ache.

"They call you the Lady of the Night Wood," Bridie commented. "If they do not revere you, then why have they granted you a title?"

"The name wasn't given me by the people of the Night Wood. You know what happened, Bridie. The tales that were told when I never returned to Kaldon. All it took was one person seeing me leading a Night Wood caravan through the Aulend for the tongues to wag."

"Did you truly leave because of Roderick?" Bridie wondered.

Nic carefully helped Gelsey from where she leaned on the table, lifting her coat. She grimaced as she put one arm then the other into the sleeves, letting Nic button her up. Warmth began to tingle over her body once she was covered again, offering little comfort despite the continuous throbbing in her side.

"Yes, Bridie, I did," she answered.

The girl stared in silence for a moment before reaching for their bags. Tugging a blanket loose, she spread it on the dusty floor. Gelsey accepted the unspoken invitation, more anxious to sit down than anything else. Nic helped settle her, the exhaustion of their little battle coming over her rapidly. Bridie appeared with another blanket, swinging the soft coverlet around Gelsey's shoulders before creating a pillow from one of the bags.

Carefully, the girl helped her lie down, lowering her ever so slowly onto her back so she was tucked warmly in the blankets with her head comfortably sinking into the bag. Gelsey exhaled loudly, her chest deflating as she went completely limp. Nic grasped her hand, leaning over her, dark eyes glinting with concern. She patted his knuckles.

"I'm fine, Nic," she assured him.

He kissed her forehead softly. "I'm going to check on the others."

Gelsey nodded, letting her weighted eyes close as he slipped away from her. If she knew her betrothed husband at all, she knew he would not sleep tonight. Instead he would sit at her side, watching her to be sure she never stopped breathing.

She was beginning to drift, the exhaustion taking over her body.

"How did you stay away from your family?" Bridie asked, her voice barely above a whisper.

Gelsey's eyes opened. She turned her head to look at the young woman sitting beside her. Bridie was staring at her hands in her lap, her mussed hair falling across her shoulder to shadow her face in the flickering torchlight.

"I do not even get along with my family, yet I cannot imagine leaving them forever." Bridie lifted shimmering eyes to her. "You loved your brothers so fiercely. I know, I saw how you felt about them every time I visited you in Kaldon. How did you stay away?"

"My heart broke every day," Gelsey rasped, a tear slipping from the corner of her eye before she could stop it. "When I first went into the Night Wood, I was alone. I almost died, and every day I thought of what my brother, Jabon, would do. He kept me alive and never knew. I wanted to tell him, so many times. But returning to him would mean returning to a life I had come to despise."

Bride reached over, her hand brushing against Gelsey's knuckles. She gently grasped her fingers, loosely holding her hand.

"I could never be so brave," Bridie sniffled.

Gelsey smiled. "I think you underestimate yourself, Bridie Kael."

"Really?" the sweet woman's voice lifted with hope.

"Yes, really."

A yawn stretched her mouth before she could resist. Bridie folded the blanket tighter around her, making sure she was firmly tucked in.

"You should get some sleep now."

"Hmm," Gelsey purred in agreement as she drifted off.

When she opened her eyes again hours later, Bridie was sleeping to one side of her while Nic sat to the other. She looked up at him with a sigh, hugging her arm across the tight bandages beneath her coat.

"She is more than we thought, isn't she?"

Nic glanced at Bridie, nodding. Gelsey followed his gaze, watching the girl she'd known since childhood resting so peacefully a foot away. When had the world turned in such a harsh manner for the pretty young noblewoman? When had her life become one of solitude in the country? Out of everyone's sight, the world had completely forgotten about gentle Bridie Kael.

Until now.

"Yes, love, I believe she is," Nic agreed.

"I misjudged her horribly, didn't I?"

"Yes, you certainly did."

Gelsey wrinkled her nose, frowning at him. "Must you always agree with me?"

Nic chuckled as he stroked her hair.

"Go back to sleep, Gelsey. We have a little more time before we must decide where to go next."

Her stomach twisted into a knot, her wound throbbing painfully when her heart began to pump faster in her chest.

"If our information is correct, we should head north," she murmured. "I believe Adlae Sundragon could have but one destination in mind."

Nic's solemn face darkened, his mouth turning down. "The Tower of Tears."

"Who else would she go to but her sister, now she's vanished?" Gelsey's shoulder lifted slightly, her question resting heavily between them.

"We have half the people of Sunkai resting on the upper floors of this tower." Nic ran a hand down his face, a hoarse breath trembling through his lips. "Children who've never seen a winter before are with us. Tears is far, Gelsey."

She took his hand. "What other choice do we have?"

He stared at her—mouth pressed tightly closed. Everything had gone wrong so quickly. Right now, she should be resting in one of the soft beds in the Blood Keep, not lying wounded on the floor of the Tower of Truce. The silence stretched between them, his reluctance to answer her question telling her all she needed to know. Because, deep down inside, they both knew the answer.

There was no other choice.

Tomorrow, they would begin their journey to the Tower of Tears.

CHAPTER FIFTEEN

Falshire
The Capital of Draedin

Leaning back, elbows propped on the rail of the ship, Lathan allowed the fresh warmth of the sun to bathe his face. The shadow had completely retreated from Draedin now, blackening the Nfaros Sea as the clouds rolled toward Molderëin, bringing a thicker darkness to the distant country. He opened his eyes, looking toward the ramp as Damari attempted to coax some of the younger dragon folk onto the vessel. He grinned, observing young Paefra place one toe on the deck before bouncing back with a squeak.

"Can I not just fly?" Paefra asked, her silvery dragon skin beginning to glow.

Damari giggled. "All the way to Molderëin? I think your wings will give out, dearest."

Lyssia tilted her head, managing to place one foot then the other onto the deck. She took a step, then backpedaled onto the ramp once more, shaking her head.

"So unsteady! I do not like wooden structures," she growled, her thick braid swaying with the shake of her head. "If we flew to our full potential, we would be in Molderëin within hours."

"We should all arrive together. We will need the Draedinian army, else we will lose lives unnecessarily."

Lathan nodded, silently agreeing with Damari as she continued to quietly coax the girls onto the ship, putting her arm around Paefra's shoulders in encouragement. Evingar came to his side, leaning back against the side of the ship with him as they both watched.

"Have you spoken with her about your rebirth?" Evingar asked.

"No." Lathan cleared his throat, brow knitting when he turned to glare at the man. "You said she wouldn't notice right away. She noticed."

Evingar grinned. "Who knew you'd grow?"

Lathan nudged him in the ribs with his elbow. Evingar chuckled, his golden hair rippling in a sudden breeze.

"No man has ever gone through the rebirth who wasn't of the mountain. Krow and I did not know how the experience would change you." His new friend shrugged, folding his thick arms over his chest. He frowned at Damari, who was still attempting to urge the young women onto the deck.

Lathan turned his back, looking out over the vast, dark blue water stretching before him. The surface swelled and dipped, rolling for miles as far as the eye could see. He bowed his head, their destination weighing heavily on his mind. If Clea had truly taken Brecken's word to heart, survived the journey, and was now in Molderëin, then the shadow was about to reign its wrath down upon her.

She's seventeen. Talented, certainly. Powerful, yes. But she's far too young. Lathan breathed deeply.

"What did you see?" he asked hoarsely.

Evingar twisted slightly to look at him. "During the rebirth?"

"Yes."

"We all see different things," he answered. "You are experiencing death, Lathan Jandry. Only a surrendered life can be reborn. I, personally, saw my life."

"Your childhood?"

Slowly, Evingar shook his head. "No, my friend. I saw Malindra. She is my life. Without her, I would be nothing."

Lathan nodded. "I saw Damari. Many times. In so many different ways. As my wife, the mother of my children … normal. Living in Sunkai."

"Perhaps what you saw was the life you'd dreamed of before her true purpose was revealed."

"I also saw …" Lathan hesitated, looking over his shoulder at his beloved. Damari had finally gotten the girls on board, standing between them holding their hands as she took them one step at a time across the deck.

"When I was reborn," Evingar murmured, drawing his eyes away from her. "I saw my death. There are many ways a man can die, Lathan Jandry. I do not know which death is meant for me, only that if I was not expected to be prepared for the moment my life is to end, the Creator would not have shown me such things."

"I did not see my death. I saw her descending upon me from the heavens, the intent to save my life shining in her eyes so brightly I could feel the life returning to me." Lathan paused, a shuddering breath slipping through his lips. He closed his eyes, head bowed low. "Did I do her more harm than good by my rebirth, Evingar? Will she take an eternity of this power upon herself to save my life? Because I—"

"Do not want her to?"

He lifted his head, eyes colliding with Evingar's. The compassion he found there—the glow of understanding in his soft smile—was of little comfort as the truth glimmered through all of the emotions playing across his face.

"Years ago," Evingar rasped, his baritone voice thicker than before. "Twenty years to be exact, the Abyss came for Falshire. There was a young man who scaled the highest peak of Hadroul's Mountain to capture the evil creature in an attempt to destroy him forever. The boy failed, and a piece of the Abyss … entered my heart."

Lathan's brow winged, mouth parting in surprise. Evingar placed his hand over the center of his chest, a tremble rippling across his body.

"I was dying, losing the battle for my soul. I would have rather died fighting, but Malindra refused to stand by. My wife surrendered her mortal soul in a sacrifice to expel the Abyss from me. She saved my life, nearly losing hers in return. In doing so, she embraced immortality. A choice she made knowing we will both most likely live long after our children are dust."

The man looked out over the sea, the salty air lifting the delicate strands of his hair. He shook his head slowly, a sheen of moisture layering his eyes.

"What you must understand, Lathan Jandry," he continued. "Is she will do as she wishes for love of you. Every one of us who loves a woman of the mountain would choose any other life for them. But tell me this, if our *Almaër Dominje* lay dying, and you had the choice to let her go or sacrifice your mortality for her, what would you do?"

Lathan inhaled sharply, his lungs aching. "You know the answer, Evingar. I believe my rebirth was answer enough."

The corner of Evingar's mouth twitched, but he resisted the smile. "Yes. Is that not my point? Do you think you love her more than she loves you?"

Lathan looked over his shoulder, watching her. Damari's hair whipped around her head. The breeze caught every delicate golden strand, rippling

151

them in the air as she guided Paefra a few feet further across the deck. The sunlight glistened off her arms and shoulders, defining the diamond-like shine of her pure white dragon skin. How different she was from the girl he'd grown up with! Yet the same softness, the same courage and love, still shone in her beautiful blue eyes.

"I think she's loved me far longer than I realized," Lathan said quietly. "I regret every day I held my tongue, refusing to tell her how I felt, because the world we lived in told me we could never be together."

Evingar grunted. "What a strange world you northerners live in."

"Is her power like the Winter Queen's?" Lathan asked. "Will the magic take its toll? Will she go mad?"

The grim downturn of Evingar's mouth was answer enough. Lathan ground his teeth, jaw creaking and blood pounding.

"No," he murmured. "I won't let her live an eternity with such a power. I will not be the cause of her eventual torment."

Evingar gripped his arm tightly. "If the time comes, Lathan Jandry, the choice will be hers alone to make. Unfortunately, there will be nothing you can do to stop her."

Lathan's stomach dropped as he watched him walk away, the finality in those words shaking him to his core. Across the deck, Damari had managed to get the girls all the way to the captain's quarters, nudging them through the door before turning to him. When she looked at him—those sparkling eyes connecting with his, the way she smiled at the sight of him—his blood rushed. Warmth pooled low in his belly.

He would do anything—be anything—for her.

But at what cost did I make my choice?

"They are quite strange, are they not?"

Zorina rolled her eyes sharply to the right, looking up—*way* up—at Bannon. The two of them were tucked in a dark corner of the captain's cabin, watching the dragon people gather around the large oak desk covered in maps. The golden-haired woman the People of the Dragon called their *Almaër Dominÿe* sat in the chair, her hands folded tightly on the edge of the desk as she listened to the men and women circled around her argue.

152

Half of the dragon people were afraid to set foot on the ships. The other half were debating whether they even wanted to leave the safety of their mountain. Now, staring at their *Almaër Dominÿe,* who'd come down from the mountain to rescue Falshire, Zorina was never happier to be a simple soldier with very few decisions on her shoulders. She need only to follow where her commanders led, while the extraordinary woman before her had to actually make the choice where to lead her.

"Do you plan to follow her to Molderëin as she requested?" she asked, angling her head in the *Almaër Dominÿe's* direction.

Bannon's thick eyebrow curved. "Don't you?"

Zorina scrunched her nose, observing the dragon folk once more. One of the young girls—the silvery one who'd been frightened to come on the ship—noticed she was looking. She smiled warmly, curiosity lighting her odd ginger-colored eyes. Zorina looked away, heat creeping up the back of her neck for having been caught staring.

"What if our commanding officers choose not to offer our armies?" she wondered. "If they do not go, we will be defecting, Bannon."

"I believe your brother has already made the choice."

Zorina's head snapped up, lips parting in surprise.

"He was speaking last night in the barracks of traveling to Molderëin with the Mountain People. Torin seems quite set on going, Zorina. I believe he will defy any officer who attempts to order he remain."

She shook her head. "He could be executed for desertion!"

"Not if the *Almaër Dominÿe* protects him." Bannon shrugged his big shoulders before clasping his hands behind his back. Abruptly, he changed the subject. "I have been meaning to speak to you."

Zorina cleared her throat, averting her gaze. "Oh? What about?"

"In the heat of battle, many things can occur by accident, not design."

"Indeed." She tightened her lips to keep from smiling.

"I hope you would not think I—"

"Bannon, if you are afraid you've been trapped into a betrothal because we were forced to touch, please put your mind at ease." Zorina grinned up at him. "I will not bind you to me because of an accident. Besides, I am far from ready to put down my sword."

He snorted. "You seem quite content to put aside Draedin tradition."

"I was content to do so when I was a child." She puffed a breath, her cheeks inflating.

"You know," he mumbled, stepping a little closer to her shoulder. "The People of the Dragon have their own betrothal traditions."

"Oh?"

The heat of him spread to her, sending an unfamiliar tingle over her body. She could feel his breath near her temple, disrupting the delicate strands of hair that had escaped her tightly woven braids.

"My mother spoke of them many times," he continued. "They were strange to her, of course. For love of my father, she adhered to his ways."

"And do you now live by these rules?"

"I do not know."

"Why not?" Zorina turned her head in his direction, chin brushing the top of her shoulder.

Bannon chuckled, the sound closer to her ear than she'd anticipated. "I suppose I have not found the right woman. Perhaps, when I do, I will then worry about the traditions."

"Hmm," Zorina hummed, her mouth lifting in a half-smile. "What a sight that will be! The fierce soldier, Bannon, taking a wife."

"Is such a thing truly unfathomable?"

"Not at all." She looked into his eyes, grinning so wide now she showed teeth. "But the thought is a bit funny."

Bannon scowled, only heightening her amusement. Before he could respond, the door to the cabin burst open, Torin stumbling through. Face red, breath heavy, he approached the desk without inhibition and bowed low at the waist.

"Your ... Majesty?" Zorina's twin hesitated, looking up at the *Almaër Dominje* in question.

The dragon woman dipped her head once. Torin straightened, holding a rolled parchment out to her.

"Word just reached the city," he whispered.

The *Almaër Dominje*'s guard took the parchment for her, the paper crackling in the suddenly quiet cabin as he opened the missive.

"The Heir has been declared in Molderëin," the man said, dark brow furrowing. He lifted his gaze to his queen's face. "Clea Jandry has been crowned Queen of Molderëin."

Zorina watched the play of emotions on the couple's faces. The *Almaër Dominje* rose from her chair, leaning over her guard's arm to look at the parchment herself. Her crystal-like eyes glimmered as she lifted them from the paper, gazing at everyone in the room in turn. When those piercing eyes fell on her, Zorina looked away, never feeling so intimidated in her life. The woman's power seeped from her so strongly, even she—a being who'd never touched the smallest amount of magic—could feel it.

The woman looked up at her guard again, resting her hand on his thick forearm.

"Did you know?" she asked.

Slowly, he shook his head, unable to look away from the parchment. "Clea didn't know either, I'm certain."

"Brecken?"

"Yes. Brecken must've known. This is the reason he sent her there, it must be!" He crumbled the paper in his fists, closing his eyes tight.

Zorina tilted her head, wondering what the new Queen of Molderëin could possibly mean to the personal guard of the Mountain Mother.

"Everything is changing so fast," the *Almaër Dominÿe* said. Then, she turned her striking blue eyes on Torin. "Has your commander made his decision yet? Will he join us?"

Torin tilted his head high. "He hasn't said. But my fellow soldiers and I want you to know we will follow you, no matter the orders we receive."

The woman's face softened with her smile. "Such dissension could warrant death, young man. I cannot ask you to defy the orders of your commanding officers."

Zorina took a step forward, drawing the attention of every person in the room.

"You didn't ask," she said quietly. Her eyes met Torin's, his proud grin lightening her heart. "We offered. This war is not over with the retreat of the shadow. If Adlae Sundragon fails to defeat the Abyss and reclaim the throne, then the darkness will return to our shores. Our duty now lies across the sea to help make sure the Abyss loses this fight."

"Do you speak for all of Draedin, young warrior?" the *Almaër Dominÿe* asked.

Bannon took a step closer.

"She speaks for all of Draedin's soldiers," he replied. "The officers may do what they wish, as they are nothing without their army."

The Mountain Queen stepped slowly around her desk, the other dragon folk moving from her path as she approached. Her eyes, crystal blue with horizontal pupils, observed Zorina curiously as they had when first she saw her.

"You are unlike any woman of Draedin I have ever met," she murmured, interlocking her fingers together in front of her. "What is your name?"

"Zorina, Your Majesty."

"She likes to be called Zo," Torin chuckled.

She glared at him before returning to attention to the *Almaër Dominje*. "My name is Damari Kael."

Bannon's brow rose. Zorina's lips parted.

"Kael?" she repeated. "As in the usurper, Roderick Kael, and the evil witch, Raphaela Kael?"

Damari winced. "There is an explanation."

"A long one," the guard grumbled.

"Lathan Jandry is my *Chalqüin*. His sister, Clea, is the new Queen of Molderëin. I think it only right you know who you wish to fight beside." Damari spun away, returning to the desk. "I do not know what will happen when we finally face Roderick and Raphaela. The future at the moment is uncertain."

Torin snorted and Zorina reached over, grabbing her twin's sleeve to yank him to her side. He shook her off, offering her a snarl which she ignored.

Damari turned to face them again, leaning back against the desk. "How soon can you gather your fellow soldiers aboard the ships?"

Zorina looked back and forth between Bannon and Torin.

"Me?" she squeaked, placing her hand on her chest.

Damari smirked. "Yes, you. All of you. If your officers will not lead your army, then I need Draedinians your soldiers trust to guide them. I think you three will do sufficiently."

Zorina's eyes bugged. Torin leaned close, his breath tickling her ear.

"Looks like you just got the promotion you always wanted, Zo."

In the Realm of Dreams ...

Clea followed the old man through the mist, his wrinkled hand holding hers with more strength than she'd anticipated. Her gown felt heavy, the hem darkening with the damp from the ground. The mist left small droplets of dew on her skin, chilling her from the outside in. The old man stopped, swiping his hand through the cloud. The fog twirled and thinned, leaving a clear dome of glass before them.

Her hand slipped from his as she stepped past him, closing the distance between her and the glass.

"What is this?" Clea asked, brushing her fingertips against the smooth surface.

"What you hold in your hand now can be a treacherous thing," the old man replied. He placed his hand over the Summer Flower, palm hovering above the petals without touching. "This flower will either be the death of you or the life. In this place, you will either grow strong or weak ... determined by what you see."

"See?" Clea's nose scrunched, her brow burrowing deeply. "I do not understand."

"Look into the glass," he ordered, backing away slowly. "Look into the glass, Heir of Molderëin, and see your friends."

Clea hesitated, her stomach winding into a thousand knots. "D-Do you know what I w-will see?"

The old man only smiled.

She closed her eyes, plunging herself into darkness. He'd said she would grow strong or weak by what she saw.

So, this is a test. A test of my strength, of my power. No matter what I see, I cannot break. Clea inhaled deeply.

When she opened her eyes, she looked into the glass.

CHAPTER SIXTEEN

The Road to the Tower of Tears

Mirae sat cross-legged before the fire, an unblinking stare fixed on the woman seated on the other side of the flames. Analli Devareigh stared back, combing her fingers gently through her long, tangled hair. Once the shock of her appearance in the woods had faded, the women rushed her into a wagon to wrap her warmly in woolen garments as the rest of them prepared the tents for some much-needed rest.

Tears was nearly in sight now, only a few more miles and she was certain they'd be able to see the walls. Which made Analli's mysterious appearance in the woods very inconvenient. Jaeger was already up in arms, his suspicious nature putting him in direct odds with Brecken once more. She could hear them arguing outside the tent—Jaeger's angry snarl followed by Brecken's softer growl.

Mirae leaned forward, clearing her throat. "I'd truly like to know how you ended up in the middle of the forest with hardly any clothes and covered in soot, Mistress Devareigh."

"Curious, is it not?" Analli replied, a secretive smile touching her lips. She began to braid her hair, hands moving like the wind as she twisted her thick tresses over her shoulder.

"Do you intend to tell me what's going on?" Mirae asked.

Analli twisted the end of her braid into a knot then dropped her shoulders, relaxed. She blinked her wide eyes at Mirae and remained silent.

"Can you at least tell me if you bring news of Sunkai? Do you know how far this darkness has spread?" Mirae reached up, closing her hand around her necklace.

A sharp burn seethed into her palm, the same sensation she'd felt the day before. Out of nowhere, Adlae's presence had been restored to her, the strangest feeling of insecurity and danger accompanying her. Mirae shuddered, rubbing her finger over the ruby eye of the dragon pendant.

"The shadow has retreated from Draedin, reaching now to cover Molderëin in darkness and death," Analli said, quietly. "As for Sunkai … I fear our beloved Mother City has fallen."

"And the circle of fire in the sky?"

"A symbol of hope for all who look upon it."

"Hope for what?"

Analli's eyes glowed in the firelight when she leaned forward. "The Sundragon's victory, of course. If the fire in the sky can be anchored by a Sundragon, victory over your enemies may very well be in your grasp."

Mirae took a breath to ask another question when the flap of the tent lifted, Jaeger striding inside followed hastily by Brecken.

"Mirae, we must speak," Jaeger said, glaring at Analli.

The woman's face lit with amusement, tilting her head as she observed the Woodlander.

"Such a fierce, suspicious nature," Analli murmured, clucking her tongue a few times. "I suppose troubling times like these produce such temperaments."

"Mirae, you know as well as I, Analli Devareigh means no harm to anyone," Brecken said, nudging Jaeger slightly out of his way. "I know you've been gone from Sunkai for awhile, but surely you remember her!"

Mirae nodded slowly. "I remember."

"If she means no harm, how is it she is so far from home? How is it she just happened upon us on our way to Tears?" Jaeger's lip curled in an ugly scowl. "Only one thing could have brought her here, Mirae. Magic."

"I cannot argue," Mirae concurred.

"Your Majesty," Brecken paused, crouching so he was eye level with her. "I have known Analli Devareigh for most of my life, as have you. She has no magic!"

"Do not be too sure, Brecken Jandry," Analli muttered.

Mirae's brow winged in unison with Brecken's, both turning to observe the woman.

"There!" Jaeger said, triumphantly. "She admits having such power!"

"She admits nothing!" Brecken shouted, spinning on his heel to rise. He seemed to tower over Jaeger in that moment, his large hands clenched into tight fists at his sides. "This woman quite possibly saved my child's life! If you go near her—"

"No more!" Mirae jumped to her feet. "I am tired of the two of you being at each other's throats! Every day we come closer to the Tower of Tears where we will face a great many enemies and obstacles. I cannot have my commanding officers fighting each other at such a time!"

"Fine." Jaeger tugged at his coat, head tilted up proudly. "But mark me, bringing this woman among our people will be dangerous."

He ducked out of the tent before Mirae could respond.

"Likes outsiders, Master Jaeger does not," Analli commented. "Strange, these Woodlanders are."

"No stranger than Quintarians." Brecken grinned.

Analli laughed. "True for a citizen of Sunkai, I suppose."

"Analli." Mirae folded her arms across her chest, bending slightly toward their new guest. "Is there anything else I need to know?"

Analli smoothed her hands over her skirt, that irritating smile brightening her face again.

"Not at this time, Your Highness."

Mirae pursed her lips. "Very well."

She spun, brushing past Brecken out into the frigid night air. Torches lined the circle of the camp to illuminate her way. Astra's protective spells rippled in the lights from the ground overhead toward the sky in the shape of a dome. Mirae walked toward the edge, head tilted slightly as she strained to see their journey's end. In this darkness, even shapes were impossible to make out. Only the flickering rays of torchlight formed the silhouettes of the trees around them and made the icy ground sparkle.

Mirae stopped at the border of the torch line, the flames sizzling and flickering two feet above the top of her head. She squinted, leaning forward slightly. Heavy footfalls behind her were no surprise, then a moment later a strong male musk wafted up her nose. Brecken stood at ease, hooking his thumbs beneath his belt as he stared into the darkness with her.

"I need you to go on a patrol," she said without looking at him. "I want to know how close we are to the tower, so we can keep the children at a safe distance."

"I'll take Griyer and Ahmet—"

"Take Faël," she interrupted. "She's a good tracker in the dark. Best we have."

Brecken's hesitation filled the space between them like a thick fog. "Mistress Eyres doesn't ..."

"Like you?" She arched a brow, looking up at him from the corner of her eye. "Yes, I know. But she's still the best night tracker I have. Take her with you."

Brecken exhaled, long and loud. "As you wish."

A moan crept up behind them on the wind, rising slowly to a shrieking pitch. Mirae and Brecken turned at the same time toward the center of the camp. Her heart raced, pulse throbbing in her wrists as the horrible cry made her tremble.

"She's not improving," Mirae whispered.

"The Abyss has a strong hold on her, Mirae. Her healing will take time, as Astra has told you many times." Brecken rested his large hand on her shoulder, the warmth of his palm seeping into her.

"If her time comes, I want Afra to pass her." Mirae faced him, watching the shadows from the torches dance across his stern face. "Will she do as I ask?"

"I'm sure she will, if she returns in time." Brecken grimaced. "I've had no word from her since she disappeared while we were at Righteousness. Once, she told me of a time she was trapped in the Place Between, permitted only to leave when the Creator willed it. Then, when she was released, she found herself on the border of the Shadowlands. She was forced to beg a ride from a passing caravan in order to make her way home."

"I thought Passers could come and go from the Place Between as they pleased," Mirae commented. They started back into the camp, Brecken moving with her between the tents.

"Normally, she can," Brecken replied. "But sometimes, the Creator requires her to stay. She says she cannot tell me what she experiences during those times, so I've learned not to ask."

Mirae played with her necklace, keeping an eye on him in her periphery as they moved further into the camp. The tents were closer together here, near the middle of the circle. Children ran in and out of the canvases, their parents keeping a watchful eye on them while they played as though they had not a care in the world. She reached out, ruffling a little boy's hair as he ran in front of them, never missing a step as he loped to the other side of the path.

"Have you discovered her name yet?" Brecken asked.

Mirae shook her head, heart heavy. "She does not speak. Or will not. I'm not sure anymore. All she does is make that horrible noise and weep in agony."

"I saw the women attempting to coax her from the wagon earlier. She nearly came out."

"Yes, then she disappeared inside once again. Back into the darkness. Back with the Abyss." Mirae kicked a loose shard of ice, shattering it into tiny pieces across the slick surface of the ground. "Now we have another unexpected traveler to worry about."

"Analli won't be any trouble. There's a reason she's here, and she will tell us in her own time," Brecken reassured her.

They stopped at the wagons, Mirae staring at the one in the center. A small lantern swung in the breeze hanging near the split in the canvas. Shuffling and whispering came from inside, the shift of a shadow catching her eye.

"Go collect Faël, Brecken," Mirae ordered softly. "The sooner you go, the closer we'll be to our goal."

Brecken bowed slightly, gripping the hilt of his sword as he turned away. Mirae turned quickly to watch him walk away.

"Brecken!"

He paused, looking back with a questioning quirk to his brow.

"Be careful," she breathed.

"Always," he replied.

Mirae waited until he disappeared among the tents before closing the distance to the wagon. She climbed up, slipping quietly inside and to the dark corner of the interior. The women had collected as many blankets as they could spare, softening the hard wood structure for the last remaining Sister of the Creed. She hugged her arms around her shins, resting her chin atop her knees as she watched the woman rock back and forth. Small whimpers filled the wagon, slipping through the poor Sister's swollen lips as tears continued to soak her red cheeks.

"Who are you?" Mirae whispered. "Please, can't you tell me who you are? Can't you tell me how to save you?"

The Sister of the Creed opened her eyes, the reddened bulbs burning Mirae until she thought her skin would peel from her bones.

"Nfaros will be won with the blood of innocents," the woman rasped.

Mirae inhaled sharply, the air hissing through her teeth. She'd nearly forgotten about Astra's prophecy, so caught up in the rush of discovering her sister was alive. How did this woman know about the foretelling the tree prophetess had given her?

"Where did you hear that?" Mirae asked. "Do you know what the prophecy means?"

The Sister sobbed, tucking her arms against her ribs as she rocked harder.

"Nfaros will be won with the blood of innocents!" she repeated in a near shriek.

She continued to whisper the phrase again and again, her voice filling Mirae's ears until she could no longer hear the wind rippling the canvas or the Woodlanders moving about their business. Until only those words echoed through her entire being.

Nfaros will be won with the blood of innocents. Mirae shuddered.

"Please," she said, hoarsely. "Tell me what the words mean. What innocents? How many more will be sacrificed so Nfaros may be won?"

The Sister closed her eyes again, head bowed sharply forward. Her pain-filled moans were the only answer Mirae received.

The dim glow of the lantern was the only light for their path as Brecken and Faël moved through the woods. The path was nearly indiscernible, with the mix of darkness and snow obscuring the way. Faël moved in silence, somehow managing to take each step without an echoing crunch of ice accompanying her. Brecken kept her in the corner of his eye, holding the lantern a little higher with the other hand firmly clasped on the hilt of his sword. Faël had an arrow poised to her bow, shoulders down and gaze fixed to the ground.

Suddenly, she bent to one knee in the snow, tucking a hand into the soft layer of powder beneath the ice. Brecken watched her raise the handful to her nose, sniffing softly before cringing.

"Smoke and ash," she muttered, slapping the snow back to the ground. She waved her hand about, small drops of moisture flying from her fingertips as she stood up again. "By the tracks, I'd say a horde came through here."

"A horde of what?" Brecken asked.

"If the ash is any indication, I'd say Black Ones," Faël answered, squinting in the darkness. "The smell also suggests Black Ones. They carry a tangy stench with them while leaving remnants of smoke on the air."

She looked everywhere but at him, bracing her bow and arrow in both hands once more. She'd pulled her dark hair back in braids, keeping the thick strands away from her face. They moved on, stepping around the soft powder where the horde had left hundreds of prints and crushed ice. Brecken wondered about the hour of the day—or night. In this darkness, it was impossible to know the time. To know even exactly how many days had passed. It felt like weeks since they left Righteousness, when in truth only a few days may have passed.

He glanced over his shoulder, the glow of the circle of fire in the sky seeming brighter than ever in the distance. The Woodlanders had been speculating about the flames' meaning since they first appeared, dozens of possibilities passing their lips. Many sought answers from Astra, who'd been unusually silent the past few days.

"You seem distracted, captain," Faël muttered. She eyed him, a hint of curiosity lighting her pretty eyes. "Are you thinking about the strange woman we found in the woods?"

"Actually," Brecken replied, clearing his throat. "I was wondering if the fire in the sky is meant for evil, not good."

"Your friend seems to think it is meant for good." Faël shrugged, the string of her bow creaking when she gave the arrow a few fidgety tugs.

"I was also wondering what my sister would have to say about it." Brecken smiled, holding the lantern further out toward the path to better light their way. "Afra is more familiar with such things."

"Do Passers have the gift of Sight?" she asked.

"Not exactly. But sometimes she knows things. She can sense things. Especially powerful things."

Faël bent to the ground, freeing one hand from the bow to pass her fingers lightly across the snow. Brecken watched her, delicate brow now scrunched together at the bridge of her nose and eyes narrowing as she stared at the trail.

"This isn't right," she said on a breath.

"What?" Brecken crouched beside her.

"Men do not march with Black Ones. Never, in any time or place, have men joined such ferocious creatures. Yet these prints ..." Faël shook her head slowly. "These are the footprints of men."

"Kael men?"

"One can only assume so. But have they strayed so far from the teachings of the Creator as to walk beside such evil things?" Faël recoiled, slapping at her clothes as if to brush away the filth of the revelation she just imparted.

Brecken rose from his crouched position. "We knew this was a possibility, Mistress Eyres. Roderick and Raphaela did not just win the creatures of the Abyss when they gave their souls to the darkness. They took the hearts of men as well."

"How sorrowful you sound." She tilted her head, watching him.

"I trained many of the men who now march with Roderick," Brecken explained. "Some are still boys who've never seen a battlefield. I would hate to meet them one on one."

He moved forward, the glow of the lantern bouncing on the shadowy trees. They walked a few feet in silence, Faël focusing on the path. Brecken kept near her shoulder, looking forward and backward to cover them both in case one of the shadows should suddenly take form. They turned around another cluster of trees and stopped, the trampled path forgotten as they both bent their necks back.

The walls themselves were magnificent. Thick stone battlements holding strong and menacing in the darkness, curving around one of the tallest towers north of Sunkai. Surrounded by the high curve of an embankment bordering the roaring river which crashed with large boulders of ice. Brecken let his eyes drift slowly up the round silhouette of the Tower of Tears, all the way to the flat top. Faël moved closer to him, fidgeting with her bow again.

"We should go, captain," she said. "I don't like being so far from the camp. I can feel them. Our enemies are here."

Brecken backed away in silent agreement, both of them taking precise movements for minimal noise as they distanced themselves once more from the battlements. Once under the cover of the trees again they turned in unison, taking off at a light jog back the way they'd come. Faël's shoulder brushed his, keeping close as she twisted to look over her shoulder several times, keeping watch.

A stick snapped. Brecken dropped, grabbing Faël's arm to bring her with him, keeping them both low to the ground. Rustling urged Brecken to slide his sword from its sheath, the soft hiss of the steel unnervingly loud in the quiet of the night. The shadows began to move, the glint of a sword reflecting off the dim rays of light from Brecken's lantern. He bent close, blowing out the flickering flame with one swift puff.

"Head back to camp," he mumbled.

"In the dark?" Faël replied.

"You can find your way, you're a Woodlander." Brecken smirked, even though she wouldn't be able to see.

"Captain, if there are—"

"I counted three shadows before putting the light out." He gave her a nudge. "I can handle them. Probably no more than scouts. You need to go, Faël, your son needs you."

"And your daughter needs you," she argued.

"Please, do as I say. For Rickai."

She muttered something beneath her breath, then a soft wisp of air told him she'd moved away, vanishing completely in the darkness as she left his side. Brecken remained crouched on his haunches, gripping the hilt of his sword tighter as he waited a few more heartbeats.

"I know you're there," he shouted, rising slowly. He took a few steps, letting the tip of his sword drag and scrape on the icy snow. "If you didn't recognize me in this darkness, I am Brecken Jandry, and if you are Roderick Kael's men, then we met once. Either in training or in the Sunkai barracks. Are you certain you want to do this?"

Silence answered him. Snow, crunching beneath several boots, warned him they were circling, surrounding him while using the darkness to hide themselves. Brecken sighed, raising his sword in both hands.

"Very well, then."

The first one came from the right, the slice of his sword through the air warning Brecken of his approach. He spun, dropping a few feet toward the ground as he swung his blade. The warmth of blood splattered across his face, followed by the screech of the enemy soldier. Brecken continued to twist, spinning a full circle in just enough time to catch the second one's blade with his own. The steel screamed in the quiet of the woods, echoing against the trees as he pushed the soldier back, shoving him hard until he heard him slam into one of the trunks.

Brecken grunted, the sting of a sharp edge nicking his flesh below the back of the knee. His right leg buckled, sword swinging wildly as he danced in the darkness with the three men, the *whoosh* of their weapons deep and furious as they filled the night. Then they pulled back, their steady breaths moving all around him as they circled. Brecken kept his weapon high, ignoring the throb from the cut in his leg as he followed the pattern of their breathing.

"Where's the woman?" one of them asked in a deep, gruff voice.

Brecken spun toward the voice, holding his sword out. "She's no concern of yours."

"Find her," another voice ordered.

Brecken roared, leaping at their shadows, striking wildly. Their swords clashed sharply, ringing in his ears as he took one down, his pain-filled groan followed by the thud of his body hitting the hard ground.

"Brecken!" Faël's shout rent the air.

Something *whizzed* toward him as he turned, watching the soldier about to run him through fall with a grunt. Faël's arrow pierced the man through the throat, blood choking up out of his mouth as he gasped and writhed before going still.

He could just make her out in the darkness, her smaller shape wrapped thickly in her wool cloak and her long braids piled on her shoulders. She shifted her bow from one hand to the other as she took a cautious step toward him. The shadows made her face nearly indiscernible, but when he squinted, he swore he could see her mouth tilted in a smirk.

"I told you to go!" Brecken shouted.

"You never would've survived without me," she replied calmly.

Brecken frowned, looking back and forth. "Where's the other one?"

"What?"

"There was a third." He moved in a slow circle, searching for any sign of movement. Closing his eyes, he listened. Wherever the man was, he'd be panicked with both his men down. Trying to find the best way to make a run back toward the Tower most likely.

"We need to get out of here," he said. "Do you think you can lead us back …?"

Faël gasped. Blade slicing through flesh drowned any other sound as Brecken watched her body jerk and then drop, a much taller shadow towering over her as she crumbled to the ground.

"No!" Brecken lunged, tumbling into the soldier.

They fell in a heap, both their swords flying far out of reach. Brecken slammed his fist into the enemy's side, feeling a few ribs give beneath his knuckles. A hand came around, grabbing a fistful of his hair to yank him away. Brecken shouted, fiery pain shooting down his neck as they rolled, snow and ice scraping his face and hands as they struggled blindly with each other. Brecken wrapped his arms around the soldier's lower back, gripping tight. He groaned as his opponent did the same, squeezing until he thought his spine would snap.

They locked together, trembling as they pushed to see who was stronger. Warmth and moisture pressed against Brecken's ear. He snarled, shaking his head when he realized it was the man's mouth.

"You're going to lose," his opponent hissed. "The Abyss is stronger, better, than the Creator, and he has chosen Raphaela to lead us all. You'll all be dead soon."

Brecken's wrist bumped something cool and metal at the back of the soldier's belt. He grabbed the handle, the dagger slipping loose with ease.

"Not today," he spat.

In one plunge, he sank the blade into the soldier's back to the hilt. The man slumped, his grip on Brecken releasing in an instant as his last breath wheezed from between his lips. Brecken shoved him off, scrambling in the snow toward Faël's lifeless form.

"No," he whispered, gathering the little woman in his arms. "No, please, no."

She coughed, blood trickling onto her lips and chin. "M-My boy ..."

"Hush," Brecken ordered, running his hand over her side and belly until he found the wound. A warm gush of blood spurted onto his palm as he pressed down, trying to staunch the flow.

"I should've listened to you." Faël grabbed his hand, squeezing. "Rickai ... he'll need you."

Brecken shook his head, throat tightening.

"I am sorry, Brecken," she choked, chest convulsing as she tried to breathe. "I don't hate y-you. I was angry, but the truth ... the truth is I do not know ... w-who killed my husband."

Brecken wrapped his fingers around her hand, holding onto her firmly.

"You led the charge and I—"

"I know. Quiet now, save your strength."

"Brecken, please, take care of Rickai for me. The Woodlanders will make him strong … but you could make him fierce. And I-I want him to b-be fierce!" She took a handful of his coat with her free hand, yanking him down until he could see her eyes. "Promise me!"

"I promise," Brecken said hoarsely.

Faël smiled, a tear slipping from the corner of her eye. "One more thing."

"Anything."

"Can you summon your sister?" she asked, her voice suddenly calm.

"I … I don't know if I can."

"Please try." Her breath hitched, ragged as her lips trembled. "Please … I need a Passer. I don't want to go in this dark place, near so much evil, wondering if the Abyss will snatch my soul before I reach the Creator."

Brecken hesitated. "She might not hear me."

"Try," Faël begged on a groan. "Hurry."

Brecken pulled her close, his forehead brushing hers.

"Afra," he rasped. "Afra, if you can hear me, please come. I need you. Faël needs you."

Silence.

Brecken inhaled deeply. "Please, Afra, hear me."

"I'm here, brother."

He looked up, watching the slim silhouette of his sister emerge through the trees. She appeared to glide across the snow, the train of her thick cloak dragging behind her. Afra knelt at his side, close enough now for him to see that the shadows on her face were not entirely due to the darkness overhead. Her exhaustion was apparent in her labored breaths, the pallor of her skin and the circles around her eyes.

Yet, she smiled, gently placing her hand over Faël's heart.

"Hello, Mistress Eyres," she whispered. "Will you let me pass you now to the Creator's keeping? For the journey does not end here but only begins."

Faël closed her eyes, nodding once. Afra raised her hands, palms up, and rested her forehead against Faël's. Brecken watched as the Woodlander woman's breath grew ever shallower until her chest deflated and her head lolled. His heart plummeted into the pit of his stomach.

Then a light rose from the center of Faël's body. Her soul, golden, glittering and bright, rose from her body, settling in a swirl of light more dazzling than the stars in Afra's hands. His sister looked up at him as he clutched Faël's body close.

"I will try to return soon, brother," Afra said. Then her eyes strayed, looking beyond him toward the tower. "Beware of Tears, Brecken. There is a reason this tower was given such a name."

Brecken looked over his shoulder, barely able to make out the battlements in the distance. When he turned back, she was gone. Vanished as if she'd never been there, leaving him alone with Faël's corpse still nestled in his arms.

CHAPTER SEVENTEEN

"What will happen to the boy?"

Mirae tore her eyes from the men carrying Faël's body away. Brecken stood completely straight, jaw stiff and eyes narrow. He'd not told her exactly what happened when he came running into the camp cradling Faël in his arms. Only that they'd found the tower but were attacked shortly thereafter, costing Faël her life and bringing Afra briefly back to his side. Now he stood under the glow of the torchlights surrounding the camp with a look on his face she'd never seen before. A look she couldn't even name.

"The Woodlanders believe we are all one family," Mirae replied. She placed her hand on his shoulder reassuringly. "He will be cared for and loved by his people, Brecken."

"I promised her I'd look after him," he said. "Even though I couldn't take care of my own child, I promised her I'd raise her son to be fierce."

"Of course you did." Mirae stepped in front of him, gripping his arms. "She was dying, Brecken. You made her a promise, and I know you will do everything you can to keep your word."

He finally looked down at her, the anguish darkening his eyes crying out to her heart. Mirae placed her hand gently on his cheek, her fingertips drifting over the thickening stubble on his face.

"She was a brave woman who could've left me to the mercy of those guards for the pain I caused her," he said, voice deepening with raw emotion. "Instead, she returned and saved my life."

"Faël Eyres always did what was right. She knew, deep in her heart, you were not worthy of death."

"Mirae!"

She dropped her hand from Brecken's cheek, turning to watch Jaeger approach. He stopped a few feet in front of her, his shoulders tensing when he glanced Brecken's way before looking over his shoulder at the men disappearing with the body of their friend.

"What is it, Jaeger?" Mirae asked, bringing his attention back to her.

"Forgive me, Your Majesty," he replied, bowing slightly. "I know perhaps this is not the time, but if we are as close to Tears as the captain says, and if Faël was correct in her assessment of the horde—"

"She was correct," Brecken snapped. "I saw the tracks myself. They were all headed for the tower."

"Then we must strike now," Jaeger insisted, ignoring Brecken. "The captain's confrontation could only have warned the army within that we are near and now we've lost the advantage of surprise."

"One of yours just died," Brecken snarled. "Show some respect."

Jaeger lunged.

"No, Jaeger!" Mirae jumped between the two men, placing a firm hand against her Second's chest. "We have all suffered a grievous loss tonight, do not make our pain worse with your bickering!"

Brecken growled, the animal sound sending a shiver down her spine before he stormed away, cloak billowing like a dark cloud in the breeze before he disappeared into his tent. Mirae shook her head, lifting her gaze to Jaeger's face. His eyes were dark, weathered skin crinkled from stress, and mouth turned down solemnly. He looked older—his exhaustion evident in every line on his face.

"We must honor her death," Mirae murmured. "I understand we are in a time of war, Jaeger, but—"

"No, Mirae, I don't think you do understand." He grabbed her arms roughly, yanking her closer.

Mirae shrieked, biting her lip when his fingers dug deeply into the softer flesh of her upper arms. He tilted her toward him, forcing her to look directly into his eyes.

"This is a time of war, and we do not have time for a traditional burial! We do not have time for the rituals or the fires. I am sorry for the child, but he will mourn in his tent with the women who do not fight. If we do not go to Tears now, then the Black Ones and the Kael soldiers will come to us, and we will lose more than a few soldiers in battle, Mirae."

Jaeger paused, taking a long breath. "We will lose everything. Out here we are vulnerable, Mirae. We are only strongest when we strike first. They could be on their way even now. Please, child, listen to me this once."

Mirae closed her eyes, folding her hands around Jaeger's wrists. She removed his hands from her arms, her mind spinning with everything he'd just said. She could hear the people preparing for Faël's burial even now, the women humming mourning songs deep within the camp as they prepared her body. Doing as Jaeger said would not sit well with them.

But he's right. She opened her eyes, looking up at him again.

"Prepare the men," she ordered. "I will inform Brecken."

Jaeger sighed with relief. "Thank you, Your Highness."

Mirae moved around him, stepping in the footprints Brecken left in the snow all the way to his tent. She shoved aside the flap, ducking inside. A burst of heat from the fire slapped her in the face the moment she was within the confines of the tent walls. Brecken sat staring into the open flames with Analli. Mirae crouched at his side, rubbing her palms together near the fire.

"I gave Jaeger the order to prepare the men to march on Tears," she said.

He grunted, shaking his head. "And did Jaeger convince you to do so? Did he tell you the risks of moving on Tears now?"

"Brecken ..."

"Did he tell you about the catapults? The embankments? The barricades?"

"I know you're upset about Faël, but taking Tears is the reason we're here. Now that the enemy knows we're here, we need to move quickly."

"The enemy knowing we're here is exactly the reason we need to wait!" Brecken leaped to his feet, storming out of the tent.

"Go after him," Analli urged. "Do something he will regret, he may."

Mirae sighed, her feet suddenly heavy as she did what the woman suggested. The men were already beginning to gather, Jaeger shouting orders across the camp as their numbers began to crowd the center of their circle. Weapons clattered, bowstrings twanged, and horses whinnied as the women prepared to hitch up the wagons once more to move the children to a safer location once the army marched for Tears.

In the middle of the hustle, Brecken strode straight for Jaeger, hands fisted and shoulders hunched. Mirae jogged to catch up, stomach twisting when she realized she'd be too late to stop him.

"Jaeger!" he shouted.

Her Second turned, face instantly twisting into a fierce scowl. "What?"

"Are you trying to get your people killed? Or are you so determined to disregard my experience it's blinded you to the danger before you?"

"Have you come up with a reason to go against our queen's wishes, Brecken Jandry? Perhaps you do not like she's taken my side over yours."

"This is not about taking sides, you old fool!" Brecken grabbed Jaeger by the front of his coat, yanking him closer.

"Brecken!" Mirae gasped, coming to his side. "Stop this!"

"I am trying to save as many lives as I can!" he continued, seemingly oblivious to her presence.

Jaeger knocked Brecken's hands away. "Do not speak to me like that, boy. I held a sword in my hand before you were born!"

"Then these woods have made your instincts soft," Brecken hissed. "Tears is not what it used to be, Jaeger Senne. The tower is stronger, the walls thicker, and the embankments higher. Overnight they could build obstructions to take down half this army within minutes!"

Jaeger seemed to hesitate for a single moment before his jaw firmed and he looked Mirae's way.

"Why did we come here if not to take Tears?" he asked her.

Brecken glared at him. "Mirae, I am not saying we don't take Tears. I'm saying the enemy knows we're here, and we need a new plan. We need to circle around, coming at them from a different location to take them by surprise. We can't rush in like this! We need to understand what they're planning better!"

"Or we can take them by surprise with our original plan," Jaeger countered. "Come at them head-on right now, before they've had a chance to prepare for our arrival."

"We would be much better served and have a better chance of actually taking the tower, if we wait a couple of days and watch. Take them off their guard."

Both men looked at her suddenly, awaiting her command. Mirae's eyes swung between the two of them, her head still spinning with both of their arguments. She'd brought Brecken into their fold not only because Brae had loved him, but because she knew his knowledge and experience would be invaluable. Yet, his desire to hold off their attack made her feet itch. She never liked sitting still when the enemy was so near.

Then she locked gazes with Jaeger, and her heart lifted into her throat. The man had been her mentor—a father to her when she thought she'd lost the two people in her life who mattered most. The confidence and strength she saw in his eyes now reminded her what brought them all here in the first place.

"I did not come all this way to wait and see how the enemy plans to eliminate us," she announced. "Brecken, I understand your point of view, but I think Faël's death is clouding your judgment in your fear of losing another soldier. We're at war. We're going to lose soldiers."

"Mirae, please, this is a mistake!"

"I came here to take Tears. Jaeger believes if we go now, before they've had a chance to fully prepare for our arrival, we will have the advantage and can scale the wall. So that's what we're going to do." She took a step closer to him, tilting her head back slightly to look straight into his eyes. "Now, can I count on you to be at my side leading the men?"

Brecken's mouth pressed into a thin line, but his head jerked slightly in a consenting nod. Mirae eyed Jaeger, brow arched.

"And can I trust the two of you to work together? We must now fight the enemy, not each other."

Jaeger smirked. "I have no intention of taking a blade to Captain Jandry ... today that is."

Brecken snarled before stomping away, furiously shouting orders for the bowmen to take the front line.

"Must you provoke him before battle?" Mirae mumbled.

"I enjoy riling him." Jaeger laid his hand on her shoulder. "I'm glad you saw things my way, Mirae."

"My sister needs what's within those walls. I'm not willing to wait and risk the enemy moving all of that weaponry out before we even have a chance to attack." She turned to face him, pulse thrumming wildly in her wrists. "Tell me we can do this, Jaeger, with minimal loss."

He gripped her shoulders in both hands. "We can do this, Mirae."

Mirae slapped her hands around his forearms. "Good. Because I intend to win this war for my sister, and Tears is the key to our victory."

Analli lifted one of the children into a wagon, watching the Woodlander army disappear into the dark depths of the forest, the flicker of their torchlights beginning to diminish the further they went. She turned from assisting the remaining women and children, pushing through the snow on the ground. All the tents had been taken down, the army leaving hundreds of tracks on the ground as they moved out with Mirae and Brecken at the head.

Analli stopped where the edge of the circle used to be, squinting in the darkness as the last shadowy silhouettes of the army began to disappear. She pulled her necklace from beneath the collar of her dress, closing her hand around the pendant. The golden dragon felt hot within her palm, ruby eyes burning her skin.

"Strange night, this is," a deep, smooth voice said.

Analli turned, finding a dark-skinned woman standing beside her. She frowned, facing her more fully.

"Do I know you?" she asked, the warmth of recognition filling her belly.

The woman's silver eyes glowed in the darkness, her hair as black as the sky overhead falling in tight waves to her ankles.

"My man is gone," the woman groaned. "Gone to fight. To death they march, but listen they will not!"

Analli placed a cautious arm around her, pulling her a little closer. "If they have a chance at taking Tears, they must try."

The woman moaned, pulling away from Analli's comfort. Her eyes suddenly seemed more like domes, sweat beading on her brow despite the cold air.

"Wait." Analli followed as the woman began to shuffle away. "You are from across the sea."

The woman kept walking, and Analli rushed after her, catching up to her side.

"What is your name? I know your accent! From long ago …"

The woman stopped. "I am called Astra in this place."

"But that is not your name."

Astra eyed her then grunted softly. "Clever, you are. Here, the name given me suits."

"And this," Analli paused, gently touching Astra's cheek. "Is not your true face, is it?"

Astra moved on, lifting her skirts when she came to the back of one of the wagons to climb inside. Analli followed quickly, the surprising warmth within the walls of the canvas making her shiver.

"You are of the Avarys," Analli breathed, heart pounding harder. "A land far out of reach of any mortal for hundreds of years. A land thought dead and gone. Our children do not even believe such a place ever existed!"

Astra began to hum, removing her cloak and coat before settling on the cushions covering the wagon floor. They lurched forward suddenly, and Analli squeaked, falling down on one of the pillows as they began to move. She peeked out the back of the canvas, watching as the wagons began to form a line, weaving between the trees as best they could, looking for a safer location farther from the Tower but also to a place the surviving soldiers would be able to track.

When she turned back, her breath completely left her. The woman who sat before her a moment ago was gone. Or mostly. Analli could hardly believe her eyes as she stared at the nymph across from her. Her ebony skin glowed with golden flecks, ears suddenly long and pointed at sharp angles through her raven hair. Oh … her eyes! Even brighter than before, they glowed with a power Analli dared not understand.

"The Avarys has been long protected by its invisibility," Astra said. "Left when I was very young, I did, to come to new lands with strange trees. A home here, I found, yes? The Avarys would only be endangered by my return."

"So you keep your true nature hidden to protect your country, allowing the Woodlanders to believe you come from a deep, uncharted territory of the Shadow Lands."

"These powers I hold are not for such men to comprehend. Used for terrible things, I would be." Astra sighed and bowed her head. When she raised her eyes once more, she'd returned to the woman she'd been moments before. "For I do not only See, Analli Devareigh."

"No, you do not. There are many things a wood nymph can do. I know. I studied such as you when I was a girl." Analli inhaled deeply then rubbed her chest, the odd ache nearly halting her breath altogether. "I made my brother a promise long ago. I fear I will not be able to keep my word."

"Do you ask my advice or my insight as a nymph of the Avarys?" One of the woman's delicate brows curved in question.

"I came to be here using a magic I've not touched in over twenty years." Analli's eyes stung. She leaned forward, reaching to place her hand over Astra's. "I can feel my life draining from me every moment of every day

179

because of what I've done. Please, if you know anything of my future, tell me now."

"Suddenly, you sound not like a Quintarian," Astra commented. "Now like a woman of Sunkai, you sound."

Analli started to draw away, but Astra gripped her fingers, squeezing until the blood completely drained from them, making her skin tingle. Her eyes rounded an even larger size, silver domes glowing so bright they reflected off the canvas.

"Sundragon blood flows through your veins!" Astra panted, her chest convulsing with each breath. "Promises broken … royal blood shed … a queen's heart torn!"

Analli yanked her hand loose, falling backward as she scrambled to put distance between herself and the prophetess. She watched her, the way the woman's eyes seemed to billow with grey clouds and her hair clinging to the sweat on her temples.

"Promises broken," Analli repeated quietly. "Will my promises be broken?"

Astra didn't respond. Instead, she hugged her stomach, rocking slowly while uttering one last chilling sentence.

"Nfaros will be won with the blood of innocents."

CHAPTER EIGHTEEN

The Aulend Forest

"Um, Uncle Maxx? Where's the road?"

Maxx glared over his shoulder at his niece. Noelle smoothed a hand through her hair, mouth quirked in a sassy grin. She was as tall as Gwylan now, the baby fat in her cheeks even beginning to fade behind the lean profile of a blossoming young woman. He had to admit, he was getting used to her rapid growth now, seeing both his brother and Brae in her face.

Though Brecken may not see the resemblance. If we ever find him, that is. Maxx grumbled under his breath, returning to study the 'path' they were following. Gwylan dipped their torch a little lower, snow glistening beneath the dancing light. They had to be closing in on Tears by now, and if fortune favored them, Mirae would have already taken the tower, offering them a chance at a decent rest.

"Perhaps I could use a guidance spell?" Gwylan suggested.

The darkness overhead rumbled, a coil of fiery red mixed with swirling black tendrils twisting intricately in the sky. Maxx shook his head.

"I have a feeling if you were to use any of your power, the shadow will unleash all sorts of fury down on us." He stood up, pinching the bridge of his nose as he resisted a yawn.

He hadn't slept since they left Quintaria, instead keeping watch during their brief rests so Gwylan and Noelle could save their energy for whatever lay ahead. Noelle's powers were growing every day, Gwylan certain she was nearly ready for a true show of force. Creating a few sparks, flames and moving things around with a wave of her hand was one thing. Fighting the enemy another, and Maxx only wished he had as much confidence in his niece's growing ability as Gwylan did. All he'd witnessed so far seemed to be simple magic tricks, increasing his worry the closer they came to finding Mirae.

"We'll have to just trust we're on the right path," Maxx said. He remounted his horse, wincing when his hindquarters flamed from having been in the saddle so long. Gwylan and Noelle did the same, the horses stomping about impatiently before they started moving through the woods again.

The trees groaned with every breath of wind swirling around them, followed by the crack of thunder that shook the shadow above. Maxx tilted his head back slightly, staring up into the sky. The clouds seemed to be forming twirling black tendrils. Thick ropes knotting then unfurling in a chaotic dance. The first light he'd seen in days—besides the odd ring of fire in the distance—had finally presented itself in the sky in the form of roaring red lightning. However, this had only served to worry him and Gwylan all the more.

"I saw Damari again last night," Noelle announced, breaking the tense silence.

Maxx looked over his shoulder at her, the slant of the torchlight toward his niece indicating Gwylan was doing the same.

"Tell us," Gwylan encouraged gently.

"Well," Noelle paused to clear her throat, then continued, "I saw ships. Many, many ships. I saw Draedinian soldiers aboard and Dragon women flying in the sky. They moved far south, toward Molderëin I think, and Damari was standing on the deck of the lead ship."

"And did she still have her dragon skin?" Maxx asked.

"I don't think she can be rid of it whenever she wants to, Uncle Maxx." Noelle giggled, the sweet sound bringing a smile to his lips. "Don't you believe what I see is true?"

The sudden solemnity in her voice erased his smile.

"Of course I do, sweetheart," he assured her.

"The shadow is moving!" Gwylan warned.

Maxx turned sharply to look. His horse reared, shrieking as he sent Maxx flying from the saddle. He landed hard, crashing through the ice and snow before slamming into a tree. His head spun wildly, pain shooting through the back of his skull as he tried to reorient himself in the darkness. Gwylan gasped, the torch faltering as she, too, was swept from her horse, landing in a heap. The snow snuffed the torch, plunging them into pitch black.

A shot of red lightning stretched across the sky, dimly lighting the clearing. Noelle screamed, shattering the air with her terror. The horses scattered, hooves pounding the ground until they were far away.

"Gwylan!" Maxx groaned, scrambling in the direction he thought she'd fallen. "Gwylan the torch!"

"I have it!" her hoarse response came and the next moment, the torch ignited in a silver blaze.

They spun together, finding Noelle sitting a foot deep in the snow, quick breaths huffing through her parted lips. She was staring at the sky, her head beginning to wag slowly back and forth.

"Uncle Maxx," she whimpered, voice trembling. "What is that?"

Maxx pulled his sword, eyes widening. One of the clouds parted from the shadow, billowing and tumbling down directly toward them. Gwylan thrust the end of the torch down into the snow, standing it upright so they still had light. She drew her bow, creating a flaming arrow with a wave of her hand. Maxx's brow winged.

"Doesn't that burn?"

Gwylan glared at him. He chuckled.

"Noelle, come this way," he ordered, holding out his hand.

She struggled to her feet, yanking her skirts in both fists before hurrying toward his side. The shadow suddenly parted, a black vine shooting out to slap Noelle aside.

"No!" Maxx raced forward, watching his niece slam back into the ground.

Gwylan released her arrow into the cloud, the weapon flying straight through without any result. The shadow screeched, another ribbon spiraling out to wrap around Gwylan. She groaned, lifted an inch off the ground before being released. Maxx shouted, swinging his sword through the shadow, the heavy *whoosh* of the blade slicing nothing but air. Something slammed into his stomach, hurtling him into one of the trees and onto the ground. His weapon slipped from his hand, breath stolen from him.

Maxx spun onto his belly, sinking into the two-feet deep snow. The darkness rolled toward Noelle as she scrambled back, tears streaming down her cheeks and snow coating her clothes. A Wraith Spawn claw snaked out of the cloud, the low shriek of the creature vibrating in the air.

"Uncle Maxx!" Noelle screamed, barely a spark lifting from her outstretched palm. "Aunt Gwylan!"

183

His head spun, vision finally clearing when he saw Gwylan sprawled on the ground, her body twisted in a limp heap. Whatever this thing was, it did not care about them.

Noelle. It's after Noelle!

"No!" Maxx shoved to his feet, lunging toward the darkness when something flashed by.

He fell back onto his rump, heart thundering as another dark green streak passed before him, the faint color of blood-red following. He shook his head, disbelieving, as the ghostly image appeared before the cloud, forming into a solid figure with arm stretched out toward this strange evil. When she turned her head, Maxx stopped breathing.

Wearing a gown as green as her eyes, she smiled at him, dark red hair rippling down her back with skin as fair and flawless as when last he'd seen her.

It cannot be ...

Her face twisted in a scowl as she faced the creature once more.

"Get away from my baby!" She flung her arm, a light shooting from her fingertips.

The darkness howled and trembled, retreating a few feet. The ghost moved forward, sending rays of light into the shadow until it rolled, spinning in a cyclone into the night sky. Maxx watched the woman who couldn't possibly be there turn around to walk back toward Noelle. Her feet were bare, and she left not a mark in the snow, walking on the surface as if she weighed no more than a feather.

Noelle stared enthralled, slowly taking the woman's hand when she offered. Maxx couldn't stop staring as the ghost leaned forward, whispering something in his niece's ear before she kissed her lightly on the forehead. Then she turned to him, tears shimmering in emerald eyes he knew so well.

"Thank you, Maxx," she said, her voice resounding throughout the clearing. "Keep her close. There is so much more for her to do."

Maxx stood up, his throat tight. "B-Brae?"

She smiled. "We will meet again, brother."

Then she was gone, disintegrating in a burst of light and snow dust. Noelle fell to her knees, hugging her stomach and sobbing. Maxx couldn't move, too stunned.

We will meet again. Creator's Night! He closed his eyes, a cold tear trailing his cheek.

Gwylan moaned softly behind him, cloak rustling as she staggered onto her feet once more.

"What happened?" she mumbled. "Is Noelle all right?"

Maxx could only nod, walking stiffly over to gather his niece close in his arms. She sobbed into his chest, her tears soaking his coat.

"I never thought I'd see her again!" she cried.

"Neither did I, little one." Maxx pressed his lips firmly to her forehead. "But it would seem she never left us."

"Maxx, something's still out there," Gwylan hissed, passing him with her bow once again in hand.

"Did she return?" Noelle wondered, rubbing the tears from her cheeks. Maxx pushed her behind him, yanking his dagger from his belt as Gwylan's silhouette moved in and out of shadow.

A grunt. A shout. Then the distinct sound of someone being dragged and blubbering protests reached them swiftly, followed by Gwylan reappearing in the dimly lit clearing.

"He was watching from the trees!" Gwylan accused, giving her captor one last shove.

"Are you mad, woman?" the man replied. "What did you do to me?"

"A temporary paralysis, fool. You'll live." Gwylan rolled her eyes, moving to stand at Maxx's shoulder.

Then her prisoner turned his head, legs still useless beneath him. Maxx dropped the dagger.

"Tyrese Malaki?" he rasped. "Is that really you?"

"Maxx!" Tyrese barked a laugh. "I thought perhaps my eyes deceived me in this treacherous darkness, but here you stand!"

"And here you ... lie." Maxx sneered at Gwylan.

She shrugged in response, nonchalantly strapping her bow to her back once more. He crouched to be eye level with the unfortunate man who'd encountered his betrothed.

"Where did you come from?" he asked.

"After the execution, things changed drastically in the Blood Keep," Tyrese replied, glancing cautiously at the two young women behind Maxx. "Raphaela began forcing the men to swear blood oaths to the Abyss, and most of them followed her, either seeing no other alternative or actually falling for the Abyss's lies. After you and Lathan ran, I started planning my escape. Biding my time with Raphaela before I was forced to make such an oath. Then I ran."

"You've been out here alone all this time?" Gwylan asked, doubtfully.

Tyrese grunted, grabbing his legs to fold them more comfortably under him. He punched his knees a few times, indicating feeling was returning before he scowled up at the woman.

"No, not all this time. I managed to find Klade Overlage." Tyrese looked pointedly at Maxx. "And his army."

"They're here?" Maxx murmured.

Tyrese nodded. "They've been searching for Mirae as Adlae ordered them to."

"You've seen the Winter Queen?" Gwylan's brow winged.

"I haven't, but Klade did. He's been making slow progress toward the Pilvaa ever since. The woods have been rampant with Wraith Spawn and Kael spies. We've had our share of bloodshed along the way." Tyrese frowned at his legs, carefully positioning them beneath him.

Maxx reached out, gripping the man by the arm to offer some support as he rose unsteadily to his feet. Tyrese exhaled loudly once he was standing again, slapping the snow from his clothes.

"Joining Klade Overlage and his army may serve us well, Maxx," Gwylan commented, head tilted in thought. "Since we are all looking for Mirae Sundragon, the protection of his men would be good for Noelle."

Tyrese turned, one brow arching up sharply. "*Noelle?*"

Maxx cringed. "Long story."

"Hmph," Tyrese grunted. "I'd also like to know where Lathan is."

"Again, long story." Maxx raked a hand through his hair. "Would Klade object to our joining you? We seem to have lost our horses along with all of our supplies."

"Any Jandry joining our ranks would be considered a blessing, Maxx." Tyrese slapped him on the shoulder, grinning. "If Klade could have, he would've stormed the Blood Keep to rescue Brecken himself. But I suppose you'll do."

"Thanks," Maxx grumbled.

"I think we should go," Gwylan said, staring at the darkening shadows in the sky.

Tyrese mumbled an agreement, gesturing for them to follow as he began to limp through the trees. Gwylan picked up their torch, put a firm arm around Noelle, and followed quickly, Maxx taking up the rear to watch their backs with his sword ready. They moved slowly and silently, each looking up every few moments to be certain the clouds weren't going to descend once more. Maxx winced every time their boots crunched the snow or the wind made Gwylan's flames flicker and spit.

"So, Maxx," Tyrese said, breaking the silence. "Are you going to tell me how you ended up out in the middle of the Aulend with a Dominant of Eventide and your *grown* niece?"

Noelle giggled. "I am quite a surprise to you, aren't I, Master Tyrese?"

Tyrese snorted in reply.

"Lathan and I were forced to separate after we found Noelle," Maxx explained. "There were ... complications ... with Damari Kael."

"I've heard the rumors," Tyrese said. "Took everyone by surprise, that one. Especially Raphaela. Our spies say she's none too pleased with her sister's elevated rank and power."

"Once Lathan was gone, Noelle began to show signs of ..." Maxx hesitated, glancing at his niece.

"I have Eventide qualities," Noelle said simply.

"Right." Maxx cleared his throat, then continued, "I'd run into Gwylan earlier and tracked her down again to see if she could help."

"And these Eventide qualities are what made a four-year-old child grow into a young woman within a week?"

"Yes," Gwylan said. She smirked. "Do you doubt your friend's word?"

"Well, I cannot deny what my own eyes see," Tyrese replied. "But convincing everyone else she is who you say she is might be difficult."

"My father will recognize me," Noelle said firmly. "He's the only one who matters to me. He *has* to recognize me."

A rock settled in Maxx's stomach, Noelle's certainty that Brecken would know her raising the tide of worry in his heart. He'd avoided the subject of her reunion with her father as much as possible, wanting to save her from hurt if he could.

Because the truth is there's no guarantee Brecken will believe she's his daughter. He inhaled deeply, holding the breath for a few moments before releasing in a calming exhale.

"We're here," Tyrese announced.

Maxx turned, hurrying to Noelle's side as they stepped within the clearing to the campsite. Torches lit their way as Tyrese guided them down the line of tents, around the scattered fires where the men sat hunched over the flames, drawing as much warmth from them as they could. Maxx put his arm firmly around Noelle when some of the men looked up, watching them curiously as they passed. A few of them nodded deeply to him in acknowledgment, recognizing him as well as his former position as a lieutenant before he fled Sunkai.

He reached over, snatching a handful of Gwylan's cloak to pull her closer to him as well. She shrieked, nearly losing her footing as well as the torch before she frowned at him.

"What are you doing?" she asked.

"Just stay close to me."

"Why?"

Maxx rolled his eyes. "These are good men, Gwylan, but even good men can be ... curious ... when a beautiful woman parades through an army camp without warning."

Gwylan snickered. "I can take care of myself, Maxx Jandry."

"Yes, I know. You've told me. Must you *always* remind me you don't need me or the protection of my sword?"

Gwylan started to respond when they came to a sudden halt, Tyrese gesturing for them to stay outside before he ducked into one of the tents. A moment later, the flap lifted again, Tyrese stepping out quickly followed by a man Maxx never thought he'd see again.

"I had to see for myself," Klade said, shaking his head. "Maxx Jandry, we thought by now you'd be long dead."

Maxx grinned, stepping forward to yank the man into a bear hug. Klade gripped him by the shoulders, smiling from ear to ear.

"Good to see you, old friend," Maxx said. "You've come a long way."

"Yes, we have and without a leader."

"Brecken knew if anyone could lead these men through the woods, you could. So did Adlae."

"Still, I will be glad to have a Jandry heading our forces once more." Klade looked over Maxx's shoulder, thick brow furrowing. "Who did you bring with you?"

"A friend," Maxx paused, waving a hand in Gwylan's direction. "And my niece."

Klade chuckled. "Only you could joke at a time like this, Maxx."

Noelle stepped forward, her nose wrinkled. "My uncle might be the humorous one in the family, Master Klade, but I can assure you he's not playing a trick on you. I am Noelle Jandry, daughter of Brecken Jandry and Brae Sundragon."

Klade's eyes darted between her and Maxx.

"How is this possible?"

"Shall I explain?" Noelle suggested, taking the man's arm. "Actually, it's not very complicated at all. You see what happened …"

Her voice faded as she practically dragged Klade back into the tent. Maxx looked down at Gwylan, her proud smile fairly glowing in the light of her torch.

"How grown up she is," she murmured.

"Yes, thanks mostly to you. I would've been lost and useless to her if we'd not found you."

Cautiously, he put his arm around her shoulders. Gwylan leaned into his side, tucking herself perfectly against the curve of his waist. The deep clearing of someone's throat reminded him that Tyrese was watching, an irritating grin curling the man's lip.

"Are you two coming inside?" he wondered.

"Certainly." Gwylan shoved her torch into the snow, snuffing the light before pulling him along behind her into the tent.

Noelle was sitting on the floor in front of the fire with Klade, chatting softly. The man stared at her, fascination and shock lighting his eyes. He turned toward them as they joined him, Gwylan arranging herself beside Noelle so she could whisper something in her ear.

"The longer I look at her," Klade whispered for Maxx's ears alone. "The more she begins to look like Brae to me. There's no doubt in my mind anymore, she is who you said."

"She explained to you then?"

"I don't understand most of her explanation, but I trust her word." Klade sighed. "You truly saw Brae in the woods moments ago?"

"Yes," Maxx confirmed. "Her voice, her hair … her very image. A ghost, yet not a ghost."

"So this is what the world has become. The dead walk, and the light has deserted us." Klade rubbed his eyes, bringing his fingers together to pinch the bridge of his nose.

"How close are we to Tears?" Maxx asked, angling himself away from the women.

"Not close enough," Klade replied. He clasped his hands together, resting his arms on his knees to lean forward. "Mirae is closer and I fear she will march on Tears, because she doesn't know we're coming."

"Can't she take the tower? Last I remember, there weren't many men guarding the battlements."

"Not so anymore." Klade looked into his eyes, the worry and fear darkening them setting Maxx's teeth on edge. "Days ago, two of my scouts saw men marching with Wraith Spawn toward Tears. They moved at an incredible pace, faster than any mortal man could possibly move without the assistance of the Abyss. They would have made it to Tears much faster than Mirae ever could."

"You think they are lying in wait for her there?"

"Why else, Maxx?"

"If they are behind the walls, Mirae doesn't stand a chance against the weaponry now in their possession!"

"I know, Maxx." Klade's shoulders slumped in exhaustion. "Please tell me the reason Lathan isn't with you is because he's gathering loyal subjects of the Sundragon to fight with us."

Maxx cringed. "Lathan is across the sea with Damari Kael. If he can convince the People of the Dragon to join us, then he will return but—"

"He will not come in time to help us take Tears." Klade bowed his head. "I feared as much."

"We can still try, Klade," Maxx insisted. "If we go now, we could catch up with Mirae and perhaps stop her from falling right into Raphaela and Roderick's trap!"

"My men have not rested in five days, Maxx," Klade answered. "We are, at least, a two-day walk to Tears. I fear, no matter what action we take, we are already too late."

Maxx stared at him, words halting on his tongue. He stood up, spinning for the tent door.

"Uncle Maxx?" Noelle called.

He ignored her, ducking out of the warmth of the tent into the frozen night air. He drew his cloak close around him, marching through the snow toward the tree line. The dim glow of the torches bounced off the slick ground, creating a different light of its own. He stopped at the edge of the clearing, looking into the pitch blackness of the woods beyond.

Softly, an arm came around his waist, followed by the warmth of a small body tucking herself beneath his arm.

"If there is any comfort to be had in this moment," Gwylan whispered. "Would you find some in my declaration of falling in love with you?"

Maxx tightened his mouth to keep from smiling. "Is this you trying to lighten an otherwise dark mood?"

"Perhaps, but that doesn't mean what I say is untrue."

He quirked a brow, glancing down at her. She tightened her arm around his waist.

"You are an unusual man, Maxx Jandry. A rather extraordinary one too. If my mother were here, I am sure she would tell me I would be a fool not to lose my heart to such as you." She rested her temple against his shoulder and closed her eyes. "You reminded me that being of Eventide does not mean I cannot feel what others who do not possess my gifts feel. I once thought such feelings would break the rules of my Sisters."

"Will you be mad if I tell you I'm very glad you walked away from your mission for me and Noelle?"

"How can I be mad when the choice was mine alone to make? Besides, my Superiors were not what I thought they were. I cannot follow those who allow their lives to be governed by fear of the unknown. Especially those who hold such power." Gwylan trembled, wrapping her other arm around him, cuddling beneath his cloak. "My power is stronger than ever before, yet I no longer feel I am of Eventide."

"What do you mean?"

"I mean I no longer feel a connection to my Sisters. I think the Superiors have banished me, in a manner of speaking."

"Do you regret your choice?"

She shook her head firmly. "Never."

Maxx placed his hand on her hair, stroking the silky strands gently. Gwylan looked up at him.

"We are already too late to help Mirae Sundragon, aren't we?"

Maxx pressed her closer, resting his chin on the crown of her head.

"Yes, Gwylan. I'm afraid we are."

191

In the Realm of Dreams …

"You can't keep me here! My friends are going to die!"

Clea lunged toward the glass, screaming when the images vanished as quickly as they appeared. She twirled around, glaring at the old man. He, at least, had the decency to look troubled, his striking eyes staring into hers with such sadness she felt a twinge of pity. But only for a moment.

"Why are you doing this?" she demanded.

"I told you already, Heir of Molderëin. What you see will either make you strong or weak. Do you think you are strong enough to survive the truth? To survive where your friends, perhaps even your family, will not?"

"Is that what this is? You are testing me to see if I will preserve the power of the flower over the lives of my own family?"

"This is a lesson, young queen. One you must come to understand. The flower's magic can be unpredictable and may not always answer you in the way you wish. Can you command this power? Can you take so much control as to, perhaps, even rid yourself of me?" He held his hands up in question, bushy silver brows arching.

"Rid myself of you?" Clea repeated, shaking her head angrily. "You toy with me! You speak in riddles. I did not claim the Summer Flower to play games! I claimed the flower so I could help save Nfaros! Now tell me plainly, what am I supposed to learn from this?" Clea pointed to the glass behind her.

"You are meant to learn the Summer Flower does not hold the answers to your predicament. The Keeper must control the power within before the power within controls the Keeper." He passed his hand over the Summer Flower, staring at the bloom longingly.

"You are meant to learn not to make the same mistakes as the blossom's previous owners. Men who used this power to fulfill their own selfish desires and paid the consequences. No, you must learn not to make the same mistakes I did."

Clea looked down at the flower, strapped like an armband around her forearm. "You once owned the Summer Flower?"

The old man leaned close, his mouth brushing against her ear so he could whisper.

"I *created* the Summer Flower."

She reared back, eyes widening when she saw the truth in his.

"You are of the Avarys. You ... are the Summer King."

The moment the words left her lips, he receded into the mist, leaving her alone once again.

CHAPTER NINETEEN

The Tower of Tears

Mirae! Mirae get up! Please, help me!

The echoing crackle of flames flooded her ears, rising above the distant scream for help. Mirae stared into the sky, watching embers swirling higher and higher into the shadows canvasing the heavens. Blood dripped over the bridge of her nose, tickling the inner corner of her eye. Breathing was hard, her chest straining with every draw of air she managed to take. She remembered the whole disastrous event. The charge across the frozen river, the treacherous climb up the steep embankments. The reign of fiery boulders gliding in perfect arches over the battlements from the catapults within.

The screams. The blood. The creatures dropping from the sky. They'd never even reached the walls, never even had a chance to place their ladders in an attempt to scale the battlements. The enemy had swarmed on them the moment they were across the river, managing to take them down without even leaving their posts on the wall.

An arrow planted itself in the ground inches beside her arm. Mirae lifted her head slowly, rolling over onto her belly to look around. Bodies were scattered across the embankment, some still falling toward the river, breaking through the thin layer of ice to be carried away.

"Jaeger!" Mirae sobbed, crawling among the bodies, her clothes smearing in a mix of blood and Wraith Spawn ash. "Brecken! Where are you? Please …"

A large hand landed heavily against her back. Mirae spun, raising her dagger.

"Easy, my queen," Cohdel said, voice rumbling like thunder in her ears. She lowered the weapon, never more relieved to see anyone in her life. "We have to go."

She gripped his arm, leaning heavily into him as he brought her back to her feet.

"Where's Braven?" she shouted above the crash of another catapult. They crouched low to the ground as the explosion blasted across the field, sparks flying in all directions.

"Braven is gone," Cohdel answered sharply.

Mirae's eyes welled. "No ... oh, Astra!"

"There will be time for grief, my lady. Now, we must retreat."

"Where is Brecken?" Her head swung, searching the chaos. "Cohdel, tell me you saw Brecken alive! And Jaeger!"

"Mirae, we have to go NOW!" Cohdel yanked on her arm, dragging her with him down the ridge toward the riverbank.

She stumbled, twisting her arm out of his hold to move of her own accord. Cohdel kept close, one hand pressed between her shoulder blades to keep her going. They'd nearly made it to the bottom of the embankment, stumbling over the piles of lifeless bodies, when a cry rang out above the others.

"Mirae!"

She spun around. "Lara?"

"Mirae, help me! Please!" Lara's scream rent the air, rising to a chilling shriek above the crash of the catapults.

"Lara!" Mirae rushed back up the embankment, ignoring Cohdel's call for her to stop. She clawed her way over the bodies, ankles twisting and muscles straining as she tried to ignore the carnage, trying to follow the sound of Lara's cries.

"I'm coming," she gasped, her voice fading as the smoke and stench attempted to choke her. "I'm coming! Lara!"

Another ear-splitting scream turned Mirae in the other direction. Her feet went from under her, breath rushing out of her as she fell backward, tumbling end over end. She landed in a heap, head spinning and stomach churning as her body throbbed with every new bruise beginning to form. The cut in her forehead stung, fresh blood bursting to coat the left side of her face. She lifted herself onto her elbows, neck arching as she raised her head ... and froze. Mirae gasped, chest convulsing with repressed sobs.

Lara's glossy eyes stared back at Mirae, unseeing ... dead. Her mouth still open in a halted scream, face frozen forever with terror. She lay across Griyer, his body just as still, just as lifeless. Blood pooled beneath them, staining the snow bright red in the glow of the fires raging down the embankment.

"Oh, Lara," Mirae cried, placing trembling hands on the woman. "I'm so sorry! This is all my fault!"

An arm came around her waist, yanking her away from her friends. Mirae screamed, writhing as she was pulled back, lifted right off her feet to be carried away. She clawed at the arm, scratching and punching with every bit of strength she had left. Then she landed hard on her feet, head spinning from the force with which she was dropped. Big hands gripped her arms, turning her around in a fast circle to face him.

"Brecken!"

"We have to go, Mirae, right now!" Brecken said without even looking at her, his focus on the clouds overhead.

A low moan distracted her, blood turning cold when she saw Jaeger, half-kneeling on the ground with a hand clutched to his bleeding side. Mirae ran to him, grabbing him around the waist to support him.

"They're coming back," Brecken declared, moving to Jaeger's other side. He swung the man's arm around his shoulders, roughly pulling him to his feet.

Mirae kept hold of the wounded man's other side, supporting as much of his weight as she possibly could as they struggled across the battlefield toward the edge of the tree line. She saw another group of dark silhouettes moving in the same direction, slipping and sliding across the river in their frantic race to safety. How many had survived the massacre? A hundred? Ninety? She could only hope for such numbers to have escaped their foolish attempt to charge the embankment.

I should've listened to Brecken. Why didn't I listen? Mirae shuddered, squeezing Jaeger's wrist to keep him firmly against her side.

The shadow began to rumble above them, clouds swirling and thickening, preparing to rain down another army of Wraith Spawn on them. They broke through the border of the trees, fumbling about in the darkness, no longer caring if they ran in the right direction only needing to get as far away from the battle site as possible.

"Brecken!" a guttural shout made them stop.

Cohdel appeared a moment later, torch held high to light the woods.

"Did you find anymore survivors?" Brecken asked between deep breaths.

"A few. They fled into the forest, afraid to take any light for fear the Wraith Spawn would find them."

"They won't follow us into the woods. Raphaela wants them to hold the tower, and if they believe they killed Mirae, then there is no purpose pursuing the few remaining soldiers." Brecken glanced at Mirae briefly before returning his attention to Cohdel. "Jaeger needs help. Do you think you can find the camp?"

Cohdel nodded sharply, taking the lead. Brecken surged forward to follow, coming to a sudden stop when Mirae didn't move with him. She stepped away, Jaeger's arm falling limply to his side.

"Mirae," Cohdel growled. "We have to move!"

"I-I can't!" she stuttered. Her heart pounded faster, bruising her ribcage as she stepped back from them. "How can I face them? I failed them! This is all my fault!"

"Mirae, now is not the time," Brecken hissed, nervously looking over his shoulder.

"You warned me." She pointed to Brecken, finger shaking. "You told me not to do this and I didn't listen!"

"Your Majesty," Cohdel murmured, softening his voice as he took a cautious step toward her. "You mustn't blame yourself for this tragedy. No one could've predicted—"

"Brecken did!" Mirae shouted, tangling her hands in her hair.

"Enough!" Brecken dragged Jaeger forward, transferring him to Cohdel. "Take him to the camp."

"What are you going to do?" Cohdel asked, grunting as he leaned in to hold Jaeger upright.

"Just take him, he'll die if you don't go now."

Cohdel didn't need anymore encouragement, turning away hastily. Brecken stepped in front of her, blocking her view of the retreating men. The only light to be had now was the glow of the blazing fields behind them, creating an eerie golden mist around the two of them.

"Now, if you want to stand here and feel sorry for yourself while the enemy catches up with us, fine, that's what we'll do."

"Sorry for myself?" Mirae shook her head, tears falling unchecked down her cheeks. "How can you say that?"

"Because that's what this is!" He grabbed her by the arms, tugging her roughly toward him. "You are a queen who made a choice, Mirae

Sundragon. That's what rulers do! They make choices. Sometimes they end in victory, sometimes they don't! You know this!"

"But I ... I ..." Mirae could barely breathe, every word painful. "I never lost so many before. The cost was never so high before."

Brecken raised his hands to her face, cupping her cheeks in his rough palms. "You knew taking Tears would be the hardest thing you ever did, Mirae. We all knew we might fail."

"But you—"

He shook his head, silencing her. "The truth is, even if we'd done things my way, I fear the results would've been the same."

"But Lara and Griyer! And Braven! How can I leave them behind to rot on the field?"

"You lost people you loved today, but all we can do to honor their memory now is keep fighting. You *have* to return to your people, Mirae. *Now*."

A heavy wind rushed through the forest, followed by a sharp whistle as the clouds converged above them.

"Creator's Night, not again." Mirae shoved him away, sword screeching against the sheath when she yanked the weapon loose.

Brecken did the same, turning so they were back to back. Mirae watched the darkness begin to descend like billowing smoke toward the ground.

"Yet another mistake I made," she whispered. "If I hadn't stopped you, then we wouldn't both be facing certain death."

"Mirae," Brecken grumbled. "You blame yourself far too much for things you cannot control, and it is quite tiresome. They would've found us whether we'd been on the move or not, because they're after you. Remind me to put you over my knee when we make it back to the camp."

"You wouldn't dare."

"Try me." He swung his blade a few times, the heavy *swoosh* of the steel slicing air resounding in her ears.

Mirae's chest swelled, the air filling her lungs painfully. The first cloud began to roll from the sky, slowly taking the form of a Wraith Spawn, the creature's claw reaching out of the smoke toward her.

"Here we go again," Brecken mumbled.

With a cry, Mirae thrust her blade into the cloud.

199

Wraith Spawn blood was hot. Thick, black, the scalding substance splashed onto Brecken's face, followed by a chilling scream before the creature dissolved into ash. He twisted around, slamming back into Mirae once more as they waited for another group to descend. They were taunting them, coming down in groups of twos or threes to exhaust them, to steal their will to survive. How had Raphaela summoned such a force? How had she created such an evil thing as this? Until they'd charged the embankment at Tears, he hadn't truly known what the shadow overhead held.

Now I do. A legion of Wraith Spawn, simply waiting to fall upon us and take us to our deaths.

"What are they waiting for?" Mirae said, breathlessly.

"Did you think Raphaela would allow you to get away with an easy death?" Brecken replied.

"No, I suppose not."

Another shadow exploded to the ground, rising menacingly into the form of a creature so many had thought were only a myth not long ago. Only those who'd lived in the woods their whole lives knew the Wraith Spawn had always been real, elusive creatures of evil, only revealing themselves when called upon by the Abyss. Brecken watched as the creature took form, the black body nearly blending completely with the darkness, bulging yellow eyes glaring at him and long, protruding teeth dripping with dark saliva.

He lifted his sword, waiting for the thing to attack, when a soft cry echoed from within the thick of the trees. His weapon faltered in his hand when the figure appeared, dropping a flaming silver torch in the snow as she charged toward the creature.

Brecken watched the petite redhead slide across the icy ground, her long, straight hair whipping behind her in the wind and bright green eyes full of excitement. With one sharp swing of her arm, the Wraith Spawn shrieked, catapulting through the air before bursting into flames. She turned, her gaze colliding with his.

Brecken dropped his sword.

Brae?

But she couldn't be. The girl could be no more than fifteen, the soft baby roundness in her face and wide innocence in her eyes evidence of a child. Then, behind her, a woman appeared. Dark hair separated in multiple braids and the black uniform of the Eventide Sisters suggested

Draedinian roots. She leaned in, whispering something to the girl before giving her a gentle push forward.

The redhead approached him cautiously, lily-white hands gripping handfuls of her blue skirts. She stopped a few feet away from him, staring as intently at him as he was at her.

"Brae?" he whispered hoarsely.

She shook her head. "No, not Brae. Noelle, Papa. Your daughter."

Brecken stumbled back, her image blurring behind the mass of tears flooding his eyes. Then, just beyond her, he saw him. Maxx came alongside the Draedinian woman, resting a cautious hand on her shoulder. His younger brother looked exhausted, the lines around his eyes more defined with whatever he'd been through and a fresh growth of stubble shadowing his face. His eyes told Brecken the truth.

"This ... this is impossible ..."

"I have magic, Papa," Noelle continued, the sweet lilt in her voice like a comforting song. "The Creator makes this—makes me—possible."

Before he could take another breath to speak, she launched into his arms, throwing hers around his neck. She was still small, her feet dangling a foot off the ground as she clung to his shoulders. Slowly, he wrapped his arms around her, his heart thundering louder in his chest.

"I'm so sorry, Papa!" Noelle wept. "I'm so sorry about Mama!"

Brecken turned his face against her hair, breathing deeply. She smelled like lavender and honey, the same way she'd smelled the last time he held her.

"Creator's Blessing," he gasped, throat tightening. "It's really you!"

"Yes!" Noelle hugged him tighter. "I'm here now. We're going to be fine!"

"Brecken." Mirae's whisper made him raise his head.

A line of torches began to appear among the trees, silhouettes forming in the darkness. The numbers were indeterminate in the deepness of the shadow, but they were filling the woods behind Maxx.

An army.

"You're my Aunt Mirae," Noelle said, stepping away from Brecken. "Uncle Maxx has told me about you."

Mirae looked between him and his daughter, eyes narrowing. "I don't understand."

"I'll explain everything," Maxx said, the exhaustion in his voice worrying. "First, we should get to safety."

Brecken nodded his agreement, snatching Noelle back to his side. They started to move toward the crowd among the trees, Mirae staying close to his back with sword still clutched in both hands.

"Brecken watch out!" Maxx rushed forward just as Brecken heard the menacing swoosh of a Wraith Spawn taking form.

He spun, shoving Noelle behind him to raise his blade—then froze.

The creature's bulbous eyes were twice as big, his body jerking and convulsing with every grunt emanating from his bleeding lips. Brecken had never seen anything like it, the thought a Wraith Spawn could be in pain unimaginable. Then he saw her.

Afra stood behind the creature, her formerly ethereal appearance now cast in a grey mist, the veins in her eyes darkened to black lines as she held her hands out toward the creature, sucking an ash-like substance from him.

The Wraith Spawn's soul.

Brecken moved around the creature, taking slow precise steps as it seemed locked in place, unable to move.

"Afra," he said quietly. "What are you doing?"

His sister groaned, fingers clenched as she drew on the soul of the creature even harder.

"Did you think my power was limited, brother?" she asked with a heavy breath. "Did you think I could take only a willing soul? Only a pure soul?"

A drop of blood rolled from her nose, leaving a line of red over her lips. She shuddered violently, drawing more of the Wraith Spawn's soul into her hands, the being fighting back, trying to pull its life back into the body.

"I can take any soul at any time," Afra continued. "And I will do so to save the people I love."

"Afra," Maxx murmured, approaching from her other side. "Sister, you're hurting yourself. Please stop this."

"If there is any soul that deserves to be ripped from the body, it's the soul of a Black One!" Afra screamed. "You don't know what I've seen, Maxx! You don't understand!"

"I understand only as you kill this thing, you're also killing yourself!" Maxx reached out, his hand hovering over hers, nearly touching. "Please, sweetheart, let go."

"Listen to him, Afra," Brecken urged. "Listen to both of us. This isn't you. This isn't what you are meant for. You are good and pure. Do not soil your power this way."

Afra's breath quickened, the grey pallor of her skin deepening to a deathly ash.

"I-I can't stop." Afra's eyes rolled, black tears seeping from her lids. "Brecken, help me!"

With one thrust, he put his sword through the chest of the Wraith Spawn. Afra stumbled, knees nearly buckling before Maxx grabbed her, pulling her tightly into his arms. She wrapped hers around his neck, burying her trembling body against him.

"Didn't you know?" Noelle whispered, drawing Brecken's gaze away from his brother and sister.

"What?"

"Passers can be the most dangerous creatures of magic in the world," Noelle explained, big eyes bright with curiosity. "And, during such a time as this, they can also be the most vulnerable to the Abyss. Aunt Afra is fortunate, Papa. Most Passers would've surrendered to the torment of the Abyss by now."

She stepped away before he could respond, moving to whisper something to the Eventide Sister. Brecken kept an eye on her as he approached his siblings, gently placing his hand on Afra's shoulder.

"Where have you been, Afra?" he asked. "What's happened to you?"

Afra cried harder into Maxx's shoulder.

"Maxx," a familiar voice called from the tree line.

"Klade Overlage?" Brecken's brow rose as the man emerged between the line of torches. "You survived."

Klade shrugged. "Who knew I had it in me, right? Good to see you, captain."

They clasped hands, Brecken giving the man's knuckles an extra squeeze. "Good to see you too."

"We should leave this place," he said. "We need to get Mirae to safety."

"The camp shouldn't be far." Mirae appeared at his side, her nervous gaze moving between Afra and the Eventide Sister. He'd nearly forgotten she was there, her unusual silence worrying. "How did you find us?"

"Your sister sent us, my lady," Klade replied.

"Adlae?" Mirae breathed the name, the sadness in her eyes beginning to dim beneath a spark of hope. "You've seen Adlae?"

"She and Jabon Malaki were headed to the far north when we parted. Her orders were clear. We are to join your forces and she will find us when her task is done."

"What task? What other task could she have than to take back our father's throne?"

Klade's brow arched. He turned, pointing up into the sky.

"I'm not certain, Mirae. But I think perhaps her task has something to do with the fire in the sky."

Brecken squinted into the rooftop of tree branches, watching the circle of flames turn, brighter and hotter than ever before. A small body pressed against his side, drawing his attention away. Noelle cuddled at his waist, circling both arms around him.

"We need to leave here, Papa."

"I agree," Maxx said. He'd picked up Afra, cradling her in his arms like a baby. Her eyes were closed, deep breaths whispering between her slightly parted lips. "Afra needs help, Brecken."

The Eventide Sister approached, laying her fingertips against their sister's forehead.

"Yes, she does," the woman murmured. "Not the sort you can give her, either. I must have a quiet place to tend to her."

Brecken squeezed Noelle's shoulders. They turned deeper into the trees, moving slowly toward the soldiers' torchlight. The silhouettes began to move, Klade vanishing amongst them as he pushed forward with Mirae to lead the way.

"Do you think Master Klade is right about the fire in the sky? Do you think Aunt Adlae has something to do with it?" Noelle wondered.

"I don't know, Noelle. I hope so." He looked down at her, his heart sinking toward the pit of his stomach all over again.

She stared up at him with those bright green eyes so much like her mother's it hurt to look at her. He patted her arm awkwardly, still trying to fully grasp the truth that this young woman was indeed his daughter.

My daughter who was four years old a week ago. A rock blocked his throat. *One thing at a time, Brecken Jandry. For now, get Noelle to safety.*

Brecken held her closer, quickening his pace to keep up with the others deeper into the forest.

CHAPTER TWENTY

A Forest with No Name

For years, the people of the Shadow Lands were feared in Sunkai. Not because of the land they called their own, shrouded under an eternal grey cloud, but because of the power running rampant in their villages. Such magic, people said, should not exist. Only those who were born to it could understand and wield this power. Sitting before their fires now, watching the women dance while the men chanted, Adlae could understand the fears of her people.

They fear what they do not understand, Winter said.

Adlae nodded, twirling a finger around the top of her staff. The snowy billows within the glass ball rolled, spinning with every twist of her finger. From the corner of her eye, she watched the Devareigh boys, her heart still in turmoil over what Healer Faw had divulged. So many secrets revealing themselves where Adlae never expected—so much for her to take in. Processing the truth in the Healer's revelation was more difficult than she ever could have imagined, especially with the ring of fire hovering over them.

"Sundragon flames to help my people within my reach, and I cannot use them," Adlae grumbled.

You will find a way.

"How?"

Winter didn't respond, the silence deafening. The tickle of someone's breath on her cheek made Adlae turn her head, eyes downcast as her body rushed with tingles from his presence.

"Will you walk with me?" Jabon asked, holding his hand out to her.

She placed her hand in his, allowing him to tug her gently to her feet beside him. He kept a hold of her, interlocking their fingers as he led her away from the camp, deeper into the darkness of the trees. Her staff began to brighten, emanating a misty light to guide them. Jabon's breath steamed in front of his face the closer he kept her to his side. She wondered how deeply he felt the chill of her touch—wondered what her skin must feel like to him. His hand felt odd, her inability to feel true warmth stealing even the memory of what his touch once felt like.

What she *could* feel were the callouses on his palm. They were harder than she remembered, the time they'd spent apart creating more scars on the man who'd stolen her heart five years ago. Adlae stared down at their twined fingers, suddenly struck by the memory of Glaydin's hand. How strange his touch had felt! The excruciating heat burning her skin whenever he'd place his hand on her arm or shoulder. The only heat she'd felt in years had come from him first, and then—in an instant—he was gone.

He is at peace now, Adlae. Soon, we will destroy the shadow that took him from you. Winter's soft presence filled her, easing some of her guilt.

"Are you going to tell me what you're thinking?" Jabon asked, stopping among the trees.

The chant of the people had softened the further they went. The distant sound of their song was strangely comforting, as if she'd heard the tune before long ago as a child. If her mother had ever taken her to the Shadow Lands when she was small, she did not remember the journey. All of Sunkai knew Queen Zelaria longed to see her home again one day, but as far as Adlae knew, her father had never allowed her to go.

Life had been difficult enough as the people of Sunkai had not been entirely accepting of a new queen from the Shadow Lands. Most wished Vihaan had chosen a bride from Quintaria or Kaldon, perhaps even a Draedinian noblewoman they could've accepted. But not a woman of the Shadow Lands.

"I was thinking," Adlae whispered. "My sister is battling her way through the Aulend while I sit and stare at a circle of fire in the sky. A weapon I cannot control but for whom I must find a wielder."

Jabon's brow arched. "Is that truly what you were thinking, or are you keeping something from me?"

Adlae winced. "You always knew when I was holding back."

"Some things don't change, Adlae."

She hummed softly in agreement, slipping her hand from his as she took a few steps away. Tilting her staff toward the sky, she summoned a breeze, reaching deeply for the snow. But the shadow was blocking her call, allowing only a fierce, frozen wind to batter against their bodies. Looking back, she saw Jabon shudder, the cold deepening the color in his face.

"Mirae and I are not the last of the Sundragon line, Jabon," she said, holding his gaze. "Sundragons have been walking the streets of Sunkai all this time and no one knew. In their own way, Dedric and Thane have a right to my father's throne as well should anything happen to me and Mirae."

"Nothing is going to happen to you, Adlae."

"You don't know that." She turned away, gripping her staff in both hands. "I simply don't understand why their existence is so difficult for me to accept. Why the thought of one of them taking the throne if both Mirae and I perish in the battle yet to come is causing such trouble in my heart."

"You have lived the last five years plotting and planning to win back this country. To take Sunkai, as is your right by blood and birthright. Your feelings about another sitting upon the throne are completely understandable." His hands pressed down on her shoulders.

"Since we left the Tower of the Dead, I have been even more confident in our victory, forgetting that some prophecies can change as the world turns. Now I begin to wonder what will happen if we fail, and the thought tortures me." Adlae groaned softly, fresh ice slithering from her fingertips around the staff. "And now here I stand in the middle of the woods, helplessly staring at a weapon that could help my sister. I am more useless now than I've ever been in my whole life!"

"And if we hadn't come here?" Jabon spun her to face him, his fingers sinking painfully into her upper arms. "You would never have discovered the flames of the Sundragon. Perhaps Healer Faw would not have found you in time for this weapon to serve its purpose. If we hadn't separated from the others when we did, then perhaps these flames would still sleep."

"What good is awakening them if I cannot wield them?" Adlae shoved out of his grasp, backing away from him. "I am the Winter Queen, Jabon. If my ice magic cannot save Nfaros from the Abyss, then why was I given such power? If only fire can save Nfaros, then why did the Creator bring me here?"

"You heard Healer Faw. You must find the wielder."

"And if I cannot bring myself to place the burden of fire magic on an unsuspecting soul?"

Jabon paused, an unspoken question lighting in his eyes. He stepped toward her, she stepped back, maintaining the distance between them.

"Adlae, do you know who the wielder is?" he asked.

Do not say! He should not ask such a question, for even we cannot know for certain. Winter cautioned.

"How can you ask me such a thing?" Adlae answered. "I may know many things, Jabon Malaki, but no one knows who is capable of wielding those flames."

"If the Sundragon line is responsible for this fire magic," Jabon said, as if she'd not spoken at all. "Then it stands to reason you once possessed fire before you were … changed."

"I never wielded any sort of power before I became the Winter Queen."

"Perhaps not, but there was always something about you and your sisters. Anyone whoever stepped into your presence felt the rush, especially when the three of you were together."

"No one will ever have such a feeling again, considering the three of us will never be together again," Adlae snapped. "Brae is dead."

Her words fell heavily between the two of them, plunging them both into uneasy silence. They stared, eyes locked, their breaths so heavy they were the only sound to be heard among the trees. Jabon shifted, the snow crunching beneath his boots and the breeze rustling his cloak. He looked older somehow, in this moment, the sadness dimming his face creating lines she hadn't noticed before.

"I know what it means to lose a sibling, Adlae. Not so long ago, I lost Brax."

"Yes, I know. Forgive me."

Adlae sighed, looking away for a moment to rest her staff against the nearest tree. When she turned back, Jabon was right in front of her, taking both her hands in his. He raised them to his lips, pressing a soft kiss on her knuckles.

Tears rushed to her eyes before she could stop them, memories of him kissing her hands the exact same way years ago coming back. He'd always greeted her this way, a warm kiss to her knuckles, her fingers disappearing in his much larger palms. He never bowed to her, as everyone else had in reverence to a princess of Sunkai. She'd never minded with him, because she'd never wanted him to bow to her.

"If none of this had happened," Adlae breathed. "If my father had not been killed and Roderick Kael had never taken the throne, I would've found a way to be with you."

Jabon smiled. "And I would've found a way to be with you."

He raised a hand, stroking the top of her hair lightly. Adlae tilted her head against his palm and closed her eyes.

"When this is over—"

"Shh." Adlae reached out, placing her fingertips on his lips. Flecks of ice crackled over his mouth, slithering and melting on his cheek. A tear slipped from her lashes and she brushed the crystal drop away hastily. "I don't want to talk about what will happen when this ends, because we do not yet know how this will end. For now, simply be here with me."

Jabon nodded, leaning forward to press his forehead against hers.

Perhaps you should tell him, Adlae Sundragon. Perhaps you should tell him what was foretold to you at the Tower of the Dead. Winter suggested.

Adlae ignored her, smoothing her hands up Jabon's arms and around his neck. He cupped her waist in his palms, drawing her nearer. Then, ever so cautiously, he tilted his mouth against hers. She sighed, her heart thundering out of control and body rushing with tingles she hadn't felt in years.

Then, for a moment—just a moment—Adlae swore she felt warmth. Genuine, human warmth from the very top of her head to the very tips of her toes. She relished the feeling, longed for it—would die for just a few moments more of this heat that simply wasn't possible for her.

Yet, even as he continued to kiss her, the wonderful feeling of warmth vanished as quickly as it arrived, leaving nothing inside except the icy chill of the Winter Queen.

Kaldon

A mix of saliva and blood seeped from the soldier's mouth. He clawed at her wrist, her fingers were clutched tightly around his throat. Raphaela lifted him a few inches off the ground. Her blood rushed hot in her veins, excitement mingling with her rage as she glowered at the messenger.

"I sent you to Tears," she hissed, spittle moistening her lips, "to kill Mirae Sundragon. So what news do you bring me from the tower? You've killed a few hundred insignificant Woodlanders and allowed the Sundragon girl to escape!"

She threw him across the room, the man crashing into the wall before crumbling to the floor in a trembling heap.

"W-We are still searching the fields, my lady!" he gasped. "We could still find her body among the carnage!"

"Do you think I am blind?" Raphaela leveled her staff toward his head. "Do you think I cannot see what is going on in every corner of Nfaros? This weapon, created for me by the Abyss himself, gives me eyes! I watched the girl slip away from you in the company of Brecken Jandry and Klade Overlage! Not only did you fail to kill her, you allowed her to run off with a *new* army! Equipped with men trained in the highest skills of warfare!"

She thrust her staff in his direction. The messenger slammed into the wall—body stiff as he was held against the stone by invisible restraints. The door behind her creaked. Roderick sauntered in, a smirk twisting his features. He crossed his arms, leaning against the wall as he looked between her and the soldier.

"Another plan of yours gone awry, Raphaela?" he mocked her. "Perhaps this interminable darkness isn't working out for you the way you expected?"

"My shadow has nothing to do with this," Raphaela snarled. "Your men are to blame for this! They let Mirae Sundragon slip through their fingers!"

"What about your legion of Wraith Spawn? Did they not also fail?"

"You begin to irritate me, brother."

"And you already irritate me, sister." Roderick took a step closer. He lowered his hands to his sides, clenching and unfurling them. "I want this darkness lifted. I want your monsters called off. You had your chance to destroy the Sundragon girls, now step aside and let me take care of them."

Arrogant boy! the Abyss shouted in her head. *Does he think he is more capable than we? Does he think he can accomplish what we cannot?*

Raphaela curled her lip. "You wouldn't last a day without me, Roderick."

"Who is king here, Raphaela? Who do the men truly follow?" He towered over her, tilting close until his nose nearly touched hers. "Me, sister. They follow me. Not you. No, you they fear, but me they respect. Their fear of you drives them to obey your orders, but have they yet succeeded in any of your missions?"

"Be quiet, Roderick." Raphaela turned away, scowling at the messenger. "Go away, now. I have punishments to administer."

"I think not." Roderick sidestepped in front of her. "Release him, Raphaela."

A thundering pulse began in her temples, pain shooting down her neck and heating her blood.

"What did you say?"

"Release him," Roderick repeated, hissing like a snake. "I am not asking, Raphaela, I am ordering you. Release this man."

Do you intend to obey him, my daughter? Who is he to order you, a powerful creature of magic? He is nothing! He does not deserve the crown! The Abyss sent a burning rush through her veins, making her entire body tremble.

Her free hand shot up, fingernails digging into the curve of Roderick's throat. Her brother's eyes went wide, fingers curling around her wrist. She barely felt the pressure of his grip on her arm, slowly lifting him an inch off his feet. He sputtered, struggling against her hold.

"Who do you think you are to command me?" she asked on a heavy breath. "You are nothing but a figurehead, Roderick. A puppet with a crown. Soon, *brother*—very soon—I will not need you anymore. Once this war is won, and the people see who truly rules their kingdom, you will be expendable."

"Y-You c-c-cannot do t-this!" Roderick panted, feet kicking frantically for solid ground. "I won Nfaros once without you! I can do so again!"

"No, you can't." Raphaela sneered. "Do you actually believe you can win a war against the Winter Queen? Against the *Almaër Dominÿe*? Our little sister is coming, Roderick, and she brings with her an army of dragon people. You may fool the stupid men who follow you into believing you have a chance against them, but they will know the truth once on the battlefield. I am the only one who can defeat Adlae Sundragon and our traitor-sister, Damari!"

She tossed him across the room. Roderick moaned painfully when he sank to the floor, cradling the side of his head where he'd hit the wall. Raphaela turned away, pointing her staff at the messenger.

"As for you," she whispered. "I have one more message for you to deliver."

"Yes, my lady," the messenger whimpered. "Anything, my lady. Just please ... spare me."

Raphaela rolled her eyes. "Oh, how they beg when death stares them in the face."

She swung the staff over her head before bringing the other end down on the messenger's chest. He seized, eyes rolling so deeply into his head she could see only the whites of them. Foam and blood burst from his mouth, the color draining from his face. His skin began to wrinkle, leaving his cheekbones prominent and eyes sunken.

A wheezing breath rushed out of him, his rapidly decaying body now lying at her feet lifeless.

Hmm ... The Abyss hummed, delighted. *Well done, my child.*

Raphaela snapped her fingers, and the guard marched inside.

"Deliver this man to Tears so the others will know my displeasure," she commanded.

The guard grimaced, lifting the body under the arms to drag him from the room. Raphaela ignored Roderick where he continued to whine on the floor, strolling leisurely across the room to the window. She stared up into the darkness, the blaring circle of fire in the sky seeming to mock her even from a distance.

"If our army cannot kill Mirae Sundragon, then surely this weapon you've given me can," Raphaela whispered.

You must strike her where she is most vulnerable, the Abyss replied. *You must destroy her before she has a chance to discover what those flames mean! Before Analli Devareigh tells her what they mean to her.*

"But if she is not vulnerable on the battlefield, then where?" Raphaela asked.

The Abyss chuckled. *Who does she love most in the world, my child?*

A slow smile tilted her mouth. "Adlae."

Yes, sweet daughter. Now is the time to attack the Winter Queen. You have command of the shadows ... now use them!

CHAPTER TWENTY-ONE

The Aulend Forest

Screams filled the air, echoing like a gong in her ears. Mirae sat beside Jaeger's cot, holding his limp hand tightly between both her palms. She could still hear Astra, her wails when Cohdel gave her the news of Braven's death still filling the camp, settling on Mirae like a shadow darker than the one covering all of Nfaros. The weight of the woman's loss had brought Mirae to her knees, no longer able to stand on her own. Quickly, her grief had been followed by the grief of others, their cries mingling with Astra's until the entire camp was overwhelmed with sorrow.

Brecken and Klade had been hunched together near the fire since they reached the camp, whispering and planning their next move. Maxx had stood quietly to the side, merely observing while keeping a close eye on the striking Eventide Sister and the young girl he claimed was Brae's daughter, until he was called away with the Draedinian woman to check on Afra. She certainly had all the features to be Mirae's niece. From the top of her red head to the tips of her worn boots, she declared herself of Sundragon blood in both looks and manner.

Now to understand how. Mirae sighed, bending over to lightly kiss Jaeger's knuckles.

He still hadn't woken, even when they cleaned and bandaged his wounds. The only signs of life left in him were his uneven breaths accompanied by pain-filled moans when they bound the gash in his side. The Eventide Sister had even attempted to use some of her power to relieve Jaeger's pain, but there'd seemed to be little improvement despite her good intentions.

Mirae jumped when Noelle appeared beside her, plopping down with legs crossed and skirts bunched. She smiled at her, green eyes sparkling in the flickering firelight coming from the center of the tent.

"How is he?" she asked, lightly tapping her fingertips together in her lap.

"No change," Mirae answered.

Noelle lifted her hand, lightly brushing a strand of Jaeger's hair from his forehead. "You care about him a great deal."

"He has been my mentor and friend since I ran from Sunkai five years ago." Mirae sighed, squeezing his fingers tighter. "I owe him my life."

"I think owing someone your life must be a very heavy burden to bear," Noelle commented.

Mirae remained silent, placing Jaeger's hand gently on his chest before she sat back. She bent her neck from side to side, stretching in an attempt to relieve some of the tension shooting down into her shoulders. Every muscle in her body burned from the recent battle, the memory of their horrifying defeat creating nearly as much physical pain as her cuts and bruises.

"I know you don't believe I am your sister's child," Noelle blurted suddenly.

Mirae's brow rose. "Noelle, I never said—"

"You didn't have to." The girl's cheeks puffed with a dramatic sigh. She scrunched her little nose, eyes narrowed to slits. "I probably wouldn't believe this possible either. Gwylan says such a thing has only happened once before, nearly twenty years ago in Draedin. My early development of magic means I'm special—that the Creator has a very specific purpose for me."

"What might that be, Noelle?" Mirae wondered.

Noelle shrugged. "No one knows. Not even Gwylan. I have no choice but to believe her because ... well ... look at me."

"I have been looking at you," Mirae replied. "The more I do, the more I begin to believe Maxx must be telling the truth. You really are Noelle Jandry. You are the image of your mother."

She stroked the girl's silky hair, her fingernail catching on one of the delicate strands. Noelle's eyes filled with tears.

"All the people I care about," she said, her voice catching. "Look at me with such pain in their eyes. I hate that I look like her, because our resemblance brings nothing but grief to those who loved her."

"Don't say such things, Noelle." Mirae put her arm around her niece's shoulders, pulling her closer. "Yes, her beauty shines within you and reminds us how we loved her. But you do not bring pain with you, Noelle. You bring hope."

"I'm glad you think so." Noelle rested her temple on Mirae's shoulder, cuddling against her side. She touched Mirae's necklace, tracing her fingertip along the dragon pendant. Mirae felt her sigh, her small shoulders rising and falling with the heavy breath.

"Can you really feel Aunt Adlae because of the necklace?" she asked.

"Yes, I can."

"Is she in trouble?"

Mirae frowned. "Why would you ask that?"

Noelle shrugged, keeping her gaze down. "I just ... I feel things too sometimes, that's all."

The girl rose before Mirae could question her further, hurrying across the tent to her father's side. Brecken stared at her for a few heartbeats, awe and split-second disbelief flashing across his face before he put his arm around her, drawing her as close as he could get her.

How long will he look at her like a stranger? Why is this happening? First, he loses Brae, then Noelle loses her childhood ... I don't understand. Mirae rubbed the tears away before they could fall, breathing deeply to calm herself.

The tent flap lifted, Maxx and the woman Noelle called Gwylan entering. Mirae pushed to her feet, moving in unison with Brecken toward the couple.

"Afra?" Brecken's voice was more a croak, worry dimming his eyes.

"Sleeping," Gwylan answered calmly. "I do not know what she was shown on her Journey, but whatever was revealed to her weakened her greatly. For a moment, I did not think I would be able to bring her back."

"Auntie Afra went on a Journey?" Noelle murmured in awe. "I ... I thought you told me Passers do not Journey anymore."

"Most don't, dear one." Gwylan's smile was compassionate as she took Noelle's hand, squeezing. "The danger is far too great. But clearly, your aunt thought a Journey was necessary."

"Why didn't she tell us what she was going to do?" Brecken asked. "Why didn't she tell *me*? I could've helped her!"

"Creatures of magic do not share such things, Brecken Jandry. Especially a Passer. Journeys are extremely personal, and whatever she saw ... well, such a thing is not for us to know unless she wishes to tell us."

"But she will recover," Mirae inquired cautiously.

Gwylan glanced up at Maxx, the uncertainty on her face raising gooseflesh on Mirae's arms.

"She has touched the soul of a Black One." Gwylan spoke slowly, as if choosing her words carefully. "If I am honest, I do not know what we'll be facing when she wakes."

The tent flap rose again. Jhase popped his head inside, a cold wind accompanying him, making the fire flicker wildly.

"Mirae, it's Astra," he said before disappearing outside again.

Mirae hurried after him, glancing back briefly at Jaeger before stepping out into the camp. She caught up to Jhase, jogging across the camp toward the edge of the circle. Astra was outside her tent, pacing back and forth mumbling to herself. Cohdel stood by, watching with hands fisted and trembling at his sides.

"Cohdel, what's wrong?" Mirae asked, trying to catch her breath.

"I don't know. I calmed her after giving her the news about Braven but now …" Cohdel raked a hand through his hair. "She just went wild! I haven't seen her this bad in a long time, Mirae. A *very* long time."

Astra shrieked, gripping handfuls of her hair as if to tear her tresses right from her scalp. Mirae lunged, grabbing the woman by the arms to pull her near. She wrapped her up in a tight hug, holding onto her to keep her as still as possible.

"Everything's all right, dearest," Mirae whispered. "You're safe."

"No!" Astra wailed, struggling against Mirae's hold.

"Please, Astra, stop!"

"NO!" Astra shoved her, stumbling away. Tears streaked her cheeks, the silver domes of her eyes shining like crystals in the darkness. "Nfaros …"

"What, Astra? What are you trying to tell me?" Mirae softly took her friend's face between her palms, massaging her cheeks soothingly with her thumbs.

"Nfaros will be won with the blood of innocents."

Mirae froze, the familiar prophecy washing through her like liquid fire. Astra gripped Mirae's wrists, her fingers digging against her pulse.

"Look around, Mirae Sundragon," she breathed. "Where are the Woodland children?"

The fire in her blood quickly turned to ice. Mirae tried to pull away, but Astra's grip was unrelenting.

"For there is no innocence like the innocence of a child. Where are the children?"

"This cannot be. You cannot mean ..."

"Look for the children, Mirae Sundragon, and know the truth." Astra released her.

Mirae didn't hesitate, sprinting across the camp. She ducked by several tents, peeking inside to search for any sign of them. The more she searched the more she recalled what had been lacking when they returned to the camp. There'd been no sound of children, no familiar patter of small feet running in the snow. No sound of light, burden-free laughter every child of the Woodlands possessed, even in this darkness.

Where are they? Creator's Night where are they! Mirae couldn't breathe, hot tears flowing down her cheeks as she moved from tent to tent, startling the inhabitants. Jhase and Cohdel were moving through the camp now as well, questioning everyone they saw. The camp began to come alive with the sounds of panic as more and more of the Woodlanders realized the children were missing.

Suddenly, she slammed into someone, nearly losing her footing. Brecken grabbed her by the arms, steadying her.

"Mirae, what's going on?"

"The children, Brecken," Mirae gasped. "They're all missing! Astra's prophecy ... the blood of innocents ... this is what she meant! The children!"

"Are you sure?"

"They're *gone*, Brecken! Of course, I'm sure!"

She shoved him aside, stumbling toward the center of the camp. Her breath came harsher—her pounding heart attempting to break her ribs.

This cannot be happening. Mirae tangled her hands in her hair, turning a full circle as she watched the camp—moments ago overwhelmed with grief—now falling into frantic chaos. Every voice seemed to be calling for a child, the sound rising to an ear-splitting timbre. She fell to her knees, covering her ears to try to drown out the sound, trembling in the foot-deep snow.

Then, as quickly as the sound rose, it fell. Mirae lowered her hands from her ears slowly, looking over her shoulder at the sound of Brecken's voice bellowing on the wind.

"Quiet!" he shouted above all the other voices, bringing every eye onto himself. "Listen!"

She frowned, brushing the snow from her breeches as she rose again, knees knocking together from cold or fear, she wasn't certain. Brecken had managed to calm the people, everyone standing as still as could be while they obeyed his command. Mirae closed her eyes, trying to listen. Trying to hear anything above the sound of her own beating heart.

The sound came softly. Distantly, beyond the camp, within the trees she could hear them singing. The language she didn't know, but the sound … the tune … so light and sweet. Such a song could melt the heart of the coldest of creatures. The innocence in their tiny voices carrying on the wind to bathe her in a warmth she hadn't felt since the first snow fell.

"I can hear them!" one of the women exclaimed. "Can't you hear them?"

Mirae opened her eyes, gaze colliding with Brecken's.

"They're outside the circle!"

They turned in unison, racing toward the sound. Brecken grabbed one of the torches at the edge of the circle, never breaking stride. Their voices were getting louder as Mirae weaved around the trees. The snow was deeper here, fighting her haste to get to the children before the shadows fell upon them in the form of Wraith Spawn.

Rounding another cluster of trees, Mirae came to a halt, Brecken bumping into her from behind. He started to speak, and she held up her hand, silencing him as she watched. The children—perhaps fifteen in all—had gathered in a circle, surrounding the Sister of the Creed. She still rocked, moaning in pain with black saliva dripping from the corner of her mouth. She was worse than she'd been before Mirae left her in the wagon, her eyes overflowing with bloody tears and her skin a sickly green.

The children continued to sing, holding hands and swaying side to side with the tune. She'd never seen children their age so serene, so focused. They took no notice of her or Brecken as they approached cautiously, keeping a small distance while following the circle the children had formed.

The song stopped. Everyone went still, the children's faces brightening with big grins as they glanced between each other. One of the little boys stepped forward, a rock carved into a tiny blade clutched in his hand.

"Rickai," Brecken murmured. He moved forward, but Mirae grabbed his arm, stopping him before he could interrupt.

"I don't think this is what we thought," she whispered.

"What else could this be? The child has a weapon!"

"Brecken please, let's just … wait."

Rickai looked back at them suddenly, his eyes full of such pure, unadulterated happiness looking into them was almost painful to her grieving heart.

"The Abyss cannot have her now," the little boy announced.

Mirae held her breath as he lifted the stone blade. Then, he turned the weapon, pressing the sharp point to the tip of his finger. A tiny drop of blood formed, rolling down the length of his finger before he reached for the Sister. Rickai drew a line across the woman's forehead, tracing two more over her cheeks before finishing by running his finger along her lips.

"The Abyss cannot live inside what the innocent have touched," Rickai said, sounding more like a grown man than a child.

"We have to get them back inside the circle, Mirae," Brecken hissed near her ear.

Mirae waved him off, watching the Sister of the Creed double over, hugging her stomach. Rickai backpedaled, rejoining the children's little circle. Tiny gasps echoed from their mouths when black tendrils began to pour out of the Sister, slithering along the ground before vanishing altogether beneath the snow.

The substance seemed to liquefy when it touched the ground, disintegrating into dust before disappearing. She didn't know how long the process took—she didn't care. The piece of the Abyss that had possessed the Sister was creeping out of her, clearing her eyes of the horrifying red to a beautiful honey-gold.

As abruptly as the darkness started seeping from her, it stopped. The Sister raised her head, clear, clean tears rolling from her eyes now and a hesitant smiling tilting her mouth. Rickai went to her, taking her hand to draw her to her feet.

"The blood of innocents," Mirae said, voice breaking. "They needn't die to save us all."

Brecken placed his hand on her shoulder, gripping tightly.

Rickai guided the Sister of the Creed out of the circle, stopping before the two of them. She took Mirae's hand, squeezing her fingers. Shivers rushed up Mirae's arm, covering her in the strangest sensation of safety.

"My name," the Sister said, her voice thick with emotion. "Is Darya."

In the Realm of Dreams ...

"You've taken me from my friends. From my family. Now you abandon me?" Clea pursed her lips, blowing a swirl of the fog away from her face. She'd turned away from the glass, unable to bear watching the events unfolding.

"You forget, you are in my domain now," his voice came to her in the distance, resounding all around her with no clear source. "I will not leave you, young heir."

"I cannot promise you I will consider the flower's safety over my own people. But I can promise you the Summer Flower will never be used for selfish purposes. Only to bring justice and peace to a world rife with mayhem and evil."

"And if you win? Will you put the flower away so it may not bring strife and temptation to any other?"

Clea looked down at the blossom, stroking her fingers over the petals. "Yes. I swear I will return the Summer Flower to its home beneath the tower once this is all over."

His silence covered her like a shroud, the mist thickening and moistening her skin. When he spoke again, the words were a mere whisper from far away.

"Then I release you to see the Creator's will done."

The ground fell out from beneath her feet, her scream slicing the air as she fell down, down, down ...

CHAPTER TWENTY-TWO

Molderëin

"Form ranks! Morgren, get them into lines!" Grange shouted, pushing through the cluster of soldiers gathered in the courtyard. He already had bowmen stationed on the battlements, foot soldiers scattered in the city, attempting to evacuate citizens from their homes and within the safety of the tower walls.

When the clouds had begun to descend, Kalea warned him now was the time to begin preparations for battle. The shadow had grown dense, forming into groups of nearly solid round boulders, glistening like glass with churning grey-green fog inside. He didn't know what would happen when they reached the ground, but he wasn't going to be caught off guard. Kalea's word that danger was to be had, and soon, was good enough for him.

Now if only our queen would awaken from her sleep. He bellowed, his orders resounding against the towers. Morgren's voice joined his own, pushing the nervous soldiers into line, snarling at each of them.

A long time had passed since they'd had to form ranks, since they'd had to take up their swords to defend Molderëin. One of the largest armies in all of Nfaros and they were horribly out of practice. Their training had slacked, in no small part due to his father's negligence and false sense of security.

A Lord Ruler who thought nothing could touch him or his city. Now he rots in a cell and I, his son, am not sorry for it. Grange attempted to push those thoughts from his mind, making his way toward the gates.

"Molten!" Nadav, his right-hand man, shoved his way through the group of soldiers rushing about, trying to get themselves into proper formation. "We need to choose some men to stand guard over the Peace Bridge. The shadow grows strong above the passage."

Grange cringed, turning in the direction of the bridge. Hundreds of miles long, wider than the most spacious street in the city, the Peace Bridge was the only manmade link between Molderëin and the outskirts of Sunkai. A journey across the bridge would take days—perhaps weeks depending on the pace of the travelers. If one didn't take the overpass, they would be forced to go by sea, a form of travel most didn't care for.

"All right, Nadav, take—"

"Riders!" Morgren yelled.

Grange jogged toward the gate, Nadav on his heels as the clatter of horses' hooves on the cobblestone filled the city. By the sound, he'd say at least a hundred men on horseback were racing down the streets, heading straight for them.

"Keep preparing the men, Nadav," Grange said, trying to catch his breath as he pulled his sword. "Morgren, with me."

The older man nodded, placing an arrow to his bow as they moved together out of the gate. Grange glanced at Morgren when they stopped just outside the walls. They hadn't really spoken since Clea had fallen into her slumber, only barking orders back and forth at each other when the shadow had grown darker. If there was one thing to unite the two of them, it was their common knowledge and skill in battle.

A group of at least twenty horses came around the corner, the rest halting, hiding their remaining numbers from Grange's sight. Cloths covered their noses and mouths, hiding most of their faces. They wore no uniforms, instead ragged coats and filthy britches with worn out boots. His stomach burned, blood rushing like a raging river through his veins—the familiar tingle of power seething through his body. He reached out to the lead rider, feeling for any sign of hostility. They were heavily armed, that he could see, but searching deeper, he felt no intent from them to attack.

The lead rider came to a halt a few feet in front of them, his brownish-blonde hair an unusual sight in Molderëin, dark eyes glistening above the edge of his kerchief. Swinging his leg over his horse's neck he slid from the saddle, a strange clatter accompanying his landing. Grange frowned as the man sauntered slowly toward him, holding the torch in his other hand higher for a better look at the stranger.

He wasn't what one would consider to be a tall man, but his lean figure and long legs gave him the illusion of being so. Neither could he be described as appearing overly strong, with long thin arms and square shoulders. Despite this he carried himself with confidence, head tilted proudly and eyes full of sparkling mischief.

But what caught Grange's eye in the end, were the objects hanging from his belt. Iron chains equipped with cuffs. The source of the noise he'd made when he dismounted.

Glárdëon! Grange's upper lip curled.

"What do you want here?" he asked, tightening his grip on his sword.

The stranger yanked down the cloth, revealing a toothy grin. "Well, well, well, the mighty Grange Molten doesn't recognize me."

"Should I?" Grange squinted, looking closer at the young man. His accent was more suited to the north, another reason his presence here—as well as his occupation as the leader of the *Glárdëon*—was so odd.

"How many years did we train side by side before your father saw fit to throw me from the city?" The stranger moved closer, thumbs hooked in his belt and chains thumping against his leg. "How many years since I was forced to survive the only way I could outside these walls?"

"As a slave trader?" Morgren growled.

"I would not speak of things you know nothing about!"

Grange's forehead smoothed, brow raised. "Shay. Shay Landorin!"

Shay raised his arms, palms up to either side of him. "One and the same."

"I thought you long dead!" Grange thrust his blade back into the sheath at his belt.

"We can go over my history later. For now, we are here to help." Shay turned, moving back toward his horse.

"Why?" Morgren asked.

Shay paused, looking over his shoulder. "Why not?"

"You are *Glárdëon*," Morgren spat the word. "I have friends who were sold by the likes of you. You care for nothing but yourself and your own survival."

Shay smirked. "You may believe what you wish of me, but I would gladly shed these chains in exchange for a sword to use in defense of my country."

"You're no Molderëinian."

Shay lunged at the man. Grange stepped quickly between them, laying his hand flat on his old friend's chest to hold him at bay.

"We have no time for this!" Grange glared between the two of them. Then he settled on Shay, giving him an extra push backward. "If you remove those chains from your belt right now, then perhaps I will believe you."

Shay looked into his eyes, his hand hovering over the offensive articles. The men behind him shifted, their horses dancing about on the cobblestone nervously as the shadow overhead roared with muted thunder. In one swift move, he unhooked the chains. They dropped with an echoing *clack* onto the stones at Grange's feet.

"There," Shay said with a smirk. "Satisfied?"

"Are you truly going to tell me you believe he is walking away from his trade because of this?" Morgren gestured to the chains in disgust.

"We need the men," Grange replied under his breath. "And we're running out of time."

"I have no intention of picking up those chains when this is over," Shay announced. "This is my chance to be what I was always meant to be. I was trained as a soldier when I was a boy before I was unjustly banished from this city. I did what I had to."

"You mentioned that." Morgren put his bow away. Then he looked at Grange, the thunderclouds in his eyes darkening his entire face. "I will not march beside him."

He strode within the tower walls without a backward glance. Grange watched him go, knowing he could handle Morgren later if he had to.

"I need you to hold the Peace Bridge," Grange said, looking back at Shay.

Shay sneered. "With pleasure."

He jumped lithely back into the saddle, spinning the animal harshly around. His men followed without question, stampeding north toward the bridge. Grange shook off the surprise of his old friend's reappearance, backing away into the courtyard. Now was not the time for memories. The shadow's rumblings were growing louder, the threat coming closer with every passing moment.

Turning, he ran smack into Kalea. She looked up at him with her wide, white-diamond eyes, pupils shuddering into horizontal lines and amethyst-colored skin glowing. She was wearing a thin, cream-colored dress, the skirt cut with two long slits to allow freer movement and haltered around her neck to keep the back open. The style reminded him of a Draedinian woman he once met—just as revealing and scandalous.

"Has she woken?" he asked, hoping beyond hope.

Kalea shook her head. "I am sorry, Grange Molten. She still sleeps."

He thrust a hand through his hair. "Have we cleared the city?"

"No, the men are still trying but—"

A heady *whoosh* from behind distracted them both. He faced the gates, standing shoulder to shoulder with the dragon woman as the black globes began to descend, fading into billows of smoke before shaping into the creatures northerners called Wraith Spawn. They landed on the streets, screams hastily following as the remaining citizens scattered, looking for an escape.

"Creator's Mercy," Grange whispered hoarsely. "How is this possible?"

The sharp tear of skin, followed by a strange rustling noise, made him turn his head. Kalea's eyes shimmered with determination, jaw clenched firmly. Behind her, soft lavender wings lifted from her back, sloping and rising in perfect curves.

"Let us ponder the how later," she said. "The war has come to Molderëin."

She shot into the sky, her wings carrying her with incredible speed toward the shadow. A burst of purple flames released from her palms, igniting one of the shadows before the creature could reach the ground. Yanking the weapon from its sheath, Grange raised the blade high, looking over the sea of men before him, spears clutched in their hands and armor glistening in the quivering torchlight.

"Soldiers of Molderëin!" he bellowed. "Defend our city in the name of the Creator and our Queen!"

The ends of their spears clapped against the ground, a resonating rumble filling the air. The billows were descending in the hundreds now, shrieks of the creatures flooding his ears. Grange charged, the thunder of the soldiers boots pounding the cobblestone following after him. Red lightning shot down from the blackened sky, sending a streak of pink light across the streets as the city erupted with the sound of battle.

Someone had changed her clothes.

This was the first thought Clea had as her eyes fluttered open. She was wearing thin, white shirtsleeves with a black sleeveless bodice clinging to her waist and hips, falling down into a flowing split skirt. Upon her feet, someone had placed a snug pair of black boots, shimmering as if freshly shined. The cool sensation of the silver circlet across her forehead, fastened securely in the two small braids holding her hair from her face sent a tingle through her cheeks.

Beside her on the bed, the *Kläerjaen* rested, the hilt rubbing against her elbow. Around her right arm, the Summer Flower coiled tightly, solid like another part of her body. Pulsing with a heartbeat all its own and reawakening the strength of her own magic deep in her soul. Her hand slid from her midriff, curling around the hilt of the sword. Clea sat up gradually, lifting the blade from the mattress when she placed her feet on the floor.

Every part of her body felt light, her muscles aching as she took slow, deliberate steps toward the window. The desperate sounds of battle raged through the city, pounding feet and screams of agony flying on the wind. Clea stared through the glass, chest tightening when she saw Grange struggling through the crowds of Wraith Spawn flooding the streets.

She walked away, shuffling from the room, the tip of her blade screeching against the stone floors. Clea made her way down the hall toward the bridge between the towers, laying her palm flat on the door to press it open. The bottom scraped on the floor, hinges groaning in protest. A harsh wind caught her hair the moment she stepped outside, whipping the dark strands in front of her face to temporarily blind her.

"Clea?" Rheatha's hesitant call drew her eyes up.

Her faithful maidservant was standing in the middle of the bridge with Izeana at her side, bow and arrows ready should the creatures scale the walls. Clea lifted the *Kläerjaen* toward one of the torches, watching the flames glint off the markings etched into the flat of the blade.

"Protect the towers," she ordered, her voice throaty. Then she raised her eyes to the sky, watching as lavender flames cut through the darkness, attempting to hold the creatures at bay.

Inhaling deeply, Clea charged, leaping over the edge of the bridge and raising her left arm toward the sky.

"Kalea!" she shouted as she began to drop toward the ground.

A hand gripped her wrist, halting her fall before carrying her over the walls, racing above the chaos of the battle below. Grange seemed to be gaining control of the streets, urging the men forward with his courage.

Beyond, the darkness was growing fiercer, Wraith Spawn beginning to descend on the one link between Molderëin and Sunkai.

"To the Peace Bridge!" Clea ordered.

Kalea turned, lifting Clea high over the stone buildings, past the high peaks of the mountains before dropping her toward the ground once more. They landed hard, Clea's ankles throbbing as she slid against the loose pebbles before coming to a final halt at the edge of the Peace Bridge. Her heart was nearly bursting in her chest, watching as the Black Ones took their true form, raising their heads with guttural cries and claws slashing the air. Kalea landed beside her. With a wave of her hand, a blade of pure fire took shape from her fingers, the crackling hilt landing in her palm at the ready.

"And who might you be?" an unfamiliar voice asked.

Clea looked over her shoulder, finding the owner of the voice standing close. He was holding a flail in each hand, the spiked balls swaying on their chains when he shifted, anxiously waiting for the fight that was coming. Behind him stood at least two hundred men, each holding similar crude weaponry and not a plate of armor among them. She was struck, briefly, by the leader's lack of true Molderëinian features before returning her attention to the bridge.

"I am your queen," she answered.

Sword held high, she charged, meeting the Wraith Spawn on the bridge. Kalea remained at her side, swinging her fiery blade, violet flames glowing in the darkness as she sliced through the onslaught of creatures. Clea's light burst from her right hand, the Summer Flower humming on her arm. The power from the bloom surged through her, her light brighter than ever as she released it on the creatures, the *Kläerjaen* shining through the black blood now staining the steel.

"Look!" one of the men shouted. "In the sky!"

Clea spun as the soldiers surrounded her, holding off the attack while she stared stunned into the sky. Wings of all sizes and colors began to appear overhead, taking the form of the Mountain People as they descended on the city. In the distance, the thunder of boots reached her, entering the city from the direction of the Nfaros Sea.

"They've come," Kalea breathed. "I wasn't certain …"

Clea couldn't speak. She watched as the People of the Dragon swooped on the city, gathering children in their arms who'd not made the towers before the attack began. Lifting straggling men and women right off their feet before shooting back into the sky, carrying them away to safety.

Then one descended in a rush, landing in the middle of the chaos. Her azure wings rose against her back, a wider span than any of the others Clea had spotted so far, her arms entirely ablaze with flames the color of a clear, clean sky. She raised them, streams of fire gushing from her hands, engulfing the Wraith Spawn in a raging blue inferno.

"Navaria!" Kalea exclaimed, clutching her chest. "She survived the northern lands!"

Clea spun with a gasp, thrusting the *Kläerjaen* up into the chest of a Black One. The creatures had broken the line of soldiers who'd circled around to protect them, forcing Clea back into the fight. She raised her hand, preparing to unleash another torrent of light when something—or someone—dropped in the thick of the enemy. Clea's eyes bugged as she watched the man battle his way through the enemy, practically using his bare hands on some of them before he came to stand before her.

He was tall—taller than she remembered him—with arms so corded with muscle he could tear a Wraith Spawn completely in half without the use of the wide-curved blade in his hand. His black hair was longer, bare chest glistening with sweat, illuminating his lightly sun-kissed skin. A tear rolled down her cheek when her eyes met his. For no matter how else he'd changed, there was no mistaking those beautiful blue eyes she loved so much.

"Lathan!"

Her big brother grinned, then together they turned, weapons raised and backs pressed together to protect each other as they fell into the fray.

CHAPTER TWENTY-THREE

Damari rose high in the sky, watching Zorina lead the Draedinian army through the gates of the city. They had the Wraith Spawn surrounded on either side now, the Molderëinian soldiers pressing them back from the towers while Zorina pushed them toward the center of the city. The shadow was beginning to retreat with her presence, rolling back toward the Peace Bridge, clearing the sky behind her.

The rumbling voice, vibrating from the center of the shadow, called out to her, "So, we meet again. Will you pursue me to the ends of the earth, *Almaër Dominjë?*"

"If I must," Damari replied softly.

"Then why don't you come closer?"

The evil thing had retreated to the Peace Bridge, leaving the Wraith Spawn in the city to fend for themselves. The clouds coiled, spitting red fire above the heads of Clea and Lathan as they battled with a troupe of Molderëinian soldiers, their numbers lessening by the moment as the soldiers began to fall under the overpowering strength of the Wraith Spawn. Only a small group surrounded by the creatures remained, a dragon woman among them as they formed around Clea like a wall of protection.

Damari shot across the sky, hovering above Lathan in moments, wings spread wide as she faced the darkness. She squinted into the black clouds, watching them roll. They appeared to form a face—a horrible, twisted face with eyes deep and dark as coals. An endless chasm staring back at her with such malicious intent she thought her fire would snuff out, taking the very life from her. The shadow felt stronger here, pulsing like a heartbeat before her very eyes.

Below her, the Wraith Spawn were sucked away, pulled from the Peace Bridge against their will once more into the shadow. The remaining Molderëinian soldiers below tilted their heads back, staring up at the darkness expectantly. Their weapons wavered in their hands, curiosity lighting their faces as they waited to see when or if another attack would come.

"You will leave this place," Damari ordered, voice rough. "Just as you left Draedin, you will leave Molderëin and never return."

"You banish me further and further to the north. Do you think you can follow me even there? That you could stop me once I retreat to those shores? For I have already destroyed the place you so lovingly call the Mother City!"

Damari inhaled sharply, lungs aching with the withheld breath.

The shadow's face seemed to smirk. "You cannot destroy me, only chase me away."

"I can try." Damari snapped her wings, flames licking at her body from the tips of her toes, up her legs, over her hips until nearly her entire body was engulfed in the pure white fire.

"Damari, no!" Lathan shouted, his voice muted as if even farther away than he was.

Ignoring his call, she flew straight into the face of the shadow, shattering the image in a billow of black smoke. Darkness consumed her as she soared through, her fire steadily streaming from her body, fending off the oil-black tendrils attempting to snatch and trap her. Chilling laughter roared all around her, and Damari stopped, her flames crackling on her skin, beginning to fade. The black vines twisted all around her, closing in on her slowly.

"I *will* banish you from this city," Damari hissed. "One way or another."

"Perhaps," the shadow replied. "But what destruction will you sow by doing so?"

Damari frowned, faltering. One of the vines snapped out, wrapping tightly around her wrist. She cried, out, sending a ball of flame against her captor. Her attempt did little good, another tendril binding around her waist and wings to pin them against her back. She struggled, stomach churning with sudden fear. Closing her eyes, she delved deep within herself, strengthening her power until she was engulfed in her flames. Even her hair blazed, yet didn't burn away, every single inch of her a weapon against the evil holding her captive. The vines started to sizzle, light grey smoke rising as they began to burn away.

The laughter increased, rising to an ear-splitting bellow. "Foolish little *Almaër Dominÿe*. How will you save your precious Mother City if there is no bridge for the Molderëinian people to cross?"

Damari wheezed, the black ropes attempting to choke the breath out of her.

"How will your ships fit the entire Molderëinian army? For I have destroyed the entire fleet of Molderëin ships, and now … now you have helped me destroy the Peace Bridge!"

Damari screamed as she was shoved down, falling at a rapid pace, her flames still burning wildly all around her as she desperately attempted to break herself free. Her wings burst forth first, snapping the vines away. But as quickly as she broke them, more came, twisting around her even harder as she plummeted toward the bridge below.

"Everyone off the bridge!"

Lathan backed away slowly, the few surviving Molderëinians pushing past him in their haste to evacuate the Peace Bridge. Clea was pulling on his arm, her hand slick with black Wraith Spawn blood. Her pleas for him to leave the bridge were muffled in his ears. All he could see were the white flashes of Damari's fire, blasting through the shadows.

He stumbled over the edge of the bridge, Clea snagging his waist with her arm to hold him steady as she tried to pull him even further from the danger. The darkness was descending hastily toward the overpass, bringing the dimming light of Damari's fire with it. Lathan clenched his fist, tapping the point of his blade against the cobblestones.

"Come on, love," he whispered. "Get out of there."

"What's happening?" Clea asked, breathlessly. "What is she doing?"

"I don't know."

"She is trying to burn the shadow from the inside," the dragon woman with his sister said. "A valiant attempt but unlikely to succeed."

Lathan glared at her. "You don't know my girl."

She arched a brow. "Though you look like one who has been reborn as one of my people, I will understand the power of an *Almaër Dominÿe* better than you ever will, northerner."

"Kalea," Clea said, a hint of warning in her tone. "Please do not speak to my brother in that manner."

Kalea dipped her head slightly in respect but still eyed Lathan guardedly. He returned his attention to the shadows. They were tumbling now, like black boulders rolling from a mountain toward the bridge. A few balls of red fire dove from within the billows, slamming into the Peace Bridge, breaking the stones apart and scattering bits of rock. Clea leaped back, her grip so firm she brought him with her.

"Lathan Jandry!" Evingar's voice boomed behind him. Lathan turned, watching the man shove his way through the soldiers grouped behind him. "The shadow intends to take the bridge! We must—"

He came to an abrupt halt, eyes locked on Kalea. Lathan looked between the two of them, frowning when Kalea's breath seemed to hitch and Evingar's eyes welled.

"You ... you're alive," Evingar whispered.

Kalea smiled warmly. "Hello, brother."

In two strides, Evingar had her in his arms, lifting her right off her feet in a tight embrace. Lathan's momentary confusion over the exchange vanished when the bridge cracked loudly behind them. He spun, watching in horror as the shadow crashed into the stone, spitting rock in every direction.

"Damari!"

He surged toward the bridge, but Clea still had a hold of him, dragging him back instead of forward.

"Lathan, it's too late!" she shouted before her voice was swallowed by the explosion.

They fell back. The force of the shadow, combined with Damari's fire, hitting the bridge, lifted them right off their feet. Lathan slammed into the solid stone ground, head spinning and ears ringing, blocking all other sounds. He couldn't move—could only stare up into the sky, watching the shadow fade into bright, thin white strips of cloud gliding across a blanket of stars.

A resounding crack tore through the air. Lathan's temples ached as he raised his head, his vision clearing as he watched the center of the bridge collapse, crashing into the sea below. Bursts of water sprang into the air like a fountain as half of the structure came down one piece at a time. Flaming boulders still rocketed from the shadow as the black clouds rolled away from Molderëin, clearing more and more of the sky.

"No!" Lathan struggled to his feet, shuffling around the debris. He crawled desperately toward what remained of their half of the bridge, looking for any sign of her fire.

"Lathan, stop!" His sister grabbed him, clinging to his waist.

She pulled him onto his feet, her cheek pressed firmly against the center of his back and her arms folded across the front of his belly. She had her fingers locked together against his ribs, keeping him where he was. He felt the cool moisture of her tears on his bare skin.

"She's gone," Clea whispered. "It's over."

Lathan clasped his hand over hers, squeezing her fingers as tight as he could without hurting her. His whole body ached with a pain that had nothing to do with the fall he'd taken when the bridge collapsed.

The dust was settling, pieces of the bridge still splashing into the water while the shadow above continued to retreat from Molderëin across the Nfaros Sea toward Sunkai, deepening the darkness to the north.

"What was it all for if not to destroy this evil?" Lathan hissed. "Now she's died a meaningless death."

"Don't say such things!" Clea swept around to face him. She took his face in her hands, forcing him to look down at her. "She tried, Lathan, as we all did."

Clea swept her thumb in a gentle circle on his cheek, the press of something solid between one of her fingers and his skin making him frown. He took hold of her right hand, turning her wrist so her knuckles were before his face. The blossom on her finger was like none he'd ever seen before—warm and throbbing, as if alive.

"Clea what have you done?" he asked. "What is this?"

"I will explain everything later. For now—"

A heavy rustle, followed by the scrape of movement on the destroyed bridge, interrupted her. Lathan moved around her, throat drying when he breathed in the remaining dust in the air, stepping carefully around broken rock and strewn bodies. The stars were at their brightest now, surrounding the most beautiful moon he'd seen in days, glowing white light down on the quieting city.

First, he saw her wings, tainted with smoke, trembling up from her shoulders. Then her head popped up, golden hair mussed and glistening

233

in the starlight. She struggled up over the edge of the bridge, groaning and panting all the way before rolling onto her back. Her body arched as her wings folded into her back, vanishing from sight. Then she settled, chest rising and falling rapidly with desperate breaths.

Damari turned over, pushing herself up on her elbow before curling her legs beneath her to sit up. Her eyes met his, face and arms smudged with ash, dimming the natural shimmer of her dragon skin. A strangled sound ripped from his throat. Lathan sprinted forward, jumping over the debris until he fell to his knees before her, yanking her into his arms. Damari buried her hand in his hair, pressing her cheek to his.

"I'm all right," she said, her breath warm against his ear. She pressed him back, laying her palm flat on the center of his chest. "Your heart's racing."

Lathan took her face between his hands. "I thought I lost you."

Her eyes flooded. "For a moment, I thought you had too."

He pulled her to him and kissed her fiercely, combing his hands through her tangled hair. Memorizing the silky feel of her tresses and the marble smoothness of her skin. The way her breath hitched with every moment of his kiss and the sweet, content sound that slipped from her lips when he stopped to catch his breath.

Taking her hands, Lathan helped Damari to her feet. Clea approached from behind, looking briefly at the two of them before her gaze moved past him.

"I never thought the day would come when this bridge would fall," his sister whispered.

Lathan looked at the destruction before them. The Peace Bridge had been cut in half, the gap between where they stood and the other half so long, he could barely make out what remained of the overpass on the other side. He put his arm around Clea's shoulders, drawing her close. His sister leaned heavily into his side, her eyes darkening with worry and lower lip clamped between her teeth as she looked at Damari curiously. He massaged her arm comfortingly.

"Neither did I, Clea," he replied.

Damari took a step forward, her toes near the jagged edge of the broken stone. The wind caught her golden hair, lifting the delicate strands like a veil across her face. When she looked back at them, her pupils thinned to horizontal lines, revealing her worry as she spoke.

"If the shadows told the truth about the Molderëinian ships … then we have lost our way into Sunkai."

CHAPTER TWENTY-FOUR

The Aulend Forest

Adlae dismounted lightly from Starlight, patting the mare's neck as she moved closer to the edge of the clearing. Healer Faw had called for a halt, the strange tone in his voice warning her something was amiss. She'd sensed the anxiety rushing through the caravan since they entered the Aulend, most of these Shadow Landers never having been this far from their homes before. The tension was rising—the sense they were coming nearer and nearer to something with evil intent growing stronger amongst them.

Jabon appeared at her side, his hand brushing her knuckles as they kept stride with each other toward the front of the line. She thought back to the kiss they shared in the woods, the memory of the elusive warmth he'd given her for the briefest of moments still tingling in her belly. If she could live that moment over and over again, she would, if only to feel what she'd not felt in so many years.

When you regain the throne, perhaps you will have the life you always dreamed of with him. Winter encouraged her.

Adlae smiled softly, whispering under her breath, "What about the secrets we keep, Winter? What about the prophecy the shadows gave us?"

Winter didn't answer, her sadness creeping into Adlae's own heart. Jabon took her hand, locking their fingers together. He seemed to be growing accustomed to her talking to herself, never questioning it, only accepting. She wondered how truly content he was to go with unanswered questions. How soon would he demand answers from her again? The way he had when they parted from Klade Overlage?

They reached the front of the line, stopping beside Healer Faw at the border of the clearing. The old man was staring straight up into the sky, watching the flames sizzle above them.

"They have stopped," Healer Faw murmured. "The flames have stopped moving."

Adlae looked up, watching the circle. The fire still dipped and swirled, but Healer Faw was right. They were no longer moving forward, no longer guiding them where they needed to be. She slipped away from Jabon, sliding her hand out of his as she moved toward the center of the clearing. The clouds overhead seemed darker against the brightness of the Sundragon flames, coiling and slithering like millions of black snakes. Red lightning flashed through the sky, coming dangerously close to the tops of the trees.

Is this the place we are meant to be? Is that why they've stopped? What are we to learn from this, Adlae Sundragon? There's nothing here! Winter said, frustrated.

Adlae lowered her eyes to the ground, brow pinching when she saw the dozens of tiny footprints left there. Crouching low, she traced her fingers around one of the prints, the light from her staff catching on a few drops of blood staining the pure white powder.

"Someone was here," she whispered. "Children, I think. The footprints are so small!"

"What would children be doing out here alone?" Jabon asked, still standing at the edge of the clearing.

"They weren't." Adlae scooted over, pressing her finger into a larger footprint. "Someone came for them."

Woodlanders?

"Possibly."

Your sister?

"Blessed Creator, I hope so."

She stood up, leaning against her staff. Closing her eyes, Adlae summoned her power, the frozen pulse of winter magic racing through her blood as she searched for answers. The first thing she felt was the taint of the Abyss on the clearing, struggling to keep his hold on a creature of purity. The next thing she felt was his banishment, sinking into the ground as the blood of an innocent was shed to release a captured soul.

But what nearly took her back to her knees were the tears. Tears of a Sundragon, warm and glistening, melting the snow where they'd fallen.

Mirae. Adlae breathed again, the sense of her sister's proximity lightening her heart.

"Adlae!" Jabon called, the hiss of his sword leaving its sheath echoing in her ears. "Adlae, come back to me!"

She opened her eyes. Figures moved among the trees on the other side of the clearing, their silhouettes crouching low as they approached with caution. They kept their torches low, leaving their faces hidden in darkness so they wouldn't be recognized.

They are not Black Ones. Black Ones do not carry torches.

"Torches do not mean they are friends." Adlae started to back away slowly, started to raise her staff in defense.

"Adlae?"

She froze.

"Blessed Sun!" Mirae raised her torch, illuminating her beautiful face in the darkness. "You found me."

Her sister started forward, Brecken Jandry appearing at her side as each Woodlander slowly lifted their torches, revealing themselves. Adlae found her feet moving of their own accord to close the distance between her and the only sister she had left.

The darkness bellowed overhead, bringing all of them to an abrupt halt. Shadows slammed down from the sky, knocking Brecken and Mirae off their feet. Adlae spun, sending a spear of ice into the sky. It shattered like glass before even reaching the darkness, useless as a dome began to form around the clearing.

"Adlae!" Jabon shouted. "Get out of there!"

She ran, trying to escape the trap closing around her, cutting her off from her people. A sharp *snap* cut the air, something tight and rough wrapping around her wrist. Adlae screamed, yanked back from Jabon. She landed hard on the frozen ground, groaning as her staff rolled away from her, out of her reach.

She couldn't move, the black vine wrapped around her wrist squeezing until she thought the bone would crack. Adlae stared into the sky, watching the darkness swoop down upon her. The Sundragon flames continued to roar in the sky, as useless to her now as they'd ever been.

No, no, no! Mirae stared in horror as Adlae was lifted off her feet, a thick black coil wrapped around her throat. Crystal tears streamed from her sister's eyes, sprinkles of ice fluttering from her toes and fingers. Her eyes lifted to the fire brightening the sky. Something stirred in her chest, a boiling liquid rushing like a river through her blood at the sight of them. The strangest of sensations as she stared at the flames turning overhead, formed in a perfect crown as they spat and roared against the darkness.

Adlae gasped, drawing Mirae's attention away from the sight in the sky. Her sister was desperately clawing at the blackness trying to choke the life from her, eyes rolling in her head. Jabon was shouting on the other side of the clearing, throwing himself against the invisible wall the Abyss had raised to separate them from Adlae.

This cannot happen! Blessed Creator please! Mirae's head swung, looking for a solution. Any answer to save her sister from this overwhelming darkness.

Then she saw it. Lying a few feet away, glistening even in the blackness of the night.

Adlae's staff. Mirae started toward the weapon. She felt them watching her, her Woodland people who understood so little about winter magic. Slowly she reached for the staff, just as another lily-white hand curled around it.

Mirae looked up, her heart jumping when Noelle smiled at her.

"Together?" Noelle whispered.

Mirae nodded, seeing Brae in the twinkle of Noelle's eye. "Together."

They spun, raising the staff toward Adlae. The thick pole popped, shooting ice and light into the invisible force surrounding Mirae's sister. Adlae's gaze shifted, watching them. A tingle rushed up Mirae's arm, the power fusing through her so strong and frozen she thought she might break in half. Noelle seemed not to notice, focused and steady as the wall sputtered then dissipated. Smoke and steam rose as the strength of the ice magic created an opening for them.

Mirae and Noelle leaped within the barrier, looking back to watch the temporary space close behind them, cutting them off from the rest of the woods. Noelle clasped the staff in both hands, her brow lowering as she marched toward the darkness. Swinging the magical weapon over her head, she brought it down on the tendril suffocating Adlae.

A flash of light exploded when the staff made contact with the darkness, sending Noelle flying through the air. She landed hard in the snow, limp. Adlae screamed, reaching a hand for their niece.

"No," Mirae hissed, drawing her sword. "Not today."

With a shout, she raised the blade above her head, an unknown force pulsing through her. The crown of flames above her head emanated a blaring roar, growing brighter and fiercer. It lowered in a whirlwind toward her, sucked down from the sky. The moment the flames touched her sword, Mirae's breath left her. Her eyes rolled back, the burn fierce and unrelenting as the fire rolled down the steel into the tips of her fingers. Her eyes smoldered, hand shaking as her sword consumed every last flame.

"Let go of my sister," she hissed.

Mirae clasped the hilt of her sword in both hands, raising the reddened steel over her head. Screaming, she brought the blade down on the darkness. The claw-like vine shattered like glass, shards scattering to the wind.

Adlae gasped, dropping in the snow as the tendril broke from her. Shrieks and moans echoed in the air as the barrier lowered, the darkness spiraling up, up, up into the sky before disintegrating.

Mirae fell to her knees beside Adlae, watching the sky clear for the first time in days, fading behind the gentle dark of night and revealing twinkling stars no longer hidden by the power of the Abyss. Fingers curling around her wrist made her look down, finding Adlae staring at her with bloodshot eyes.

"The girl!" she rasped.

Mirae's eyes widened and she spun away, scrambling through the thick snow to her niece's side. Brecken was stirring a few feet away, his groans letting her know he was alive.

Thank the Creator he did not see this ... Mirae turned Noelle over carefully.

The young girl's brow crinkled, and she moaned, reaching up to press her hand to her temple.

"Ouch," she muttered.

An elated laugh burst from Mirae's lips. She gathered the girl close, pressing her face into her hair. Noelle giggled, hugging her back.

"Is Aunt Adlae all right?"

Mirae looked over her shoulder in time to see Jabon helping Adlae to her feet. They stood quietly for a moment, Jabon grasping her hands. Her sister gave his fingers a squeeze before she turned away.

Their eyes met. Mirae's heart stopped. Would Adlae judge her for her failure at the Tower of Tears? Would she blame her for putting them all in this position?

Will she hate me for trying to take the throne? Mirae trembled.

Noelle gave her a nudge with her elbow, awkwardly rising from the ground while trying to slap the snow from her skirts. Mirae did the same, ignoring how the ice clung to her britches and boots, eyes still locked with her sister's.

Adlae inhaled. "You look like our mother."

Mirae's eyes flooded. Of all the things she'd expected her to say ...

In three strides, Mirae had her in her arms, ignoring the sting of ice from Adlae's body. Her eyes fluttered closed as she rested in her big sister's embrace. She'd dreamed of this moment ever since she found out Adlae was alive, and to be here now was almost too good to be true.

"Adlae ..." Jabon's wavering voice claimed both sisters' attention.

They turned, finding Noelle standing there, Adlae's staff in one hand and Mirae's sword in the other. The young girl frowned, looking back and forth between the two objects. Mirae's sword gleamed orange and red as if freshly taken from the forge fires. Adlae's staff crackled, fresh ice forming round the pole.

"Winter and fire magic," Noelle murmured. "Joined as they've never been joined before. It is unprecedented ... impossible."

Brecken was on his feet now, moving cautiously forward to stand at his daughter's shoulder.

"Gwylan says fire magic cannot mix with winter magic. They will destroy each other and yet ..." Noelle shook her head. "The Sundragon flames beat in the Woodland Queen's sword and the Winter Queen's staff grows ever stronger in the fire's presence."

Adlae stepped forward, gently taking her staff back from their niece. "I am the Sundragon, child. I possessed fire long before I was claimed as the Winter Queen."

"But you cannot wield fire magic." Noelle's eyes widened curiously.

"No." Adlae looked back at Mirae. "But she can."

Every eye fell upon her, their surprise as fierce as her own. Mirae reached over, taking her sword away from Noelle. She raised the blade in front of her in both hands, watching as the burning glow began to fade back to the gentle sheen of silver steel. Even as the heat faded, she could still feel the new power pulsing in the blade.

Adlae placed her hand on Mirae's shoulder. "These flames were always meant for you, sister. But beware their strength. For there is no greater temptation toward evil than there is with the burden you now bear."

Mirae lowered the weapon, turning to thrust it hastily away in the sheath at her belt. She looked into her sister's eyes, reaching up to grasp her fingers. A warm contentedness filled her belly, nearly drowning the sensation of the magic now pulsing through her blood. Ignoring the strange feeling, she forced a smile.

"Come away from this place now, Sister," she murmured. "There is much we need to talk about."

CHAPTER TWENTY-FIVE

Hood pulled low over her forehead, she made her way through the camp. After the events earlier that evening, the Woodlanders were finally calming down. Nerves eased and hearts lighter than they'd been since she'd arrived. Adlae Sundragon's presence seemed to go a long way toward accomplishing the peacefulness now settling over the grieving people. With the children safely returned to their families and the shadow completely gone from the sky, leaving a blanket of beautiful stars to smile down on them, the world seemed to be put right again.

Yet it's not. Far from it. She sighed, quickening her pace toward the edge of the circle.

She came to the tent she desired, erected right at the border of the protective circle, separated from the rest of the camp for privacy. Hesitation froze her feet on the ground, heart pounding ever faster as she struggled with doing what she knew she must. With finding the answer she desperately needed. So many visions flashed before her eyes now, whether during sleep or when wide awake. She couldn't stop them—wasn't sure she wanted to stop them. But there was one who could help her with, at least, one of the questions she had.

Without waiting to be allowed entrance, she ducked between the flaps. Cohdel jumped up from where he'd been sitting, dagger in hand. She didn't flinch, simply stared back at him as he took a moment to recognize her. He snarled at her, shoving the dagger out of sight once more.

"You should not scare a soldier like that, girl," he reprimanded.

"Forgive me." She turned away, for he was not her objective.

The woman she sought sat in the corner, staring dejectedly into the fire warming the tent.

"Lady Astra," she said, sitting down directly in front of the woman, folding her legs beneath her.

Astra looked at her, the hollow depths of her silver eyes sending a chill down her spine.

"I have been waiting for you," the prophetess said, voice rough from crying. "I knew you would come to me, eventually."

Noelle removed her hood, the fire glinting off her bright tresses when they spilled over her shoulders. "I am sorry for your loss, my lady."

Astra sniffled in reply, blinking rapidly when the glitter of fresh tears appeared on her lashes. "Loved that man, I did. With every beat of my heart."

She took the woman's hand between both her palms.

"He is at peace now. I am sure of it."

"Yes, I suppose he is." Astra straightened her shoulders. "You have come to me for another reason."

Noelle nodded slowly. "How long have you known?"

Astra just blinked in silence. Leaning closer, Noelle managed to recite the words that had been repeating in her mind for days now.

"Nfaros will be won with the blood of innocents."

The Tree Prophetess's eyes dimmed with sadness, her fingers twisting around Noelle's to an almost painful grip. Breathing deeply, Noelle pushed the question from her lips, ignoring the sting of a tear sliding down her cheek.

"How long have you known your prophecy ... was about me?"

To Be Continued ...

ABOUT THE AUTHOR

ERICA MARIE HOGAN was born in New York but now calls Texas home. She has three cats and two dogs, was homeschooled, is a member of American Christian Fiction Writers, and when she's not writing, she's reading. Erica can be found on Facebook, Twitter, and Goodreads, along with her monthly blog, "By the Book: Diary of a Bookaholic."

ERICA'S OTHER BOOKS

The Winter Queen, Book 1

Dance of Shadow, Book 2

www.ingramcontent.com/pod-product-compliance
Lightning Source LLC
Chambersburg PA
CBHW072210170626
46813CB00003B/880